KATE CHUDLEIGH;

OR,

THE DUCHESS OF KINGSTON.

BY THE AUTHOR OF "EDITH THE CAPTIVE."

WITH FIFTEEN ILLUSTRATIONS,

DRAWN BY F. GILBERT.

LONDON:
JOHN DICKS, 313, STRAND, AND ALL BOOKSELLERS.

KATE CHUDLEIGH;

OR,

THE DUCHESS OF KINGSTON.

THE FRACAS BETWEEN CAPTAIN HARVEY AND THE DUKE OF HAMILTON.

CHAPTER I.

A BALL AT LEICESTER HOUSE IN THE OLDEN TIME.—THE YOUNG BEAUTY AND HER ADMIRER.—A MAID OF HONOUR.—THE TRAITOR, AND THE ATTEMPTED ASSASSINATION.—CATHERINE CHUDLEIGH AND HER TWO LOVERS.—A DEFIANCE—A SAD HEART AND AN ARRANGED MARRIAGE—NIGHT AND DAWN.

ON the evening of July the 10th, in the year 1725, when George the Second held his Court at

Leicester House, frequently called Saville Palace an entertainment was given, at which so much lavish magnificence was displayed, that the whole of London was attracted by the preparations, and the neighbourhood was in a state of blockade from the throngs of people, the thick lines of equipages, the sedan-chairs, the Royal Guards, and the thousand and one obstructions and excitements which made up the blaze and riot of the scene.

The front of the Palace blazed with lights.

No. 1.—KATE CHUDLEIGH.

The King's Hanoverian Guards kept watch and ward at the entrances; and numerous were the squabbles which those unpopular troops—so unpopular, that one of the first acts of George the Third, on his accession to the throne, was to disband them—had with the people.

Within the saloons of Saville Palace all was beauty, light, mirth, music, and gay delight.

A thousand guests thronged the reception-rooms of the monarch.

A thousand wax-lights lent their united lustre to the illumination of the courtly throng, chasing away every shadow from the magnificent apartments, and reflecting the sparkle of jewels into the remotest corridors of the palace.

A thousand Guards kept watch without—for Jacobinism was in full vitality; that is to say, the partisans of the deposed Stuarts were still contending for the throne.

The King walked, spoke, eat, drank, and lived in an atmosphere of danger.

The ball was at its height.

The air was full of music—of gay laughter—of pretty little shrieks of distress, as the ladies' trains would suffer in the crush of the saloons.

All that was fair—all that was rich, powerful, and noble in England, upon that occasion had met, to assume a loyalty that probably was really felt but by few.

The King was indisposed. Fears had been entertained for his life. It was roundly asserted at the coffee-houses, and even hinted by the newspapers of the time, that some secret poison was undermining his existence.

But it is eleven o'clock.

The great gilt folding-doors of the principal saloon, and which conduct to the private apartments of the monarch, are thrown open.

George the Second, leaning on the arm of his physician, appears.

Pale, and sallow, and ghastly looks the King.

A set smile is on his face—a smile created more by the mere retraction of his lips from the teeth, than by any other movement of the muscles of his face.

"Long live the King! Long live the King!" shouted many a voice.

The music—the dance-music, was suspended on the instant, and the first notes of the Royal Hymn commenced.

"Long live the King!" cried one gentleman, in a most conspicuous dress of what was called Pompadour velvet.

"From over the water!" added another voice.

The sharp report of a pistol followed immediately, from no one knew where. Some thought it came from the floor, some from the ceiling—some from one side, some from the other; and not a few were ready to declare that it came from without.

The effect was magical.

Terrible as well as magical.

In one instant the whole assemblage—those thousand guests of the King—were seized with a panic.

Ladies screamed and fainted by the score—gentlemen drew their swords.

There were loud cries of "Treason! treason! Guard! guard! Save the King! Help! help! The Palace is on fire! Down with the Jacobites! A plot! a plot! Treason! treason! treason!"

Hundreds rushed to the doors of the ball-room to escape.

Those doors were speedily blocked up by a living mass.

The officers of the Hanoverian Guards without, ordered their men to force an entrance to the protection of the King.

The struggle—the fight—the oaths—the shrieks—the cries for mercy—the clash of swords—all made up a scene of tumult that was at once fearful and indescribable.

The King had turned a shade paler. His thin, retracted lips drew further back still.

The physician stood by his side, supporting the King's arm; but upon the face of that physician was such a look that even those who in the fight and excitement of the moment chanced to see it, turned away their eyes with terror.

The disengaged hand of the physician was upon his breast.

With the other arm, as we have said, he still upheld the King.

Then a gentleman fiercely sprung forward. He was in the uniform of an officer of the royal navy, and with his drawn sword in his hand, he placed himself before the King, crying out, as he did so, "Let the next traitorous bullet rather find a home in my breast than in that of the King!"

"No! no! Not your breast! Not yours!" shrieked a female voice.

A young girl, almost a child—in that debateable state of existence between the girl and the woman, which, while it still retains the youthful freshness of the one condition, has acquired some charms from the maturer state—darted forward, and half fell to the floor at the feet of the King, and of the physician, and of the gentleman in the naval uniform who had so chivalrously stepped forward.

"No, no! Not your breast! Mine rather; oh, much rather mine!"

She looked up as she spoke.

The look was angelic.

Never had lovelier eyes shot forth such flames of tenderness and emotion.

Never had such loveliness as this young girl presented blossomed on the earth, to "witch the world with beauty."

Description is useless; there are no words to paint the charm of expression. Eyes—brow—hair—mouth,—all were perfect; and the combination produced a sparkling dazzle of female loveliness, which even extracted an exclamation of admiration from the cold heart of the sick King.

Then the physician, with one deep sigh, fell to the floor.

The mystery of the terrible look that had come over his face was explained.

The pistol-shot that had been intended for the breast of the King, had reached his breast instead. A wonderful courage and constancy of purpose had kept him up for those few minutes, and now that he fell to the floor, he fell a corpse!

The King staggered back, and was only upheld by the arm of another gentleman, who at that moment stepped up to the royal circle.

The fair young girl who, either from sympathy with the monarch or with the gentleman in the naval uniform, had rushed forward with so much emotion, now shrieked aloud.

The tide of guests that had made so mad a set towards the doors of the saloon ebbed somewhat back again before the Hanoverian Guards, and a couple of hundred swords flashed about the King.

The gentleman in the Pompadour coloured coat then stepped close to the fair young girl; and, as he stooped, he whispered to her, "Catherine!— Catherine! what means this emotion?"

She struggled to her feet.

Two arms assisted her.

One was that of the gentleman in the Pompadour coat,—the other was that of the naval officer, who, in a curt tone of voice, said, "I was not aware that Miss Chudleigh was so well acquainted with the Honourable Mr. Pultney, the friend of the Prince of Wales."

"Nor was I at all aware," replied the gentleman in the Pompadour coat, "that Miss Chudleigh had any acquaintance whatever with the Honourable Captain Harvey, the son of the Earl of Bristol."

"Sir?"

"Well, sir?"

"Gracious heaven!" cried the gentleman into whose arms almost the King had fallen, when he stepped back after the death of the physician. "Gracious heaven! It is—it is Catherine!"

At the sound of his voice, the young lady, whose name was really Catherine Chudleigh, and who held the position of Maid of Honour to the Princess of Wales, uttered a cry of dismay.

The gentleman who was supporting the King placed him on a settee close at hand; and then, bowing low, he said, "Will your Majesty graciously permit me to leave you for a moment?"

"Yes, yes, my Lord Hamilton—yes! We retire—we—we retire from this scene; and soon— soon from all scenes—from all scenes——"

The gilt folding-doors were thrown open by the royal pages.

"Way for the King! Way for the King!"

The sick monarch alone—alone in heart—alone in affection and in hope—left the saloon.

The doors were all doubly guarded by the officers of the Hanoverian Guard, and several general officers, who had assumed the command, and the order of events, determined that no person should leave the Palace without such a scrutiny as should present the best chance of detecting the conspirator and assassin who had fired the pistol-shot at the King.

Catherine Chudleigh, for a moment, seemed disposed to accept the protection of the naval officer, Captain Harvey; and the gentleman in the Pompadour coat, seeing that, made a low bow, saying, in a sad and regretful tone, "Farewell, then, Miss Chudleigh!"

Some feeling of remorse, for an unkind act to one who had been for long a kind and indulgent friend, came over her.

She rejected the arm of the naval officer.

"Oh, no, no! I am not ungrateful, dear Mr. Pultney!"

But he was gone.

Tears came to the eyes of Catherine Chudleigh. She was still young, and the pure founts of tender emotion were not yet dried up, *as they were to be.*

Captain Harvey stooped, and whispered to her.

"Dear, dear Catherine, who loves you as I love you? Who——"

"If you please, sir," interposed the gentleman who had been so recently supporting the King,— "if you please, sir, I will relieve you from the care of Miss Chudleigh."

"You, Duke?"

"Even I, Captain Harvey!"

The young Duke of Hamilton seemed, at that moment, to forget that he was in a crowded ball-room, for he flung his left arm around the slender waist of Catherine Chudleigh, as he added, "It is well that Captain Harvey, the well-known libertine, should be warned that the lady is my affianced wife."

Captain Harvey was one of the people who turn white and tremble when very angry.

He did both, now.

"Your wife? You—you—affianced? Ha! ha! ha!"

"No!" said the young girl, as she hastily disengaged herself from the half embrace of the Duke of Hamilton. "No! The flowers that are neglected, fade and die. They love the hand that fosters them in the hour of their desertion."

As she spoke, she placed one of her beautiful, dimpled, small hands in that of Captain Harvey.

The Duke of Hamilton pressed his left hand upon his breast, as if some assassin's bullet had struck him, as it had struck the King's physician so short a time ago.

No doubt he felt, in the pangs of disappointed love, very nearly as acute a pain.

"Oh, Catherine! Catherine! Catherine! Is this——"

His voice faltered. He stepped half aside, and then letting his sword hang from his wrist by the silken and bullion tassel that was about the hilt, he covered his face with both his hands.

A scornful laugh burst from the lips of Captain Harvey.

The sound of that laugh at once turned the tide of feeling in the heart of the Duke of Hamilton, and he faced his rival firmly.

"False friend!—false subject!—false lover! Have at you, then!"

The Duke's sword flashed in his opponent's eyes.

Catharine Chudleigh shrieked aloud. Captain Harvey had just time to put himself on the defensive, the glittering sword-blades rang together, and then a rush of guests and several officers separated them.

But Captain Harvey's arm was bleeding

Catherine Chudleigh looked with grief and terror on the crimson drops.

"It matters not," he whispered, "if you love me?"

"I will! I do!"

"You consent to be mine?"

"Arrange all with my aunt, Mrs. Hanmer."

"Then I am happy; for, Catherine, as sure as that to-morrow's sun will shine, I love you."

CHAPTER II.

CATHERINE CHUDLEIGH AT MARLBOROUGH HOUSE. —A STRANGE PHENOMENON—THE INFLUENCE OF WIT AND BEAUTY. — AN EXPEDITION OF DANGER. — NIGHT IN ST. JAMES'S PARK.— THE DRUNKEN SENTINEL — A DUEL IN THE ROYAL ENCLOSURE.—THE DUKE OF HAMILTON BIDS HIS FIRST LOVE FAREWELL.

THE ball at Leicester House was over.

The tumult had subsided; the King was very sick, and attended by all his physicians.

Catherine Chudleigh, as forming part of the suite of the Princess of Wales, had retired with her royal mistress to Marlborough House, which had been that season placed at the disposal of the Prince of Wales by its ducal owner.

The Maids of Honour of the Princess of Wales were not very splendidly lodged.

A collection of small rooms at the top of the house was spared to them with difficulty; and it is in one of these that we shall now, at the hour of two, when London was silent, and sleep sat upon the eyelids of all but herself in the royal abode, find our heroine.

Catherine Chudleigh!

That young creature, whose marvellous beauty had already begun to fire the hearts and turn the heads of some of the noblest and the richest of the Court.

That girl, almost a child yet in years, for she was scarcely sixteen, who was the theme of ballads, the inspiration of wits, and who, at that one Court ball at Leicester House, had won more hearts than the most practised coquettes could have disposed of in a lifetime.

In that little apartment she one by one takes the jewels from her hair—from her fingers—from her wrists, and from her fair neck. She places each on the toilette-table—some with a sigh, some with a gay laugh.

They were all presents.

Anonymous presents.

She had found them on the threshold of her room, addressed to her—on her toilette-table—placed beside her on her seat at church—sent to her in letters breathing adoration.

And she wore them all, and laughed at the senders.

A more finished coquette than that young girl of sixteen could not have been found.

"I wonder, now," she said, as she took from her ears a pair of beautiful earrings, each made in imitation of a sea-shell, with a pearl enclosed in it,—"I wonder who sent these? Ha! ha! Well, I don't care! This ring with the rubies is prettier, and this bracelet with all the diamonds is prettier still. How I shall laugh at all these men—how I shall make sport of them! I wonder if I am so—so very beautiful, as they all say I am?"

She took a long look at herself in the glass—she smiled, as she saw that the bright light of her own eyes far transcended all the lustre of the jewels. She smiled again, as she saw that in that first smile there was a world of witchery.

A third time she smiled, for the second one had disclosed such pearls of teeth, and had produced two such pretty dimples, that she was almost in love with herself.

Then she turned from the glass, and called out, "Bella! Bella! Where are you now, Bella?"

From the room which immediately joined that which was in the occupation of Catherine Chudleigh, a plain, sallow-looking young woman appeared.

Any one would have thought, from the manner in which she was summoned by the Maid of Honour, that she was the waiting-maid.

But such was not the case.

Bella Steinburgh was a Maid of Honour likewise; but she was plain. She lodged in the room adjoining Catherine's.

By some strange infatuation, she had brought herself to consider that because Miss Chudleigh could boast of such wonderful personal attractions, she was a being to be looked up to and worshipped as something super-excellent, and more than human.

Contrasting her plain, homely features with those of Catherine Chudleigh, poor Bella bowed down before the majesty of beauty.

She must, whether she put the idea into words or not, have considered it impossible for Nature to work by contraries, and place in such a fair casket other than some rich and noble jewel of a mind and soul.

So Bella Steinburgh might be said to have set up Catherine Chudleigh as an idol.

An idol that she was always content to worship night and day.

An idol whose behests, whose caprices, never could be wrong.

"Bella, are you sleeping?" asked the spoilt beauty.

"Oh, no, no!"

"Well, that's a good thing! You know I am never sleepy; and it's quite enough rest for me to lie down while the Princess takes her own rest, after dinner. Well, what does the child stare at?"

The "child," as Catherine Chudleigh called Bella, was two years her senior.

"Nothing—nothing, dear Catherine! But you know I cannot help looking at you, you are so very beautiful!"

"Oh, stuff! We did not make ourselves."

Bella sighed. She thought that if she had had the making of herself, it would certainly have been on the model of Catherine Chudleigh.

"Now, listen to me, Bella."

"Yes, dear Catherine."

"The Duke of Hamilton has come home. You know—for I never thought it worth while to keep a lot of secrets—that I was to have been married to him, but he neglected me. He did not write to me from Vienna as he should have done; and Captain Harvey, who is so well known to my Aunt Hanmer, is—is—well, he is good-looking, and will be a great lord, some day, and I shall be Lady Catherine, the Countess of Bristol. Do you hear all that?"

"Oh, yes—yes! It would not be too much if you were to be a queen—an empress."

"Well, I don't suppose it would. But you are so dull and stupid, Bella!"

"Alas! I am very sorry; but I think——"

"Well, what do you think?"

"That I should not appear so to any one else and it is because you are so clever, and have such wit and such judgment, that you think me so."

"Perhaps so. Well, it can't be helped, I suppose. So, Bella, I intend to marry Captain Harvey!"

"Oh! oh! oh!"

"What's the matter?"

"I shall see you no more."

"Stuff! Do you think I am going to leave the Court on account of any man?"

"No?"

"Certainly not. I know what will happen to-morrow, well enough. The Duke of Hamilton will speak to the Princess of Wales, with whom he is a favourite; and he will persuade her to send for me, and she will urge me to fulfil my promise to marry him; and he will make some excuse for not writing from Vienna; and—and——Heigho!

" ' I'm afraid, I'm afraid
Too many lovers will puzzle a maid.' "

" Dear, dear Catherine! how beautifully you sing! The sounds seem to fill up my heart, as if some angel's voice were in the air!"

Catherine Chudleigh did sing divinely.

She laughed.

" Well, Bella, you don't half attend to me; for I am telling you all my secrets."

" Yes—yes! Oh, yes, I do!"

" Very well, then. I want to be quite sure, before I reply to the Duke of Hamilton, that Captain Harvey intends marriage at once."

" Yes—that is right."

" Then I must see him to-night."

" To-night!"

" To be sure! His ship is lying off Tilbury Fort."

" Tilbury Fort!"

" To be sure! Did the girl never hear of Tilbury Fort before? Well, I don't intend to go there. Don't open your eyes so wide, Bella. There is the King's state barge, to which Captain Harvey has been appointed as commander, this very day. It is at Kew; and the Lord Chancellor told me, just for the pleasure of having a little chat with me, of course, that it was a custom, when any naval officer received the appointment of commander of the royal barge, to sleep on board it the first night, although he, in all likelihood, never saw it again."

" Yes, dear Catherine; I hear."

" Well—that's where I'm going."

" What?"

" W—h—a—t! Ha! ha! My poor Bella, you look scared out of your wits, such as they are —indeed you do. But I have made up my mind —I will see Captain Harvey to-night; so it will be of no use for you to say one word about it. Get me my sailor boy's dress that I had for the Queen's *fête* at Chiswick. Be quiet, do! Don't I tell you I am going to Kew, eh?"

" Oh, Catherine!—Catherine!"

The little beauty stamped with her feet—she clenched her hands, and uttered little half shrieks, which so alarmed Bella, that she hastily procured from a wardrobe the complete dress, more fanciful than true, of a sailor boy.

In ten minutes Catherine Chudleigh was equipped.

Bella flung herself upon her neck in a passion of tears.

" Dear—dear Catherine, you are too adventurous—indeed you are! You will fall into some danger."

" No! I can take good care of myself, and always could. To-morrow I shall be the wife of Captain Harvey, or of the Duke of Hamilton. But I prefer Harvey, and therefore I will see him to-night. Now, Bella, there is a groom of the name of Hutchinson; he sleeps in the stables looking on to the Park. You will go and find some way of rousing him up."

" I cannot—I cannot!"

" You can—you must, I tell you. He is a man —a young one—almost a boy; but he will kill himself if I tell him. And what I want him to do

is to get out a horse for me—one of the Princess's jennets that came from Hanover. I mean to ride to Kew."

Catherine Chudleigh walked up and down the little room, and whistled like some blackbird on a thorn.

That was one of her accomplishments.

What had prodigal Nature denied to that wayward, wilful heart?

Bella, as was always the case, obeyed her. The stable lad was aroused—the jennet was at the private gate at Marlborough House. Three o'clock struck from the clock of the Palace, as Catherine Chudleigh, at a smart trot, left London for Kew.

But she was not destined to get so far on her journey. A few moments' reflection decided her, rightly or wrongly, that her nearest and best way would be through the Park of St. James's.

It was not an hour in which any ordinary passengers were abroad in the royal enclosure, but the household of the Princess of Wales could at any and all times walk, ride, or drive through it. The mere words, " On the service of the Princess of Wales," usually sufficed; but if a sentinel happened to be stupid or suspicious, they one and all had a written pass to produce.

In her sailor boy's dress, Catherine Chudleigh had not this pass.

But she trusted to the words, " On the service of the Princess," being sufficient.

Turning, then, towards the gate in Pall Mall, Catherine confronted the sentinel, and cried out the pass-words sharply.

They were sufficient.

A leaf of the iron gate revolved, and she rode into the Park.

But it was early in July. The days were at their longest nearly; and already the eastern sky had the dull, leaden look, here and there tinted with yellow of a faint and purply hue, which proclaimed the approach of the new day.

It would take her a good hour and a half, if not more, to ride to Kew.

Catherine Chudleigh counted the time mentally.

Half past four, at Kew; half an hour there— five; half past six, back to Marlborough House. That would be still two hours before the royal establishment was astir.

" That will do!" she said.

At a sharp trot she made her way across the Park.

" Sentinel!—sentinel! Hilloa!—hilloa! On the service of the Princess!"

" Can't help it! You—you—(hiccup)—you— don't pass my post—neither of you!"

The sentinel was in an evident state of intoxication. He said " neither of you," so that it may fairly be presumed that he saw two jennets, and two sailor boys on their backs.

" Stupid!" cried Catherine Chudleigh; " I tell you I am on service of the Princess of Wales."

The only reply of the half-drunken sentinel was to bring his firelock to the charge, and make a plunging thrust at the jennet.

The horse reared in alarm, and Catherine Chudleigh had some difficulty to keep her seat in the saddle.

The chimes of St. James's Church announced half-past three.

" Wretch! beast!" she cried, in violent anger;

"I will see your colonel, and have you shot to-morrow!"

She turned her horse's head from the drunken sentinel; the light in the east was on the increase; a thin, white mist was over the duck-pond in the centre of the damp wilderness which was called the enclosure, in the middle of the Park, and which now forms such a recreation ground for nursery maids and their neglected charges, and tired, sleepy pickpockets.

Through the mist she saw some moving figures.

In the sharp, silent morning air, she heard voices. One of them was familiar to her, as it uttered the words, "Prove your pretensions sir, then, at your sword's point. I do not surrender mine but with my life!"

"Ah!" said Catherine Chudleigh, "that is my old lover, the Duke of Hamilton."

She alighted at once from the jennet, which, with her usual carelessness, she let go loose; and clinging to the paling that enclosed the wilderness and the duck-pond, she strove to look through the white mist at what was going on.

Had she a shrewd suspicion of the identity of the person to whom the Duke of Hamilton had uttered those words?

To be sure she had!

That Captain Harvey was there, and that her projected journey to Kew had been luckily delayed, were facts that she quickly decided in her own mind.

But, as yet, she could only see the dim outline of moving figures; she heard, though, the clash of swords.

She clapped her hands together, as she said, half aloud, "These men fight for me—all for me! Because I am beautiful, and they are both madly in love with me, one of them will kill the other! Shall I give my hand to the survivor? We shall see! we shall see!"

As she spoke, she made her way lightly, and with all the ease and aptitude of an alert and agile boy, over the palings; she ran along the damp grass, and reached the scene of the combat.

Four persons were there present.

Two were seconds.

Two were principals.

The principals had their coats off, and were hotly engaged: then the foot of one of them slipped on the grass, and he was for half a second at the mercy of his antagonist. It was Captain Harvey who had so slipped. The sword of the Duke of Hamilton was at his throat, when Catherine Chudleigh caught up from the ground the sheath of one of the weapons which had been carelessly cast down, and, darting forward, she dashed up the blade of the Duke's sword, and stood between him and Captain Harvey.

Each of the combatants uttered an exclamation of surprise.

The two seconds ran forward.

Catherine Chudleigh had just time to whisper a few words in the ear of Captain Harvey, and then the Duke of Hamilton was about to rush upon him again, when his own second stayed him, and held him by the hand, saying, "No, your Grace—no! Both Lord Minto and myself now declare this duel at an end. Captain Harvey is wounded, and so is your Grace. When blood actually falls, the seconds can stop the combat."

"Be it so," said the Duke of Hamilton; "but perhaps Captain Harvey is as little satisfied as I am, and so we may meet again."

"With pleasure, your Grace," said Captain Harvey; "although, were I otherwise inclined, it would seem a little hard that I should be continually called upon to fight you because I had won the affections of the fairest of her sex."

The Duke of Hamilton made an impatient gesture, as he replied, "But for the unseemly interference of one of your ship-boys, whom I am half inclined to lay my sword sheath over, your difficulties and hardships would now have been over."

Catherine Chudleigh burst into a ringing laugh, and the Duke of Hamilton clasped his hands together, and turned pale.

He had in that laugh recognised the tones of the fair Maid of Honour.

"And is this," he said,—"is this the end? Oh, Catherine, Catherine! is it for this that I have loved you? Go, false one, go! No fate, however sad—no tears that I could wish you to shed, can be so bitter as those which will spring from your own acts! Captain Harvey, I contend with you no more. Enjoy your prize, and be merciful when the period of satiety shall come, and beauty shall fade away like this morning mist."

"Only to leave the living presence of still more resplendent beauty behind it," said Captain Harvey, as he held Catherine Chudleigh to his breast, and for the first time pressed his lips to hers in a burning kiss.

The Duke of Hamilton fled from the spot, and his second followed him. The second of Captain Harvey, probably thinking that two was company, but three was none, followed their example, after a bow to Harvey and to the seeming sailor-boy.

CHAPTER III.

CATHERINE CHUDLEIGH MAKES CONDITIONS IN LOVE.—THE PROJECTED MARRIAGE IN LONDON.—THE FINESSE OF A YOUNG HEART.—THE ROUTE TO LEICESTER HOUSE.—A FEW WORDS ABOUT MR. PULTNEY.—THE NIGHT AT THE ROYAL RESIDENCE—DOES HE, TOO, LOVE ME?—THE MIDNIGHT SOLITARY.

"HARVEY,' said Catherine Chudleigh, "in the first place, I won't have any more kissing; and in the second place, you must marry me to-day."

"I will."

"Truly?"

"With all my heart! I love you to distraction. I have fought for you—I bleed for you. I would marry you ten times over, if that were necessary to make you mine."

"Keep away!"

"Dear, dear Kate!"

"Keep away, I say, will you? Let me think. Yes. I shall have no turn of duty to-day at the Palace. I shall be at my aunt's house in the Birdcage Walk. You will come there?"

"On the wings of love!"

"But I am under age. You cannot get a license to marry me, I'm afraid."

"Dear Catherine, I thought of that."

"How?"

"A good month since you as nearly as possible promised to be mine. In a freak—an inspiration—call it what you will, while my ship was lying off Southampton, I went to Winchester and put up the banns of marriage between us. We have but to go there, and we can be married at any canonical hour we please."

"Impudence!"

"Oh, Catherine, forgive me! It was love—true, ardent, devoted——"

"Hush! Who is this? Some one gets over the paling. It is a boy—he waves his cap to us—to me! What does he want? Ah, I see who it is!—the boy-groom Hutchinson, who drives the Princess's ponies. What can he want?"

The boy reached Catherine and Captain Harvey, panting and heated.

"Miss Chudleigh—if you please, Miss Chudleigh, the Princess was taken ill, and Miss Steinburgh said that you had slept at Leicester House to-night, and so excused your not attending, as the Princess asked for you; and she has sent me—that is, Miss Steinburgh has sent me to ask you not to come home."

"With me, then, dearest?" said Captain Harvey.

"Certainly not!"

"But—but——"

"Will you be quiet? I will go to Leicester House; Lady Pultney is there, and will admit me to a share of her rooms, no doubt. Harvey, you will give this boy a guinea."

"With pleasure. No one, dear Catherine, shall have to complain of a want of liberality on my part who has been of any service to you."

"Come along, then. You must see me safely to Leicester House, but I don't know how you will leave the Park, for I was not allowed to do so."

"I have a golden key, my dear girl. I bribed the sentinel at the Birdcage Walk."

"Yes; now I comprehend how it was that he was so drunken that he stopped me from leaving. But if I had left, I should not have seen you, and by this time I should have been nearly at Kew, where I thought you would have been sleeping on board the royal barge."

"I should have been so, my Kate; but at the call of honour I met the Duke of Hamilton here."

"And if you had been killed?"

"Would you have mourned for me?"

"Perhaps!"

The wilful beauty looked with a coquettish smile into his face, and Captain Harvey sighed. Perhaps, even then, the shadows of future events were projected on to his heart by the pure light of destiny behind them; and if he had examined his own feelings closely, he would have come to the conclusion that the most ill-starred step in life he could possibly take would be to ally himself with the beautiful Maid of Honour, Catherine Chudleigh.

But when does passion reason?

When does infatuation, such as that which filled up his heart and brain, ever permit the calm and sober voice of common sense to be heard?

Did he not know that the very genius of caprice had taken up its abode in the heart of that fair young girl?

Did not he gather, or might he not have gathered, from his profession a simile that would have but too truly illustrated her character?

From those baffling, fitful winds which blow apparently in all directions at one and the same time, among those groups of fair islands in the South Pacific, he would certainly have found a sailor's illustration of the capricious temper of the girl to whom he was about to commit the fortune of his life.

But she was so beautiful! Oh, fatal gift! Fatal to its possessor, and fatal to all who shall come within the giddy, mad whirl of its influence.

Happy, happy are they who, without being repulsive in form or feature, can yet please the fastidious eye, while the undazzled intellect is left freedom of action.

"No," cried Catherine Chudleigh, suddenly,—"no, I won't! That's decided!"

"What, dear one?"

"I won't be married at Winchester!"

"No?"

"But, my angel——"

"I say I won't—that's quite decided! It must be in London somewhere. Lady Flora Deloraine, one of the Maids of Honour, was married last month. All the formalities previous to the marriage were gone through, somewhere in Shropshire; and then the Bishop, or the Archbishop, or somebody, gave leave for the ceremony to take place in London. I won't go to Winchester!"

"My dear girl, all shall be as you wish."

"As I wish? I suppose so! Ha! ha! Would it not be a little too soon to tell me I was not to have my own way in everything? But here we are at Leicester House. You must arouse the night porters, and ask for Lady Pultney."

"Yes, dear—yes!"

"Be quiet! I won't be called dear, so don't do so any more, if you please."

"Well, well!"

Captain Harvey with some difficulty aroused the night porters who kept watch, or were supposed to do so, at one of the private entrances to the royal residence.

"Tell them," whispered Catherine Chudleigh, "that the nephew of Lady Pultney has come home from sea to stay with his aunt, and that she must be aroused to welcome him."

"Yes, Kate. How fertile you are in resources!"

"I had need be!"

Captain Harvey was fortunately known personally to the grooms of the Palace, and his word for the seeming young sailor-boy was sufficient.

The fair, delicate, and rather *petite* Maid of Honour, in her boy's clothes, did not look above twelve or thirteen years of age.

To admit such a lad into the house, and on the word of Captain Harvey, of the royal navy, who was well known as the son of the Earl of Bristol, did not appear to be any dereliction of duty.

"Good night, Harvey," said Catherine. "Remember me to all on board the good ship."

This was for the hearing of the grooms; but she added in a whisper, "Remember—I won't be married at Winchester."

"My dear love, your wishes shall be my laws."

"Very good; as long as you keep in that mind, we shall get on well together. Good night!"

"Good night, dear one!"

Once within the royal residence, Catherine Chudleigh knew her way perfectly well about it. There was a grand staircase, a secondary staircase, and a third staircase. The grand one led to a corridor of great length which was magnificently carpeted and hung with choice pictures ; and to the right of that corridor were the King's apartments.

The secondary staircase communicated with the grand one at the end of the corridor, and there was a range of rooms which were in the occupation of the various officers of the Court.

Those rooms lay to the left, so that it was only the staircases that made any difference in the mode of reaching the corridor.

Down the grand one the royal family only descended.

The other was used as a common thoroughfare by the lords and ladies in waiting.

The third staircase was for the domestics.

Darting, then, light as a fawn, up the grand staircase, for there was no etiquette awake at that hour in the Palace, Catherine reached the royal-looking corridor.

In the open air it was now daylight, but the blinds, curtains, and shutters of Leicester House sufficiently shut out the early sunbeams to make the oil lamps that were carried in the hands of life-size statues, and which burned in the corridor, quite necessary.

Catherine looked at several doors, and then she tapped at one as she said to herself, " This is Lady Pultney's chamber. I will stay with her, and get her, out of her kindness to me, to say that I was here all night. What a strange thing it has always been !"

Catherine smiled as she uttered these words, and to the reader they would be perfectly inexplicable without a few words of explanation.

The Honourable Mr. Pultney had married a lady in her own right to whom he had been tenderly attached in early life. He was a man now past the middle age—learned—wise—a politician —a philosopher, and the great friend and ally of the Prince of Wales.

Mr. Pultney and Colonel Chudleigh, the father of our Maid of Honour, had been school companions, and it was the interest of the Pultneys that had procured for Catherine her official position in the household of the Princess of Wales.

From the day that the beautiful young girl had come to London, Mr. Pultney had set about the task of forming her mind and manners with the greatest assiduity. He had read to her and with her ; he had devoted all his leisure to her, and neglected as her education had been, and as the education of most girls was at that period, it was to him she owed all the solid information she possessed.

She was an apt pupil, and he was amazed at the rapidity with which she learnt all that was requisite ; so that the learner, with so able an instructor, was better informed than many of the so-called learned ladies of the age.

But we have heard Catherine, as she stopped at that door in the royal corridor, say to herself, " What a strange thing it had always been !"

This was the strangeness.

Mr. Pultney had not fallen in love with her !

Everybody else did !

Why not he ?

Was he too wise ?

Was he too good ?

Or did he, from that wisdom, just perceive the small venom that lay like a coiled snake at the bottom of the heart of the young coquette ?

We shall see.

Catherine then tapped lightly at the door of that suite of three rooms which she knew to be in the occupation of Lady Pultney, as Mistress of the Robes to the Princess of Wales.

No notice was taken.

She tapped again, but still lightly, for nothing was further from her intention than to arouse any of the inmates of that part of the Palace beside the one she sought—Lady Pultney.

Then she heard a hasty movement within the room, as though some one moved aside a chair with a sudden action.

The door was opened, and disclosed a sitting-room with a table, on which was a reading lamp, which shed a subdued green light from its tinted glass upon a profusion of books and papers.

Shading his eyes with his hand so as to enable him to look towards the door, was Mr Pultney himself, the indefatigable member of Parliament, and friend of the Prince of Wales, and Leader of the Opposition to the Ministry.

CHAPTER IV.

THE STRUGGLES OF A BRAVE HEART.—CATHE-RINE CHUDLEIGH'S TRIUMPH —AN ADVENTURE AT THE PALACE —THE SOLITARY STUDENT. — DOES ALL THE WORLD LOVE HER ?.— THE POWER OF BEAUTY.—THE CHAMBER IN THE ROOF.—THE OLD CHEST —DOUBTS AND FEARS OF THE MAID OF HONOUR.—A TERROR AND A SURPRISE.

FOR a few moments Mr. Pultney looked with a puzzled air towards the door, and could not see who it was that disturbed his studies. Perhaps his eyes were confused by reading at lamp-light, and when he should have been taking healthful repose.

But that state of incertitude did not last long.

He then saw the slight, graceful figure of the apparent sailor-boy on the threshold of the room, and he called out somewhat harshly, " What is it ? who is it ?"

Catherine Chudleigh advanced three paces; she lifted from her head the sea-boy's cap, and some portion of her beautiful hair fell in shining massive ringlets on to her shoulders.

A ray of light fell upon her face, which wore a radiant, half mocking smile as she looked into the eyes of the grave, sage man who thus had been " consuming the midnight oil."

" Catherine !" he exclaimed.

She made a saucy kind of sailor-boy's bow and a scrape with her foot, as she replied, " Mr. Pultney !'

" Good heaven !"

" Amen !"

" You here, Catherine ! You, my—my—that is you, Miss Chudleigh—and in this disguise !"

" Just so ! I want Lady Pultney !"

" She is at Buckingham House to-night."

" Oh !"

Mr. Pultney took her by the hand and led her into the room. How handsome—how fascinating she looked ! What brightness in her eyes—what roses on her lips—what glowing pearls between

THE HANDSOME STRANGER ALARMS CATHERINE.

them, as she smiled! She felt his hand tremble and turn cold as he held hers within it.

"Catherine, what is the meaning of this?— what freak?—what—what design?"

She laughed.

"Nothing—nothing! I will go up to the top of the Palace—that is to say, to the top rooms, where the Maids of Honour used to sleep while the Electress of Brandenburgh was here; for I must stay here to-night—or, rather, for the remainder of this morning—now that I am here!"

"Cath—Cathe—rine!"

"What, dear Mr. Pultney?"

"You — you won't forget all that I have taught you?"

"Never! I recollect, even, all the Latin."

"That is well, Catherine—dear, dear Catherine!"

"Hilloa!"

She whistled in her sweet blackbird tones.

No 2.—KATE CHUDLEIGH.

"What—what is the matter?"

"You called me 'dear Catherine' for the first time, that's all. But how pale you look! Perhaps it's the green lamp? No! Bless us all, dear Mr. Pultney, you are ill!"

"No, Miss Chud—that is. Catherine—oh, no! God bless you! Go—go!"

"But are you sure you are not ill?"

"Quite—quite sure."

"Well, I'm glad to see you to-night, because I have something to tell you."

"Me? to tell me?"

"Yes; I am going to be married."

"Married—married! You married? No, no, no! Oh, no —impossible!"

"I don't see that it is at all impossible, dear Mr. Pultney, and I want you to give me away."

"Give you away!—you?—you? Give away my heart, my soul, my life! Oh, heaven help me! what am I saying? Catherine, Catherine

—dear, dear girl—I, even I, the—the sedate man of many cares—the politician—the grave senator—even I——"

"What?—oh, what?"

She approached close to him; she looked with a world of witchery and mischief into his eyes; she placed one of her little hands upon his breast.

"What, dear Pultney?—what?"

"I love you!"

Mr. Pultney sank back upon a chair, and, clasping his hands over his eyes, he sobbed bitterly.

The cry of exultation died away upon the lips of the Maid of Honour. She was human, after all, and that man's grief touched her heart.

"Don't cry, Mr. Pultney—don't cry! I will love you, too, if you won't cry."

He moved his hands from his eyes; he uttered a gasping sob of half-despair, half-delight, and he folded her to his breast.

For the first time, he pressed his lips to hers in one passionate and loving kiss.

For the last time, too.

He lifted her up, then, as though she had been some little child, and carried her through that room to the door of another, which he opened. That other was a costly and elegant bed-chamber. He first placed her across the threshold, and then, in choking accents, he said, "Heaven will bless you, my Catherine, and hold you in its holy keeping! Good night—good night!"

He closed the door, and retraced his steps through the outer room and out into the corridor—out of the Palace, into the open air, and against the iron railings opposite he rested his heated brow, and wept.

Then he uttered one word.

That word was "Victory!"

He felt that he had triumphed—that he had won the hardest battle man can win—the battle with himself and his own affections.

Catherine Chudleigh was alone.

"He loves me!" she soliloquised—"everybody loves me! I suppose I am really very beautiful. I must be very beautiful; and beauty is—is——Yes, to be sure—beauty is power; and I want power, and I will have it. Wealth, beauty—the command of men's hearts! Ah! I shall be very happy! Of course I shall be very happy! What is to hinder me? I will marry Henry; he will be a peer, and I, in the robes of a princess, shall look more beautiful still! He loves me; Hamilton loves me; Mr. Pultney loves me; Bella loves me! Bah! she is a girl, and what do I care for her love?"

Catherine Chudleigh had little thought for the storm of feeling that was sweeping over the heart of the strong man who had been enforced to tell her that he loved her.

She strutted about the chamber into which he had shown her in a conceited style.

Then she stopped before a large cheval glass, in which no doubt Mrs. Pultney was in the habit of settling the disposition of her Court robes.

That mirror reflected now the plain sea-boy's dress in which Catherine Chudleigh was attired.

But she looked very lovely.

The trim, delicate little figure, straight as a wand, and upright, lithe, and active as some graceful, tall, tropical flower that carries a coronet of beauty on its slender stem.

So sat the fair face of Catherine Chudleigh on the faultless form.

She laughed.

What witchery there was in the laugh!

She leant forward, as though she were about to kiss the reflected fair features in the glass; and then she assumed a coquettish attitude, and beckoned to it, and then she laughed again.

"Oh, yes; it is no matter what I am dressed in, I am still beautiful!"

She then glanced at the huge old costly bed that was in the room, and she shook her head, making all her fair curls dance like sweet sunlight about her.

"No, I won't stay here—I won't! I don't like this room. The lodgings of the Maids of Honour are up-stairs. I shall be sure to find some room unoccupied, and in the morning I can send for that stupid, useful, good-tempered Bella; and she can bring me some horrid girl's clothes from Marlborough House. Oh, how I hate girl's clothes! I think I should like to be a man—a gay young spark upon town! Wouldn't I tease the girls!"

Catherine put on the sea-boy's cap again, but she was heedless of the long, wavy, and beautiful hair that hung far beneath it, dancing around her fair face, and kissing the jacket of the sham young sailor.

There was little chance of awaking any one at such an hour in the morning, and she trilled forth, like some early lark, an air as she tripped out of the bed-chamber, and took her course along the corridor, after passing through the outer room where she had seen Mr. Pultney.

The oil lamp with the green glass shade was still burning there, but the night student was gone. Never, perhaps, again would he be able to sit down with the calmness of an unclouded intellect to those pursuits that had once been his delight.

Catherine Chudleigh smiled as she passed the table, and saw the confused heap of papers lying upon it; she smiled with gratification as she whispered to herself, "Oh, yes, I felt certain he would say he loved me some day! Poor Mr. Pultney!"

She reached the gorgeous corridor; she began to whistle in that sweet, bird-like way that she had taken infinite pains to acquire, and which shocked some people and delighted others to hear from the lips of a young Maid of Honour.

Then, reaching the stairs that led to the upper part of the Palace, she had ascended three of them, when a strange cry arose upon her ears.

Catherine stopped the whistling.

She turned abruptly, for the strange cry had come from the corridor she was leaving.

Prostrate on the lowest step of those stairs, with his hands clasped together, was a young man, almost a boy, in the morning costume of one of the royal pages.

Accident, no doubt, had brought him, at that early hour, across the corridor; and he had seen and recognised Catherine Chudleigh.

She was annoyed at the attitude he assumed, and still more so at the words he uttered; for she did not recollect to have ever cast a single glance at him, and had no recollection of his features.

"Oh, Miss Chudleigh, Miss Chudleigh, if you will be so good, so charitable, so merciful as to kill me now, here, at once, if—if you cannot love me a little—only a little; for I do love you with all my heart—all, all my heart!"

Catherine put on a look of scorn.

"What do you mean?"

"Only that I love you—adore you! We—we —that is to say, all the pages love you! We quarrel about you—we fight about you; but I— oh, I love you best of all!"

"Of course you do."

"You think so—you believe me? You will —will be a little kind to—to one who——"

"Are you mad?"

"Nearly—nearly, dear Miss Chudleigh; and it is all for love of you!"

"Not another step!"

The poor love-stricken page had shown some inclination to crawl up the stairs, but at this imperious mandate from the Maid of Honour he shrunk back.

"Well," she added, "is that all?"

"All? all?"

"Yes. Have you said all you have to say now?"

"If—if I were to speak, to weep, to pray, to cry out to you for a month, I could only say that I love you, I love you!"

"Shall I tell you why?"

"Tell me anything, so that you condescend to speak to me. I feel happy then."

"Well, then, you love me because—because——"

"Yes; because?"

"You cannot help it! Ha, ha, ha!"

With a ringing, musical laugh, that seemed to echo through the heart of the poor enamoured page, she turned, and, quick as a ray of light, darted up the staircase.

The Page rested his face upon that step on which she had stood, and burst into a flood of tears.

"Very good," said Catherine Chudleigh, when she reached the landing-place, from which opened the bed rooms of the Maids of Honour, "very good; it is quite clear that everybody falls in love with me the moment they see me, and I shall have everything my own way, I see. What a glorious life I shall lead, to be sure. What sport it will be to see the whole male nation at my feet, ha, ha! Oh, I shall be as happy as the day is long. I must be very, very beautiful!"

She opened, quite at haphazard, one of the numerous doors she saw about her.

It did not much matter to her whether that door led to one of the occupied rooms of the Maids of Honour or not.

Catherine Chudleigh felt quite certain that she would run no risk by trusting the secret of her disguise to any of them.

But no, it happened she lit upon an empty chamber. She began to feel tired. Her first impulse was to cast herself upon a chair and go to sleep, there and then, at once. Then, with the impulsiveness of her nature, she resolved to go to bed. She opened a wardrobe that was in the room; and, in the most reckless manner,

tumbled out its contents, until she found some night clothing.

"All right, that will do. Why, it's nearly morning, I declare, quite getting light. Good-night now to all my lovers, great and small, high and low; and I hope they will torment themselves and each other as much as possible. This is a hard bed; well, it don't matter; I feel rather sleepy, and shall thoroughly enjoy a few hours rest. Eh? What?"

Catherine Chudleigh had closed her eyes, and in a few minutes would doubtless have been fast asleep, when a slight noise, of she knew not what in the room, aroused her.

It was that sort of arousing, which, as if by the touch of an enchanter's wand, dashes all sleep, and all desire to sleep, from the mind and body, and leaves us preternaturally wide awake, with every sense in a state of tension.

Catherine started half up in the bed, and looked about her.

The faint grey morning light was in the room.

Objects were all plainly visible, and that light, cold and white as it was, having increased each moment.

But what was it that had startled and alarmed her?

What was it that had struck such an alert at her heart?

All was still now.

She looked round the room, which was not a very large one, and, as her eyes wandered from one piece of furniture that it contained to another, they at length rested upon a large, old-fashioned, handsome, oaken chest, that stood beneath the window.

It was a chest that might at one time have stood in the sacristy of some old church, and held the muniments of the sacred building.

So it might have been the chest in which some family of lineage kept the deeds, the charters, the grants and privileges of a noble house.

Or the chest in which a miser might store his gold.

But be it what it might, the eyes of Catherine Chudleigh regarded it with a kind of fascination that could not be resisted.

It was in vain that she strove to turn her gaze away—to close her eyes entirely to outward impressions — still she ended by gazing at that old-fashioned chest, and sleep no longer oppressed her.

"How foolish I am, how very foolish. I thought I heard something; but, no doubt, that was fancy. I wonder I did not take a good look at that old chest before I got into bed; but I can now. I can easily now. What is to hinder me, from doing so, eh? Nothing, nothing. I will, too. Ah!"

Catherine Chudleigh was not of the screaming class of young ladies.

Neither was she of the timid or fainting sort.

But when she saw the lid of the ancient oaken chest commence slowly to open, she might be excused for the exclamation of surprise, not unmingled with a degree of terror, that burst from her lips.

CHAPTEL V.

A MYSTERIOUS ADVENTURE. — THE HANDSOME
STRANGER.—CATHERINE CHUDLEIGH'S DANGER.
—WOMAN'S PITY AND MAN'S DESPAIR.—THE
ALARM IN THE PALACE.—A SEARCH IN THE
DORMITORIES. — THE SECRET OF THE OAKEN
CHEST. — CATHERINE'S DEFIANCE OF THE
DUCHESS.

SLOWLY and quietly the lid opened.

She saw a hand.

She saw an arm.

The blood seemed for some seconds to stand
still at her heart, and then, as if to make up for
the lost pulsations, it rushed like wild-fire through
her veins, and she could hear the violent beating
of the vital organ.

But she did not cry out now. Curiosity, intense, all-absorbing curiosity, got the better of
every other feeling.

Her eyes were rivetted upon the oaken chest.
She felt them begin to ache from the painful
character of the fixed gaze with which she regarded it; but she would not have looked away
for worlds, and she could not, if she would.

Wider and wider still the lid of the box opened,
until it was cast quite back; and then she heard
a low, sad, soft voice, that in its sweet and gentle
accents, seemed to smite her almost to tears.

"Oh, gentle heart of maiden fair, as ever the
bright sun shone upon, have pity, pity, pity!"

She tried to speak, she wanted to say something, she knew not what; but the words did
not come forth from her pearly teeth and cherry
lips. Perhaps, something like a sigh she did give
utterance to, and that was all.

The sigh was echoed from the mysterious
occupant of the chest, and then she saw a face,
and she felt that she could gaze on it for ever.

Youth bloomed, or should have bloomed, upon
that face, although now it was very pale. Perhaps, that made it the more interesting to
Catherine Chudleigh; but the face was mournfully beautiful; masses of hair, dark as midnight,
hung about the pale brow, and descended low
upon the shoulders of the young man, who now,
with a low and graceful movement, raised himself up from the chest, and stepped out of it on
to the floor of the chamber.

He was attired in a plain suit of black velvet,
about which glistened a trimming of bugles.

The slight moustache upon his lip was dark as
the raven's wing, and with it, the full, fair lips
disclosed at the slightest motion, a glittering row
of teeth that shamed real pearls.

He spoke again.

Again, the low, sad tones struck upon the ears
of Catherine Chudleigh.

"Maiden, ever gentle, ever piteous, can I think
that you will betray me?"

Catherine, by a violent effort, found words in
which to reply.

"Betray you? you? you? Oh, never!"

A sweet smile played like a sunbeam over the
face of the mysterious stranger, and he bowed
low; lowly and gracefully he bent before the
young Maid of Honour, as he said, quietly, "In
the fair soul of woman, let us ever look for
peace, for pity, and for love!"

With a slow and stately step, and yet one that
had much persuasive gentleness it it, he approached the bed side. There was a cushioned
chair close to it, and on that he sat down; and
taking one of the hands of Catherine Chudleigh
in both his own, he looked into her fair face, as
he said, softly, "You are very young?"

"Six—six — teen!" she gasped, rather than
said.

"Yes, about that same age I should have
guessed, and you are very fair."

"I—I—if you—think so!"

"I dare say other eyes have seen it, other lips
have told you that you are beautiful!"

"Yes, oh, many; but——"

Catherine Chudleigh paused, she had been
about to say that if he only thought that she
was beautiful, the opinion of others would be of
little moment.

The mysterious stranger smiled quietly. There
was such a quiet assumption of superiority over
her in all he said and in all he did, that she found
it in vain to struggle with the feeling.

He touched the little delicate hand he held,
lightly with his lips.

It was scarcely a kiss.

And yet the touch, half caress only though it
was, thrilled from heart to brain of Catherine
Chudleigh.

"Who? who? Oh, tell me who you are?"
she gasped. "Tell me, for the love of
heaven!"

"A traitor, they call me here, in London."

"A traitor!"

"Yes. Can you not guess?"

A terrible suspicion, a guess that brought with
it a world of terror, came to the imagination of
Catherine Chudleigh.

Was it possible, that in this mysterious, interesting, fascinating stranger, she saw the assassin of the King's Physician, and the man who
had intended the bullet to reach the heart of the
King?

She shrunk back.

She withdrew the hand that he still held
clasped in both his.

"Oh, now indeed," she said, "I do suspect!"

"If," he replied, in the same sad, but soft
musical voice, in which he had already addressed
her, "you suspect me, and you have but to call
out aloud, to give such an alarm as it is easily in
your power to give, and I am a dead man!"

"Dead!"

"Yes. Nothing can save me, I must die by
my own hand, or by the hand of some other,
who would perform the act less gently or perhaps——"

"Perhaps—what?"

"Ah, no, I wrong you! I was going to say,
that, perhaps, you would earn a reputation for
loyalty that would be the theme of ages, and
yourself kill me!"

He drew from its coal black sheath, a long,
steel sword, the blade of which shone like
polished glass, and held it by the blade, with
the hilt towards the hands of the Maid of
Honour.

"No! oh, no!"

"You will not?"

"I cannot, and if I could—no! no!—I do

not want your life! but now I know that it was you who fired a pistol at the King."

The sad, pale face bowed guilty.

"I serve," he said, "another, who is the rightful King of these realms, and it was my duty to rid him of the presence of an usurper, if possible. I have failed, and perhaps you will consider it to be your duty to give me up to the executioner, the hurdle, the gibbet, the axe, the flames!"

"Oh, heaven, no!"

The stranger rose from the devotional chair and, spreading his arm over Catherine Chudleigh in a mysterious kind of position, he said, "Then, fair girl, you love me?"

She felt as if some nightmare of the soul were creeping over her. She made an effort to assume her ordinary composure; as she did, she heard, lying down as she now was, perhaps more distinctly than as if she had been up, a confused noise, in the lower part of the palace.

Then come the tapping of a drum.

The confused noise came nearer and nearer.

It was coming up the building, along with it she heard the clash of arms.

"I fancy," said the stranger, "that there is some alarm, and that by some means the impression is on the minds of the authorities that I am still in the palace."

"Yss; they come to seek you."

He smiled sadly.

"I hear them on the stairs, nearer, nearer still. It is for you to sacrifice, or to save me!"

"No, no! Oh, no! not sacrifice!"

Catherine Chudleigh had turned the key in the lock of the chamber-door, and now, before another word could be said by either herself or the mysterious stranger, there came a sharp knocking at the door.

"Answer!" said the Jacobite, for such he undoubtedly was.

"Who—who knocks?"

"Who sleeps here?" asked a female voice. "Which of her Majesty's ladies occupies this room?"

"I—Miss Chudleigh!"

"Chudleigh, Chudleigh! You don't belong to the royal household. You are one of the people of the Princess of Wales."

"Yes, madam!"

"Who is it?" whispered the stranger.

Catherine had recognised the voice of the person on the outside of the door.

"It is the Duchess of Portman, Mistress of the Robes to the Queen."

"Oh, that malignant Orangist!"

"Open the door, if you please," said the Duchess. "A general search is taking place through the palace for the assassin who fired at the King, and I have undertaken to conduct this part of it."

"Farewell," whispered the Jacobite, to Catherine Chudleigh. "I fled last night from the royal saloon, and found a refuge here. I secreted myself in that chest, which can no longer be a hiding place, since you know of it. Farewell, I will not stain the threshold of your chamber with blood, or I might defend myself."

"No, no! Oh, heaven, what shall I do?"

"Will you open the door, minion?" cried the Duchess, in a rage."

"Yes—no! That is, yes, madam!"

"Quick, then!"

Catherine Chudleigh looked like some fair, white apparition, as she glided from the bed. She grasped the arm of the stranger, as, with scarcely breath to do so from agitation, she whispered to him, "Into the chest again, into it again, and I will save you. I will, I will!"

He gave her one sad, mournful,—but oh, so grateful a look, and slipped into the chest.

The Duchess of Portman rattled at the door.

Catherine Chudleigh flung into the chest above the mysterious stranger, who packed himself into a small space at the bottom of it, a quantity of the clothing, ribbons, lace, and flowers, she had cast out in her reckless way from the wardrobe, and then she closed the lid.

The Duchess beat eagerly against the door.

Catherine cast about her a robe with fur trimmings, and then shot back the lock.

The door was open.

The small gallery without was crowded by guards, and the Duchess of Portman, accompanied by two other of the Honourable Ladies of the Court, stepped into the room.

"It's a very odd thing that you are here at all, Miss Chudleigh," said the Duchess.

"And a still odder thing," added one of the other ladies, "that she should keep us so long at the door."

"Yes," said Catherine.

"Yes, indeed," said the Duchess. "Is that all you can say?"

"Yes."

Catherine Chudleigh sat down on the top of the oaken chest.

"You will have to account for yourself, Miss Chudleigh," added the Duchess, "I can tell you!"

"Yes."

Catherine meant to be provoking, and certainly nothing could very well be more so than the constant iteration of the one word "yes," in answer to all that was said to her.

CHAPTER VI.

THE FRUITLESS SEARCH IN THE MAID OF HONOUR'S CHAMBER.—CATHERINE CHUDLEIGH'S CLEVER MANAGEMENT. — THE OAKEN CHEST ESCAPES EXAMINATION.—IS HE DEAD?—THE MAID OF HONOUR'S DESPAIR.—LOVE AT FIRST SIGHT! AND DEATH IN THE CHEST.—AN EXPEDIENT.

IT was not good policy on the part of Catherine Chudleigh, seeking as she did, most unquestionably, to save the handsome young stranger, who had thrown himself upon her mercy, to be so aggravating to the Duchess of Portman.

But she could not help it.

Catherine Chudleigh had a resisting temper, which had not yet been sufficiently schooled in the fiery opposition of the great world, on the threshold of which (only a child in years) she stood, to be controlled.

In none of the chambers of the dormitory of the Maids of Honour had the Duchess of Portman instituted anything like the search that took place in that apartment which Catherine had appropriated to herself on that night, or rather on that early morning.

It was not that there was the remotest suspicion on the mind of any one, that any of the ladies of the court were harbouring the assassin; but as, when the act was committed, which had thrown the Palace into such confusion, all the Maids of Honour, and other officials of the building, were up and about the saloons: the possibility that the traitor might have made his way up to those topmost chambers, and be still hidden there, naturally arose.

And he might be hidden quite unknown to the occupants of the rooms.

That the guess of the authorities was a good one, we are aware, for was he not actually in that chamber to which the Duchess of Portman now directed such special attention.

The chimney was peeped up.

The wardrobe was looked into.

The outside of the window was glanced at.

But there was no discovery.

"Well, Miss Chudleigh," said the Duchess, "I congratulate you."

"Yes, madam."

"I congratulate you upon the fact, that no concealed traitor is found here."

"Yes, madam."

"Don't speak to me, girl, in that way. I do wonder what men can possibly see in your doll's face to think you pretty."

"Yes, madam."

The Duchess shook Catherine Chudleigh.

Catherine kicked at the Duchess.

"What is she sitting on?" said one of the other ladies. "Is it a box?"

The Duchess was a woman of bone and sinew, and she shoved Catherine Chudleigh off the lid of the oaken chest in a moment.

The lid was raised.

"Clothes and trumpery."

The lid was shut down again with a bang.

"Yes, madam!" said the Maid of Honour.

"You may be quite sure," added the Duchess, looking tremendously irate, "that I will make it my special business to inquire how it is that you sleep here when the Princess of Wales is at Marlborough House!"

Catherine said "Yes, madam!" once more, and the infuriated Duchess left the room.

She waited until the search at that part of the royal dwelling was over, and then the Maid of Honour again turned the key in the door and flew to the oaken chest.

"Saved, saved!" she said. "I have saved you, and as all the world loves me, if you, too, will——Oh, heaven! Oh, what—what?"

She had flung from the chest the various fancy articles that had served so well to conceal the presence therein of the handsome courtier, and she saw him again.

But he moved not.

He spoke not.

"Dead, dead!" screamed Catherine. "He is dead!"

There was a rapid footstep in the corridor, and the door was violently pushed. It was well that it was locked, or a discovery must have taken place.

The loud scream that for once had been extorted from the lips of Catherine Chudleigh had reached the ears of the Duchess of Portman just as she gained the foot of the stairs leading from those dormitories, and she was back to the door of the room in a few seconds.

Catherine closed the chest.

She flew to the door, and opened it.

Pale and agitated, she stood face to face with the Duchess.

"Well, girl?"

"Well, madam?"

"You screamed! You cried out!"

"I did."

"What for—what for?"

"Sport!"

"Sport? Dare you say so to me? Sport?"

"Yes, madam!"

Catherine Chudleigh began to whistle.

"Was there ever such impudence?" exclaimed the Duchess.

Catherine Chudleigh still whistled.

The Duchess looked for a moment or two as though she contemplated some personal violence to Catherine, and then, afraid to engage in any further altercation with one who was such a mistress of the art of aggravation, she abruptly left her.

The Maid of Honour closed the door again, locked it, and rushed back to the oaken chest.

There lay the handsome stranger, with his eyes closed, apparently dead, smothered, suffocated in that chest, rather than utter a groan or a sigh which should convict the young girl who had risked so much to save him.

Not that Catherine Chudleigh, the young Maid of Honour, knew exactly then what she had risked. She did not reflect that she was guilty of actual treason, and that her life would be forfeit to the laws—laws which were then carried out often with a horrible and barbarous stringency—for "harbouring, aiding, comforting, and abetting a regicide and a traitor."

She wrung her hands.

She wept, sobbed, and groaned.

"Oh, do try to live! Do speak! Do move! You cannot be dead! You, so handsome—you, whom I will love—whom I did love! Oh, why am I forced to say did? Why are you not alive, that I may say I do love you? Love, love! Oh, the pang—the agony of a lost, lost love!"

She stretched her arms over the box, she sobbed as if her heart would break.

Was this retribution? Where now was the bold, the insolent, haughty, tricksey spirit of the heartless Maid of Honour who meant to make human affections her sport and pastime?

Did she now feel some of the pangs which she had taken such delight in making others feel?

Could it, indeed, be possible, that the only person who had really enthralled her fancy, had appeared before her as a vision of beauty, but to fade away from her sight the next moment into the misty regions of death.

Now she felt that she had never really loved the Duke of Hamilton—never loved Captain Harvey, whom she had promised to marry.

Never loved any one until she looked into the soft, melancholy eyes of the would-be regicide.

"Awake—awake!" she cried, wild sobs ming

ling in convulsive throes along with the words. "Awake—awake! I will save you and I will love you, or perish with you! Awake from the trance of death, and look on me, and speak to me once again!"

No; it was surely not to be.

The form of manly beauty in the oaken chest might still for a few fleeting hours be fair to look upon, and then the grave will claim it.

Grave! What grave?

Catherine Chudleigh clasped her hands together, and with difficulty suppressed a shriek of dismay as the thought occurred to her that she was in as great, if not a greater, perplexity with the dead body than she had been in with the living traitor who had misplaced her protection.

What should she do now?

How could she hide the corpse?

In what manner should she be able to account for its presence there?

She knelt down by the side of the chest, completely prostrated by fear.

The morning, however, had come; all would soon be life, bustle, and commotion in the Palace; she would not be able to remain in that room except on the plea of indisposition, and even that would not insure her safety.

Mr. Pultney would come to see her.

Sympathizing Maids of Honour, belonging to the Queen's household, would be thronging the chamber.

No, no, that would not do.

She felt that she must make some effort to remove the dead Jacobite out of that chamber into some other.

She started to her feet.

An idea had struck her.

The page, that royal page, who is so deeply, so madly, so devotedly in love with me; he will do anything that it is possible to do at my desire; and he will attempt even what is impossible, if I tell him Ah, how useful it is to be beloved, and what a glorious thing it is to be so beautiful!

Catherine stole a glance at herself in the little mirror that was in the apartment, and one of her old coquettish smiles came over her face.

It was doubtful, after all, if even the death of the handsome Jacobite would affect her for long.

She looked eagerly among the heap of clothing she had in her pettish, careless way flung from the wardrobe, for some articles of dress that would suit her, and was soon sufficiently attired to make her way through the Palace.

She wondered whose bed she had slept in, and whose clothes she had made so free with.

Again and again she clenched her little hands, and made as ugly faces as her beauty would let her at the thought of the insulting conduct of the Duchess of Portman.

But for that visit, too, she would not have been in her present difficulty.

Who could have said that she slept in that room of all others, then? She might have aided and assisted the Jacobite to escape, and then transferred herself altogether to some other chamber.

But, as it was, she would now be associated with the transaction in the most disagreeable manner.

She could not dissever herself from the room, and therefore, it became necessary that the dead body of the handsome regicide should be removed.

"Yes," she said; "yes, I will seek that page who bowed down so low before me on the staircase, and who was ready to give his life for me—he shall help me."

The Palace was astir.

Some of the officers of State were already assembled in the breakfast saloon.

Pages, grooms of the chamber, gentlemen ushers, and officers of the guard, were passing to and fro, and ascending and descending the staircases.

Catherine Chudleigh met several who bowed to her in passing.

She wanted to find out the page who was so smitten with her charms; but although she met several of his fraternity she did not see him among them.

If she had known his name she would have asked for him; but that she did not, and she was, at length, compelled to seek the pages' waiting-room, as a handsome apartment adjoining the royal apartments was called.

She was near the door of that room, when the object of her search appeared.

Pale and dejected, the young page, with a look of suffering upon his brow, came out of the room with slow steps.

Catherine Chudleigh stepped up to him. She did not speak at the moment, but with a glance, she gave him a slight touch on the arm.

He turned and saw her.

He cried out with joy, and tremblingly cowered down before her as though he had suddenly met with an angel in his path, and could not bear the blaze of immortality.

"Your name?" asked the Maid of Honour, hastily.

"Carolus Aime."

"Well, I think that—that you love me!" queried Catherine.

"Love you? Love you? Oh, heaven! all the love the world ever knew does not make up the dear affection that——"

"Be quiet! That will do! Thinking that you did love me, I thought, at the same time, that you would be glad to do me a service to prove it."

"My life—my life! Do you want my life? Say so, and it is yours!"

"No, your life would do me no good; but I want courage and fidelity."

The page placed his hand upon his sword.

The other hand he pressed to his heart.

"Very well; follow me to my chamber."

"Your—your chamber?"

"Yes."

She laughed maliciously.

"Yes, my chamber. It is in some confusion and litter; but you will excuse all that?"

"Oh, heaven!"

"Come, do not stay romancing and ejaculating here! Follow me, and I shall find out if you really love me, or only have pretended to do so. This way—follow—follow, quick!"

CHAPTER VII.

THE PAGE THINKS HIMSELF IN A HEAVEN OF FE-
LICITY.—CATHERINE CHUDLEIGH'S DUPLICITY.
—THE STOLEN KISSES.—A STRANGE PROPOSAL
AND AN ALARM.—A MYSTERIOUS DISAPPEAR-
ANCE.—WHERE IS THE HANDSOME JACOBITE?

THE page was bewildered.

Whether he floated after the fair Maid of Honour, or actually trod the rich carpets of the Palace, he know not. All he felt conscious of was, that before him was the image of his heart's idol, and that she had told him to follow her.

And whither?

To her own chamber!

The chamber in which she had slept, and which she apologized to him for being in something of a litter.

"Am I mad?" he gasped. "Am I mad—or am I in a dream?"

Up the staircase, along the corridor—still he saw her, and still he followed her. She paused then a moment at the door of the room, in order that he might come up to her, for she had outstripped him by some twenty or thirty paces.

He reached her, panting, not with fatigue, but with delight and excitement.

She took him by the arm.

She placed a finger on her lips to awe him into silence, and she led him into the room, and closed and locked the door.

"Carolus!"

"Angel—angel!"

"Listen to me."

"Music—oh, such music!"

"I am about to trust you with my life, and with something yet dearer to me—my reputation—do you comprehend me?"

He fell on his knees at her feet.

"I look into your dear eyes—oh, Miss Chudleigh, may I and can I call you Catherine?"

"Yes; because after to-day I shall look upon you as my friend. I want to ask you one question, now, which I hope you will be able to answer me?"

"Yes, oh yes, your friend! Well, friends may love so dearly."

"Be quiet."

He had ventured to lift the edge of the robe which she wore, and press it to his lips.

"The question I want to ask you is, if you know where in the Palace the Mistress of the Robes sleeps?"

"The Duchess of Portman?"

"Yes."

"The Duke is in Flanders, and the Duchess occupies the small room, known as the Queen's boudoir."

"Good! Are you strong?"

"Strong? I think, I hope, I am! Oh, dear, dear Catherine! my love is strong; for it seems that it would enable me to remove mountains if they stood between us. Oh, believe me! Let me, now that I am here——"

"What?"

"Let me kiss your dear hand—your little fingers—let me for one moment!"

"Nonsense, Carolus! Do you think you could now—do you think if I were to ask you—

if I were, having brought you here to my room—do you think, boy as you are, that—that——"

"Catherine, my own Catherine, I love you!"

"Get away!"

He sprung to his feet, and clasped her in his arms.

He rained kisses on her face, her eyes, her cheeks, her lips!

"Will you get away, you wretched boy—will you? How dare you? Take that!"

A hearty blow, repeated with both hands on each side of his face, staggered the page; and he was still further staggered, when the fair Maid of Honour added: "All I wanted to know was, whether you thought you would be strong enough to carry a dead man on your back?"

The page looked both surprised and terrified.

He repeated her words.

"A dead man on my back?"

"Yea, Carolus. If you can, and will do so, and if you have the skill and cleverness to place him anywhere in the bed-chamber of the Duchess of Portman, you may call me 'dear Catherine,' and I will call you——"

"Oh, yes, say the words!"

"Dear Carolus!"

The page was sick with joy.

"You consent?"

"Yes, oh, yes! But a dead man? What dead man? Oh, it cannot be real. It is all a dream—all a delusion of the fancy!"

"No—alas, alas!—it is not!"

Catherine Chudleigh laid her hand upon the lid of the oaken chest, and burst into tears.

The sight that she knew was there, waiting to meet her sight, overcame her, and she wept abundantly.

The page was deeply affected; but still there had come a strange, glaring look into his eyes.

The frowning look of jealousy.

Who was this dead man of whom Catherine Chudleigh spoke? Who was he for whom she shed such precious tears? What was the meaning of it all?

"Carolus, Carolus!"

"Yes, dear Catherine."

"Open this chest, and tell me what you think of what you see."

She crouched down on the floor, and hid her fair face in her hands; and the tears trickled through her fingers as the page obeyed her.

She heard him open the lid of the chest.

But he uttered no exclamation, either of surprise or affright, as she fully expected he would. On the contrary, he spoke quite calmly, as he said, "Yes, dear, dear Catherine, I have opened it."

"And—and you see——"

"Yes, dear."

"A dreadful sight?"

"Not any."

"What do you see?"

"Some feathers, some ribbons—very gay ones; some clothing; and among them the dress of a boy; a hat and feathers, too; some trinkets; some——"

"No, no; you deceive me. Oh, can there be such callousness—such, such indifference even to death in the heart of a boy like you? Ah! What—what? No, no! Gone?"

Catherine Chudleigh had turned her gaze to the chest. One glance was enough.

KATE ESCAPES FROM HER BRIDAL CHAMBER WINDOW.

The dead body of the handsome Jacobite was gone.

The page was upon his knees.

So was she.

They looked at each other in silence and in surprise, with their faces so close to each other that each saw his and her image in the eyes that were so close at hand.

Catherine Chudleigh then drew a long breath. It was scarcely one of relief—for the mystery of what had become of the regicide was one that wanted explanation.

The page drew a long breath, too; for he was puzzled and perplexed in the extreme as to what could be the meaning of all this terribly-exciting and mysterious conduct on the part of the Maid of Honour.

She looked again into the oaken chest.

She plunged one hand and arm into it. She

tossed out some of its miscellaneous contents. No; there was no handsome Jacobite there. She touched the actual wood of the bottom of the chest.

"Gone, gone—utterly gone! Most inexplicably and most mysteriously gone!"

What was she to do now? What was she to say to the page? How explain all that would seem perplexibly bewildering in her conduct?

It could not be done. Whatever his state of mind for the future as regarded her, she must leave him in it. There was no other resource.

"That will do, Carolus," she said. "You can go now."

"Go now?"

"I said go now."

"But—but——Oh, dear!"

"There is the door."

The page looked at the door—then he looked at Catherine. He projected his face towards her, and his lips looked as though a kiss lingered upon them.

There was no mistaking the action.

"No, no, no," she said—" go!"

"Oh, Catherine!"

"Oh, Carolus!"

"One—only one—one poor——No, I don't mean poor—one dear, sweet, delicious kiss—so dear, so precious to me, so, so very easy to you!"

"You will go then?"

"Yes."

"At once?"

"At once, dear heart!"

"There, then."

Their lips met—met over the corner of that most mysterious oaken chest; and then they both started, and nearly knocked their heads together; for there came a sharp, decisive bang at the door, which was locked.

The page would have uttered some ungenteel exclamation, but Catherine Chudleigh clapped her hand upon his mouth, and stopped him.

The sharp tap at the door was repeated.

Then there came a voice from the other side.

"Miss Chudleigh is requested to open the door in the name of the King!"

The page would have spoken again, but Catherine Chudleigh stopped him by a threatening, upheld finger.

"Open—open, in the name of the King!" said the voice again.

It was a man's voice.

The Maid of Honour called out in reply to it.

"Who dares ask me to open this door?"

"I, Miss Chudleigh; I am compelled to do so. My name is Major; I am of the Chamberlain's department, and am ordered to examine this room."

"I resist, sir."

"But, my dear young lady——"

"Sir, I resist; and you have just given the reason. I am a young lady. Begone, sir; and if it be necessary, tell the King that now he has lived a King, he should be likewise a gentleman, and respect the presence of a lady's chamber."

A confused murmur of voices now came from the outer side of the door, and then a fresh voice cried out, "Miss Chudleigh's delicacy need take no alarm, for Mr. Major will only be called in if necessary."

"Oh, madam, are you there again?" cried Catherine, as in those tones she recognised the voice of the Duchess of Portman once more.

"Yes, I am here, minx; and I have had to order it, and this door will be broken down."

"Everybody knows your Grace's extreme sensibility, modesty, and delicacy," retorted Catherine Chudleigh. "So, in the full conviction that you would not hesitate to come with half a dozen pages of the Palace to look into any one's chamber, I will in a few seconds open the door."

"You had better, hussey."

"Oh, yes, I will. But I warn you, my Lady Portman!"

"You warn me! Of what?"

"Why, the Life Guards do not sleep here! You will find a troop of them at the King's Mews?"

"Break the door down!" screamed the infuriated Duchess. "I can stand the violence of this wretched girl no longer!"

"In with you!" whispered Catherine Chudleigh to the page, as she pointed to the chest—"in with you! It is your only chance, and that but a small one!"

"Shall I be suffocated?"

"Never mind!"

The page got into the chest. The Maid of Honour covered him up, even as she had covered up the handsome Jacobite, with the odds and ends of clothes and frippery from the wardrobe, and then shut down the lid. Did she hope that he, too, would mysteriously disappear, as had disappeared the handsome stranger?

CHAPTER VIII.

CATHERINE CHUDLEIGH APPEARS TO BE LOST.—THE SCOTCH MAID OF HONOUR HAS HER SUSPICIONS.—WHO IS IN THE CHEST?—A TREMENDOUS DISCOVERY.—THE REPROACHES OF CAPTAIN HARVEY.—THE DUCHESS OF PORTMAN APPEARS TO ENJOY A TRIUMPH. CATHERINE CHUDLEIGH EXTRICATES HERSELF FROM A DILEMMA.

CRASH!

The door was broken open.

Catherine Chudleigh was arranging her hair. She did not even look round. But she began to whistle, because she thought that would annoy the Duchess.

"Mr. Vigors," said the Duchess of Portman, in tones of passion, "do your duty, sir!"

"It is my painful duty, Miss Chudleigh," said the official from the Chamberlain's office—"it is my painful duty to accompany the guard, which is now without, to this apartment, in which, at an early hour this morning, the Lady Augusta Home, who sleeps in the room adjoining, says she heard the tones of a man's voice."

"No doubt," replied Catherine Chudleigh—"no doubt the Scotch Maid of Honour you have mentioned is well enough acquainted with the tones of men's voices in bed-chambers, but, in this case, she has probably mistaken my man for her own."

"Wretch! I'll tear your eyes out!" screamed an infuriated female, who now dashed into the room from the corridor beyond.

"Oh, you are there, too, my Lady Augusta!" laughed Catherine. "Ha, ha! My kind lover, Mr. Pultney, always used to say that nothing put people in such a passion as a good home truth."

This pun upon her name, and the bitter sarcasm that accompanied it, so exasperated the Scotch Maid of Honour, that she made a rush at Catherine; and no doubt, as she was double her size and weight, she might have inflicted upon her some sudden injury, had she not fallen over the identical oaken chest which contained the page.

"Ladies, ladies!" said Mr. Vigors. "Pray don't—oh, pray don't, I beg of you!"

"Good heavens, what is all this?" cried a voice from the corridor. "What is it? I am told that there is every suspicion attached to Miss Chudleigh!"

Catherine shook a little.

It was the Captain Harvey, to whom she stood in so close a relation as to be his affianced wife, who thus spoke from the corridor.

She felt all her danger.

But Catherine Chudleigh had the heart of a lion. She called out aloud, "Oh, Harvey, thank heaven, you are there! These women want to kill me!"

"No, wretched girl," said the Duchess. "If you are guilty of secreting a traitor, it is not I who will kill you. The public executioner will get rid of such a disgrace to the Court. Mr. Vigors, be so good as look in this oak chest, for, on my faith! it looks large enough to hold a man, and it was not examined before."

The Maid of Honour gave herself up for lost.

It was but a degree better that the page should be found in the chest instead of the regicide.

In the latter case, the penalty would have been death.

In the former, it would be dishonour; for how could she, in any way that could save her reputation, account for the presence of the page in that room?

She turned pale and red by turns.

The Duchess of Portman saw these effects, and triumphed accordingly.

The Lady Augusta Home saw these likewise, and she flew at the oaken chest like a tigress.

"Stop, stop, dear lady," said Mr. Vigors, as he stood with his sword drawn on the defensive. "Stop one moment, if you please. These arch-traitors are dangerous, and, in their desperation, would spare neither age nor sex."

This was an unfortunate speech for Mr. Vigors to make, as the Duchess of Portman was what is called "tenacious" on the subject of age; and had she not been so deeply interested in the oaken chest as to devote all her attention to it, Mr. Vigors would have heard of it.

Catherine Chudleigh chuckled at the edge of the little dressing-table, and said not a word.

Mr. Vigors advanced to the chest.

With an air of solemnity, he laid his hand on the lid.

On the chance, then, that it might contain the object of his search, he shouted out, as he flung the lid back, "Resist, and you are a dead man!"

The page uttered an odd cry, and sat up in the chest.

The official from the Chamberlain's office flung himself upon him, crying aloud, "Treason! treason! treason!"

Captain Harvey, who had from a feeling of respect for Catherine remained on the threshold of the room, now advanced four paces.

Those four paces brought him to the chest.

"Good heaven!" he cried. "Is this possible?"

It was Lady Home, then, who first announced who and what the occupant of the chest was.

"Carolus, the page!" she cried. "It is Carolus, the page!"

"Page? One of the pages?" sneered the Duchess, in unfeigned surprise.

"Oh, Catherine, Catherine!" said Captain Harvey, in a mournful tone of voice, that carried with it a world of reproach.

The page looked from one to the other in a state of stupefaction.

Catherine Chudleigh clasped both her hands over her eyes with powerful tension. What should she say? What should she do? Would any amount of cleverness - any amount of audacity—suffice to free her from the entanglement into which she had fallen? For a few moments —during those few moments of surprise, when nobody knew exactly what to do or what to think—her brain was in a perfect whirl with excitement.

Then she turned to Captain Harvey.

"You—you? Can you believe me guilty?"

"Catherine! Catherine!"

He pointed to the page.

Then she uttered a little sharp, short scream, for she had thought upon the possibility of an escape from the peril that surrounded her, as well as of a means of turning the tables upon the Lady Augusta Home, whose officious zeal had brought that trouble upon her.

"I swear," she said, "by the everlasting heaven above us—I swear that, about half an hour since, when I left this room, I opened this chest, and Carolus was not there; nor was he anywhere else in this chamber. Speak—speak, wretched boy, and save me, even if you confess what will hurt yourself? Did you come in here, while I was absent, from the adjoining room, and hide yourself in this chest?"

"I did," replied the page.

Lady Augusta Home made a rush at him, but the page ducked his head, and down went the lid of the chest again, with a bang.

"Oh, Harvey, Harvey!" said Catherine Chudleigh, with a smile.

"Catherine!—dear Catherine! can you ever forgive me? Oh, speak!"

"Easily."

She placed her hand in his.

The Duchess looked confounded.

Lady Home was yellow with rage.

The page opened the lid about half a foot, but she made another scream and rush at him, when he let it come down again sharply.

"Really," said Catherine Chudleigh, "you might, I think, let the boy alone now."

Captain Harvey was forced to make the most painful efforts to keep himself from laughing aloud.

"This is all very inexplicable!" cried the Duchess of Portman. "Of course, the page will be at once dismissed from the royal service; and you, Miss Chudleigh, will recollect that you have still to invent some good reason for being here at all."

"Your Grace," said Captain Harvey, "may leave that to me. I know the reason why Miss Chudleigh slept last night here; and I know it to be a good one."

"Nobody better, I daresay!" sneered the Duchess.

"Madam, this young lady is about to become my wife; and such being the case, her honour is as dear to me as my own."

"And my honour!" sneered Lady Augusta Home. "What is to become of my honour?"

"Oh, my dear," said Catherine, with an arch

look, "*you must turn over a new leaf, since it appears you have lost the page!*"

As she spoke, Catherine, with her hand still in that of Captain Harvey, left the room ; but as she did so, she said, gaily, " There is one thing you must do, Harvey, or I won't be married for six months longer."

" Great heavens! what is it?" asked Harvey in surprise.

" You must manage, somehow, to get that boy—the page, I mean—out of the scrape he has got himself into."

" But, Catherine——"

" No, no ; I will hear nothing. It is of no use your saying a word about it. He told the truth, you know, when he might not ; and so saved me from a good deal of stupid, unpleasant suspicion."

" Well, I will try."

" That won't do. Your rival secured a good bye for six months."

" Oh, Catherine, you will make me begin to think that you look with an eye of favour upon the boy."

Catherine Chudleigh uttered one of her pretended little screams of surprise.

" Do you doubt it? Of course I do. The boy is a nice boy—good-looking, handsome. I'll give him a kiss some day. Dear me, Harvey, one would think you fully expected I was going to be constant to you! Of course I admire the boy. I'll kneel down, and he shall kneel down some day, and he shall kiss me, and I will kiss him. Oh, dear, yes! Well, what do you say now, eh?"

" Nothing, nothing, Catherine ; but that I will do anything you wish, if you will but be a little serious, only now and then."

Captain Harvey looked upon the speech that Catherine Chudleigh had made, as one of those ebullitions of her high spirits and preverse disposition, of which he had already had some stringent proofs.

Little did he dream that she was speaking of something that had actually already taken place within the hour.

But the conversation between them was abruptly put an end to by the arrival of the young girl from Marlborough House, who was so blindly full of admiration of Catherine.

Poor Bella had spent a night of the greatest alarm, and at the earliest opportunity had made her way from the Princess of Wales to seek Catherine, whose whereabouts at Leicester House she had guessed from the casual expressions which the young groom, Hutchings, had reported to her he had heard from Catherine in the Park on the occasion when he had warned her not to return to Marlborough House.

Poor Bella quite astonished Captain Harvey by the passionate manner in which she fell upon the breast of Catherine and sobbed with delight at seeing her.

" Be quiet, do, Bella!" cried Catherine. " There, that will do. Captain Harvey, this child loves me truly and better than you ever will. Now, don't put on a face of contradiction, for what I say I mean."

———

CHAPTER IX.

CATHERINE CHUDLEIGH ASCERTAINS SOMETHING MORE ABO T THE HANDSOME JACOBITE.—THE FURIOUS RIVALS.—CAPTAIN HARVEY DOUBTS AND YET LOVES.—THE CONDITIONS OF THE SPOILT BEAUTY.—MRS. HANMER IS PERPLEXED BY RIVAL OFFERS.

" I AM haunted," said Catherine Chudleigh to herself, as with Captain Harvey, at about half-past ten o'clock on that day she went in one of the Court carriages to her aunt's house by the Green Park. " I am haunted by the visage of that young man with the brown hair and the pale face, and whose mysterious disappearance will be the plague of my life."

She sighed.

Captain Harvey looked at her with apprehension.

" Ah, Catherine, are you unhappy, when I hope that this day may still see you as my wife."

" No—no. But——"

She sighed again.

" You are, indeed, out of spirits, dear Catherine. Can I do or say anything to please you ?"

" No. I was only thinking—what a handsome—I mean what an ugly wretch that must have been who so nearly took the life of the King."

" What, the Jacobite?"

" Yes! I shall be so glad when he is taken. Is he taken?"

" I fear not ; but from what I heard General Sondes say, there is some clue to him."

" Indeed, indeed! What clue?"

" It is thought that he is a very distinguished personage, indeed, no other than the grandson of a certain person never mentioned in the atmosphere of the Palace."

" Ah, you mean, then, that he is a Prince of the deposed House of the Stuarts?"

" So they say."

Catherine Chudleigh sighed again.

" But," added Captain Harvey. " I have no doubt he will be caught and executed."

" Not if I know it!" answered Catherine, with a sudden energy. " Not if I know it—that is to say—to—to say, unless I have a good place to see it all, for who would spare the traitor who would aim at the life of the King?"

She had seen the dark cloud gather on the brow of Captain Harvey, as she had commenced speaking, and she had no wish to quarrel with him.

She thought that to be Countess of Bristol, which there was so good a chance of, since he, the Honourable Captain Harvey, was the next heir, and the present Earl was childless, was not a piece of fortune to be thrown aside for a dead man.

She still considered that the handsome Jacobite was no more ; and the only possible explanation that even her ingenuity suggested, of the disappearance of the body, was, that he had more associates and adherents in the royal residence than any one was aware of.

While she was employed in her search for the

page, Carolus, they might have removed the suffocated Jacobite from the chest.

It was a little far-fetched this explanation, but still it was the only one that bore even the semblance of a theory that was at all plausible on the subject.

The young Maid of Honour had too keen and acute an intellect to be superstitious, so she did not look into the realms of the supernatural for an explanation of events taking place in this every day sublunary sphere.

In such-like conversation, then, the Honourable Captain Harvey and his bride elect, reached the house of Mrs. Hanmer, the aunt of Catherine, who had brought her to London, and whose house was still her nominal home.

A horse, held by a groom in rich livery, was at the door of the house.

Captain Harvey bit his lips as he said :—

"Catherine, that man is in the livery of the Duke of Hamilton, and he is no doubt at present with your aunt, making some proposals for your hand."

"Very well ? What then ?"

"He may dazzle her."

"Well."

"Oh, Catherine !"

"Oh, Harvey : If the Duke of Hamilton dazzles my Aunt Hanmer, why let him marry the person he dazzles, for I will not have him."

"You enchant me, but still—a scene—a—kind of fracas—a sort of sentimental meeting in a room with your aunt and with Hamilton, would not be the most agreeable thing in the world for all parties."

"And why not," said Catherine Chudleigh, with vivacity. "I should enjoy it above all things. Come on, I am not afraid of all the aunts and all the Dukes in the world."

Catherine sprung from the coach, closely followed by Captain Harvey, who had a pale, stern look upon his face. She hastily ascended the steps of her aunt's house, and crossed the hall.

To the right was a reception-room, called the "Rose Room," from those ornaments in sculptured oak being on the cross-beams of the ceiling.

Catherine flung the door open, and the first thing she saw was the Duke of Hamilton on his knees at the feet of her aunt.

She caught a few words which the Duke was uttering, in fervent tones, at the moment of her entrance.

"Yes, kind Mrs. Hanmer, second my views; stop this marriage of Catherine with Harvey, which can only end in misery, and half my estates shall be yours."

Catherine understood the situation instantly; she knew, too, that her aunt was not exactly a stoic where the goods and chattels of this world were concerned ; and she found some effect had been produced by the large, liberal offer of the Duke.

Mrs. Hanmer had power, as she, Catherine, was still a minor, as her nearest relation in London, to stop so important a step as a marriage, but Catharine adopted a course in a moment, that confounded her aunt, and covered the Duke of Hamilton with confusion.

Making a comic kind of rush into the room, she cried out in her loudest tones, "Bless you! bless you both! May you live long and die happy! Come in, Harvey, come in. His Grace of Hamilton is going to be my uncle, for he has just made an offer to my Aunt Hanmer, and he says he will settle on her one half of his estates."

Mrs. Hanmer swooned.

"Confusion !" cried the Duke, as he, with some difficulty, scrambled to his feet.

"I congratulate your Grace," said Captain Harvey, with a low bow.

"Well, Nunkey Hamilton !" said Catherine. "How are you, eh !"

"Catherine ?"

"I'm here."

She began to whistle.

"Is it possible, Catherine, that you can make a sport of my feelings in this manner."

"Feelings ? feelings ? What do you mean by feelings. I have feelings at the tips of my fingers, and that is all I know or want to know about such things."

"On my faith !" cried the Duke. "I begin to think so, Catherine ; you have cured me."

"Like a ham do you mean ? You look rather dry and smoky."

"No. But you have cured me of a passion which was almost an insanity. Harvey, we are no longer rivals ; on the contrary, you have my —my most sincere sympathies and condolences."

"Indeed, your Grace, I am not aware that I require either."

"Oh, yes, you will marry Catherine Chudleigh."

The Duke moved towards the door.

Catherine pretended to burst into tears.

The Duke frowned.

"If those tears came from the heart, Catherine Chudleigh," he said.

"Oh! oh! oh!—they do, they do! I—I want to say a—a something to you !"

"Say it now, dear one ! What is it ?"

"I want to—to tell you something. Harvey, do you mind me telling him something ?"

"Hang him !" muttered Captain Harvey.

"Your Grace, you know there was once a—a; oh, dear! there was once a—a——"

"What, Miss Chudleigh, what ?"

"A fox, and he wanted some grapes that he jumped after in vain, and offered half his estate for, but when he found he could not reach them, he said they were sour—ha! ha! ha! Good-bye, Hamilton—good-bye! If you still persist in your offer to Aunt Hanmer, I consent—Ha! ha! ha!"

The Duke of Hamilton rushed from the house in a state of mind bordering on distraction.

Mrs. Hanmer looked vexed.

"Catherine, Catherine," she said, "you let your high spirits run away with you."

"Never mind, aunt, so long as I keep the men from doing so, since that is what they all want to do. But come now, Harvey! when you are the Earl of Bristol, I am quite sure Aunt Hanmer will have no cause to complain of a want of liberality."

"Certainly not—most certainly not ; and as it is, I was about to offer to Mrs. Hanmer, as some little recompense for the loss of your society, Catherine, my manor of Chillham, in Essex."

Mrs. Hanmer put her handkerchief to her eyes.

"What feeling can I have but one, and that is, for the happiness of this dear child?"

"That's settled, then," said Catherine, "I intend to be married to-day."

"To-day, child?"

"Yes, or not at all."

"I am charmed at your determination, Catherine," said Captain Harvey. "I have had an opportunity of already consulting my uncle's chaplain, who happens to be in town, about it; and he says, that if Mrs. Hanmer will make an affidavit that she stands in the relation of what is called *loco parentis* to Catherine, a special license can be procured, and the marriage can take place this day with ease."

"All's right!" cried Catherine. "Come, aunt, you can do that, you know. *Loco parentis*—the place of a parent. Mr. Pultney taught me Latin. Come on, be quick about it. You be off with Harvey, and settle all that——Stop! yes I will!"

"You will what, dear Catherine?"

"I will be married in the chapel at Whitehall."

"The Chapel Royal?"

"That's it."

"But my dear Kate!"

"Now, you are going to make some objection, and I won't hear it. The Princess of Wales can easily manage that, and I will go and ask her, while you make all the other arrangements. The Chapel Royal, I say, or nowhere. I will show you all the conditions of my consent when you come back."

"Conditions?"

"Yes: do you think that I am going to marry any man in the ordinary hum-drum, stupid kind of way, eh? Not I. I have thought it over. But don't bother about that now, you can always, even at the altar, you know, refuse. I don't care a bit; there's lots of men!"

"Oh, Catherine!"

"What now?"

"This—this levity!"

"Levity—levity! Do you call that levity?"

Catherine Chudleigh jumped upon a chair, and then to the table, and then, with a push, displacing a statuette that was on a porphyry pedestal, she took its place, and assuming a charming attitude, she made a light robe she wore float over her head in graceful folds as it caught the agitated air around it.

"A goddess! A goddess!" cried Captain Harvey. "Yes, dear Catherine, your own way you shall have in all things, for your life is my life, and I love you dearer than tongue can tell!"

Catherine sprang down from the pedestal, and Captain Harvey, with Mrs. Hanmer, left the house to carry out the arrangements for the marriage.

The spoilt beauty then ordered her aunt Hanmer's carriage, and as she stepped into it she said: "To Marlborough House."

A very short time sufficed to carry her to the temporary abode of the Princess of Wales, who, at that time was in a chronic state of bad health, and loved to encourage the belief that she was in so delicate a condition that her hold of life was very slight.

Catherine Chudleigh flattered, and coaxed, and sympathized her out of an order that she was to have the use of the Chapel Royal for her marriage, and, moreover, the Princess gave her a superb necklace of pearls and opals, and wished her all manner of happiness.

"My dear girl, I would myself," said the Princess "be present at your nuptials, but you know the state of my health."

"Alas!" replied Catherine, with a sigh; "I do, too well. It is fearful."

"It is, indeed."

"Oh, dear—dear madam! what will this nation—this world do when they lose you?"

"I am afraid but indifferently," said the Princess of Wales, who had no more idea of dying than of leaping out of the open window. "But the misfortune is, that although my health is so bad, there is nothing in all my complaints incompatible with a very long life, with which I hope to be blessed for the sake of others."

"That is the only hope," said Catherine, as she, with another deep sigh, left the royal presence, just as a tray was brought in with a roast duck, a quantity of manchets, and a full flask of sherris, for the delicate and royal sufferer's lunch!

Catherine, as she neared an apartment that was very curiously shaped, having a staircase descending from the centre of it, saw Mr. Pultney slowly coming up.

The light shone down upon his head in such a way that she, for the first time, saw how very grey he was getting.

It appeared to her that since she had looked upon him last, he had wonderfully aged.

Was he suffering?

And was it for love of her?

She shrank back a bit behind the hangings of a window.

Mr. Pultney came right up the stairs, and passing across the room with a slow and stately step, he opened a door that led into a small library, and, passing in, shut it behind him.

She heard how he caught his breath in short, half-spasmodic inspirations as he passed her.

"Ah!" she said, as she emerged from the window-curtain.

"I begin almost to think I ought not to marry, since my doing so only pleases one, and drives so many other men to despair."

She went to the door of the little library, and listened, but she could hear nothing.

Then she turned the handle.

No one spoke.

She looked in, Mr. Pultney was at a table, resting his head upon his hands.

Catherine Chudleigh tripped into the room, and touched him on the shoulder.

He started up with an exclamation of alarm, and then he cried out, "No, no, leave me! Serpent, enchantress, scorpion! Oh, no! angel, angel! Leave me—leave me! No, no! This heart—this poor heart, for ever!"

"Be quiet," said Catherine Chudleigh, as she took a spring, and sat on the edge of the table. "Be quiet, my good friend, I want to speak to you."

"To me—me! Yes, yes, Catherine, I am here—Heaven bless you ever and ever! Do you come for a lesson as of old?"

———

CHAPTER X.

CATHERINE CHUDLEIGH LEAVES MR. PULTNEY IN GREATER DESPAIR THAN EVER.—THE MARRIAGE AT THE CHAPEL ROYAL PROCEEDS AND MEETS WITH SOME SINGULAR AND UNEXPECTED INTERRUPTIONS.—LOVE CONQUERS ALL, AND OVERLEAPS ALL OBSTACLES.

No," said Catherine; "but I want to ask you something."

"Me, dear one?"

"Yes. Who fired a pistol at the King?"

"A would-be regicide."

"I know that; but what I want to know is, who was he?"

"That I cannot tell you with any certainty; but there is an idea about that it was the Prince, James Stuart."

"I never heard of him."

"Few people have. He is a younger brother, it is said, of the 'young man.'"

This phrase of the "young man," was commonly used to denote Prince Charles, the son of the Pretender.

"What is he like?"

"It is said that he is so femininely handsome that a term is often applied to him which is commonly only applicable to feminine charms."

"What term?"

"Beautiful!"

"Yes, he is beautiful!"

"You say so? How is it possible you can know?"

"Why, if you say he is what he is!"

"Yes, he has they say—for I never saw him, and doubt, now, that there is any such person as a Prince James—he has the perilous gift of beauty."

Mr. Pultney fixed his eyes sadly upon Kate Chudleigh as he spoke.

She smiled.

He clasped one hand over his eyes, as though he would shut out from his brain the bewitching enchantment of that smile.

"Well," she added, "what I want you to do, Mr. Pultney, is to let me know at once when he is taken, if taken, or any news regarding him alive or dead."

"I will."

"Thank you—good-bye!"

Catherine Chudleigh had a fashion, at the end of a lesson, when Mr. Pultney had been her kind and able instructor, of coming up to him, and holding back with both her hands the clustering ringlets from her brow, to allow him to kiss her between the eyes.

She did so now.

The kiss came, and the eyelashes of Mr. Pultney, heavy with tears, just touched the fair forehead.

"Good-bye!"

Catherine whistled gaily.

"Good-bye, Catherine dear!"

"Oh, I forgot."

"Yes, dear."

"I am going to be married to-day."

"Married!"

"Yes, to Captain Harvey."

Mr. Pultney turned his head.

"All happiness—all earthly happiness be yours. I am going to Vienna as ambassador."

"Oh, indeed!"

"Yes, Kate, but I ought not to hesitate to say to you what all the world says, and what many persons say they know."

"What is it?"

"That the Honourable Captain Harvey is a man of violent, vindictive, and imperious temper."

Catherine laughed.

"Well, then, he has met his match, good Mr. Pultney, so good-bye. I shall be married in the Chapel Royal. Won't you come and give me away? No—you won't—well, if you won't why then you won't—good-bye."

"Do you love me, master? No?"

Mr. Pultney knew the quotation from Ariel's tender speech to Prospero, but he could not reply for a moment or two, and it was only in choking accents that he could at last say,

"Dearly, dearly, my delicate Ariel!"

Then Catherine Chudleigh, singing the song of the fair spirit in the Enchanted Island, tripped lightly from the room.

Mr. Pultney fell to the floor, and lay like a man in a swoon.

"Home!" said Catherine Chudleigh, as she stepped into the carriage again, without a thought of the desolate heart she left behind her at Marlborough House. "Home, and as quick as you can, for I see that it is past the hour of noon."

The carriage quickly whirled her to the house of Mrs. Hanmer, where she found Captain Harvey and her aunt waiting for her.

Harvey sprung towards her, and would have caught her in his arms, but that she eluded him, and he embraced the empty air.

"My dear girl, all is arranged. The special license is procured, and the ceremony may take place as soon as we can reach the Chapel Royal."

"What ceremony?"

"Good heavens! Catherine, what do you mean?"

"What do you mean?"

"Our marriage—our happy, happy union! Oh, Catherine, do not now play with the heart that is all your own."

"Do you or any man think that I am going to be married in this dress, eh?"

"My dear," said Mrs. Hanmer, "I have seen to all that. Mrs. Knowles, the Court milliner, was engaged to make a wedding-dress for the young and charming Princess Marie of Modena, and what do you think Harvey and I have done? Why, we have carried it off bodily at the price of three hundred pounds, and here it is."

The door opened, and a *modiste* appeared, followed by two young girls, carrying parcels and bundles. The dress and appointments were exhibited, and Catherine, for once in the way. was pleased.

A sky-blue satin, all covered with lace, that hung about it like fleecy clouds, and brilliants, and pearls, at each point of gathering.

Oh! it was a charm to behold that dress, and even Catherine Chudleigh clapped her hands.

She flew with "Aunt Hanmer" to put it on, and in half an hour more she re-appeared fully attired for the ceremony.

Joy sparkled in the eyes of Captain Harvey.

"Mine, mine, now!" he cried. "My own fairest of the fair, Catherine!"

"Not yet. Now stop a bit! Hem!"

Catherine opened a folded paper she had in her hand, and read—

"Item. I am to have as much money as I like, and to spend it how I like.

"Item. I am to have four rooms all to myself, into which the husband is not to venture without knocking.

"Item. I am to have all my own letters brought to me inviolate, and the husband is not to have the presumption even to look at the outside of them.

"Item. I am to have my own way always, in everything, and about everything."

She looked up at Captain Harvey.

"Will that do?"

"My dearest——"

"Will—that—do?"

"Catherine!"

"Oh, very well. Aunt Hanmer! Aunt Hanmer! Help me off with this dress, I won't be married! I am not going to be married!"

"Yes, yes!" cried Captain Harvey, "it will do. I consent! I consent!"

"Sign, then!"

He signed the memorandum, and Catherine Chudleigh, with that agreement in her pocket, went to the Chapel Royal to be married.

She had written a hasty note to Bella to be at the Chapel, and Captain Harvey had bidden to the hasty nuptials three of his friends, who were to meet the party in Whitehall.

The one carriage driving up to the chapel created no sensation, and although two or three persons paused, as the fair apparition in sky-blue satin, and lace, and diamonds, and pearls, got out of the coach, no one tried to enter the chapel.

The clergyman was there already.

A dimmed, golden light pervaded the sacred edifice, which, with all its splendour, showed to greater advantage than when half-hidden by a large congregation.

The three gentlemen, who had been hastily bidden to the marriage by Captain Harvey, were there.

Bella, all tears and sensibility, was ready to faint away at any moment.

Mrs. Hanmer, even, looked a little flurried and anxious, and perhaps, after all, the calmest, and the coolest, and most indifferent person there present, was the bride.

The clergyman was robing in the sacristy.

The little group formed round the altar.

A wrapt stillness—a holy calm—pervaded the chapel. Slowly, then, and quietly, the organ gave forth a hymn. There were no voices to join the sacred strains, and by the time the last notes had died away, the clergyman took his place by the rails of the communion table.

Captain Harvey approached Catherine, and lifted the veil from before the sweet face.

"Bless you, my Kate."

She was truly beautiful, but very child-like. The prettiness of Eden was in her eyes, and the clergyman for some few moments regarded her with wondering eyes.

But everything, so far as he was concerned, was right and formal, and he opened the book.

There was a faint kind of bustle at the door of the chapel.

The clergyman paused, and looked in that direction, as did the bride and bridegroom.

Some persons approached.

"Hush!" said the chapel clerk, for the manner in which these persons approached did not say much for their appreciation of the sacred character of the roof beneath which they were.

Then Captain Harvey uttered an exclamation of surprise and rage.

Catherine Chudleigh, even, could not help a few words of astonishment.

Pale as a spectre, the Duke of Hamilton made his appearance by the communion rails. He elevated his hands above his head, and in a voice that was agonizing by its depth of feeling, he cried—"Catherine! Catherine! I have no pride— I have no common resentment—I am not so bold and defiant as this worm you might tread upon —I only know that I love you, and that life without you is a blank—a night without a moon or stars—a day without sun! Now, even at the last moment, I lay myself and my coronet at your feet!"

He cast himself to the ground, and grasped the edge of the sky-blue robe.

"Anybody else?" said Catherine.

Captain Harvey placed his hand upon his sword, but the clergyman held his arm.

"Yes," said a voice, in reply to the question of Catherine, and a gentleman stepped forward. "Yes, Miss Chudleigh, do you know me?"

"I do."

"Who am I?"

"You are His Grace the Duke of Kingston!"

"True, and I love you. I have long loved you in secret, and hoped that the day would come when political differences would no longer separate me from the household of His Royal Highness the Prince of Wales, and that then I might hope for the hand of one who has long been the secret object of my attachment, and to whom I now make an offer of both hand and heart!"

"Insolence!" exclaimed Captain Harvey, with his face inflamed by passion.

"Whatever of insolence," added the Duke of Kingston, "you may fancy that my conduct exhibits, I am ready to justify at a fitting time and in a fitting place, sir."

"And to me, too, Kingston!" cried the Duke of Hamilton, with an angry flush.

"Yes, to you, too—and to all the world, if necessary."

"Anybody else?" cried Catherine Chudleigh, in her highest tone of glee,—"anybody else? Let us have it all at once, my lords and gentlemen!"

A young lad staggered forward, and cast himself at her feet in a passion of tears.

It was the page, Carolus.

"I, too—I, too, Miss Chudleigh—I, too, love you; and it would be a just mercy if any one would kill me!"

———

THE MARRIAGE CEREMONY INTERRUPTED.

CHAPTER XI.

THE MARRIAGE CONCLUDED.—CATHERINE CHUD-
LEIGH'S EARLY REPENTANCE.—A SUPPER AT
MRS. HANMER'S, AND ITS RESULTS.—THE FIRST
QUARREL AND THE LAST.—A LOCKED DOOR.—
A MYSTERY.

" ANYBODY else ?" cried Catherine, again.

" Gracious heavens !" said the clergyman, as
he closed his book, " what can be the meaning of
all this ?"

" The meaning, dear sir," said Captain Harvey,
his lips white, and quivering with passion—" the
meaning is, these gentlemen, in open and public
defiance of all the decencies and all the proprieties
of civilised life, seek to tear from me, even at the
altar, the bride who has rejected them, or, failing

No. 4.—KATE CHUDLEIGH.

that, they wish to plant in my heart a thorn
which time nor tide shall eradicate !"

Both the Duke of Hamilton and the Duke of
Kingston strove to speak at once.

The former, however, prevailed.

" No, Captain Harvey," he said,—" no. For
my own part, you wrong me. There are circumstances under which the most incongruous actions
may be performed—and justly, too. When a fire
is raging, you, or I, or any gentleman, may intrude into the chamber of a queen. Alas! there
is a fire in my heart which will scorch me to
death, unless you, Catherine, have pity on
me !"

" Rather on me !" cried the Duke of Kingston.
" I tell you, Catherine Chudleigh, that you are
fated to be my wife, and far better will it be for
you now to become the Duchess of Kingston
than after, perhaps, years of turmoil and of grief."

"And I, too—I, too!" screamed the page,—"I too, love you, oh! Miss Chudleigh."

"This is the most unseemly scene," said the clergyman, "that ever I heard, saw, or read of, within the walls of such an edifice as this."

Catherine smiled.

"Well, sir," she said, as she placed her hand in that of Captain Harvey's, "notwithstanding all these blandishments and all these inducements here, even at the altar steps, I adhere to my determination. Harvey, I am yours!"

The page screamed aloud.

The Duke of Hamilton staggered from the Chapel Royal, like a man bereft of his senses.

The Duke of Kingston held by the rails of the communion table, and seemed resolved to be a witness of the marriage.

Captain Harvey turned towards the clergyman, as he said, in tones that struggled with passion, "I pray you proceed, reverend sir. We shall be extremely grateful to my Lord of Kingston for his name to the church register, as a witness."

The Duke of Kingston let go his hold of the rails of the communion table, and very slowly left the chapel.

Captain Harvey, by accident—for he quite forgot that any such person was present—trod upon the arm of the young page, as he lay at the feet of Catherine Chudleigh.

The boy only sighed.

The marriage ceremony then began.

The chapel, each moment that it proceeded, to the surprise of the party there assembled, grew darker and darker. A dense fog had suddenly swept over London from the low-lying districts of Westminster and Lambeth, and the darkening vapour was making its way, in rolling cloud-like masses, into the Chapel Royal.

Deeper and deeper still grew the darkness.

The forms of the bride and bridegroom at the altar became indistinct.

The clergyman could only be dimly seen.

A feeling of superstitious dread came over the mind of the officiating reverend gentleman, and his voice shook and faltered to that degree that he could scarcely continue the service.

The clerk of the chapel crept away to the small robing-room, where the sacred vessels and vestments were kept, and returned with a light.

A tall wax-candle, in an antique candlestick of silver, was what he brought; and as he held it with both hands, somewhat above the height of his head, it shed a strange unnatural lustre over the chapel.

The ceremony was nearly over.

But Captain Harvey had forgotten a ring. In all the hurry, the bustle, and the excitement of that hasty marriage, he had totally omitted to provide himself with a wedding-ring, so that when the moment came at which it was necessary to place that symbol of the union on the finger of the bride, he had not the means of doing so.

The clergyman paused.

Catherine Chudleigh held out her hand.

Captain Harvey was thoroughly vexed and confused.

The clerk divined the dilemma. Perhaps, he had had experience of such a circumstance before, but whether that was the case or not, he came forward to the rescue.

Producing a ring from his waistcoat pocket, he slipped it into the hand of Captain Harvey.

"Take that, sir—take that. You can buy another for the lady, and give it me back again."

Captain Harvey was glad of any aid in the sudden emergency.

He took the ring, and slipped it on to the finger of Catherine Chudleigh.

A minute and a half more, and the ceremony was over. The benediction was pronounced.

The clergyman closed his book.

Catherine Chudleigh was Catherine Harvey, the wife of the heir apparent to the earldom of Bristol.

Was she happy?

Ah, no!

Was she commonly contented? Had she gone to the altar as so many brides go, satisfied that it is a kind of fate they should be married and content with the man Providence, or chance—call it which you may—has assigned them?

Certainly not.

When would the ambitious, restless mind of Catherine Chudleigh's ever be content—ever be at peace?

Never!

Yes—yes! There was to come a time when peace would be the portion of that restless, scheming, plotting, vanity-stricken brain. That time would be when the green sod rested on it, and when the costly marble of some mausoleum enclosed it.

But not till then.

From the moment that the marriage ceremony was concluded—from the moment that the benediction was uttered, and she was really and truly the wife of Captain Harvey, Catherine Chudleigh regretted the words of assent she had uttered.

Then the constant passion of the Duke of Hamilton looked beautiful in her eyes.

Then she thought His Grace of Kingston a most desirable consort.

Then she had pity even for the young page, Carolus, who, perhaps, in his boy's heart, really loved her best of all.

She looked up into the face of Captain Harvey—her husband—and she did not like the expression of triumph she saw there.

He spoke.

"My wife!—my own!"

Catherine Chudleigh pouted.

"You are in a great hurry to call me your own."

"And are you not?"

"Certainly not. You may fancy me a piece of property, but you are mistaken."

"Oh, Catherine!"

"Oh, Harvey!"

"Have you not sworn to love?"

"No!"

"To honour?"

"No!"

"To obey?"

"No. That least of all. I took good care not to pronounce those words, or to let them pass by without a mental protest."

"Come, come, dear one, we will not quarrel on our wedding day."

"Ah!"

From the gallery of the church, or in some mysterious manner in at the open door, there floated a thin slip of paper. It fell right upon the breast of Catherine.

What could it mean?

There was writing on it.

Captain Harvey caught it from Catherine's veil, and his cheek flushed, and a dark scowl came upon his brow as he read it.

"The lost heart and the saved head quits the young bride, who shall not be a wife!"

"What, in the name of all that is impertinent and detestable, is the meaning of this?" cried Captain Harvey.

Catherine felt the hidden meaning of the words rapidly translating themselves to her heart. Who could they come from but the Jacobite traitor? That more than brilliantly handsome stranger, whose "head" she had saved, but whose "heart" she had enslaved for ever.

She smiled with satisfaction.

Her husband saw the smile, and for the first time he looked upon her with feelings akin to bitterness.

They had been into the vestry of the chapel. The register was duly signed, and it was on the threshold almost of the sacred edifice that this little episode took place.

"Catherine, Catherine!" cried Harvey, "I again ask you, what does this mean?"

"And I tell you I don't know, and if I did——"

"What then?"

"Ha, ha! Can you doubt?"

"I should like to doubt!"

"Then do so no longer, for, I tell you plainly, I would not tell——"

"You—you would not?"

"Ah! The brute! He is beginning ill-usage already! Help, help! Who will save me?"

"Good heaven, Catherine, what do you mean?"

"You pinched my arm!"

"Nay, nay!"

"You know you did! Good people all, I take you to witness that this man, because he is my husband, began to ill-use me at the very door of the Chapel Royal!"

"My dear child," said Mrs. Hanmer, "pray do get rid of these fancies!"

But Catherine was wilful, and would get rid of no fancies.

She whimpered and pretended to cry, and be unhappy all the way home to Mrs. Hanmer's house; and perhaps one of the wretchedest of men in all London, at that time, was the bridegroom who sat by her side.

"Now, don't come near me! You are a brute!"

"Then, Catherine, it is a great pity that you are the wife of a brute!"

"Dear me! that is just my opinion! Let me see. Did I say I would go out of town? I don't know whether I did or not, for whatever I say one hour I intend to gainsay the next!"

"Good heaven; and this is my fate!"

"Your fate! You were so terribly anxious to marry me, and now you call me your fate!"

"I cannot help it!"

"Yes, you can! I will be reconciled to you on one condition!"

"Reconciled?"

"Yes, I said reconciled!"

"But what have I done?"

"I hate you!"

"Hate me?"

"Yes, to be sure: Don't all fashionable wives hate their husbands, and prefer any and every other man in all the world."

"You will drive me mad!"

I hope so! Folks will say, 'There goes the beautiful Marchioness of Bristol'—that is to say, when your horrid relations die, and let you have the title—' there goes the beautiful, the charming, the accomplished Marchioness of Bristol, who has a mad husband!' "

"Alas, alas!"

"Oh, as many lassies as you please, always provided you give me a similar privilege!"

Captain Harvey looked savage and dangerous.

"Come, now," added Catherine, "what I was going to say as the price of my reconciliation to you was, that you should go out of town for a month!"

"With you?"

"Me, me? With me? Is the man mad? No; by yourself, of course! With me, indeed! Ha, ha! What put that into your head?"

——

CHAPTER XII.

CAPTAIN HARVEY SHOWS THAT A BRIDEGROOM MAY BE TROUBLESOME.—THE ROSE-PANELLED ROOM.—A LITTLE SURPRISE, AND THE DEATH OF THE GUARDSMAN.—CATHERINE IS CAPRICIOUS.

IT was in such-like discourse as the above that the bride kept her husband constantly on the fret for the remainder of the wedding-day.

Mrs. Hanmer provided a brilliant supper, in the midst of which Catherine jumped up, crying out, "I am weary! I shall retire! Good night, savage!"

This "good night" was addressed to Captain Harvey, who started up, and glared at her with truly savage eyes.

"What do you mean? What, in the name of all that's—that's——"

"Oh, don't mind me!" cried Catherine. "Swear away!"

"No, no! But——"

She vanished from the room, with a gay laugh.

Captain Harvey would have pursued her, but Mrs. Hanmer laid a hand upon his arm and restrained him.

"Patience, patience, Harvey! Let her be. She is in one of her wild humours just now. It is all acting. Sit down awhile, and then you no doubt will find her affectionate and reasonable."

"Affectionate?"

"Oh, yes, she has quite a tender heart, I assure you!"

"Hem!"

"And I likewise assure you that I feel how

very handsomely you have behaved in regard to the *post obit* you have executed on my behalf."

"Well, Mrs. Hanmer, I have kept faith with you, but what may be the nature of the bargain I have paid so handsomely for is quite another thing."

Click went the lock of the room door at this moment.

Mrs. Hanmer uttered a faint scream.

Captain Harvey sprang to his feet.

"What is the meaning of that?"

"One of Catherine's tricks!"

"Tricks, tricks?"

"Yes; she has locked us in!"

"That, Mrs. Hanmer, is a trick I will soon put an end to."

As he spoke, Captain Harvey dashed himself against the door of the supper room with a vehemence that it could not withstand.

There was a crashing sound, and the door gave way.

"Now!" he cried, "I will see if this bride is indeed to be called a wife!"

The mansion, for it quite merited that name, was large.

It stood in its own grounds, and gardens; and on the upper or first floor, which comprehended its entire height, there were no less than eighteen bed chambers.

A long corridor that went the whole depth of the house from front to back, was the common route to all these rooms, which opened right and left from it.

That corridor was dimly lighted by an oil lamp, borne in the hands of a statue.

When Captain Harvey reached the corridor, he called out aloud, "Catherine! Catherine! This is too childish! Catherine, I say, bring this farce to an end!"

There was no reply.

Rage took possession of the bosom of Captain Harvey.

"How long? How long?" he cried, "am I to suffer myself to be fooled by a girl scarce out of her childhood?"

As he spoke, he dashed from room to room of the chambers in the corridor, in the hope of finding that which was to be the nuptial chamber of himself and the fair Maid of Honour.

But in none of them could he find her, or discover any traces of her presence.

Then it occurred to him that, of course, Mrs. Hanmer could direct him at once and easily to the rooms that might be called for the occasion his, and he rushed to the top of the stairs, calling out, "Madam! Mrs. Hanmer! Mrs. Hanmer, I say! Madam!"

Mrs. Hanmer appeared on the top of the stairs with a lamp.

"Which room? Which room, Mrs. Hanmer?"

"Any one but that with the rose-coloured panels," was the anxious reply of Mrs. Hanmer.

"What?"

"Any one. No—no—I will show you, wait, wait, don't stir."

"Bah, I have no patience to wait, and suspect that that room, whichever diabolical one it may be, with the rose-coloured panels, is the one I seek!"

Mrs. Hanmer uttered a scream of apprehension, but what at, Captain Harvey could not divine.

He rushed down the corridor, and as he went, he snatched the lamp from the statue.

About half way down, he certainly saw a room-door, the panels of which were painted a faint crimson flush.

He dashed open the door.

"Catherine!"

"Bombs and devils, who is this?"

A tall man, in the uniform of a private of the Life Guards, made a rush to get past Harvey.

With a shout of rage, Harvey drew his sword, and passed its fine polished blade through the body of the intruder.

The guardsman staggered back, as he exclaimed, "Jack Holther done for at last. Bombs and furies! who would have thought of that?"

Mrs. Hanmer reached the room at this moment, and held up the lamp she carried.

"Wretch! murderer!" she cried. "What had he done to you, and what business was it of yours that you should kill him?"

"Kill him! Kill!—Kill!—This room—Catherine!"

"Murderer, this is my chamber!"

A light broke in upon the brain of Captain Harvey.

The guardsman, then, was the *cher ami* of Mrs Hanmer, and had nothing to do with Catherine.

After supporting himself for a few seconds by the side of the large old-fashioned four-post bedstead that was in the room, the wounded, or killed guardsman, fell heavily to the floor.

"Help! help! Murder!" shrieked Mrs. Hanmer.

Captain Harvey looked on this scene for a few seconds with eyes of utter bewilderment.

Then, shouting out the name of Catherine, he began a further search in the various chambers of the corridor, heedless of what tumult Mrs. Hanmer, in the indiscretion of the moment, might choose to make.

Captain Harvey pushed open a door, which immediately disclosed to him a handsome bedchamber, lighted by tall wax candles on the toilette table.

The conviction that he had found the room he sought, came with a firmness that could not be shaken to his mind, in a moment.

Yes, that was Catherine's chamber.

Captain Harvey slammed the door behind him.

He doubly turned the key in the lock.

"Catherine! Catherine! speak to me. Tell me that you love me, and that all these strange proceedings are but the frisks of a girlish fancy, and the overrunning of exuberant spirits. Say but that, and I can forget and forgive all, remembering only that you are more beautiful than tongue can tell, and that I love you."

No Catherine replied.

Captain Harvey put down the lamp he had snatched from the extended hand of the statue in the corridor, and ran round the handsome bed, with its deeply fringed silken hangings, which occupied at least a third of the room.

"Catherine, Catherine!"

She was not to be seen.

"Do not, oh, do not hide from me, Catherine, my wife!"

No. To all appearance, Captain Harvey ha'

that magnificent, for it almost deserved such a title, bed-chamber to himself.

Then, as he paused a moment, and looked at the bed, he saw that it was disarranged.

A hope sprang up in his mind, that Catherine might be there, half hidden among its draperies.

No. That hope vanished at a second glance.

Then, as he cast his eyes towards the toilette table, which was close to a window, he saw that the flames of the wax lights were violently agitated.

He felt that some strong current of cold air was making its way into the room.

He flew to the window!

It was wide open.

Tied to two of the legs of the dressing-table was the corner of a sheet, attached to which was another, and then a blanket.

The length so made reached to within three or four feet of the garden beneath.

Captain Harvey uttered a cry of dispair as he looked from the window.

Catherine was gone!

Gone on her wedding-night! Gone! fled! he knew not whither! He had but the mockery of a wife—the shadow of her apparition, if so much as that! What was he to do? What could become of him?—of her?—of all the world?

* * * * *

How did all this happen? Why had Catherine so fled from the man she had wedded on that day, in the face of heaven?

We shall see.

When the capricious and beautiful Maid of Honour fled from the supper table, she had lingered for a few seconds at the door of the room, and she had heard the words that passed between Captain Harvey and her aunt, which could have no other meaning than one.

Her Aunt, Mrs. Hanmer, had sold her to Captain Harvey for the *post obit* on the Bristol estates.

There was not much in this which should have affected the position of Catherine Chudleigh, except she could draw from it one conclusion.

That conclusion was, that the breach which had taken place between herself and the Duke of Hamilton had been of her aunt's fomenting.

If she should be able to assure herself of that fact, Catherine felt that some signal act, which would confound the whole transaction, would be the only thing to content her.

So she began by locking the door of the supper room.

CHAPTER XIII.

CATHERINE CHUDLEIGH MAKES A TERRIBLE DIS-
COVERY.—THE FAITHLESS ONE ABSOLVED.—
AN ELOPEMENT ON A WEDDING NIGHT.—THE
WINDOW AND THE GARDEN.—A SERENADE.

CATHERINE wanted time.

She wanted time to repair to her aunt's own chamber—the chamber with the door of the rose-coloured panels.

In that chamber she knew there was a cabinet of Coromandel wood, in which Mrs. Hanmer kept all her papers and correspondence.

The impression had always, she knew not why, been upon the mind of Catherine, that in that cabinet, which Mrs. Hanmer kept so religiously locked, there was a something interesting to her.

With her usual impetuosity, therefore, she resolved, on that night of all others, to test the fact.

Catherine did not, of course, imagine that locking the door of the supper-room upon Captain Harvey and her aunt, would leave her much time for action; but she was rapid in her movements, and it gave her some.

Her knowledge of the house, of course, enabled her to proceed at once to her aunt's chamber.

She started back at the door of it, for she was certain she heard a footstep within it.

But a second thought told her that that need not be a cause of alarm, although it might be one of embarrassment, as far as her designs went.

The footstep, in all probability, was that of her aunt's waiting maid.

"Constance! Constance! Constance!" cried Catherine, as she entered the room. "Is that you?"

There was no reply, and, to all appearance, the room was empty.

Perhaps, if Catherine had been very curious, and had time to satisfy that curiosity, she might have found concealed somewhere in that room, that same Guardsman, who was so awkwardly to encounter Captain Harvey during the next quarter of an hour.

But, as it was, she turned her whole attention to the Coromandel cabinet.

There it stood, invitingly, on the top of a bureau, which was its usual place.

But it was locked

Of course it was locked. Catherine fully expected that, but it was neat, delicate, and frail to a degree.

The slightest amount of actual violence would open it.

Catherine took from the toilette table a pretty Turkish dagger, which did duty there as a paper knife. It was quite sufficient for the purpose.

The cabinet flew open, although not without damage to some of its flimsy ornamentation.

There was a series of little drawers, which the nimble fingers of Catherine opened one after the other, with the speed of a juggler.

She uttered an exclamation.

She saw and snatched out a packet of letters.

The handwriting was familiar to her. It was that of the Duke of Hamilton.

Rapidly did Catherine run over the letters with her nimble fingers to the date of each.

"Vienna!" "Vienna!" "Vienna!"

Such was the place from which they were all dated.

A hot flush came over the face of Catherine.

She had been deceived! Cruelly and terribly deceived by her aunt, Hanmer! Here were all the letters from Vienna, which she had accused the Duke of Hamilton of never writing at all!

Here was the correspondence which the supposed cessation of had made Catherine throw over all affection for the Duke.

Now she understood how she had been bought and sold!

Bought by Captain Harvey!

Sold by Mrs. Hanmer!

Catherine uttered little shrieks of passion, and clenched her hands!

"Never! no, never! I swear it! Whatever may be the consequences, never will I be wife to that man! Never! never!"

We are afraid that the fair Maid of Honour, at this juncture, uttered several expletives, which in that non-sensitive age were not considered so shocking, coming from the lips of a young lady in her teens, as they would be now.

Then she shed some hot scalding tears.

Then she spoke again.

"I hate, hate, hate him!"

She did hate him.

Her husband! The man to whom she had pledged her hand and heart at the altar only that day—the man whom she had given a legal right to vex and annoy her until one or the other of them found peace in the grave!

Oh, it was shocking! It was nearly maddening!

What could she do?

"Fly! fly!" she cried. "Flight—for flight is my only resource."

She placed the packet of letters, that she had obtained possession of, hastily, but securely, in her bosom.

The hot scalding tears still fell, as she made her way to the room which had been prepared for her *and her husband*, by Mrs. Hanmer.

Oh, how hateful was that one word, husband, to her now.

There was only another that sounded so horrid in her ears.

That was the name of Harvey.

Yes, there was yet another.

That other was the name of Hanmer, for she hated her aunt now, with a hatred which only such a mind as hers, with all its ill-regulated passions, could hate.

She heard the tumult below.

The noise of the broken supper-room door.

She dashed the tears from her eyes.

"No time to lose! No time to lose!" she cried, and she ran into the handsome nuptial chamber.

Then she started, and seemed to be transfixed with surprise.

She heard a noise from the garden below the window.

The two wax lights that were on the dressing table would enable any one to see her when she entered the room.

But it was the voice, that one voice, which, of all others, was to her a concentration of all the sweetest melodies she had ever heard, which struck her.

Was it? Could it be the voice of the Jacobite spy? the assassin of the palace, who to all appearance, she had seen in death; and who had so very mysteriously disappeared, and who was now serenading her from the garden of her aunt's house.

Yes, it could be no other voice.

No tones but his could strike into her heart so deliciously.

She stood still, and, silent as a statue, some few paces from the window, to listen to the strains.

The Jacobite spy, if it were him, and not some spirit in his likeness, was singing:

"Fly, lady fly, from cold hearts about thee:
Fly, lady fly, to the fond soul that loves thee:
Come with me, come with me, over the sea:
My bark's on the ocean, the wind whistles free
Fly, lady fly."

The strain ceased.

Catherine flew to the window. It was open, she leant far out, and looked into the garden.

"Speak to me, oh, speak!" she cried. "If you be mortal, speak to me!"

The low, soft, gentle voice of the Jacobite spy replied to her:

"Ah, fair one. The ship comes home to its port, and the timid bird to its nest, so this fond heart returns to thee!"

"You love me! You love me!"

"Better than all my remaining lines, lady!"

"Re — main — ing lines? What do you mean!"

"Heed not the strong expression, fair one, and only think and know that I love you!

"Fly with me, far from the hand that will smite thee,
Fly with the heart that will ever delight thee!
Fly, oh, fly!"

"I come!"

The moon broke through a crevice in a track of clouds, and then Catherine saw how deep it was to the ground, for she was almost in the act of leaping to it from the chamber window.

The Jacobite spy was beneath, and, as the moonbeams fell around him, if she had had any lingering doubts of his identity, they would have vanished.

With fascinating eyes she looked upon that face and form of wondrous beauty

"I come, I come!"

"Careful, dear one."

"Yes, yes."

"For my sake!"

"For your sake, yes."

There was no lack of ready means in the mind of the young Maid of Honour, and she at once proceeded to the bed, to find the means of a safe descent into the garden.

She stripped off a couple of sheets and a blanket.

The sheets and blankets she tied together, as fast as she could, and then the end of one of the sheets she tied to two of the legs of the dressing table.

"I come, I come?"

A terrible fear came over her for only a moment, there was not time for it to last longer; but it was a fear, that, when she reached the garden, she should find the Jacobite spy had disappeared, and that she had been conversing with a being who was not of this world.

It was an inexpressible relief to feel his manly touch, as she almost fell into his arms.

"Ah, you are mortal!"

"Most mortal, inasmuch as I can love mortality."

"You love me?"

"Can you ask?"

"No. No, I have faith; but—I—I—am a wife!"

"I was in the chapel."

Catherine uttered a cry of surprise.

"I it was who sent you, on the obedient air, that note."

"Yes, oh, yes."

"And it has come to pass. You are a bride, but not a wife!"

"Never! never! the wife of that man!"

The Jacobite spy, uttering words of love and tenderness, led Catherine rapidly along out of the garden paths.

Lights flashed from the house.

A voice called out loudly:

"Watch! watch! There is some one in the garden!"

The Jacobite spy paused for an instant, and, amid the dimness, Catherine could see the glimmer that shone upon his sword blade, which he had hastily drawn from its sheath.

The moon, after a brief career over the chasm in the clouds, had disappeared again.

"Thieves! thieves!" cried a man, who made a rush at the Jacobite spy.

A yell of pain followed, as the Jacobite passed his sword right through the neck of the man.

"On, on!" he whispered. "On, dear girl, we shall be safe in another moment!"

Catherine was bewildered.

For once, in her life, the gallant and courageous Maid of Honour began to feel the sensation of fear.

The Jacobite spy hurried her forward, supporting her so well with his left arm, that being much taller than she was, he at times nearly lifted her off her feet.

They reached the termination of the garden in the direction they were going, and then the Jacobite whistled twice, faintly.

A door in the brick wall was opened instantly.

Catherine could see sufficiently well to know that she looked out upon the green park, and that immediately beyond the door a coach was waiting.

"St. George!" said a voice.

"And the Lilies!" replied the Jacobite spy.

He then turned to Catherine, and with a profound bow, said, "We shall meet again!"

"Ah, you intend to leave me?"

"Only for a time."

"How long?"

"Until to-morrow. We shall breakfast together; and then, oh, then, fairest of the fair, I can explain to you much which will seem now inexplicable to you!"

"But——"

Catherine paused. It seemed to her that she had surely something to say, and yet she knew not what.

The Jacobite spy held the door of the coach open.

Mechanically she obeyed the courteous gesture with which he invited her to enter it.

The door was closed upon her.

She was alone.

The coach started at a rapid pace, and Catherine began to ask herself, if it could all possibly be real, or if she were only in some horrible dream.

There was but one thing that gave her a feeling of satisfaction, and that was, that at all events, whatever should become of her, she was flying from Captain Harvey and her aunt Hanmer.

That was indeed a consolation.

They were defeated.

The coach went for some distance on the smooth soft grass of the Park, and then Catherine Chudleigh—for, after the truly strange marriage she had contracted, we feel still compelled to call her by her maiden name—felt that the wheels made a sudden transition to the gravel path.

Then came a still harder roadway, and an undefined feeling of fear came over the heart of Catherine.

Where was she going?

Who, after all, was that mysterious man, who had so thoroughly associated himself with her fate?

Why had he left her, at a time when all his avowed sentiments seemed to impel him to remain in her society?

Mortification, as well as alarm, began to find a place in her heart.

She was about to open the coach window and to call out aloud, when she was prevented doing so by the vehicle suddenly stopping.

She heard a gate revolve upon its hinges.

Some words were spoken that sounded like watch-words.

The coach then rolled under an arch, as the sound testified, and then upon some stone slabs of which, it may be presumed, some court-yard was composed.

The mystery of her position increased each moment, and almost for the first time the vague idea that there was danger flashed across the imagination of Catherine Chudleigh.

Yet, no, it could not be. That gentle voice was still ringing in her ears. She still saw in her mind's eye, the deep devotion that beamed from those beautiful eyes.

And did not all the world love her?

Was she not praised, *féted*, and made much of by old and young?

Oh, no, there could be no danger, and, therefore, there need be no fear. The climax of the adventure might be, that more human hearts might be thrown at her feet for her to trample upon.

A light flashed before her eyes.

The carriage door was opened.

"Descend, loved one, and forgive a seeming mystery for the clearness of explanation which shall be soon accorded to you."

It was the voice of the Jacobite spy.

The temporary pique that had taken possession of Catherine Chudleigh, from the circumstance of being left alone so long in the coach, passed away.

She was willing to believe that there was some good reason for all this disguise and all this mystery, which had likewise about it an air of romance, which was far from being displeasing to her imaginative disposition.

She leant heavily upon the arm of the would-be regicide as she descended from the coach—so heavily, indeed, that it would almost seem she wished to assure herself over again that he was a being of flesh and blood.

Some heavy door at that moment closed with violence, and in reply to the start which Catherine gave, the Jacobite spy spoke.

"It is nothing, dear one—it is nothing."

"What place is this? Are we alone? Oh, tell me for what purpose I am brought hither? I am not a coward, but I am yet a woman—perhaps, in your estimation, I am scarcely that, I am yet so young."

"Fear nothing. Have I not told you that I love you?"

"Love should be confidential. Who are you?"

"I am a proscribed man. Will it not content you to call me Chevalier?"

"It must, if I can have no other name by which to address you. Ah! what sounds are those? They speak of grief, and of despair!"

A low, wailing sound, intermingled with short shrieks and inarticulate ejaculations, came upon the ears of Catherine Chudleigh.

CHAPTER XIV.

A SCENE OF TERROR.—THE MYSTERIOUS EXECU-
TION.—CATHERINE CHUDLEIGH'S HORROR AND
DESPAIR.—THE JACOBITE SPY MAKES A PRO-
POSITION.—CATHERINE'S LOVE AND DOUBTS.

THE Jacobite had led her up the stone steps of what appeared to be a lordly mansion, and faint as the light was, which came from a hall of large dimensions, she could not but see that those steps were in many places overgrown with moss, and that between the stones, grass and weeds had germinated, sending up the stalks of a ceaseless vegetation which never could have survived the footsteps of many persons up and down those marble stairs.

There was an air of grandeur about the hall, which took Catherine completely by surprise.

That surprise was increased, however, to an immeasurable extent by a circumstance which was calculated to awaken every superstitious fear, either intuitive or acquired, which found a home in the breast of Catherine Chudleigh.

The Jacobite spy paused nearly in the centre of the hall, with his fair companion still leaning on his arm, and speaking in those soft, gentle accents which were peculiar to him,—he startled Catherine by addressing some one else than her.

And yet no person was visible.

"Must this sad scene be enacted to-night?"

"It must," replied a voice.

Catherine Chudleigh could scarcely forbear from uttering an exclamation of alarm; for although she saw no one whatever, and although the spacious hall seemed to contain no living persons but herself and the Jacobite, the short reply in the few words we have recorded, came to her ears exactly as if it had been uttered by some one standing a few paces from her and the Jacobite.

Catherine Chudleigh clung to the arm of her companion, with a feeling that now as strongly resembled fright as possible.

He could not but feel the pressure, and attribute it to the right cause.

In those sweet, flute-like accents, that always seemed to go direct to the heart of Catherine, and to find there a responsive echo, he spoke again to her.

"I say, fear nothing, for that which you shall see to-night will not apply, even as a warning to the heart that knows no guile."

Were these words in any degree assuring?

Had she, the Maid of Honour, who had fled so strangely from the husband of her own choice, a heart that knew no guile?

The question forced itself upon her imagination, and she trembled.

The Jacobite spy spoke again.

"Does she confess?"

"She confesses," replied the voice from the invisible speaker.

A loud shriek, that seemed by the suddenness with which it ceased, to be suppressed by some physical means, broke the stillness of the place.

Catherine lost her courage.

"Let me go!" she said; "let me leave this place, for it seems to be full of terrors!"

"Not yet," whispered the Jacobite. "Who shall harm you while I am with you to shield you with my love."

There was certainly something re-assuring in these words, but still they were scarcely sufficient to restore the composure of Catherine.

She no longer, however, asked to be allowed to go.

Where could she go to?

That was a question which more than once had occurred to her, and each time it had presented a greater difficulty to answer.

The Jacobite now led her gently along the hall towards a door covered with many faded gildings, upon what seemed to be a richly sculptured coat of arms that stood up in bold relief from the panels.

Then he spoke to her again.

"Whatever you see, and whatever you hear, let me impress upon you the propriety—nay, the necessity, I should call it, of a prudent silence."

"Yes."

The Jacobite pushed the door open.

A faint light fell upon the eyes of Catherine Chudleigh.

She found herself in a small space, not above five feet in depth, and bounded, behind her, by the door which the Jacobite had just opened, and, in front, by a couple of large doors, the upper portions of which were glazed.

The faint light which the eyes of Catherine Chudleigh had become conscious of, came from some room beyond those folding, half-glazed doors.

"Look!" said the Jacobite.

The glass was dim, dust and decay had dropped upon it, and aided by the moisture of night, had taken much from its transparency.

But still Catherine could see, however mistily and dimly, through the glass into the space beyond.

That space was a large hall or banquetting-room.

The walls were richly gilt, the windows, or where she guessed they were, for they themselves were not to be seen, were hung with many draperies of crimson velvet.

The floor, where it could be seen, from the dust and the damp of years which had settled upon it, was brilliantly carpeted from the looms of the east.

Candelabra, chandeliers, and old-fashioned

THE EXECUTION OF A TRAITRESS.

mirrors of every kind and description, filled the minute details of the hall.

But, it was rather due to that rapidity of perception—which was a feature in the character of Catherine Chudleigh—than to the time she had for observation, that she was enabled to see and notice so much.

In about half a minute, her whole attention was engrossed by a scene that took place before her horrified gaze, and which she felt that time nor occupation would ever enable her to forget.

A door opened at the further end of the hall.

Two men appeared, attired in long, black cloaks, which had a most funereal aspect.

They kept turning round as they entered the hall, as if heralding the way for some one else.

That some one else was a man who followed them, bearing in his arms a strange-looking bundle.

No. 5.—KATE CHUDLEIGH.

dle, which it terrified Catherine Chudleigh to conjecture the explanation of.

Not for many seconds, however, was she left to her own imaginative suggestion upon the subject.

The bundle turned out to be a sack of sawdust.

Heedless of the rich carpeting, the man emptied the sawdust on to the floor, and partly with his hands, and partly with his feet, he collected it into a flat heap on one spot.

That spot composed a space of about four or five feet in each direction.

In the centre, then, of the sawdust, the man cleared a small space right down to the carpet.

Then he left the hall.

The two mysterious men, in the long black cloaks, and who, likewise wore black velvet visors, that most completely concealed their features, took up their positions, one on each side of the little sawdust heap—a platform, as it might be called.

Then the man returned who had brought the sawdust.

Catherine uttered a cry.

He had brought two objects with him, that formed a terrible commentary upon his previous preparations, and at once afforded such an explanation of them, that there could be no doubt whatever about the meaning of the preparations before her.

One of those objects was an axe.

The other was a block.

Such a block as might be used for the purposes of execution.

Such an axe as once, in the old White Tower of London, Mr. Pultney had shown her.

An execution, then, was about to take place.

Whose execution?

Catherine remembered the wailing cries and short shrieks she had heard.

She remembered, too, the scream that had been so suddenly suppressed, and she felt certain that those cries and that scream were feminine.

"No, no!" she said; "I cannot, I will not be a spectator of this dreadful scene."

"But a moment or two more," said the Jacobite.

"Not one instant!"

Catherine turned from the glass doors, and made an effort to get back into the hall, but the door behind her was fast.

The Jacobite spoke again.

"Look—oh, look!"

A horrible kind of fascination took possession of her.

She could no longer find power to withdraw her eyes from the scene that was about to take place in that spacious hall, be it what it might.

And so she gazed through the dim glass panes and saw it all.

The block was placed in the little space that had been cleared in the centre of the sawdust.

The axe was placed leaning against the block.

Then a bell began to toll.

Or it was some sound which so strongly resembled the deeply-muffled notes of some cathedral bell, that it might well answer the same purpose.

Through the door, then, which had admitted the two cloaked and masked figures, and the man with the block and the axe, there came two more persons.

These, likewise, wore cloaks of the same sable hue, and masks.

They looked behind them as they entered the hall.

Catherine had lost the power to do so, or there and then she would have liked to scream aloud, for the sight she next saw was one to excite every sensibility of her nature.

A female form, enveloped in a cloak and hood —the latter thrown back from her head and face, appeared.

A bandage was over the eyes, and, indeed, the whole upper part of the face.

It was evident that this female had not the slightest glimpse of her pathway in her eyes, by the mode in which she seemed to feel her way in the darkness.

Yet she came on.

As if urged by some power that she could not resist, and which impelled her forward ; or from some internal conviction that resistance and hesitation were alike useless ; she slowly groped her way into the hall.

Low moans came from her lips.

Occasionally she wrung her hands, with that mute expression of agony which is so touching.

But still she advanced.

The Jacobite then spoke to Catherine Chudleigh.

"For your life's safe—for my life's sake, too—speak not !"

She could not speak.

Every sense was so absorbed in a contemplation of the spectacle before her, that she could neither speak nor move.

She could scarcely breathe.

Slowly the lady with the cloak, and the hood, and the bandaged eyes, came up the hall.

"Halt !" said a voice.

Catherine Chudleigh could not tell which of the mysterious persons present had uttered the word.

The prisoner, however, halted, for she had reached the edge of the little mass of sawdust, in the midst of which was the axe.

Then the same voice spoke again.

"Traitress ! traitress ! traitress !" it said "The oath was taken, and the fiat of death has gone forth !   Traitress ! traitress !"

The other persons in the hall took up the word, and with deep-toned voices, that found a sad echo about the fretted roof of the hall, they pronounced the name, "Traitress ! traitress !"

The prisoner only moaned.

Her feet struck against the sawdust.

She stooped and touched it ; she took up some in her hand.

A shriek of horror testified to the effect which its touch had upon her, and to the fact that she guessed her doom.

"Let it be done !" said a voice.

"The dead to the dead !" said another.

"Earth to earth !"

"From the blood of the betrayer let the righteous cause gather nourishment."

"Death ! death !"

The veiled and bandaged lady sunk to her knees.

"Mercy ! mercy ! mercy !"

A sign was made by one of the masked men.

Another of them knelt down close to the block, and caught the prisoner by some tresses of long hair, which hung upon her shoulder. He turned those tresses over the top of her head, until they hung as if from her forehead ; and then, by a violent jerk, he pulled her head over the block.

"Mercy !—oh, heaven, mercy ! No, not death ! Oh, heaven, spare ! spare !"

"Strike !"

The axe gleamed in the air for a moment, and then, with a horrible and heavy thud, it came down.

Catherine Chudleigh, for the first time in her life, fell into a swoon.

*   *   *   *   *

"Ah ! where am I ? Is it true ? Oh, no, a dream—a dream ! Where am I ? Oh, heaven, no ! it is true !"

Such were the exclamations uttered by Catherine Chudleigh, as she awakened from her trance, and found herself in a strange bed-room, lying on a bed, the coverlet of which was of rich quilted satin.

"Be composed!" said a voice.

It was the voice of the Jacobite.

"Ah, you are there? Cruel! cruel! You do not—you cannot love me!"

"With all my heart."

"You have no heart?"

"Yes; and it beats alone for thee."

She looked up, and saw that he was leaning lightly and gracefully against the back of a chair, which was near to the foot of the bed.

"Tell me, then, if you have either love or pity for me, if I really saw a terrible murder committed last night, or not?"

"You saw an execution."

"Execution, or murder. It was real, then?"

"It was real."

"Oh, how terrible!"

"A terrible necessity. Catherine Chudleigh, can you listen to me now, calmly?"

"Yes, oh, yes! What can you have to say to me?"

The Jacobite took the chair against which he had been leaning, and brought it forward near to the bedstead.

He sat down, and sighed deeply, and fixed his eyes upon Catherine, with an expression at once of pity and of affection.

CHAPTER XV.

THE JACOBITE SPY COMES OUT IN A NEW CHARACTER.—CATHERINE CHUDLEIGH IS AT ONCE FASCINATED AND DISAPPOINTED. — A SLIGHT QUARREL. — THE MYSTERIOUS POTION. — A PRINCE OF THE HOUSE OF STUART APPEARS ON THE SCENE.

ALL the old fascination which the marvellous beauty—the word is too feminine, but there is no other sufficiently expressive for this man—came freshly over the heart of Catherine.

She no longer regretted that she had flown from the husband she now detested.

She no longer wished undone the acts of the last twelve hours, but she told herself that, in the love of that man—mysterious, and something beyond mortality as she had reason to think him—would be henceforward bound up her existence.

He stretched out his hand, and she placed hers within it.

He spoke very sadly.

"You do love me?"

"You do not want me to say so!"

The coquettish feminine nature still revolted from an open expression of the feeling which was fast becoming a second life to her.

"No, Catherine, you need not say it,
I read it in your sparkling eyes:
And there alone should love be read.
I read it in your gentle sighs,
For so alone should love be said.

You do love me!"

"And you?"

"Ah, I love you as never mortal man loved. You are, you shall be all the world to me, if—if——"

"If what?"

"If you will consent to look upon the past and the future with my eyes."

"I do not comprehend you?"

"You shall? you shall! The man who sits upon the throne of England occupies the place of a prince who alone has a right to the title of King of these realms."

"Ah, you are one of those treasonous people Mr. Pultney used to plague me so much about."

"Indeed?"

"Yes, you are a Jacobite."

"It is true, I am an adherent of the exiled family of the Stuarts. I want to place upon the throne of England a descendant of King James the Second. When that end shall be accomplished, I shall be the first subject in rank, and in influence, and in wealth, and you shall be my wife!"

"I am a wife?"

"No. A bride, but no wife."

"But—but——"

"I see that you do not yet quite comprehend what is required of you, and I will tell you. Go into the gay court world again, from which this odious marriage with Captain Harvey would have soon taken you. Go again among all the rank and all the beauty of England, to feel that you are the most beautiful of all, and that the rank you will one day assume, when the exiled family is restored to the crown, will eclipse the highest."

"A spy?"

The Jacobite was silent.

"A private Jacobite spy?"

"Call it what you will, oh, Catherine; but remember along with it, how much I love you."

The Jacobite, as he spoke these words, clasped his hands over his eyes, and groaned, as though some bitter and sudden grief had come over him.

"Tell me one thing?"

"What is it, oh, fair one?"

"Was—was the—was the poor traitress who was murdered last night, was she a spy?"

"She was."

"Ah!"

"But she betrayed the trust that was reposed in her. The deaths of no less than eight noble gentlemen lie at her door."

"I won't do it!"

"Won't do what?"

"I won't be a Jacobite spy."

"Oh, think again. Think again. You already know too much."

"I won't—I won't. I don't care. I don't mind what I know; but I will not accept the office you assign for me."

"With my love?"

"You do not love me."

"Alas! alas! This is very, very sad. Well, be it so. Be it so. If it must be so, my life is gone."

"Your life?"

"Yes, I chanced my life upon this project of

making you aid our cause. Your refusal forfeits my existence."

"I don't believe it; if it be so, where is your generosity, that you would seek to destroy me, and make me a spy upon all those who would think me a friend, to save your life. Do you mean that?"

A dark shadow came over the face of the Jacobite.

A flashing look, like lightning from a thunder cloud, darted from his eyes.

"Be it so, then," he said; "but remember one thing, that I shall henceforward be your fate."

"My fate?"

"Yes, you shall never be able to free yourself from me. Remember, that it was you, in your own chamber, sheltered, aided, and abetted the man who attempted the life of the King."

"Ah!"

"Remember, that you have been in the company for the whole of the past night of persons who are inimical to the law. Remember, that you are compromised politically."

"No."

"Yes, and criminally."

"No, no!"

"It is so, criminally. Who will now believe in the purity of Catherine Chudleigh, who fled from her nuptial chamber on her wedding-night, into——"

"Into what?"

"These arms!"

To the eyes of Catherine all the sweetness and all the beauty of the Jacobite had vanished; and the cold, steel-like glance that came from his eyes now made her shudder from head to foot.

"Oh, heaven save me!"

"You may save yourself. You refuse, in words, to be what I wished you—namely, one who, from time to time, would gather at the Court all the information which the adherents of the exiled family require; but you will do so, in fact. When I come to you and question you, you dare not say me nay!"

Terror now hung at the heart of Catherine Chudleigh, but she strove to conceal it. She sprung up from the bed—for she was in the same clothing, without the least exception, which she had worn at her aunt's house.

"No!" she cried. "No; I will be the slave of no man, of no party!"

The Jacobite rose, too, from the chair at the bed-side, and going backwards, towards a table in the room, he took up a silver cup.

"Say you so, oh, capricious fair one?" he cried; and, at the same moment, he flung the contents of the cup into the face of Catherine.

It seemed to be nothing but clear water; but she was shocked and indignant at the outrage.

"Wretch! Villain! Oh, that I had given you up to—be—what—is—this?—Oh, save me! —I fall—I fall!"

The Jacobite caught her in his arms.

The contents of that cup must have contained some very subtle essence indeed, for the small portion of it that had reached the lips of Catherine Chudleigh to throw her into insensibility.

"Chevalier! Oh, Chevalier!" cried the Jacobite.

A door opened in one of the panels of the room, and a tall, fair young man came into the chamber.

"What is it, Johnstone?"

"Your Royal Highness has heard all?"

"No, faith—not a word."

The Jacobite spy, who was named by the tall, fair young man, Johnstone, bit his lips.

"Nay, your Highness. I did hope you had heard how much I tried to bend the stubborn girl to our purposes."

"And she won't bend?"

"She will not, your Highness."

"Break her, then!"

"Ah, your Highness; I am afraid she is one of those natures that you can neither break nor bend."

"Indeed!"

"Yes, your Highness. I believe there is no one in all the Court of England who might be of such essential service to your cause as this Catherine Chudleigh."

"Why so? She is but a pretty girl."

"If she were nothing but that, the marvellous beauty she possesses, and which, your Highness, can see, pale and inert as she is now, would arm her with a wonderful power; but she is something more than that."

"What, Johnstone?"

"She has talents—abilities of the highest order. Her wit—her courage—her general acuteness—and her audacity, if I may use the term, stand unrivalled."

"You make her out a phœnix."

"As she is, your Highness."

"And, with all this, she will not serve us; say you so?"

"No, not willingly; but she has higher qualifications still."

"You are an enthusiast, Captain Johnstone."

"Yes, your Highness. She is a great favourite with the Princess of Wales, who is half a fool, and would tell her anything; and, as the Prince of Wales is wholly a fool, the Princess knows everything."

"Ah! that is something."

"Then, again, the Honourable Mr. Pultney, who commenced his acquaintance with her by being a second father to her on the death of General Chudleigh, and who got her the appointment of Maid of Honour to the Princess of Wales, has ended by falling madly in love with her."

"You don't say that?"

"It is so. Moreover, the Duke of Hamilton, whom we wish so much to win over to us, is enamoured of her to that excess that he is almost beside himself with grief and despair that he cannot call her his own."

"You surprise me more and more!"

"The Duke of Kingston, too, is up to the ears in the delicious bath of love!"

"For her?"

"Ay, your Royal Highness, for her!"

"Why, Johnstone, she is worth twenty thousand troops in the field!"

"A hundred thousand, your Royal Highness, and all in battle array!"

"Hem! What can be done?"

"Nothing."

"Nothing! You, who are so full of all kinds of stratagems—you, who of all men have a remedy for any disaster when no one else can suggest one—you say nothing can be done?"

"At present."

"Well, I leave the affair to you! By the saints—by St. George in particular—she is a dainty piece of flesh and blood! Johnstone, are you in love with her?"

"Your Royal Highness knows that I have devoted my life to your cause, and that all I am in love with is legitimate monarchy in England!"

"Thanks—thanks!"

"And, likewise, I have——"

"Ah, we forgot! You have a wife and children!"

"I have."

"Well, but you know, Johnstone, that don't much matter! That wife and those children are at Rome, in safety under the shadow of the Vatican. You are the real heir to the Auriandale estates—which are now held by those opposed to me and my safety—only let the sign-manual of James the Third be good in this land, and we will soon change all that. She is pretty!"

The Royal Highness, who was, beyond a doubt, one of the exiled princes of the House of Stuart, kissed Catherine Chudleigh twice.

A look of pain came over the face of the Jacobite spy.

"Well, well," said the Prince, "don't take it to heart, Johnstone! Its a family failing, if it may be called one, you know!"

"I have heard so!" said the Jacobite, coldly.

"A Stuart never could refrain from kissing a pretty girl when he had a chance!"

The door in the panel was opened again, and, with a slight bow, the Prince left the room.

The Jacobite was alone with Catherine Chudleigh.

He laid her gently in the recesses of an armchair, and then he listened.

A clock was striking somewhere close at hand, and the morning breeze brought the sounds near.

It was six in the morning.

"Yes," said the Jacobite,—" yes, it must be so. I will see what comes of it, and take the chances!"

A quarter of an hour after that a coach conveyed Catherine from the mysterious house, and the next sensation of waking existence she had, was finding herself on a doorstep not far from the top of St. James's Street.

A curious throng of persons was about her.

She heard the hum of voices, and she opened her eyes with difficulty.

The smell of some fragrant essence was in the air.

"She will do now," said a voice. "How do you feel, young lady?"

A grave-looking man in black was bending over her.

The crowd of people, when she opened her eyes, pressed eagerly forward to hear her and see her better.

"Keep back! Keep back, all of you!" cried the grave-looking man in black. "Keep back! Do—do you want to smother the patient!"

Catherine felt a heaviness about the eyes, which, although it was rapidly going off, for some few seconds prevented her from looking well about her.

Then she heard some one utter an exclamation of despair and grief, and a voice cried out, "Oh, dear! oh, dear!—it is—is Miss—— "

Then the voice ceased, as if the speaker thought it indiscreet to name her; and as Catherine saw the crowd divide, and some one push himself forward, she was aware that it was the stable-boy, Hutchins, who was so ready to do her any service, and who was attached to the household of the Princess of Wales at Marlborough House.

She felt that she had found a friend, and stretched out her arms towards him.

CHAPTER XVI.

CATHERINE CHUDLEIGH ALONE AND FRIENDLESS.—THE ADMIRING CROWD AND THE FUGITIVE.—A QUACK DOCTOR OF OLD TIMES.—THE STABLE BOY AND THE SEDAN CHAIR.—SAVED AGAIN.

"Do you know the young lady?" asked the doctor, who had been hastily called to attend upon Catherine Chudleigh, as she had been found by some passers-by lying insensible on the door step.

"Oh, yes—yes!"

"Where does she live?"

"At Marlborough House."

"Oh, indeed? Well, I daresay you are a good lad, and I see you are in his Royal Highness the Prince of Wales's livery; so, if you will take the young lady home some one will call a chair, and I will look in about twelve o'clock to see how she is."

"Yes, sir."

"Hem! I'm the famous Doctor Opodildoc, good people all!"

"Quack! quack!" cried several voices, for the Doctor Opodildoc was the most noted character of the day.

The doctor soon got into a dispute with the mob, under cover of which the boy Hutchins called a sedan chair, into which he assisted Catherine, and walked by the side of it down St. James's Street.

She was rapidly recovering.

Whatever was the nature of the rapidly-acting opiate, so small a portion of which had been sufficient to cast her into a sleep, it certainly did her no permanent injury.

Probably, it was one of those anesthetic agents now so popular, but which, at that time, might have been known to a few persons.

Catherine looked out at the window of the chair.

"Hutchins!"

"Yes, dear Miss Chudleigh?"

"What has happened?"

"Alas! I don't know."

"Of course, you don't—it is I who ought to know; but—but—stop! No—do not stop the chair if you think I can get into the Palace without observation. Can it be done?"

"Oh, yes, Miss Chudleigh, if you will only condescend to come by the stables."

"Anyhow!"

"Then it can be done as nicely as possible."

"Very well. I want you to get me news if Miss Bella Steinburgh is at the Palace."

"I know she is."

"That will do. I must reach her room without any one seeing me, if that can be done. Stay, I will do it this way. I will stay in the stables until you go to her for a cloak or a shawl and a bonnet."

"Yes, Miss Chudleigh, only say what you want me to do, and it is as good as done. Oh, dear! oh, dear!"

"What's the matter?"

"Is it really true that you are married to Captain Harvey?"

"No."

"No?"

"No. It's only a jest. I am the wife of no man—no, and I don't think I ever shall be. Oh, the infamy—the villany!"

The mind of Catherine flew back to the scene in her aunt's bedroom, when from the little Coromandel wood cabinet, she had extracted the packet of intercepted letters, which the Duke of Hamilton had sent her from Vienna.

She had slid that packet into the breast of her apparel.

It was a wonder that they were preserved after all she had gone through in the long night that had just passed away.

But she had them, as she now ascertained by feeling them.

The sedan-chair had now reached Marlborough House, and, without any molestation or impediment, was quietly taken round to the stables.

The boy, Hutchins, dismissed the chairmen. and Catherine Chudleigh waited in one of the harness-rooms, while he went in search of Bella Steinburgh.

Catherine had not to wait long before Bella herself, in the greatest consternation, made her appearance, and flung herself upon her neck.

"Oh, Catherine, Catherine! what has happened? How—why are you here?"

"Stuff! don't plague!"

"But, dear Catherine, where is—is your husband?"

"My what?"

"Your husband. I thought——"

"Never pronounce that name to me again unless you want me to hate you."

"Hate me?"

"Yes, for ever and for ever, Bella. I have no husband; and, as for what you 'thought,' let me tell you it is a very dangerous thing for people like you to think."

"Alas, it is!"

"There, don't cry, now. Lend me your hat and scarf. That will do. Good-bye, Hutchins! Now, Bella, don't be stupid; I want a good long sleep, and intend to have it in your bed, and then I must speak to the Princess of Wales. Perhaps, I shall condescend, love, to give you my history for the past four-and-twenty hours; but don't call anybody my husband, or try to make out that I am the wife of anybody, or you will drive me mad."

"I won't."

"Don't, then."

Bella was all amazement; she was overflowing with curiosity, but she kept watch and ward over Catherine for a space exceeding five hours, during which the little spoilt beauty slept soundly.

Catherine awakened, thoroughly refreshed, and completely herself again.

"Chocolate, Bella!"

"Yes, dear."

"Be quick—ratafia cakes!"

"Yes, dear Catherine, anything you like. Oh! how glad I am to hear you speak in your own voice again."

"Good gracious! do you expect me to speak in any one else's?"

"No, love!"

"Ah! do go along, and get the chocolate at once, and don't be stupid."

"You are so clever."

"Will you go?"

Poor snubbed Bella went at once, and soon returned with a breakfast for Catherine, who enjoyed it with all the gusto of youth.

Bella sat opposite to her, looking at her, and sighing sadly.

"Now, what is the matter?"

"Oh, nothing! but it is so ill-natured."

"What is?"

"Lady Portman has been saying all sorts of ill-natured things, and, whatever she says, that odious thing with the red hair, Augusta Home, lifts up her hands, like pieces of raw beef, as they are, and cries out 'Yes—oh dear! To be sure!'"

"Bravo!"

Catherine clapped her hands.

"Bella, as I had once occasion to say, you are not half such a fool as you look."

"Oh, you flatter me!"

"Not a bit. But what do they say?"

"Why—a—a—they say——"

"Well, what?"

"That it was a good thing you got married, as they say you have, for you wanted a husband to keep you out of mischief."

"How kind. Well that receipt does not always answer, for Lady Portman has had two husbands, poor men, and she has been in mischief all her life, and would be still, but that she is fat, and old, and ugly; and as for Lady Augusta Home, she may have, and doubtless has, all the desire to get into mischief in the world, but as there are no baboons at Court, she will not have the chance."

"Oh, Catherine!"

"Oh, Bella!"

"How severe you are."

"Trash! Help me to dress, and then, as the phrase goes, take my humble respects to the Princess of Wales, and say that I request a private audience."

"Yes, dear Catherine."

Bella was delighted at the idea of Catherine Chudleigh becoming once more an inmate of the Palace, and a member of the household of the Princess of Wales; but yet her curiosity was not satisfied, and she threw herself at Catherine's feet, as she cried out in earnest tones—

"You did promise to tell me—indeed, you did promise to tell me all!"

"All what?"

"All that has befallen you. How you have been married, and yet how you have no husband?"

"There is nothing to tell. I don't like him,

and I won't stay with him. That is surely enough."

" Oh, yes!"

" Well—what more would you have?"

" What did he say? What did he do? What did you say? and what did you do? Will he trouble you? Can you marry any one else? Will you stay here?"

" Peace—peace— you stun me. I will tell you more after my interview with the Princess."

Bella saw that she was to get no more information just then, so she went on her errand, soon returning, with the information, that Her Royal Highness the Princess of Wales was much surprised, but would see the late Maid of Honour at one o'clock.

Catherine Chudleigh knew that that was just twenty minutes before prayers, which the Princess had punctually performed in her own closet, as a handsome room, looking into the park was named any day.

The interview would therefore be necessarily brief.

But the tardy hours passed away as all tardy hours will, and Catherine, assuming her most engaging appearance, sought the Princess in her closet.

A Gentleman Usher was at the door, at which he tapped with his wand of office thrice.

Then without waiting for an answer, he opened the door, saying, as he did so, and evidently from the orders of the Princess:

" Lady Harvey will be so good as to walk into the closet."

Catherine started as if a serpent had stung her.

That was the first time she had been called Lady Harvey.

The name jarred upon her senses most discordantly, and it awakened the disagreeable idea that not only was the marriage well known at court, but that the Princess was determined to give validity to it.

" No, never—never!" said Catherine to herself—" Never will I be that man's wife."

She was on the point of saying something angrily to the Gentleman Usher, but she controlled the wish, the more particularly as the closet door was open, and the Princess would be sure to hear any word that was spoken.

Another moment, and Catherine Chudleigh, as she was resolved still to consider herself, was in the presence of the Princess.

Her Royal Highness was alone.

She looked cold and severe.

Catherine knelt before her.

" Oh, madam—dear mistress—why did I ever dream of leaving you?"

Probably Catherine thought by this demonstration of personal feeling to prejudice the Princess at once in her favour, but she was mistaken. She had a cold, inflexible heart, in which there was no romance, and very little feeling to deal with.

The reply of the Princess was prompt and decisive.

" I suppose that you left my service in order to get married to the man of your choice!"

" Oh, no—no!"

" No. Do you mean to tell me that you have committed the great indelicacy of getting married to any one who was not your choice?"

" Yes, royal madam!"

" You astonish me!"

" Oh, madam I am so young, I did not know my mind, and what is more, I did not know the man whom I married was capable of two monstrous iniquities."

" Iniquities! What do you mean by iniquities?"

The Princess was getting curious. It was one of her passions, curiosity, and a love of a little bit of scandal, if that was comprised in the matter.

Catherine was playing her game well.

The Princess of Wales tried hard to keep up the air of cold indifference with which she had commenced the interview, but she could not.

" Tell me at once what you mean?" she cried. " Tell me directly, Catherine Chudleigh, all that took place?"

" Ah, madam—royal mistress—you do not cast me off! You call me Catherine Chudleigh still!"

" Then, I was wrong."

" Oh, no, no—a thousand times, no! I have no desire to hear any other name from your royal lips!"

" Well, well, you don't tell me what happened. Pray, be quick!"

" Then, madam, the marriage, in a very informal manner, took place in the Chapel Royal; and I made up my mind that I would stay that night at my aunt Hanmer's, instead of leaving London. We supped, and then——"

" Prayers, your Royal Highness!" cried the Gentleman Usher, flinging open the doors of the Princess's closet, as he had a general order to do on the arrival of the chaplains, whose turn of duty it was to officiate.

The Princess was vexed.

" Soon—soon! In a few minutes!" she said. " Leave us now!"

The Usher turned, and closed the door again.

" Well, Catherine — well! After supper! Well, what then?"

" Oh, I cannot tell your Highness!"

" But you must! I will know it! I tell you I must and will hear it! Come, come, child, recollect that I am not only your mistress, but a married lady beside ; and so—and so—— Well, I was going to say, that whatever you have got to say to me, there will be no impropriety in telling me."

" None in the least, madam. After supper, then, he became—he—he became——"

" What—what?"

" Violent. He broke down a door—drew his sword—made no end of disturbance—and uttered such frightful language, that I was compelled to threaten him with your Royal Highness's displeasure ; upon which——"

" Well, upon which?"

" He said he did not care a straw for your Royal Highness, or your displeasure ; and he further said, that the beauty of Germany had suffered no sensible diminution by your Royal Highness's departure from there."

" The villain!"

" Oh, yes! Goaded to despair, I—I fled. I could not—I would not stay with such a man. I fled from the house by the open window, and am here to claim your royal protection. Oh, madam, have mercy upon me!"

A tap came to the closet door.

"What is it?" cried the Princess, in a tone of some anxiety.

"Prayers, your Royal Highness!"

"Go to——"

Where the Princess of Wales intended the Usher and the Chaplain to go to on that occasion history does not inform us; but she indulged in a pinch of snuff, which had become a habit even in those early days, and added, "Let prayers be said in the Picture Gallery. We will come if we can, but at present we are indisposed."

CHAPTER XVII.

CATHERINE CHUDLEIGH HAS AN INTERVIEW WITH THE PRINCESS OF WALES.—AN INTERRUPTION. —AN ESCAPE AT THE PROPER MOMENT.— CAPTAIN HARVEY IN DISGRACE.—THE FRIEND AT THE PROPER MOMENT.

THE royal closet was closed again.

"And," said the Princess, with some vivacity, "do you mean to tell me, child, that that is all?"

"Yes, your Highness."

"Then—you are a wife——"

"Ah, no!"

"A bride?"

"Yes; but still your Royal Highness's Maid of Honour."

Tap! tap! tap! came at the door of the royal closet.

The Princess of Wales certainly this time swore in German.

"The Honourable Captain Harvey presents his humble and respectful duty to your Royal Highness, and prays the favour of an audience."

"Ah!" shouted Catherine.

The Princess of Wales was troubled. She perhaps had a slight suspicion that Catherine had been romancing a little in the account she had given her of the conduct of Harvey.

"Come in ten minutes for an answer," she said to the Usher.

Catherine clasped the Princess's hands, and shed a shower of tears.

"Oh, madam, I have not told you all! My aunt Hanmer and Captain Harvey——"

"Ah, what is it?"

"Something else happened——"

"Speak out! I am a Princess—I am a wife! I don't mind what I hear! Tell me all, Catherine!"

"Then, madam, in a Coromandel wood casket in my aunt's bedchamber, I found all the letters which were written to me by the Duke of Hamilton while he was at Vienna, and which had been suppressed by my aunt and Captain Harvey, who actually paid her to advocate his claim to my hand."

"Is that all?"

"It is, indeed!"

"Then, child, you have been badly treated; but I don't see what I can do in the matter. You cannot remain in my service as a Maid of Honour. The scandal would be too great. We don't like scandal, but I will still allow you your salary out of my private purse, and——"

Tap, tap, came at the door of the royal closet again, and the pertinacious Groom in Waiting appeared.

"Your Royal Highness was pleased to say that in ten minutes——"

Catherine Chudleigh had just time to dart behind a Japan screen that was in the room, when Captain Harvey appeared, and made a low bow on its threshold nearly to his shoe ties.

The Princess of Wales looked desperately provoked.

"It seems," she said, "that we cannot have any privacy! Yonder is our bed-chamber! Beyond that a dressing-room! Pray walk in."

Captain Harvey bowed again.

"Your Royal Highness, I am the victim of some cruel mistake! I thought that your royal commands had been brought to me that I should present myself to you in ten minutes."

"No such thing!"

"The Usher——"

"Is von fool!"

The Princess of Wales lost her English as soon as she got into a passion.

Captain Harvey bowed again, and was on the point of retiring, when the foible—curiosity—of the Princess began to exert its influence, and with the desire to know what sort of complexion he would put upon the affair, she spoke in milder tones.

"Then, sir, you are not to blame, and we grant the audience."

"Oh, madam, you are all kindness and condescension!"

Captain Harvey did not wait for a second invitation or permission to enter the royal closet, but at once advanced, again bowing to the Princess as he did so.

"Gracious madam, yesterday I was married."

"Well, sir?"

"My wife is the young and charming Catherine Chudleigh that was, but now the Honourable Mrs. Harvey!"

"Well, sir?"

"In the most strange and unaccountable manner she fled from me last night, and report says that she has found a refuge near to the person of your Royal Highness. Oh, madam, consider what must be my feelings, and make tho truant wife return to her duty!"

"We are surprised, sir, that upon so delicate a subject you should apply to us! His Highness the Prince or the King were fitter."

"Oh, no! Catherine was one of your Maids of Honour—she loved you, no doubt, and you regarded her with kindness!"

"I cannot interfere!"

Captain Harvey turned a shade sallower, as he said, "May I be so bold as to say, that as your Highness has already interfered to some degree——"

"Insolence!"

"Not so, your Highness. I am an injured man! I am so—so maddened—so stung with shame—so—so perfectly beside myself, that I cannot cultivate all those little petty everyday courtesies which the butterflies of the Court excel in!"

THE PRINCESS CHIDES CAPTAIN HARVEY.

"Sir!"

"Nay, madam! Pardon me, and have some consideration for human passion and human suffering. As I live, I think Catherine is in your keeping, and I implore you to deliver her to her husband!"

The Princess rose to her feet.

"I demand my wife!"

The Princess stood before the Japan screen, and turned white with rage.

Captain Harvey stepped forward a pace.

"Help! help!"

There was a look of death-like resolve and despair on the face of Harvey. All that was evil in his resolve seemed to be at boiling point.

"My wife—my wedded wife!" he cried. "I demand my wife! All laws, human and divine, verify and justify my claim. She is mine, and mine in the sight of heaven and of earth; and

No. 6.—KATE CHUDLEIGH.

not all the Kings, all the Princesses, and all the Princes of the world, shall keep her from me!"

"Help! Guard! Guard!"

"Guard! Guard!" shouted a voice in the ante-room.

"Nay, then, the end justifies the means!" cried Captain Harvey. And he sprang past the Princess of Wales, and tore down the Japan screen.

A female form was there, and uttered a shriek as he rudely seized her by the arm.

A couple of officers of the Guard at the same moment, with drawn swords, reached the closet door.

Captain Harvey was confounded. The female whom he had so rudely seized was Bella Steinburgh, instead of that wife whom he claimed so barbarously, and with such a total disregard of the polished etiquette of a palace.

The Princess of Wales was probably no less

astonished than Captain Harvey, although a few moments' reflection would enable her to find a solution of the mystery.

Adjoining that royal closet was the bed-chamber of the Princess, and adjoining that again was a small dressing-room, to which was attached a bath-room—not that the latter was ever used by a German Princess—and from that bath-room descended a small flight of stairs to the library of Marlborough House.

It was possible enough, therefore, that by that route Catherine might have escaped.

It was easier to imagine the escape of Catherine, however, than the appearance of Bella Stein-burgh.

She certainly had no business there at such a time.

She accordingly screamed, and looked all the terror and confusion she felt.

Captain Harvey, pale with passion—we have already said he was one of those persons who turn pale when greatly excited—had actually caught the Maid of Honour by the arm.

The Princess of Wales, although at first frightened, and regretting that she had on the impulse of the moment called for help, was now well pleased that she had done so.

It placed Harvey in a worse position, and made the awkward error into which he appeared to have fallen much more apparent.

The Princess put on a look of deeply offended dignity.

"This outrage is beyond all human patience!"

The two officers of the Guard, who knew Harvey perfectly well, were astonished to see in him the perpetrator of any outrage against Royalty.

His predilections in favour of the reigning family were well known, and he was about the last man they would have expected to see in such a predicament.

They did not calculate upon the overwhelming power of those other human passions which had found a home in his heart.

Disappointed love.

Jealousy.

The rage of one who had set his happiness upon one cast in life, and lost the venture.

He could not speak.

He could only look in the face of Bella Stein-burgh, as if doubting the evidence of his own senses, and expecting each passing instant to see her transformed back again into Catherine Chud-leigh.

Bella shrieked again.

"Silence!" cried the Princess.

Then Captain Harvey found power to utter a few words.

"Madam, I suppose I should apologize for being the victim of some clever trick, in which it is not dignified for your Highness to have a share."

"Intolerable insolence!"

"Nay, madam——"

The Princess stamped with both her feet alternately on the floor with rage.

"Gentlemen, gentlemen!" she said, addressing the two officers. "Have I not power to order this man into arrest?"

"Certainly, madam," said one of the officers.

The other shook his head, for he knew very well the Princess of Wales had no such power; but turning to Harvey, he said, "Captain Harvey, I am quite sure you will not stand upon abstract rights now; but, at the request of her Royal Highness, you will give up your sword."

"Certainly not."

"Then I am sorry."

"So am I. Let me advise you, Colonel Ben-tinck, not to complete your sentence. What apology I can feel myself called upon to make to her Royal Highness I will within the next four-and-twenty hours make with pleasure; but I cannot help thinking that Marlborough House, although only the temporary abode for royalty, should not be made a refuge for runaway wives."

"Every place should be a refuge for a wife when she flies from a brutal husband," said the Princess of Wales.

That was about the wisest, as well as the best-expressed speech the Princess had yet made on the occasion.

Captain Harvey had his hand on his sword when the Usher, who had made himself already so busy by his various inopportune announce-ments, suddenly cried out, "Admiral Gascoigne!"

An officer, in the full dress of an admiral, appeared at the door of the royal closet.

Captain Harvey bowed low to him, and was passing out, when the officer, who had received so curt a reply from Harvey about his arrest, cried out, "Admiral, you are the superior officer of Captain Harvey, and he has affronted her Royal Highness the Princess of Wales most grossly."

The admiral paused, and put on a look of severe astonishment.

His errand to the Princess of Wales was to get her to use her influence with the Prince, or, rather, not to use her bad offices, in a matter that personally concerned him.

He wanted a royal grant of a tract of land in Cornwall, which, although then but a barren waste, was afterwards to be the wealthiest for-tune of the Gascoigne family, under the title of Earls of Falmouth.

No wonder, then, that the Admiral looked severe.

"An officer of the royal navy," he said, "affront our gracious and beautiful Princess!"

The Princess of Wales was remarkably plain, so she felt all the delicacy of the compliment.

"If you do flatter," says Millarde, "lay it on thick."

That was decidedly thick.

"Yes," replied the Princess, "under the ab-surd notion that I could make his ill-used wife return to him, he has almost assailed me."

The Admiral drew himself up to his full height; it was not high, but he looked as digni-fied as he could.

"Captain Harvey."

"Admiral."

"I am surprised, astonished, annoyed!"

"All of which expressions seem to me," said Harvey, "to mean the same thing."

He was goaded into such a state of frenzy that he would have made such replies to the King himself had he been there.

The Admiral now felt that he had a personal quarrel with Captain Harvey. He looked red and then blue with rage, as he added, "Sir, you will consider yourself under arrest; and you will at once repair to the flag-ship, in Portsmouth Harbour, and give up your sword to the officer in command, and, if I live, I will try you by court-martial!"

Harvey shook a little.

"No, Admiral, no!" he said. "This day I shall lay my commission at the feet of the King!"

"But until his Majesty graciously accepts your resignation, and permits you to withdraw from the service, you are under my command. I have given my orders, and expect them to be obeyed. If not, I shall take means to enforce them."

Captain Harvey bowed sarcastically, and left the royal closet.

The Princess smiled, and fanned herself, for she had the infirmity of getting hot and red when anything vexed her very much.

Bella was kneeling, and resting on a chair with her head and hands, and crying.

"Admiral Gascoigne," said the Princess, "I will see you in a few hours. At present, I am very much engaged."

The Admiral bowed low.

"I am only too happy to have been of the slightest service to your Royal Highness."

He was resolved that she should not forget the obligation, however slight it might be.

When the Princess of Wales then once more found her royal closet clear of intruders, she turned to Bella Steinburgh, and saluted her with a sound box on the ears.

"Hussey! how came you here?"

"Oh, Madam!"

"How came you here, I ask?"

Another box on the ears.

The Princess was rather fond of boxing the ears of those of her Maids of Honour who would put up with it.

It is reported of one, a spirited young girl of the name of Ferris, that she returned the favour one day with a promptitude and effect that made the Princess see such an illumination in both her eyes as no Court *fête* had ever presented to her.

But Bella was made of more impenetrable stuff.

She put up with the Princess's violence without attempting to return it, and only cried.

"Will you tell me, wretched creature that you are, how you came here?"

"Yes, oh, yes—the—the staircase—to—to the bath-room!"

"And how dared you come that way, and where was the Page, eh, hussey?"

"The—the Page of—the stairs?"

"Yes; where was he!"

"He—he wanted to hear, too, as he is so fond of—of——"

"You, you ill-looking——"

"No, no; of Catherine! So when I came to the stairs, and told him she was here, we both crept up together, and—and—Catherine came then behind the screen and fled, and the Page ran after her, and I staid—and that is all!"

"All, indeed! So that is all! You are no longer a Maid——"

"Oh, do not say so!"

"Of Honour to me!"

"Alas, alas! Oh, your Royal Highness, forgive me this once, and I will promise never to transgress your commands—never—oh, never—

and—and—if the Count Skelmevslegginski ——"

The Princess uttered a scream, and clutched at a table for support.

"If he should come again—I—should only be too happy to—too——"

"Hush!"

"Yes, madam."

"Be a good girl. The Count is—is a sort of distant cousin to my family; but his Royal Highness the Prince of Wales has taken a dislike to him, and that is why I meet him now and then at home."

"Yes, madam."

"You quite comprehend?"

"I think I do, madam."

"Then I forgive you."

"A thousand thanks, dear, dear mistress. I shall live only to be useful to you, and to my dear friend Catherine Chudleigh."

"Well, well, find her out, and tell her that I forgive all that has passed, and that I do not wonder at her flying from such a man as Harvey, although I do wonder very much at her marrying him at all! There—go—go!"

Bella was not a little pleased to escape so well.

Two boxes on the ear, and a good scolding, and then an ample and complete amnesty, did not to her appear in a very bad light.

She was extremely anxious about Catherine.

The facts of the escape of the ci-devant Maid of Honour were exactly as Bella had related them.

When Catherine Chudleigh ran behind the screen, she had no hope of being able to leave the apartments of the Princess of Wales without an encounter with Captain Harvey.

It was a most agreeable surprise to her, therefore, when she almost fell over Bella Steinburgh and one of the Pages of the Princess's household.

They had both, no doubt, heard all that had taken place.

In fact, they could not do otherwise, for bit by bit, they had got right into the royal closet, and were exactly on the other side of the Japan screen.

"Save me!" whispered Catherine.

"Follow me, dear Miss Chudleigh," said the Page. "I, at least, will never, no never, call you Lady Harvey."

Bella had sunk down in a half faint, and Catherine paid no attention to her, but followed the Page of the private staircase.

The library was not a large room, and the moment they reached it, the Page fell on his knees, and, in the most audacious manner, clasped Catherine round the feet, crying out, "Kill me, oh, kill me, or—or——"

"What do you mean? Are you mad?"

"No! Kill me or kiss me!"

There was something so serio-comic about the manner of the Page, that Catherine, in the midst of all her perplexities, could not help laughing.

"Now," she said, "I see you are mad!"

"No, no! It is Carolus, the king's Page, who is mad for love of you. I love you as well as he does, but I think it much better to keep my senses, in the hope that I may be of service to you."

"Very well. Good bye?"

"No, no!"

"Will you let me go?"

"Not yet! Not yet! Here? There is my sword—take it. The hilt is next to you. Take it, and kill me, or—or— You know what I said?"

"No."

Catherine liked to hear it again.

"Or, kiss me?"

"Foolish boy! How old are you?"

"Seventeen."

"There then, you are only a child I find, after all."

Catherine kissed him lightly on the brow, and, at the moment she did so, a deep groan came from some one who was surely in the library.

The Page sprung to his feet.

Catherine uttered an exclamation; and as she did so, she saw a figure emerge from behind a thick velvet curtain, which shut off a portion of the room which was merely the deep embrasure of a large bay window.

A glance was sufficient to let her know who that was.

It was the unfortunate but noble-minded Mr. Pultney.

He who loved her so well, but who was resolved that his love should never be a reproach to him, or to her.

CHAPTER XVIII.

CATHERINE CHUDLEIGH FINDS A FRIEND IN NEED.—THE INTERRUPTED EMBRACE.—MISUNDERSTANDINGS.

THE Page's first impulse was to fly from the spot, but he was a smart and clever, as well as an audacious youth, and after a moment's reflection, he saw the propriety of keeping his ground.

"Mr. Pultney," he said, "you are a man of honour and a gentleman. You will not betray me, because you are quite incapable of betraying any one!"

Mr. Pultney did not look at him. His eyes were fixed upon Catherine, who for the moment blushed and looked distressed.

She respected Mr. Pultney, if she did not love him.

"And so, sir," added the Page. "I will take my leave of you, convinced that no evil report to the prejudice of any one, will come from the lips of the truly honourable Mr. Pultney!"

The Page knew perfectly well, that should the little escapade reach the ears of the Princess of Wales, his instant dismissal would be the consequence.

But still Mr. Pultney paid no attention to him.

Silence, he considered, gave consent, and as he saw that Catherine looked distressed, he thought his best plan was to leave the library.

"Who knows," he said to himself, "who knows, but Mr. Pultney, though he is so grave, and looks so desperately wise, may want a kiss himself. I only wish I could catch him at it, that's all."

Mr. Pultney then was alone with Catherine. She smiled.

It was one of her old smiles, such as she had so often looked up in his face with, when he was teaching her, it might almost be said all she knew, for she was indebted to him for her education.

The smile was like a gleam of sunshine to his heart.

"Dear, doa Musa," he said.

"Ah, you have called me Musa once more!" she cried. "That was the pet name you used to call me when I was quite a little girl."

"Yes. It was, indeed, and now, good heaven. Now, what are you?"

"Your Musa still."

"No, no. A thousand times, no."

"Yes, ten thousand times, yes!"

"It's impossible, Catherine. What shall I call you, Chudleigh—Harvey. What?"

Catherine made a grimace.

"Anything but the last."

"And yet—and yet you stood at the altar with that man."

"I did. But—but——"

"But what!"

"That is all."

"All? all? What do you mean by that is all?"

"I hardly know. I am young, ignorant, perhaps foolish, but what I mean to say is, that if I am the wife of that man, it is only by name, that is all."

Mr. Pultney sighed deeply.

"What is the meaning of all this, dear Musa? What am I to think of it. You married that man yesterday, and to-day I find you here, using strange expressions."

"It means—it means——"

"Well, Musa!"

"You must say dear Musa."

"Then, dear Musa, what does it mean?"

"That I hate him."

"Your husband?"

"No, no. The man named, Captain Harvey, who shall never be husband of mine."

"Good heavens!"

"Yes, I hope so, and I hope, too, that you will be good to me."

"As how! What can I do? What can I say? Oh, Musa, what can I think? Why have you done what you have done? and, then, why do you stop short and act as you are acting?"

"I don't know."

"Alas! alas!"

"I don't know what to do next, I mean. Mr. Pultney, you know that my father is dead. You know that I was dependant upon my situation in the household of the Princess of Wales, which you procured me, and upon my aunt Hanmer, who pretended to love me as if I were a child of her own."

"She has often said so."

"Yes. But it was not true!"

Mr. Pultney shook his head.

"Why do you doubt."

"Because, I cannot help fancying that all the world must love you!"

Catherine laughed.

"Ah, Mr. Pultney, you judge of all the world by yourself."

She laid one of her little hands upon his breast, as she spoke.

He changed colour.

"Oh, Musa, Musa, my dear Musa. Tell me what I can do to aid you, and if my life is necessary to the service, I will cheerfully lay it down for you my—my—my——"

"What!"

"Darling."

Catherine clapped her hands.

"That is right, I am your darling. I always was. I knew it, but you wouldn't say it. You had to keep it a secret, and you thought you did, but I knew it. Well, then, that's settled. I want a divorce."

"A what!"

"A divorce from Captain Harvey. I hate—hate—hate him."

"You must hate him, indeed, to speak of him in such a way!"

"I do; and I have found out my aunt Hanmer—she has betrayed me. Stop—what is a—a *post obit?*"

"A deed by which a sum of money or an estate may be secured to some one by its expectant heir on the death of its present possessor —say a father!"

"That's it—Captain Harvey has given my aunt a *post obit*, for her services in getting me to marry him—and I hate him, and I hate her—and I will never cross her threshold again, and I am no longer in the service of the Princess, and so what am I to do?"

"Do? do?"

"Yes—am I to beg?—am I cry water-cresses? Here's your sweet, fresh gathered cresses, from the brook! Come gentles all, and madames fair, oh look, oh, only look!"

Mr. Pultney took out his pocket-book. He extracted from it several bank notes, and handing them to Catherine, said:

"Take these, Catherine—take these. I will consider what can be done!"

"About the divorce?"

"Yes, yes. But if there was no informality in the marriage——"

"Stop!—what would make any informality?" asked Kate, eagerly.

"Did you sign the register?"

"Yes—that is—no!"

Catherine had signed it.

"Then, my dear Musa, let him bring his suit against you, and the defence you can set up is informality. The suit may pend for years, and some stroke of fortune may free you from his persecutions, if he can, in the face of the world, stoop so low."

"So low! Am I so little?"

"Dear Musa, you misunderstand me, I mean if he can stoop so low as to persecute anyone to live with him, who hates him as you do."

"As I do with all my heart, Mr. Pultney. Where shall I go? Where shall I live?"

"There!"

Mr. Pultney wrote on a leaf of his pocketbook, which he had with him, the words, "Mabledon House, Bloomsbury Fields."

"Where is that?"

"Close to old Montague House. It is one of my houses. Go and take possession of it. There is an authority."

Mr. Pultney wrote under the address the following words:—

"MR. WORTHINGTON,—

"The bearer of this, Miss Catherine Chudleigh, is to be received and considered as the mistress of Mabledon House."

"G. PULTNEY."

"Oh, Mr. Pultney, how can I sufficiently thank you!"

"By embracing——"

Mr. Pultney did not see the door open very slowly, and the Page peep in at it.

"Embracing!" cried Catherine, with an arch look, as she extended her arms.

"My—my offer!" added Mr. Pultney, as he turned perfectly white, and his heart seemed to stop beating.

Catherine rested on his breast.

"Oh heaven—save me!"

It was not Catherine who cried out "Heaven save me!"

It was Mr. Pultney.

He pressed one kiss on her fair cheek, and then tore himself from her. Oh, how he loved her!

What a hero was he!

What a battle he fought and won—a battle with himself, in which victory was despair—defeat, death!

But he won it.

And he went his way in despair.

"I do think," said Catherine Chudleigh, "that he loves me best of all. Well, I shall do now! Mistress of Mabledon House—a fine old mansion, all red bricks, and stone facings, and no end of terraces, and pretty vases, and statues, and Italian garden walks. I will defy Captain Harvey. Let me see—these notes—Oh!—a thousand pounds in all. I will set up my coach. I will let the wretch go to law with me, if he like. I—I——"

Accidentally Catherine felt the packet of letters that she had taken from the Coromandel wood cabinet in her aunt's house, and which were the intercepted letters of the Duke of Hamilton.

"And I might have been a Duchess," she said; "a Duchess! I have lost that chance; and all for what? to be the wife of a man whom I hate, and who will persecute me as long as I live. Oh, it is horrible!"

She paced the room with agitated steps.

"What shall I do? What can I do? Shall I see Hamilton? I ought—I will—Yes, I—oh!"

As Catherine turned in her walk up and down the room, she met, face to face, a lady in a dark silk robe, and a travelling hat.

Catherine knew her instantly.

"Mrs. Pultney!" she exclaimed.

"Yes, Miss Chudleigh."

"Ah!"

Mrs. Pultney had never spoken to her in such tones before; she was evidently agitated with profound emotion.

"Yes, Miss Chudleigh. I hope you will be happy in Mabledon House, but never more —never more presume to look as if you knew, or had ever known Constance Pultney."

Mrs. Pultney turned, and left the room.

Catherine was so struck with astonishment, that she was gone before she could say a word.

Then she cried out after her.

"Stop! stop! What have I done? Stop! stop!"

Mrs. Pultney was gone.

"Well!" said Catherine, "I suppose she is jealous. I can't help it. I did not ask Mr. Pultney for Mabledon House. I wonder what will happen next? But it don't matter. I don't want to be plagued with women. I have wit enough and beauty enough."

She looked aslant at herself in a mirror, and smiled.

"Yes; I have beauty enough to attract to Mabledon House any men of rank and fashion in London, and I will do so, too. I will be the leader of the gay world—the Achilles of fashion; and if Harvey should seek to annoy me, there shall be a hundred swords ready to leap from their scabbards to defend me."

Catherine walked slowly towards the room that Bella called her own.

She fully expected to find her there, and she was not disappointed.

With her ears tingling from the smart discipline of the Princess of Wales, Bella Steinburgh was eagerly expecting Catherine.

She flung herself upon her neck.

"Oh! dear, dear Catherine!"

"Get away."

"But I do feel for you, indeed, and in truth, I do!"

"I don't want you."

"You are cruel to one who loves you."

"Of course."

"Should that be of course?"

"To be sure it should. Who is one to be cruel to but those who love you? Other people don't care anything about it."

"How clever you are."

"Oh, stuff!"

"You put things in such a clear light."

"No—do stop! Bella, you have said all that a hundred times before, and I don't want to hear it. I am going to set up a grand establishment of my own at Mabledon House, close to Bloomsbury Fields, and what you are to do is this——"

"Come with you?"

"No."

"No! I will if you please."

"No! I think you can be more useful to me here in the service of the Princess of Wales; but you must manage to come to me often, and let me know all the affairs of the Court, and everything that is going on. You comprehend?"

"Oh, yes!"

"Well, then, if you do that, I shall think more of you than ever, and shall be always glad to see you."

"And what are you going to name yourself, dear Catherine?"

"Name myself?"

"Yes; Harvey or Chudleigh?"

"Oh, gracious!"

"Don't be angry!"

"Angry! It is enough to make any one angry! Do you suppose for a moment that I could think of calling myself by the name of that wretch? No, I am Miss Chudleigh still!"

"Yes, dear."

CHAPTER XIX.

CATHERINE CHUDLEIGH AT HOME.—THE HEAD GARDENER. — PERDITA. — THE LETTER.—THE NEW COSTUME.

CATHERINE took possession of Mabledon House that evening, quite heedless of the effect which the transaction had evidently had upon poor Mrs. Pultney, who, in times past, had treated her with so much kindness.

She had made a resolution which was bold, and might alter her destiny.

She wished to visit the Duke of Hamilton at his lodgings, in what was then called The King's Warren.

These consisted of a low dingy range of buildings, close to the river, which were, in fact, the last remains of the ancient extensive Palace of Whitehall.

On the restoration of Charles the Second, so many needy cavaliers and landless noblemen, who had suffered confiscations and spoliations in the civil wars, crowded the court for compensation and reclamation of lost properties, that they were allowed to take possession of old Whitehall, which became called in consequence, by the wits of the court, The King's Warren.

It was there, that the Duke of Hamilton, by nature of some office that he held at Court, had what were called lodgings.

Catherine felt that if she could only procure the alliance, so to speak, of the Duke of Hamilton in the affairs which she wished to set going, more than one half of the difficulties she would have to encounter would be overcome.

She had no scruple whatever in the use she made of any body for her own purposes. The damage, immediate or prospective, to them never entered into her imagination to consider.

And yet, what it was precisely she meant to ask the Duke of Hamilton to do, she was not fully prepared to say.

Vaguely and uncertainly she thought that the man who loved her, or who had loved her so fondly and devotedly as he had, would be sure to think of some mode of extricating her from her troublesome position.

But previously to visiting him, Catherine was resolved to adopt some means of escaping from any sudden attack on the part of Captain Harvey.

From her opinion of him, she had every reason to believe that he would not scruple to endeavour to accomplish by force, what he had failed to do by persuasion.

Acting upon the right or the supposed right that she was his wife, he might attempt to take Mabledon House, which the love-stricken Mr. Pultney had given her possession of, by storm.

To defeat such an attempt, Catherine Chudleigh called to her aid a young woman who had been maid to the ladies of the bedchamber at Marlborough House.

This young woman had been dismissed from her service, for matters, the least that is said about, being the best.

But she was clever, and to a certain extent, accomplished.

She was very unscrupulous, too, which, perhaps, was her principal characteristic, if not her principal qualification.

Her name at the Palace was not in high favour, so Catherine called her Perdita.

With this person, then, she made a thorough examination of Mabledon House.

The servants of Mr. Pultney, with two exceptions, had received their new mistress graciously enough.

These two exceptions were an ancient butler, and an equally ancient housekeeper.

They were both shocked at the idea of being commanded by a young girl of seventeen years old, who, as the butler said, was quite an infant.

And who, as the housekeeper said, "was no better than she should be, if half so good."

So they packed up, and left.

Catherine was delighted to get rid of them.

She told them that she had not the least doubt in the world but that they had been robbing Mr. Pultney for the last fifty years, and hinted at a search of the cart-load of luggage they took away from Mabledon House.

It may be supposed, therefore, that these two old pampered domestics separated in the midst of a squall.

"Now, Perdita," said Catherine, "you will be my own maid, as well as housekeeper."

"Yes, my lady."

"Stop! I don't exactly know whether I will be called my lady or not."

"Oh, madam, you ought to be a duchess!"

"I know I ought; and, what is more, I intend to be one!"

"Of course, madam—oh, of course! And I feel sure that nobody would become a coronet——"

"Stop!"

"Yes, my lady."

"Upon consideration, you may call me my lady."

"Yes, my lady."

"But there is one thing that you have no occasion to do, because Bella Steinburgh will be here, perhaps, and she does it to perfection."

Perdita looked surprised.

"What can that be, my lady?"

"Flatter me!"

"Oh, I am incapable!"

"Of course."

"And, besides, it cannot be done; for it would be quite impossible to say of you, my lady, anything that you don't deserve."

Catherine smiled.

"That will do. Now come with me, and bring with you that bunch of keys which the housekeeper threw on the table so disdainfully."

"Yes, madam."

Catherine then commenced the examination of the house.

Those of our readers who have any recollection of old Montague House, which for so long did duty in Great Russell Street as the British Museum, will have a good notion of what Mabledon House was.

Red brick and blue tile, and stone corners and facings, and huge bay windows, and wildernesses of rooms, made up the structure.

Catherine was delighted with her new home.

But most of all she was pleased with the rooms, that opened the one into the other on the first floor.

One of those rooms was most beautifully panelled and carved, and the ceiling was painted by Favio, in one of those allegorical subjects—all sprawling gods and goddesses.

But the effect was grand.

The room opened into a smaller one, with an exquisite chimney-piece in Carrara marble, and beyond that was a smaller compartment, that commanded a pretty view of the garden of the old house.

"This will do!" said Catherine. This first room shall be my bower chamber. In this second one I shall often sleep; and the third shall be a private boudoir, from which I can, when I please, descend into the garden. You will now, Perdita, call that man with a blue apron, who is trimming those trees and bushes."

"Yes, my lady."

The man was called, and turned out to be the head gardener. He informed Catherine Chudleigh that he had two assistants, and that among them they contrived to keep the garden in good order.

Catherine thought that, considering its limited size, it might have been done without the two assistants at all.

But she made no such remark to the head gardener, since, after all, it was no matter to her what sort of establishment Mr. Pultney chose to keep at Mabledon House.

But she gave him her orders.

"You will transplant from other parts of the garden, or get them elsewhere, some trees and bushes that will completely screen this window."

"Screen that window?"

The gardener shook his head. People of that kind always shake their heads, and look doubtful, when asked to do anything unusual.

"Very well," added Catherine, "you leave at the end of the week."

"Leave—leave?"

"Certainly."

"Oh, miss, I—a—can easily screen the window, and anything else you please."

"Then, you stay. See that it is done at once."

By the evening, some tall trees and shrubs grew up, as if by magic, outside the window.

Catherine, in the meantime, had made some other acquaintances.

The dress she had worn as a sailor boy, when she started on the expedition from Marlborough House which had involved her in so much trouble, she handed to Perdita.

"You will take this suit of clothes, Perdita, and you will go to some tailor, who can set his men to work at once, and have six suits made, all to the same measure as regards size and length, but as different as possible in respect to look and fashion."

"Yes, my lady."

"One dress shall be a quiet every-day walking-dress."

Perdita nodded.

"Another shall be the dress of any of the Court pages."

Perdita nodded again.

"Another shall be the dress of a drummer-boy of the Foot Guards."

"Yes, my lady."

"Another shall be that of a poor lad, who

may be supposed to sing ballads in the streets; and as for the others, I shall leave it to your ingenuity to get them."

"Oh, my lady, let one be the charming dress of the Light Horse! You would look so beautiful as a—a what do they call it?—a young Cornet in the King's Light Horse!"

"You are right! I should get that made by all means. And now, be quick, Perdita, for I am on the commencement of a course that may tax all your ingenuity and all your courage to keep up with."

"Never fear me, my lady."

"One moment before you go."

"Yes, my lady."

"It is now two o'clock—I must have the young gentleman's walking-dress by eight, at the outside, which gives them six hours in which to make it. You can call at a perruquier's, too, and bring me some fashionable wigs to choose from."

Perdita started at once.

Catherine then wrote the following letter to the Duke of Hamilton.—

"To his Grace of Hamilton,—

"One who has had an opportunity of watching the progress of an honest attachment, and seen how it blossomed—was blighted, withered, and died—is anxious to give the Duke of Hamilton some particulars of the perfidious treachery to which he has been subject, and will call on him at his lodgings, at the King's Warren, at nine o'clock to-night, as punctually as anything human, and to some extent dependent upon the actions of others, can ever hope to be."

The letter she despatched at once to the King's Warren, and then she waited with some degree of impatience for the clothes, which Perdita brought back word would certainly be at Mabledon House by eight o'clock.

Bella arrived at about seven.

The news she brought was, that her, Catherine's, marriage was the talk of the whole Court, and that the general impression was that Captain Harvey had been compelled to obey the orders that had been given him by Admiral Gascoigne.

"That is well, Bella! If it be so, I am free of him for a time, at all events!"

"Oh, yes, and her Royal Highness feels very much for you, and will not withdraw her favour from you on any account!"

"Good! All is well—all is well! Who will say that out of all this seeming evil I may not extract a great deal of good? and, already, I am the mistress of a great, grand house, with a retinue of servants! Surely, I have made a step in life!"

Eight o'clock struck.

Almost before the sound had died away, Perdita announced that the suit of clothes had arrived.

Bella began to get alarmed, for she saw that some expedition was on foot that, from her experience of Catherine's adventures, she could guess might be one of hazard.

"Oh, dear, dear Catherine, be careful, and do not risk too much! You are so young, so fair, so—so——"

"Stupid, I suppose you mean to say! Out with it!"

"Oh, no, no! You are as clever as you are beautiful, and that must be very clever indeed!"

Catherine laughed.

"Dismiss your fears, Bella! I am not going on an expedition of any danger, and you should recollect, now, that I am no longer a Maid of Honour, and therefore have no mistress to account to for my actions!"

Catherine was equipped in the course of twenty minutes.

She looked like a charming youth. Her hair she brushed under one of the new peruques which were then all the rage, and which went by the name of cherokees, so that none of it was visible.

She wore at her side a dress sword with a silver hilt, and when she cast about her a cloak of very dark purple cloth with a hood to it, such as were worn then by the young courtiers when on duty at any of the out-door fetes of the Court, and she looked, in the language of the period, "A very pretty picture," although somewhat *petite.*

Catherine, now, had but one doubt or regret about her personal appearance.

She was unquestionably little.

But that could not be helped. She put up with it as well as she could, and certainly, if, as old Matthew Fuller says, "When Nature builds a tall house, she does not put anything very valuable in the attic story," the converse of the proposition in Catherine Chudleigh's case was true, for she possessed within that compact small head of hers as much ability as would have furnished forth a company of Amazons.

"Good night, Bella!"

"Let me go with you!"

"Bah! pho! I don't want to be bothered with women!"

"But, Catherine——"

"Mr. Sydney, if you please!"

"Oh, dear!"

"Well, what now?"

"You always frighten me!"

"Do I? I am glad to hear it! It is the duty of a young fellow, such as I am, to frighten the girls! Oh, if I were only a man!"

"What, then, dear Catherine?"

"Never mind. I would lead a nice life, I daresay. Good night! Come to me to-morrow, Bella, and bring me all the news of the Court."

"I will—I will!"

Catherine had previously sent for a coach, with orders that it should be waiting for a gentleman at the corner of Holborn nearest to Montague House.

But she had not quite completed her arrangements.

Instead of passing out of the room in which she had dressed through the bed-chamber, and so on by the panelled apartment with the gods and the goddesses on the ceiling, she approached the window that looked into the garden.

That was the window outside which the gardener was told to put the screen of vegetation.

Catherine opened the window-seat, which had a lock and key to it, the latter of which she had

CATHERINE CHUDLEIGH PERSONATES A GHOST.

hidden in a little secure place behind the shutters, and took from the interior of the window-seat a very curiously constructed rope.

It was a tolerably thick cord, knotted all over with silk and worsted, that in thick masses were twined about it in such a manner that it was as thick as one's arm, and afforded a capital hold both for hands and feet.

To the surprise of both Bella and Perdita they found that while Catherine had been alone she had not lost time.

Outside the window, and hidden among the thick herbage of a cherry tree, that grew up in great luxuriance against the wall of the house, she had fastened a strong hook between two of the bricks.

There was another hook at the end of the rope so that it could be attached easily.

Catherine dexterously, then, slid out of the

window, and while standing on the sill she closed it.

Another moment, and she slid down the rope, and disappeared.

The rope itself was pretty well hidden then and lost to sight, as it fell perpendicularly down the wall among the blossoms and leaves of the cherry tree.

A slight shake from below sufficed to hide it still deeper, and as the silk and the worsted by which it was surrounded were of the colours of brown and green, it would have required quite a critical eye to detect its presence.

Catherine was off.

She sped along one of the garden paths, and, taking a little key from her pocket, she opened a small door in the brick wall, and quietly emerged into the thoroughfare in front of Montague House.

No. 7.—KATE CHUDLEIGH.

CHAPTER XX.

A NIGHT ADVENTURE.—AN UNEXPECTED EN-
COUNTER.—A COWARDLY ATTEMPT.—THE COLD
BATH.—RIGHTEOUS RETRIBUTION.—IRRESOLU-
TION.—THE SHRIEK.

CATHERINE saw the coach which she had ordered
to be in waiting for her.

"So far, so good!" she said. "If I can but
restore myself to the heart of Hamilton, all may
yet be well."

She walked deliberately towards the coach, and
called out to the driver:

"Now, my man, you are waiting for me?"

"Yes, sir — if your name be Master Sydney."

"All's right. Whitehall Stairs."

"Yes, sir."

Catherine leaped into the coach, and it started
in the wheezing, lumbering, but far from un-
comfortable, fashion of those ancient vehicles.

She had made up her mind to approach the
King's Warren by water.

The vast extent of the old Palace of Whitehall
—the demolition of which is surely one of the
regrets of society—made it approachable in a
variety of ways.

That part of it, which then remained, and was
called the King's Warren, from the reasons we
have stated, was close upon the river.

The Thames at that period was, if one may be
allowed the expression, much more of a private
public way than it is at present.

"Of course, there can be no comparison
between the numbers of persons carried now by
the river steamers, and those that in the reign of
George the Second made use of the silent highway;
but at that time people were in the habit of hiring
wherries at the rate of a hundred to one com-
pared to the present demand for them.

. The whole surface of the Thames, between
Old London Bridge and Westminster, would be
at times the most animated scene possible, with
the crowds of small boats that thronged it.

The state of the Strand was not such as to
make it a tempting thoroughfare.

After dark, footpads, Mohocks, and the whole
tribe of depredators of the Court and the City
were to be found at every corner.

The Thames, therefore, up to quite a late hour,
was decidedly the safest, and the choicest, and the
shortest route from one place to another.

The various stairs were then as well known as
the cab stands of London are now, and the
drivers of the few Hackney coaches and the
chairmen of the sedans, never needed to be told
twice where to go to, if a river landing place,
however obscure it might be, were named.

Now-a-days, the oldest inhabitant of London
knows not of the existence of one half of them.

Whitehall Stairs was then quite a noticeable
landing and embarking place. The miserable,
dull, prison-like groups of building that make up
Whitehall yard, and its adjuncts, have destroyed
that spot of the river, which might be one of the
first in London, from the bend which the Thames
takes about that point.

But to our story.

It was quite dark when Catherine Chudleigh

alighted from the Hackney coach, close to Whitehall Stairs.

She had to look carefully as she descended the
worn and slippery steps towards the river, to see
one of them from the other.

A crowd of wherries were grinding and
bumping against each other in the rising tide.

"First oars!" cried Catherine.

"Ay—ay—sir!"

She jumped into a wherry.

"As close as you can go in to the King's
Warren."

"Ay—sir—that will be the Seven Steps."

Those seven steps made up a well known
landing place; so called after the seven bishops
who were said to have come that way on their
memorable interview with James II.

It was said that the river tide, which used to
come up high over all those steps before that
event, ever since stopped at the seventh step, and
left all above it high and dry.

The rising tide was running at speed among
some craft that lay moored a little way out into
the stream.

A compact fleet of small boats was so close
to the shore, that the waterman who had charge
of Catherine Chudleigh and her fortune was compelled to row some distance out into the river, to
"weather" them.

This brought the wherry fairly into the current of the stream; and it had just been turned
inwards, to go in a diagonal fashion to the
Seven Steps, when a long boat, manned by no less
than eight men, pulling vigorously, came down
the river at a rapid rate.

"Wherry a-hoi!"

"Where are you coming to, you lubbers?"
shouted Catherine's waterman.

"Run the fool down!" sung out an angry voice
from the long boat.

Catherine knew that voice on the instant.

No one but Captain Harvey could lay claim to
it.

She could not forbear an exclamation, and she
half rose in the boat.

The long boat came with a rush, and its pointed
prow ran over the low gunwale of the wherry.

There was a rocking motion for a few moments, and then the wherry filled, and surged
over.

It surged over, bottom upwards.

Catherine Chudleigh uttered a shriek.

The waterman swore.

"Pull on! pull on! Confound the fools! it's
their own fault!" shouted Harvey.

Catherine was active and young; had she been
encumbered with the clothes of her sex, it is
doubtful if she could have saved herself. As it
was, however, she contrived, just as the wherry
gave way under her, to jump from it into the long
boat.

She alighted on Captain Harvey.

"Curse you, sir! What do you mean? Do
you think I am without feeling?"

"Perfectly," replied Catherine, in a feigned
voice.

"Go to the——"

"After you, sir, if you please! What do you
mean by rowing along the Thames like a river
pirate, which I believe you are, and swamping
everything smaller than yourself?"

Captain Harvey uttered several very energetic expletives, such as were common enough at that period, and for many a long year afterwards, on the quarter-deck of the vessels of the Royal Navy.

"Pitch him over! I don't want passengers. Pitch him over!"

"Indeed!" said Catherine. "It may suit a runaway officer under arrest to commit murder on the river; but I doubt if any of you, my men, feel inclined to be hanged because Captain Harvey is in a bad temper!"

"Ah! you know me!"

"Know you! Of course, I do!"

"Who the ——— are you, then?"

"A gentleman!"

"I will know what gentleman, or some good reason why."

"Certainly. The good reason why is, that I am here alone, and unarmed, except with this little toasting-fork of a rapier; and you are a bigger man than I by one-half, and have eight stout seamen with you. Brave, gallant Captain Harvey, why the whole nine of you may actually get the better of young Squire Merton, of the old Grange, at Petworth. Oh, dear, what an exploit, to be sure!"

The sailors laughed.

"Silence!" roared Captain Harvey.

"Come, sir, if I land you, you must promise one thing."

"What?"

"Not to say you met me to-night."

"Oh, one don't wilfully, you know, acknowledge one's little disgraces!"

"Little disgraces? What on earth, sir, do you mean?"

"We are on water now, so I am not obliged to mean anything particular on earth; but what I did mean was plain enough. Accident has brought me into bad company, and it is not likely I shall speak of it."

"Insolence!"

"Yes."

"Very well. Let no man take the responsibility upon him but myself."

Captain Harvey made a dart forward to fling Catherine into the river; but she had kept her eyes keenly upon him, and at the moment he did so she clung to two of the seamen on that side of the boat; and Harvey, missing his aim at her, fell over into the river.

Catherine flung herself, then, overboard, on the other side of the boat.

She could swim like a fish.

"Captain Harvey," she cried, "if I see your wife, I will tell her you are taking a cold bath!"

"He's down!" shouted one of the sailors.

"He has the cramp!" cried another. "I know that cry. Jack Adams went down in just such a way."

Captain Harvey had uttered a strange sort of yell.

Catherine paused a moment, and only trod the water to keep herself afloat in one spot.

Was it possible that the man who, only a few moments before, she would have said might probably be the bane of her existence, was drowning?

Was fate, indeed, about to be so kind as to take from her her only encumbrance?

On that, the first night when she was beginning to take some steps to fight what might be a long battle with the man who called her his, was she to see him dimly, by the pale night light, fade away into death?

There was a good deal of confusion on board the long-boat.

"Hoi! hoi! Here you are, sir! Back oars! —back stroke-oar, there!"

Catherine looked over the waving surface of the water.

No one was visible.

She began to feel cold.

"By ———, he is gone!" she heard a voice say.

Then she began to swim to the Seven Stairs.

A feeling of thankfulness was at her heart.

Was she free? And if so, what should she do? What should she call herself? His widow? Oh, no, no! She would forget him—at once and for ever, forget him!

She reached a wherry close to the Seven Stairs.

She scrambled into it, and then to another, and so reached the steps themselves; and dripping like a water spaniel, she made her way to *terra firma*.

Then Catherine asked herself if she should, or should not, carry out her intention of visiting the Duke of Hamilton; and while she was thinking of it, she heard a series of screams from the river. Drawing back into the deep shadow of some of the old buildings about the King's Warren, Catherine determined to discover what had happened before she took any steps one way or the other.

CHAPTER XXI.

A TRUE FRIEND.—THE DEAD NAVAL OFFICER.—RECOGNITION. LOVE AND DESPAIR. THE SPECTRE. — FLESH AND BLOOD.—PARDON. JOYFUL REUNION.

A BOAT shot up from the river to the landing-place.

A female staggered out of it; and by the dim light Catherine Chudleigh could see that she was wringing her hands in an agony of grief and despair.

"Oh, heaven! She is drowned—she is lost! Oh, have mercy upon me—have mercy upon us all! She is killed—drowned—drowned!"

To the intense surprise of Catherine, she recognised the tones of Bella Steinburgh in these frantic accents.

The truth flashed upon her in a moment.

Bella really loved her, and with some presentiment that evil was about to befall her, had that time followed her on to the river.

"Lost—lost—drowned! Oh, poor, poor Catherine! So beautiful—so good———"

"Hem!" thought Catherine; "I am a living contradiction of the proverb, that 'listeners hear no good of themselves,' for it is quite the contrary."

A flash of light came from a window not far off.

A man's voice spoke from the window.

"What is all this? What has happened? What is it all?"

"Ah!" said Catherine to herself, as she drew still further into the shade. "So I am nearer to Hamilton's lodgings than I thought, for that is he."

"What is it? Speak, somebody! What has happened?"

Yes; there could be no doubt whatever about the voice.

Catherine felt certain that it was the Duke of Hamilton who was requesting information from the window of his lodgings in the King's Warren.

"She is drowned; she is lost; she is no more!"

That was Bella.

"Who—who is no more? Speak again! Surely, I ought to know that voice?"

"Yes; and I yours, your Grace."

"Ah! you know me?"

"I do; and I in you recognise surely one who——But I will not name myself aloud here in the open air, with so many ears listening to me; and if your own heart does not name the one for whom I shall ever grieve, you never loved her."

"Good heaven!"

"Ah! now I know that your heart and your fears do name her."

"They do—they do! Oh, my poor—poor Catherine!"

"Yes; it is of her I speak; it is for her I grieve."

"A moment—only a moment! You convulse me with grief—only a moment! Good heaven! Can I live to hear such tidings? Wait only a moment, I will come down!"

The Duke of Hamilton then disappeared from the window.

Bella Steinburgh remained below, wringing her hands, and sobbing bitterly.

"It seems," said Catherine Chudleigh to herself, "that, at all events, when I do go out of the world, some one will grieve for me."

She kept still in the shadow of a buttress of the old wall, and she saw by a light that flashed from an open door, that the Duke of Hamilton had come down himself to admit Bella Steinburgh, the Maid of Honour.

"Come in—oh, come in!" he said; "and tell me what has happened!"

"Ought I?"

"Oh, yes—yes."

"But I am alone."

"Never mind. I, too, am alone."

"That is worse!"

"Good heavens! what is worse, Miss Steinburgh; can you stand here, parleying with me on grounds of propriety, when my heart is wrecked with anxiety to know what you have to tell me of one who, whatever her conduct may have been, I loved sincerely, and cannot help loving still."

"Good!" said Catherine, in a low tone, that could reach no ears but her own.

"That is true—that is true!" said Bella; "and you are a nobleman and a gentleman."

"Of course I am."

"A man of honour!"

"Who will doubt it?"

"I follow you, then; and I will tell you all I know."

Bella Steinburgh went into the lodgings of the Duke of Hamilton, and, in his agitation, he forgot to shut the door after him.

Or, Bella it was, perhaps, who left it open.

The opportunity was a golden one, for Catherine Chudleigh, and she did not hesitate for an instant to take advantage of it.

With her characteristic boldness and decision, she slipped in at the doorway.

There was a small, square hall just within, lit by one lamp, that stood on a gilt bracket.

A chair of formidable size, almost as large as a couch, was in the hall, and behind it Catherine easily found a temporary refuge.

It was well for her, supposing that she meant concealment, that she found so snug a hiding-place on the impulse of the moment, for the Duke of Hamilton, who, by some means, was alone in his lodgings on that night, came down stairs again rapidly.

"When will that knave, Mitchell, come home?" he said; and, as he spoke, he closed the door and shot a bolt into its socket.

"I come, I come!" he cried, as he rapidly flew up the stairs three at a time—"I come, Miss Steinburgh; but, for your sake, I wished to close the door."

Catherine emerged from her hiding-place behind the chair.

"So far, so good," she said. "Who knows, but this will be a lucky accident after all, providing that my wet clothes do not give me a death cold. Well, I'll take my chance of that! I am young and strong."

She ascended the stairs lightly.

At the top of them, she saw an open door, and the apartment within it was dimly lighted.

Neither the Duke nor Bella were in that room, but Catherine made sure they were in the apartment beyond it, for she heard the sound of their voices.

She tripped lightly onwards.

She had nothing in reality to fear.

Even if she were discovered, all would be well with her, and she would only see the man she had come to visit.

But she wanted to hear what he should say to Bella; and, with all the natural curiosity of her disposition, she anxiously concealed herself, and was careful that her footsteps should make no sound.

Bella was weeping.

The Duke of Hamilton was uttering exclamations of despair.

"Yes," said Bella. "Her sole hope was in you and in your love. I don't know to this moment what could have induced her to marry that odious Captain Harvey."

"Nor I, nor I! Caprice, caprice, Miss Steinburgh! Excuse me; but your sex, you know, is rather noted for—for—what shall I call it?—that kind of infirmity of purpose in affairs of the heart that gets the better of all your reason!"

"Alas, alas!"

"Yes; I, too, say, alas!"

"She did not love him."

"Ah, me!"

"And now she is no more. I guessed, or rather I should say that I knew, she purposed a visit to you, and my heart misgave me that she would fall into some danger, so I followed her."

"Can it be possible that you, a weak, timid girl, felt so much for her?"

"I did, I did! She would have been angry with me if she had known that I followed her, so I was compelled to do so secretly. I took a boat after her, and I saw the wherry she was in ran down by a larger one, and she is drowned!"

"Oh, Catherine!"

"Oh, Catherine!"

"My love!"

"My friend!"

Bella and the Duke of Hamilton mingled their tears.

"House, house! Hilloa, there! Help, help!" said a voice from the outside.

The Duke of Hamilton ran to the window.

"Who calls—who calls?"

"Help, sir, whoever you are! Here is a gentleman who has swam on shore!"

"Ah!"

"Oh, it is not Catherine!" cried Bella; "and yet if it were?"

"A tall gentleman!"

The hearts of the Duke of Hamilton and the Maid of Honour both sunk from hope to despair.

"It is not Catherine."

"Alas, no!"

"A tall gentleman in the uniform of an officer of the Navy," added the voice, "and he is dead now. He drew his last breath as soon as he got to the Seven Steps."

Catherine clasped her hands.

Who could this man—this tall man, in the uniform of the Navy—be, but Captain Harvey?

Was he dead? Had he indeed drawn his last breath as he reached the top of the Seven Steps?

What a question!

How full of interest for her.

"I will come down, directly," said the Duke. "Whatever may be one's own private griefs, the instincts of common humanity must be obeyed."

Catherine had just time to hide behind the door, when the Duke ran past her.

She heard a confusion of sounds below, and in the midst of them all, the Duke cried out, "No. This man is my enemy, and if anything fatal should happen to him in my lodgings, a venomous world would make the worst conjectures. I cannot say if he be dead or not, but Doctor Ponsonby has lodgings at the next door. Take him there."

"Aye, aye, sir! but if so be the gentleman is known to your worship, I would only say we are poor men, sir——"

"You want me to pay you for your care of that man—well, take this guinea. It shall not be said that I hesitated in such a case."

The Duke of Hamilton then came back again, passing Catherine as before.

"Miss Steinberg," he said, "event upon event, and each more strange than the other, crowd upon me; and that man who has been brought in there half or wholly drowned, is Captain Harvey himself."

"No! no!"

"It is so, indeed."

"The wretch—the monster—the murderer!"

"Murderer?"

"Yes. Do you not see that it was his boat which ran down the little wherry, in which our Catherine was coming to see you?"

"Ah!"

The Duke of Hamilton uttered a terrible cry.

"Don't you see that although some accident has happened to him, at the same moment he wanted to drown her, and has done so, for the poor dear has not come on shore?"

The Duke uttered another cry.

That cry was echoed by a scream, and the curiosity of Catherine being strongly excited, she crept forward a few yards, so that she could command a view of the next room.

The Duke of Hamilton, with an awful expression upon his face, had a sheathed sword in his hands, and Bella, on her knees, was holding him by one arm, to stop him from sallying forth upon the terrible purpose that had found a home in his heart.

"No, no. Spare him! Oh, do not kill him, if he still lives. You cannot restore her by a thousand deaths!"

"Oh heaven! hear me!" cried the Duke. "I love her as never man loved woman! I would travel to the earth's confines! I would endure heat, frost, thunder, storm, tempest, and despair, but to look upon her face again!"

"And I!—Oh, I!"

"Alive or dead!"

An idea flashed into the mind of Catherine.

She pushed the door slowly open; she composed her countenance to a terrible calmness; and moving forward with a strange gliding motion, while her damp clothing presented a strange appearance, and she looked much paler than usual, from fatigue, and want of rest and warmth, she entered the room.

Bella screamed.

The Duke turned of a death-like paleness, and stood with the sheathed sword in his hand, quite transfixed by the seeming vision.

The movement of Catherine Chudleigh was entirely successful. There could be no doubt but that both the Duke of Hamilton, who ought to have soared above such a superstition, and the more credulous and weaker-minded Bella, both believed that they looked upon the apparition of Catherine.

The drowned Catherine.

The Duke felt and exhibited all that creeping sensation of horror which the presence of anything surpernatural is said to produce.

Probably his feelings of absolute horror upon the occasion were more acute than Bella's.

Neither of them could speak.

Absolute horror froze their faculties, and it was reserved for the ghost to say something, unless the silence was to remain unbroken.

At last, Catherine began to think so.

Slowly she traversed the room, passing them both.

Their eyes followed her.

She went right round a table, and then, with a slow and majestic movement, she took from the breast of her water-soaked apparel the packet of letters which the Duke had sent her from Vienna, and placed them on the table.

She then passed on towards the door again.

Bella fell flat upon her face to the floor, in a swoon.

The Duke spoke.

It was only by a great effort that he could so far recover his faculties as to command the power of speech.

"Vision of my Catherine—shade of my lost loved one, speak to me—oh, speak to me, if it be but one word, to give me a hope that in the world to come we may meet again !"

"Again !" said Catherine, solemnly.

She passed on.

But the Duke of Hamilton was rendered desperate. He made a plunge forward.

"With you—with you, my Catherine, in life or in death—with you, ever !"

He caught her by the arm.

"Ah! flesh and blood !"

"No."

"Yes, say I."

"Unhand me—I—I——"

"Oh, Catherine! is this worthy of you ?"

"No."

The Duke sighed deeply, and tears started to his eyes.

"No," said Catherine again ; "but the man who truly loves, forgives—forgets all but that he is loved again."

As she spoke, she rested her face upon his breast, and looked up in his face.

Could mortal man resist that mute appeal.

The Duke was human.

With a cry of joy, he folded his arms about her, and pressed her to his heart.

CHAPTER XXII.

CATHERINE CHUDLEIGH RECEIVES A PLEASING EXPLANATION FROM THE DUKE OF HAMILTON. —A DARING ENTERPRISE.—THE CHAPEL ROYAL.

"CATHERINE, Catherine—my Catherine ! Dearest —best—ever beloved——"

"That will do !"

She disengaged herself from his clinging embrace.

"Dear, dear love !"

"There—that's enough ! You forget that I am——"

"What—oh, what can you ever be but the idol of this fond heart !"

"The wife of another."

"Never !"

"And a ghost !"

"Oh, Catherine, do not trifle with me now ! Why did you come to me, if it were only to make a plaything—the toy of an idle hour — of the poor heart that beats only for you."

Catherine was touched a little.

"What would you have me do ? What can I do ?"

"Fly !"

She laughed.

"No, no ! Free me from the chains that are about me, and I am yours."

"Chains ?"

"Yes ; Captain Harvey claims me."

"He is dead."

"I doubt it. The river has given him up. He will live—live yet to be the bane and the terror of my life."

She shuddered as she spoke.

The Duke of Hamilton had felt that her sleeve was saturated with water, and he saw that her whole apparel was in the same condition.

"You will die of cold, my Catherine !" he said. "I have other clothes here. Change those wet clothes at once."

"Oh, thank you !"

"I will help you !"

"You are too kind. I am afraid you would prove but a clumsy lady's maid. Besides, I am half dry now, and don't mind it a bit."

"But !——"

"Be quiet. Listen to me."

"With all my senses. I hear you, and see you, and I am happy."

"I married Harvey——"

"Alas ! yes."

"I went with him to my aunt's house. I supped with him !"

"Oh, spare me ?"

"I retired to—to a chamber; but—but—as I went, some impulse prompted me to examine a cabinet in my Aunt Hanmer's room, and there I found that packet which contains all your intercepted letters to me."

"While I was in Vienna ?"

"Yes."

"I wrote once each weekly post !"

"I never received a single letter !"

"What treachery !"

"It was. My aunt sold me to Captain Harvey, and I found too late that I hated him !"

"Too late ! Too late !" groaned the Duke.

"I secured the letters, and I went then to the bed-chamber, that had been set apart for me and —and——"

"No, no ! Do not name him ?"

"My husband !"

"Catherine, Catherine, why will you thus torture me ?"

"Ah, does it torture you to be told that I loathed him—that I only stayed in that chamber long enough to strip some of the clothing from the bed, and make of it a means of escape to the garden ?"

"You did ?"

"I did !"

"On your life—on your soul—you fled from him ?—when he reached that chamber he would miss you."

"I was gone !"

"My Catherine !"

"Get away, do !"

"Oh, joy !"

Catherine Chudleigh began to whistle, and sat composedly down.

"Dear, dear, heroic girl !"

"Come, come. When you are rational I will speak again !"

"I am ! I am !"

"Very well. I must resist Harvey. I must by some means prove myself not his wife legally. How can that be done ? What will he first do when he seeks to prove that I belong to him ?"

"The register of the Chapel Royal will afford a proof."

"That was what Mr. Pultney said."

"Mr. Pultney ! Have you consulted him upon the subject ?"

"I have. He is a true friend, and a most honourable gentleman!"

"Who shall doubt it?"

"Ah, Hamilton, Hamilton. I told him that I had not signed any church register, and if you really love me, you would find some means of making my words come true."

"Some means?"

"Yes. A register is a book."

"A—book?"

"To be sure, and a book has leaves; on one of which it is worded that you, Catherine, are the wife of Captain Harvey. Do you see——?"

"I—think—I—do!"

"Well?"

"If—if it could be done."

"What?"

"The—the register of the Chapel Royal. If it could be reached!"

"What an idea, Hamilton. You want me, then, to tear out the leaf of the register, so that when Harvey wants it to prove me his wife, he will only find a blank!"

"That was your idea!"

"No—yours!"

"Mine?"

"To be sure, and a good one it is. I will help you. Do you think that now—to night, you could find your way into the Chapel Royal by any route?"

"Hush!"

"What do you fear?"

"Nothing, nothing; but—but Catherine—if I were to do this act——"

"Well?"

"If, then, I should be discovered, I should have no power to keep you, and the first name in the rolls of my country's nobles would be sullied past all purification. Oh, what shall I do when honour and love contend for mastery in this poor heart and brain?"

"I don't want you to do it!"

"I thought you—you did."

"No. What I want you to do is to suggest some mode by which I may get into the Chapel Royal. What business I have there let remain my secret."

The Duke looked flushed and alarmed.

"This part of old Whitehall," he said; "which is called the 'King's Warren,' is beneath the same extensive irregular roof as the Chapel Royal."

"I know it is."

"A great heap of old ruined chambers lie between here and the chapel, but——"

"They may be traversed."

"They may."

"And the Chapel reached. That is what you mean, Hamilton, and you will not help me, I will go alone."

"Dare you?"

A scornful look came over the face of Catherine Chudleigh, and she made no direct reply.

"Well, I will help you, dear one, so far; but tell me, if you can preserve a clear conscience in this matter, so that if I am so blessed as to be able to call you mine in the face of all the world, I may be able to do so without a blush."

"As you please. What is the harm?"

"Hark?"

"What clock is that?"

"The Horse Guard's. It strikes the hour of eleven! Are you still intent upon this expedition?"

"I am!"

"And so am I!" suddenly cried Bella Steinburgh, as she looked up. "And so am I. Where you go, Catherine, I go!"

"You shall, Bella, and while my Lord Hamilton's conscience is so nice and fine, we two girls will carry out this little adventure between us."

"No, by heaven!" cried the Duke. "I am with you for weal or for woe!"

"I thought so. Now I do begin to think that you really love me!"

"Did you doubt it?"

"N—o!"

"Oh, Catherine!"

"Come, come! We have, perhaps, some hours work before us, so let us commence it. How do we begin?"

"By following me."

The Duke of Hamilton looked pale and determined, as he took from the table the wax light in the silver candlestick that stood upon it.

Catherine kissed the hand of Bella, for she could not but be sensible of the real and true affection which had prompted one so naturally timid and uncertain in her actions to make such efforts and resolutions in her behalf.

Such a recognition of Catherine's approbation of her conduct, slight though it was, quite sufficed to satisfy Bella Steinburgh.

She felt strengthened, and armed to encounter anything.

"Listen to me, both of you!" said the Duke of Hamilton, as he stood by the door of the room, with the candle in his hand.

"Yes, yes, Hamilton, we do, we will!" cried Catherine Chudleigh; "and your reward shall be this!"

She placed her hand in his disengaged one.

"For such a reward," he said, "I would dare anything!"

Catherine laughed.

There was a world of fascination in her laugh, and she knew it.

"I was about to say," added the Duke, "that your coming here this night is the most fortunate thing that could have happened!"

"Indeed?"

"Yes; for to-morrow night the enterprise in which we are about to engage, would be impossible!"

"How so?"

"A great portion of old Whitehall has been condemned to demolition, and to-morrow that part of it which lies between here and the Chapel Royal will be handed over to the contractors and architects, in order that they may set to work."

"But to night," said Catherine.

"To night is our own!" added the Duke.

Catherine saw that he went to a drawer, from which he took out a pair of exquisitely wrought and inlaid pistols.

These he carefully looked to as regarded their priming, and then placed them in a breast pocket, so that they might be ready for action at any moment.

He then loosened his sword in its scabbard, and turning to Catherine, with a look of great sweetness, he said, "Since I accompany you on this expedition, it must not fail."

"That is right."

"Follow then, and love assist us."

The Duke went out on the landing place at the top of the staircase, and listened.

A profound stillness was in and about the King's Warren at that moment, but the stillness did not last long.

Shouts and cries, and vociferous plaudits suddenly arose from some other rooms in the Warren, accompanied by a jingling of glasses and rapping upon the tables.

All these sounds were distinct enough, although somewhat muffled and subdued by distance.

"What does that mean?" asked Catherine.

"I can hardly tell you. A gentleman who calls himself Sir Stafford Guy resides in the Warren, and although at ordinary times he is as grave and sedate as a judge, yet, at times, he gives these riotous parties."

"Heed him not. They do not lodge in our route, do they?"

"Oh, no!"

"Come on then, Hamilton. I am not only anxious, but curious; so lead the way, I beg of you!"

"Follow, then!"

The Duke of Hamilton led them up a long flight of stairs, which were a continuation of those from the hall.

———

CHAPTER XXIII.

THE CHASM IN THE FLOOR.—THE STORY OF THE PHANTOM CHESS-PLAYER.—THE CHAPEL ROYAL IS GAINED.—THE STRANGE LIGHTS.—THE JACOBITE PASSWORD.

CATHERINE followed her admirer and conductor with a great deal of curiosity up the old staircase; which, from the ominous manner in which it creaked beneath their weight, seemed completely to justify the determination which the Duke had said had been come to in regard to the demolition of some part of Whitehall.

At the top of these stairs there ran a corridor of considerable length, but of very low pitch as regarded its roof.

Various rooms appeared to open from this corridor, and as they were at the topmost story of the house, Catherine was in a state of wonder as regarded their onward progress.

The Duke of Hamilton produced a key from his pocket, and opened one of the rooms.

"Come in! come in! there is nothing to fear."

They all three stood on the floor of rather an extensive kind of loft or attic.

The roof was so low, that even Catherine could touch it by elevating her hand.

The attic seemed to have been converted into a kind of lumber-room for old furniture and decorations of Whitehall.

What particularly attracted the attention of Catherine were a number of half-decayed and broken picture frames, each of which had a gilt crown on the top moulding.

Great quantities, too, of these gilt crowns, more or less mutilated, and made of wood, carved very finely, were in the attic.

"I see," said the Duke, "that you wonder how all these insignia of royalty came here."

"I do, indeed!"

"The only explanation I can offer is, that when Cromwell, after the death of Charles the First, took possession of Whitehall, these picture frames, which enclosed some of those beautiful paintings of which the King was so fond, were cast aside just because of the crown."

"And these other gilt crowns?"

"Look at them again, and you will see that they have belonged to the backs of chairs, which, no doubt, were in the state rooms of the Palace."

"Ah! yes. I see now."

"Oh, Catherine, Catherine!" cried Bella, "can you venture here?"

The Duke of Hamilton had opened a cupboard in one corner of the attic, and on the floor of the cupboard he had raised a trap-door.

The chasm beneath looked black and profound.

"Do not fear it," said the Duke; "it only goes to a depth of about ten or twelve feet to the floor below. You can drop it with ease."

He placed the light on the edge of the trap as he spoke, and dropped lightly and easily through it.

"Come, Catherine, dear, and fear nothing."

Catherine let herself down, and was received in the arms of the Duke, who could not forbear giving her what might be called a loving embrace.

Under the circumstances, Catherine appeared not to notice this little infraction of the kind of agreement that had been entered into between them.

It was a more difficult matter to get Bella down the narrow trap, as she was in feminine costume, but it was accomplished; and then, as the Duke held up the light, they saw that they were in a very different kind of apartment from that they had just left.

That portion of the extensive range of buildings known under the general name of Whitehall was but one story in height.

The principal rooms, therefore, were upon the floor in which the duke and his brave companions were.

When we say one story in height, in regard to Whitehall, we do not include as a story the nests of little rooms in the roof, which could hardly be considered to constitute another story to the building.

The apartment, then, in which Catherine Chudleigh found herself, was one that awakened a great deal of interest and curiosity in her imagination.

It was anciently and cumbrously furnished, and although that furniture was in a state of decay, yet there were quite sufficient traces of past grandeur and magnificence about it to stamp it as the adornments of a palace.

The Duke spoke in a low voice as he said: "This is the first of a suite of rooms which it is said the spoliator, Oliver Cromwell, had closed up on the evening of the execution of Charles the First."

"For what reason?"

"The story is a very strange one."

THE VERGER PRODUCES THE REGISTER.

"Then you will tell it to me at another time."

"Nay, a minute will suffice, and I think it better that we should not seek the Chapel Royal until that roystering crew that Sir Stafford Guy has in his rooms to-night depart."

"Will they depart?"

"Yes, at half-past eleven precisely; I have heard them often."

"Then, why did Cromwell shut up these rooms?"

Catherine Chudleigh, in her careless, graceful way, vaulted to the side of a table as she spoke, and sat on it.

"Ah!" she added, "turn over some chessmen, and it looks as if a game had been disturbed."

"That is the story."

"What is the story—a disturbed game at chess?"

No. 8.—KATE CHUDLEIGH.

"Just so."

"Let me hear it, then."

"And I, too," said Bella, "am all curiosity, although I think I heard the Baron Gros, the minister from Prussia, once say something about it."

"Well, it is this, Cromwell was fond of chess; but finding out that those about him let him win purposely, no doubt on account of their finding out that it put him out of temper to lose, he adopted the odd custom of playing with and by himself."

"Odd, indeed!"

"He used to come here to play; these are the chessmen he used; and while the King lay in durance, first, at Hurst Castle, and then in London, the Lord Protector would pass away some weary hours with these odd games at Chess."

"Ah, yes!" said Bella. "I recollect all about it now."

"But I want to hear it," said Catherine.

"Well, then," added the Duke, "it is said, that being sorely troubled in mind after the execution of Charles the First, he, Cromwell got up in the night, and came into this room with a solitary night-light in his hand, to play with himself a game at chess."

"Well, well!"

"He set the pieces and made one move, and then his hair bristled on his head, and his heart stood still; for a phantom hand was stretched over the board, and a move was made on the other side."

"Well, I like that!"

"It makes my blood crawl and creep in my veins," said Bella.

"Go on—go on, Hamilton! What happened next?"

"On the fore-finger of the phantom hand, there was a ring, in which was an onyx stone, which Cromwell knew well had been worn by the King at his execution, and he then knew that the ghost or shadow of Charles the First was sitting opposite to him, and playing with him the game at chess."

"Horrible!" cried Bella.

"Interesting!" said Catherine.

"Cromwell was a bold man, and made another move.

"The spirit of the King did the same.

"Then a deep, hollow voice cried out 'checkmate!'

"The King won.

"I don't know, but Cromwell rushed from the room with his hair on end, and terror in every feature of his face. The next morning he had this suite of rooms closed up, and I hardly think, except from curiosity, they have ever been looked at since."

The chimes of some clock announced the half-hour past eleven.

In a few more seconds, a single horseman was heard clattering past upon the old stone pavement of Whitehall.

"That is Sir Stafford Guy," said the Duke of Hamilton. "Who or what he is, I cannot divine; but I suspect he is not what he seems."

"Well, Hamilton," said Catherine, "shall we now proceed?"

"Yes; this is the way."

The Duke of Hamilton led them through the suite of rooms in which the ghostly game of chess had been played, to a long corridor, which was called the King's Walk; and from that they entered, perhaps, the most ruinous portion of old Whitehall.

A suite of no less than eleven rooms, the one opening into the other, was passed through.

Decay and dilapidation seemed almost to have done their worst in those apartments.

The hangings, once so gay and so gorgeous, hung in damp, dismal-looking shreds from the walls.

The rich carpeting was frayed and worn; and as all the valuable articles of furniture had been long since removed, and some of the grand, noble chimney-pieces had been taken away, the rooms had a very peculiar aspect.

The last of them opened into a square hall.

The Duke then paused, and spoke to Catherine.

"It will be necessary," he said, "to make our way into the Choral Loft, as it is called, near the roof of the Chapel."

"Anywhere, so that we reach it."

"Follow, then."

Up an ancient staircase, through four rooms, and then through a small door in one of the panelled walls, the Duke took them.

They found themselves in what had evidently been a private oratory; and the Duke whispered, as though mortal ears could hear him.

This is said to be the oratory to which James the Second used to retire, after being forced to sit out the Protestant service in the Chapel Royal, to pray to the Virgin Mary to forgive him his sins.

"Then we are close to the Chapel?"

"We are."

The Duke approached a portion of the wall of the little oratory, and drew aside a massive thick cloth curtain.

A rush of cool air sprang inward, and in two steps they found themselves in the old Choral Loft of the Chapel Royal.

The whole area of the Chapel was below them.

It looked like some vast and deep cavern.

The darkness was of that deep, profound character that it affected the eyes with that delusive appearance that makes it seem to move about in dense rolling masses.

"We can descend," whispered Catherine.

She did not know why she spoke only in a whisper.

It was the genius of the place that influenced her. There are spots on which it appears a kind of sacrilege to raise the voice.

Who ever thinks of speaking aloud in the long, quiet, sacred nave of some old, grey cathedral?

"Yes," replied the Duke, "our course is quite easy before us."

"Hush!"

"What is it?"

"I thought I heard something."

"Indeed!"

"And so did I!" said Bella.

"Surely not."

"Hush!" added Catherine. "There again! there again!"

A slight sound had come up from out of the profound darkness in which all the lower part of the chapel was shrouded.

What the sound was it was difficult to determine.

But the Duke had heard it this second time, although he had failed to do so at first.

They all three stood as still as statues.

They hardly breathed.

All was still.

The darkness before them still seemed to move about in those massive convolutions, which would almost persuade unreasoning people that darkness was a substantive something of itself, and not a mere name expressive of a negative condition of the air from the absence of light.

Then, however, Catherine suddenly laid her hand upon the arm of the Duke.

It was well that she did so, or he would have fetched the light which he had left in the oratory.

Far down, through the darkness, she saw a small star-like light.

"Look!" she said. "Look! what is that!"

"What? what? Ah, I see, a star?"

"No. A light!"

They all then watched the phenomenon with the most intense curiosity.

It did not seem to have power of illumination sufficient to send any halo or atmosphere of light about it, and yet Catherine, whose senses were fine and acute, thought that there was a darker substance than the air accompanying the little star-like light below.

She whispered to Bella.

"What do you see?"

"The—the—light——"

"Why you shake with fright!"

"I do."

"Pho! pho! Don't be a coward!"

"Oh, Catherine, it is all the same you know."

"What is all the same?"

"I mean, that as everybody, you know, cannot be so handsome as you are, so everbody cannot be so brave."

"Oh, nonsense, what stuff you talk, Bella."

"Hush," said the Duke.

Another little star-like light made its appearance.

Then the two stars approached each other.

From the lowest depths of the Chapel Royal, there came up to the ears of the three persons in the Choral Gallery the faint whisper of a voice.

"Roses and Lilies!"

"Ah," said Catherine. "I have heard words similar, if not exactly like that once before."

CHAPTER XXIV.

THE STAR-LIKE LIGHTS IN THE CHAPEL ROYAL.—THE COURAGE AND HEROISM OF CATHERINE CHUDLEIGH.—THE JACOBITE SPY AGAIN APPEARS ON THE SCENE OF ACTION.

CATHERINE remembered that it was a watchword, and very similar, in fact, to that which she had heard on the occasion of being taken by the Jacobite spy to the mysterious mansion in the neighbourhood of the Green Park.

The idea of the supernatural, which had began to take possession of her quickly now faded away.

She whispered to the Duke.

"Do you know what that means?"

"No, Catherine!"

"It is a Jacobite pass-word."

"Indeed!"

"Yes, I have heard it before, or something very like it."

"How? where?"

"That I will tell you another time."

"Oh, look—look!" whispered Bella.

A third star, a fourth, a fifth, and a sixth made their appearance.

The stars then all grouped together on the floor of the chapel, and by their united light, small as even that was, there could be seen the dim outlines of several men.

Indeed, there could be little doubt but that as many little star-like lights as were there, there were men to carry them.

But what did they mean?

What could be the business of six men meeting so near to the midnight hour, in such darkness, and with such secresy, in the Chapel Royal?

The Duke of Hamilton was very greatly interested.

"Catherine," he whispered, "I pray you to remain here, while I descend and listen to what is going on."

"No—no."

"Nay, do not oppose my going—it may be that I shall hear——"

"Hush! oh, hush!"

Catherine had heard a voice.

Could she mistake it?

It was the rich, low voice, in its soft, musical accents, of the Jacobite spy; with whom she seemed to be so well acquainted.

"No—no, Hamilton, let me go down and listen."

"There may be danger!"

"Not the least. You may trust to my report."

Catherine did not wait to argue the point with the Duke; but feeling her way in the dark, to which her eyes were now getting somewhat accustomed, she found a narrow staircase, and commenced a slow descent into the body of the Chapel Royal.

As she descended lower, she could hear the sound of voices more distinctly.

"This, then, being resolved upon, my lords," said a voice, "the death of the Prince is certain, and the consequent confusion in the nation will be the mist from which shall be evolved the light of a bright and a happy restoration."

Catherine could not doubt for a moment but that this voice was that of the Jacobite spy.

She crept a little closer.

The Jacobite was speaking again.

Either the musical cadences of his voice made them more easy to catch, or she was accustomed to the same, and, therefore, heard what he said; while what was replied to him, was but a confused jargon of sounds, of which she could make nothing.

But he spoke again.

"I know one about the person of the Princess, from whom I shall get what information may be useful."

"What one?"

"A mere girl, but of marvellous beauty; and of great intelligence."

"You mean Catherine Chudleigh," said another voice, "for she is the only one who answers to your description."

"I do mean Catherine Chudleigh. Already is she committed to our course, since she would find it impossible to free herself from the charge, once made, of having concealed me in her bedchamber when the whole of Leicester House was in a commotion to discover me after I had shot the physician."

"A good shot!" said a voice.

"Yes—I never miss. He dead, the King must go soon, for his was the only skill in Europe that could keep him in life."

This was entirely a new idea to Catherine.

It was, then, the unfortunate physician who was intended to be killed, and not the King after all.

"When will you see her?" asked a voice.

"To-morrow!" replied the Jacobite spy.

Then, one by one, the little star-like lights were put out, and all was pitchy darkness in the Chapel.

Catherine had some difficulty in finding her way back to the Choral Loft.

When she got there she had nothing particular to tell, for the idea that the most malignant and unscrupulous of the Jacobite clubs had for their object the assassination of the Prince of Wales, was too common an one to be considered as any news.

But Catherine had another difficulty to contend with, she asked herself how far it would be safe for her to be the informant of what she had heard.

Unable to decide this question in a satisfactory manner, she resolved to say nothing.

In reply to the anxious and eager inquiries of the Duke, she said that she could not get near enough to hear a word.

The star-like lights were all gone now, and the Duke of Hamilton spoke in a decided tone, as he said, "We must not retreat without accomplishing our objects, and we must set about them more boldly."

"Boldness for me!" said Catherine.

The Duke fetched the light.

If there had been any person in the Chapel below, the light in the Choral Loft must have been evident enough, but no notice seemed to be taken of it.

"Come," said the Duke, "let us descend. We shall find the register of the chapel no doubt in the Sacristy."

They all then descended the narrow staircase that conducted them right down to the body of the Chapel, and when there the Duke held the light as high as he could, to cast as much illumination as possible about them.

Not the least appearance of any one being there could be seen.

"Was it fancy?" said the Duke.

Catherine felt certain that it was not fancy, but she did not say as much. It was reserved for Bella, however, to utter an exclamation of surprise, and to cry out, "There is some one yonder!"

The Duke drew his sword.

Catherine stepped first back a pace or two, and then forward.

With short wheezing coughs, an old man, in a gown that betokened the position of verger of the Chapel, came forward with a tottering gait.

"Gracious heavens, gentles, what want you in the Chapel Royal at such an hour; or are you depredators, who will take an old man's life, and then lay unholy hands upon the sacred vessels of the house of God?"

The surprise of the Duke was great, but he took, on the instant, a velvet mask from his pocket, and put it on.

Catherine crept in his shadow.

Bella felt inclined to faint, but she managed to control the impulse.

The Duke had taken the wax candle from its silver stick, and was holding it in his left hand. He now, with a dab, stuck it to the top of one of the ornaments around the royal pew, and called out aloud—

"Come forward! Come forward! This is a matter of life or death!"

The old verger hobbled forward.

"Life or death?" he said. "Ah, me, I have lived my span!"

"Who and what are you?"

"I am Simeon Booth, the verger."

"Why are you here in the Chapel at this hour of the night?"

The old man's hand shook, partly as it appeared, with palsy, and partly voluntarily, as he said, "And why? eugh! eugh! Oh, my cough! Why are you here? sure it is not your duty, and it may be mine."

The Duke raised his sword.

"No, no!" cried Catherine. "There is a more powerful weapon than the sword."

"Indeed?"

"Yes. Old man, do you love gold?"

The old verger extended one of his hands, and opened and shut it several times, graspingly.

The action was significant; but there was one thing that much surprised Catherine Chudleigh, and that was, to see a diamond of great beauty and lustre glittering in a ring on the old verger's finger.

The circumstance ought to have excited more suspicion than it did, and probably, if the circumstances had not been those of great and immediate excitement, Catherine would have made some enquiries that might, or might not, have been replied to satisfactorily by the old verger.

As it was, however, she made no remark on the subject.

"Do I love gold?" said the old man. "Oh, when does age not love gold?"

The Duke of Hamilton shook his head. He saw what Catherine meant to try to do; but he had grave doubts of the wisdom of employing or trusting the old verger of the Chapel Royal in any such important matter.

The man who would sell such a service for gold, he considered would not hesitate to betray the secret for more gold still.

But Catherine was resolved upon essaying an escape from the difficulty by bribing the verger.

She eagerly whispered to the Duke of Hamilton:

"Pay him well, and we shall do in one half the time, and twice as well, what we want to do here."

"I yield to your wish, but it is against my better judgment."

"Nay, there is little risk. A very short time, indeed, and in the natural course of nature, he will not have the power to betray us."

"Be it so, then, dear, dear Catherine. I am the slave of your wishes."

The Duke approached the verger.

He spoke in a feigned voice.

"Do you know me?"

"No, sir; but if you will have the goodness to say who you are, I will not forget."

There was an air of simplicity about this speech, which went further to allay the suspicions of the Duke of the good faith of the verger, than anything else could have done.

"My name is Colonel Smith, and I will trust you."

"You may, sir."

"Will these fifty guineas induce you to let us look at the Register of the chapel for five minutes—alone?"

The old man made an eager grasp at the money.

"Yes, oh, yes — five — yes, ten minutes, twenty-five minutes, if you please. I have the keys!"

"It is done," said the Duke to Catherine.

"And well done."

She put her arm under that of the Duke, and they followed the old verger to what was still called the Sacristy of the Chapel Royal.

The old man now produced a bunch of keys, and after some fumbling and trying, first one and then the other, he opened the large, carved, oaken chest, which contained the Register.

"It is strange, my friend," said the Duke, "that you did not know which was the proper key?"

"I am seventy-one, sir."

The reply was so simple, that the Duke said no more on the subject.

The old man lifted the book from the oaken chest, and handed it to the Duke.

"Go," said the latter. "Wait in the chapel until I call to you."

"I obey your commands, worshipful sir, I obey your commands. Fifty golden guineas. Oh, Simeon, Simeon, you are a rich man, Simeon!"

The verger left the Sacristy.

Catherine Chudleigh eagerly opened the book. It seemed to yawn open naturally at the place where the last entries were made; and there she saw her name, and that of the man she had married, and now hated.

"It is here—it is here!"

The Duke of Hamilton looked with an agitated air and manner at the entry.

"If," he said—"if the existence of the register be the bar to my happiness, or one of the bars to it, then let it perish!"

"No—no!"

"Ah, Catherine, do you then, at the last moment, repent? Can you wish to preserve the fatal evidence that you belong to another?"

"No. But——"

"Nay, let me!"

The Duke would again have roughly torn out the page from the book, but Catherine Chudleigh prevented him.

"No, Hamilton, no!"

"Hush! Do not pronounce my name in the atmosphere of this place!"

"I will not; but lend me your sword."

"Take it, dear one. If you wish to find a sheath for it in my faithful heart, you may do so!"

"Not so—not so! This is the use I want to make of it."

Catherine with the sword-blade carefully cut out the leaf of the Chapel register which contained her signature and that of Captain Harvey.

"We will tear it now at once," said the Duke.

"Oh, do, do!" said Bella.

"No; not so," said Catherine, as she carefully folded it up, and placed it in the bosom of her dress—"not so! I will keep it; but I will take care that it never sees the light of day."

A deep, hollow groan came upon their ears, as Catherine spoke.

They all started like guilty people as they were,

With one accord they cried out, "What is that?"

The Duke turned paler than before.

CHAPTER XXV.

THE INTERRUPTION.—THE DEAD CLERK. — THE STOLEN REGISTER.—AN ENCOUNTER WITH THE MOHOCKS.

NEITHER Catherine Chudleigh nor the Maid of Honour, Bella Steinburgh, nor the Duke of Hamilton spoke for several seconds then; and the silence became so painful, that it was about to be broken by Catherine herself, when the deep, hollow groan was repeated.

This time it seemed to localize itself to one particular part of the old Sacristy.

The sound seemed to come from the deep embrasure of an old bay window.

The Duke of Hamilton did not hesitate a moment.

"Keep the door, Catherine," he said. "I know you have the courage to do so."

"I have."

Catherine Chudleigh, with the Duke's sword in her hand, stood like a sentinel on duty at the door of the Sacristy that led into the Chapel.

She heard the old verger coughing and wheezing in the dark.

"The light, Miss Steinburgh!—hold the light for me!" added the Duke.

Bella, although with a hand that trembled excessively, obeyed him.

Drawing, then, from his pocket one of those small and exquisitely-finished pistols' he had brought from his lodgings in the King's Warren, the Duke of Hamilton stepped into the deep embrasure of the corridor.

He uttered an exclamation.

Lying on his back, and apparently in the last agonies of dissolution, from a wound in the forehead, lay a man.

"Speak! Who are you?"

The wounded man made a movement with his hands, and pointed into the chapel.

"Can you not speak one word to tell us who you are, and who has done this deed?"

The man was dying.

But there was yet the spark of vitality at his heart, and by its aid he made one of those wonderful efforts which the dying will sometimes make, and shrieked out one word.

One word that echoed through the Chapel Royal.

"Treason!"

That was the word.

It was the last that the fearfully wounded man could utter.

With it went the last breath that was his in this world.

The Duke turned hastily round; and as he did so, the door, or some door of the chapel, was slammed to violently.

They were alone in the Sacristy with the dead man.

"Catherine, Catherine!" cried the Duke. "Call the old verger!"

"Hither, hither!" cried Catherine; "into the chapel! More gold, more gold!"

She thought that would be a certain invocation to the old man to appear, but it failed. He came not, nor did she now hear the least sound indicative of his presence.

"He is gone!"

"Who? The verger?"

"Yes. He has left us."

"And this one has gone, too, never to return. Look on this sight, Catherine, if you have never seen death before."

"Ah! that is the Clerk of the Chapel Royal!" said Catherine, when she looked in the face of the dead man.

She recognised him at once as the man who had helped at the marriage, and lent Captain Harvey a ring to place upon her finger.

It was rather singular that up to that moment she had quite forgotten the existence of the ring; but she now tore it from her finger in disgust, and cast it to the floor of the Sacristy.

"There is some terrible mystery in all this," said the Duke of Hamilton, "which I cannot fathom; but since we have accomplished the end that brought us here, I recommend that we retire from this place as soon as possible."

"With all my heart!" responded Catherine.

"As for me," said Bella; "I shall die of frightful dreams, for I shall never get that man's dead face out of my imagination and memory."

"Come on, then, quickly. We will leave by the way we came."

The Duke led the way, and in much less time than it had taken them to reach the Chapel Royal, through the dreary, deserted apartments of Whitehall, they once more reached the lodging of the Duke of Hamilton in the King's Warren.

It was two o'clock in the morning, then.

The Duke cast his arms around Catherine.

"Stay with me—oh, stay with me, my affianced wife—my Duchess that shall be!"

Catherine Chudleigh disengaged herself from his embrace, as she said, "The way never to be the Duchess of Hamilton, is to stay here another minute! Come, Bella, come!"

"But—but——"

"But what?"

"The hour is so late, you cannot go home."

"Can I not? You forget I am no longer of the household of the Princess of Wales, but my own mistress. Good night!"

"Now you are offended with me, and I am lost."

"No; forget a foolish speech, and take your sword, and see me in safety to Mabledon House."

"You will let me visit you to-morrow?"

"Assuredly."

"Every day?"

"Yes; every day. I will not be a mock mistress of Mabledon House while it remains in my hands, therefore, I will see who I please, and as often as I please."

"And I, dear Catherine, will wait but for your divorce from Harvey, which I fancy can surely be obtained, to make you my own."

The Duke would have had a carriage out at that late hour even, but Catherine declared she would rather walk; and as the streets of Lon-don were anything but safe, even, after dark, to say nothing of two o'clock in the morning, the Duke promised a guinea to a couple of stout watermen, who were to follow with their boat stretchers, and show fight in case of need.

The distance to Mabledon House, from Whitehall, although not very considerable, was through a part of London not very famous at that time for keeping the peace.

At the corner of the Strand, a party of half tipsy gentlemen, singing wild Bacchanalian songs, and with their drawn swords in their hands, rapidly approached.

It seemed impossible to avoid these boisterous men who were "making night hideous" with their noise and clamour.

"The Mohocks are out, sir," said one of the watermen.

"Hide yourselves!" said the Duke to Catherine and Bella. "They are too many to cope with, I fear."

It was more easy to counsel hiding than to find a place in which to carry out the suggestion.

They were close to the dead wall of Northumberland House, and at the moment Catherine and Bella paused, and looked about for some place of shelter, they were seen by the Mohocks.

These wild, lawless bands of young, and sometimes older, men, who should have known better, had revived, and the streets of London after nightfall were becoming again, as they had been some twenty years before, dangerous to traverse at night.

The mildest proceeding of the Mohocks consisted in kissing all the kissable — that is, the young and good looking—females they met, and making the men take what they called the "sword leap."

This was, to hold a sword in a horizontal position about five feet or more from the ground, according to the real or presumed agility of the party, and forcing him to leap over it.

If any hesitation were exhibited, divers prickings from sword-points in the rear generally sufficed to urge the victim, at all events, to attempt the leap.

It was not every one, though, who was blessed with so complying a humour.

Sometimes the Mohocks caught a Tartar.

Then a desperate fight would ensue, which might end in the slaying or desperately wounding of one or two Mohocks, and almost always in the resisting person being overcome by numbers, and left for dead, with a couple or more sword thrusts through his body.

Such were the sort of gentry that came down the Strand on this occasion.

They raised the peculiar shout and cry of their lawless association, and, brandishing their swords, came on quickly.

"A petticoat! A petticoat!" cried one "Whoop! Hurrah!"

"A young petticoat!" yelled another. "Luck at Charing Cross! Whoop! Tantivy!"

Then the whole band yelled out something that sounded like the murdering word, "Yahoo! Yahoo! Yahoo!"

With a rush they came to the corner of Northumberland House.

Catherine and Bella had no time to find a hiding-place.

All they could do was to go a short distance down towards Whitehall, again; while the Duke of Hamilton, with his drawn sword, barred the onward progress of the Mohocks for the moment.

The two boatmen stood their ground like men.

But the Mohocks were at least a dozen in number, so that such a contest could scarcely be doubtful as regarded its results.

CHAPTER XXVI.

THE RESCUE.—SIR STAFFORD GUY.—THE DISCOMFITED MOHOCKS.—CATHERINE CHUDLEIGH AT MABLEDON HOUSE.

"Whoop! Whoop! Leap the sword! Are your women young and sweet lipped? Yahoo! Yahoo! Down with him! He shows fight! Draw his teeth! Clip him in the wizen! Yahoo! Whoop! Tally-ho!"

With such shouts and cries the Mohocks pressed upon the Duke of Hamilton.

One tall, shambling-looking fellow, in a maroon velvet coat, and who swore beautifully, made a lunge at the Duke with a rapier of unusual length; but either the Duke of Hamilton was dexterous enough to get out of the way at the lucky moment, or wine and riot had disordered the arm of the bully.

The long rapier ran over the shoulder of the Duke instead of through his neck, where it had been intended to go.

Then the tall Mohock uttered a shrill scream.

The Duke of Hamilton's sword passed through his lungs, and the hilt fairly struck against his chest with a sullen sound.

The two boatmen had run round the Duke so as to occupy, speaking in a military sense, the flanks of the Mohocks; and they had each felled one of them senseless to the ground.

All the work of about three or four seconds.

The Mohocks were staggered. Their bullying ferocious leader was down, and two others of the party.

They paused, and drew back.

But that was only a temporary repulse.

The rattles of the watch began to make a hideous noise, for a party of the so-called guardians of the night, had seen the tumult from the steps of St. Martin's Church.

It took the Mohocks only a moment or two to see, that they had still a great preponderance of numbers.

Nine to three still made long odds.

The Mohocks turned with anxiety to avenge their fallen comrades. With yells and shouts, for they were enraged by what had happened, and anger had taken the place of the wild, frolicsome mood that had possessed them, they rushed on the Duke and the watermen.

The salvation of the Duke of Hamilton, for the moment, actually was due to the number of his foes.

They impeded each other.

The very sword blades jostled each other aside from his breast.

But this was a state of things that could be but very temporary indeed.

The Duke of Hamilton, with his back against the shutters of a shop, fought with desperation, and he felt that he was all but lost.

"Fly, Catherine! fly!" he cried. "Fly! Back! back!"

Then, to his surprise, there was a sudden pause among the Mohocks.

Right and left they fell and fled, and the Duke heard the trampling of a horse's feet upon the pavement, as a voice cried out, "What, all you upon one man! Cowards, have at you! A lot of Frenchmen, I suppose!"

A bright sword-blade flashed in the dim radiance of a lamp, that was by the statue of Charles the First, and the Mohocks fled.

They left three more of their number on the field.

That made six in all.

One the Duke had ran through the body.

Three, in all, the watermen had knocked down, and two the strange horseman had brought to the dust.

"Sir," said the Duke, "you have saved my life?"

"I hope so. What a cowardly crew, to be sure. Did they set upon you for nothing?"

"They are Mohocks."

"Ah, so I thought—so I thought. Well, sir, here lie some of the party, who, I think, will be Mohocks no longer. Is that lady with you, sir?"

"They are; and, if I mistake not, I have the pleasure of knowing your voice?" said the Duke.

"My voice! My voice! Better not! Better not!"

"Nay, sir; your name is Sir Stafford Guy, and I think you are a near neighbour of mine, in the King's Warren?"

The horseman laughed.

"To be sure! To be sure! You are right, sir! To whom have I the honour of speaking? I think His Grace the Duke of Hamilton, is my nearest neighbour?"

"I am he!"

"Then, I am right glad to have been of service to you. May I ask, if you have far to go? It is possible, although not very probable, that the rascals, who have ran away, may rally!"

"As far as Montague House," said Catherine, as she stepped forward; "at least, that is the distance, although it is not exactly Montague House itself, which is our destination."

As Catherine spoke, she looked up towards the horseman.

It so happened, that the light from the lamp at the statue, faint though it was, fell full and fair upon the face of Catherine.

It was impossible to mistake her, notwithstanding the masculine habit she wore, for other than what she was.

A young and lovely girl!

The horseman raised his hat, as he said, "Ah, I don't wonder at the Mohocks."

The Duke hastily stepped forward, as he whispered, "Catherine, Catherine, is this prudent?"

"Never mind me, your Grace," said the horseman, with a careless air. "I am the last man in all the world to spoil—spoil——Never mind me, my lord Duke; I will ride on a few paces; and

I don't think the Mohocks will come to trouble you any more."

The Duke of Hamilton was vexed that Catherine had allowed Sir Stafford Guy to penetrate her disguise so easily, but there was so much gentlemanly ease about him, and so much good humour, that he was compelled to thank him, and accept his offer.

"It would be churlish, indeed, sir," he said, "if I were to reject your kind office after what you have already done for us."

"Oh, don't mention it—don't mention it! I was riding home!"

"You ride late, Sir Stafford."

"Sometimes."

The watch, now finding that the danger was over, ran over the way, and appeared on the scene of conflict.

"I must take you all up!" cried one. "I must take you all to the Round House, as sure as my name is Diggory Shovel."

Diggory Shovel had the impudence to lay hold of Catherine Chudleigh by the arm.

Crack came the loaded end of a riding-whip, that Sir Stafford Guy wore dangling to his wrist by a silk cord.

Down went Diggory Shovel.

"Hands off, if you please!" said Sir Stafford Guy, quietly.

The party of watchmen left their chief, and ran back over the way again, and began to wind their rattles at a furious rate.

"Never mind them, your Grace!" said Sir Stafford Guy. "Let us push on; it's but dull work knocking those fellows on the head. As the Prince of Wales said to me about an hour ago, 'this is neither glory nor profit.'"

"The Prince of Wales, sir!" said the Duke of Hamilton, in surprise. "Did you say the Prince of Wales?"

"Yes, yes! It don't matter!"

Sir Stafford Guy trotted on, and the Duke followed him with Catherine and Bella.

But little conversation took place between the party, as they proceeded rather hastily to Mabledon House.

Indeed, after the careless remark that Sir Stafford Guy had made about the Prince of Wales, he seemed rather to shun any further speech.

He wore a cloak of dark brown cloth, with a collar of some kind of fur; and, as it blew aside at times, the Duke could see that he was very richly dressed.

The mystery which had always shrouded his neighbour of the King's Warren, was by no means decreased by this accidental meeting with him at Charing Cross.

The gates of Mabledon House were reached.

"I am at home," said Catherine.

Sir Stafford Guy bowed, and without any more salutation then to the Duke of Hamilton than consisted of a wave of the hand, he set spurs to his horse, and galloped off.

"A strange fellow!" said the Duke.

"And a brave one!" added Catherine.

"There can be no doubt of that."

"Good-night, then, Hamilton!"

"Good night! dear—dear Catherine, since it must be so. I will call on you to-morrow, since I have your permission to do so."

"Certainly; this house shall be no nunnery while I occupy it."

"And I will take the advice of some of our highest law men on the marriage."

"Oh, do, do! For this man—this Harvey—may yet make some most desperate effort to claim me."

"I will rather meet him at the sword's point."

"Good night—good night!"

Catherine shook hands with the Duke, but he drew her gently towards him, and kissed her cheek, as he whispered, "Oh! how can I ever hope to tell you how much I love you!"

She yielded to the fond, half-embrace for a moment, and they parted.

The Duke went home in a dreamy state of mind, thinking how he could take effectual steps for getting the marriage, which was such a mockery, between Catherine and the Honourable Captain Harvey, declared null and void.

Catherine, with a slow step, and an aspect of fatigue, entered her house.

Her house it was, for so long as Mr. Pultney chose to let her call it so.

"Bella, Bella! you will stay with me to-night?"

"Yes, dear Catherine."

"Ah, me! how tired I am!"

"Shall I sleep with you?"

"Dear me, no! I hate anybody with me. There are some half-score of fine bedrooms in the house, and you can choose which you please."

"Yes, dear."

"Now go away."

"Bless you, Catherine!"

"Bless us! good night!"

Catherine Chudleigh stamped on the floor of the magnificent ante-room to her bed-chamber in Mabledon House.

Bella would kiss her hands, however, and then left her alone for the night.

CHAPTER XXVII.

A LOVER IN SEARCH OF HIS MISTRESS.—THE MYSTERIOUS PORTRAIT.—THE STRANGE APPARITION. — LOVE SURMOUNTS ALL DIFFICULTIES AND FEARS.—THE BLACK CURTAIN.—RECOGNITION.

LEAVING the fair Maid of Honour to such undisturbed slumbers as she might be enabled to enjoy, it is necessary that we should conduct the reader to the somewhat gloomy and mysterious pile of buildings still then existing, which comprised the ancient royal residence of Whitehall.

The associations connected with Whitehall were not pleasant.

Far from pleasant to royalty.

Its chambers had been the hot-beds of intrigue.

More than one assassination had occurred within its walls.

The whole building, too, was encumbered with the recollection of the last moments of Charles the First.

Hence was it that a great portion of the building was deserted.

THE MASKED HORSEMAN SALUTES CATHERINE CHUDLEIGH.

Suites of rooms that had never been used for the last sixty years were completely shut up.

The long straggling suburbs of the building—for such we must call them—that reached down to the banks of the river were in a complete state of decay.

The wind whistled through many a crack and crevice.

The winters' damps made themselves felt on the fairly painted ceilings.

The old arras on the walls hung heavy with moisture, and Whitehall only awaited the fiat which was to doom it to destruction.

Certain proceedings were, however, to take place in this deserted building on that night, which deserve a record.

The hour of midnight has struck, and all is still upon the silent highway; which the river, even at that time, was called in contradistinction

to what was then thought the great bustle of the Strand.

A solitary wherry made its way to the private Stairs of Whitehall.

There was a sort of alcove arched with stone, and a flight of marble steps which led up to the garden gate.

Not even in the broad flush of day would any adventurous waterman land a fare at those steps.

Even the garden of Whitehall was supposed to be haunted.

At the long range of windows that fronted the river mysterious lights were said to have been seen.

And it was further reported that by waiting close to those steps in a wherry, and just rowing gently so as to save the upward or downward current of the tide, mysterious and heart-rending screams and cries might at times, in the still hours of the night, be heard from the old building.

But the occupant of this wherry we have spoken of evidently had no such fears.

With a rapid sweep of his sculls, he brought the wherry up to the moss-covered steps.

He hastily attached it to an iron ring.

Light of foot, then, he sprung up the steps and entered the delapidated garden.

"In good time—in good time," he said, "for I hear not a sound."

The darkness was great, and it was evident that this stranger—be he whom he might—was not well acquainted with the intricacies of the place.

He floundered over neglected flower-beds.

He nearly ran against some of those leaden statues with which our ancestors, at all events, used to fancy they adorned their gardens.

But at length he reached an ancient gravel path which was exactly beneath the windows of that part of Whitehall facing the river.

There he paused.

"I must get in somehow!" he said.

But the task seemed difficult.

The windows were above his reach, and there did not seem to be any means of getting at them.

So he skirted the building, and watched his opportunities.

As he did so, a strange cry came upon his ears.

It evidently proceeded from the interior of the building.

But whether it were masculine or feminine, or human at all, was beyond his power to say.

It seemed to make the blood curdle in his veins, however.

For a moment he clasped his hands over his face.

"Maude — Maude!" he said,—"can it be Maude?"

Then instantly he seemed to convince himself that such could not be the case.

"No— no!" he cried, "for if she is here she is here of her own free will, and those are cries of distress."

The voice in which he uttered these words was youthful.

There was heart-rending agony of tone, likewise, in them, which showed how largely his feelings must be interested in the adventure he was attempting to carry out.

"What is the use of me loving her?" he said. "What was the use of me flying from my father's home and entering into the service of old Welling's, the draper, in the City, so that I might be near his fair and lovely daughter, if it has been but for the purpose of discovering her frailty? But I will find it all out. I cannot bear this suspense. Thrice I have followed her at nearly the midnight hour to Whitehall."

The youth, for such he was, still continued his progress round the building.

"Thrice, he added, "she has eluded me like an apparition, but now I am determined to make my way into the building."

He came to a stone flight of steps.

Slowly and cautiously he ascended them.

They led him to a terrace—the windows conducting to which came right down to its marble flag stones.

"Now," he said; "now I shall surely succeed."

The panes of glass were but small in those windows.

The youth put on his hands a pair of thick buff gloves.

Breaking two of the panes of glass, then he wrenched aside likewise the framework between them.

The orifice was then large enough for him to pass through.

He stood within what were once considered the sacred precincts of the royal residence of Whitehall.

How still the place was!

He trod upon a carpet.

He could feel that by the softness of the touch.

The air was damp and musty.

Groping his way onwards, he touched a wall.

Moving along that wall, and loading his fingers as he did so with masses of damp dust, he at length touched a door.

Was it fast?

No.

It yielded to his touch, and still in absolute darkness, the youth passed on.

But the darkness, great as it had been, was nothing to the intense blackness of the place in which he now was.

A shuddering fear came over him.

He stretched out his arms and paused.

It seemed to him as if another step must plunge him into some deep abyss from whence there would be no escape with life.

But he had the means of procuring light.

It was only as a matter of precaution that he had not already done so.

Now, however, not being able to endure that darkness longer, he lit a match.

By its aid he ignited a small piece of wax taper.

Holding it above his head, so as to shed as many of its feeble rays about the place as possible, he found himself in a wide passage, not above twelve or fifteen feet in length, and which conducted him into a gallery of paintings of great extent.

The ceiling was painted according to the fashion of a by-gone age.

The walls were completely hung with, no doubt, estimable works of art.

It was well known that George the Second, and likewise George the Third, who were both totally ignorant of everything relating to the fine arts, sold a great number of pictures from Whitehall to foreign galleries.

Those were the identical pictures.

Covered with dust.

Covered with damp, and the heavy film of neglect.

And the young man who had thus made his way surreptitiously into the ancient palatial residence, stood in the midst of the gallery, and gazed about him.

Then he held his light towards the floor.

It was covered with dust.

Dust which lay there like a black snow-drift.

Then a half suppressed cry burst from his lips.

Glancing behind him he had seen the marks of his own foot-prints in that dust.

But there were other foot-prints before him where he had not yet trodden.

They were small and light.

Could they be the foot-prints of Maude ?

He replied to the mental question in the affirmative.

He recognised them with a lover's instinct.

He was on her track.

"I shall find her, I shall find her," he cried, "and unravel this dreadful mystery."

Even as he spoke he heard a strange sound.

A rumbling kind of echo through the building, as though something were passing along upon wheels.

Then all was still.

There was a strange fear at his heart, he knew not why.

Accordingly his eyes were directed towards a particular picture.

It was a portrait as large as life.

A full length, with the lower part of the frame resting on the floor.

He knew not what directed his attention to that portrait.

Perhaps it was that the rays of light from the little wax taper he carried happened to fall more fully than elsewhere upon the pale, sad face of the picture.

The young man approached it closer.

The portrait was that of a cavalier attired in black velvet.

The fashion of the garments was not that of those at that time in use, nor were the long peaked beard and moustache at all common then in England.

There was a peculiarity, however, about the neck of the portrait which he stepped closer to examine.

Some one, with a piece of red chalk or red paint, he could not exactly detect which, had drawn a line right across the neck, horizontally.

The portrait had all the appearance of decapitation.

Then the young man knew perfectly well whose portrait it was.

"Charles the First," he said.

He recollected hearing an anecdote once which would account for the peculiar appearance of the portrait.

Some month or so after the execution of Charles the First, the Protector, Oliver Cromwell, was said to have been in that picture gallery with General Ireton, superintending the repainting of the ceiling.

The sight of the portrait of his royal predecessor was not very welcome.

"Remove it!" was the brief command.

"Nay, General," said Ireton, "we will leave it with a correction and a difference."

He then took a brush with red paint from one of the artists who were at work upon the ceiling, and made the streak across the neck.

Then the Lord Protector smiled grimly, and walked on.

But the young man whom we have followed so far into the precincts of Whitehall now suddenly paused and started back.

Back as far as he could go, until stopped by the pictures on the further side of the gallery.

His eyes were distended !

He drew his breath short and thick !

The portrait moved !

The light he had was very dim.

It was scarcely more than sufficient to make darkness visible.

And in the confusion of the moment, amid the dim shadows of that place, he might be well excused for fancying that it was the portrait itself that stepped out of its frame and confronted him in that gloomy gallery.

There was a dim, dusky-looking figure.

It raised an arm, and moved along the gallery floor with noiseless steps.

It reached another portrait of similar dimensions and position.

There was a slight creaking sound, and the vision disappeared.

The young stranger in Whitehall summoned up all his courage, and moved in the direction in which the seeming apparition had disappeared.

It was gone.

But the portrait to which it had made its way hung strangely in its frame.

The young man examined it more closely.

He found it was movable, turning upon two points above and below on its centres, and disclosing a passage beyond.

"I accept the direction," he said; "and whether this appearance be natural or supernatural, I will follow the path it seems to have opened to me; and for the love I bear to thee, my sweet Maude, I will accept aid either from the beings of this world or another."

The young man advanced along the passage, which was immediately behind the movable portrait, and at the end of which was a door only partially closed.

He stepped cautiously, and placed himself in such a position as to see all that was going on in a rather large apartment at the end of the passage, without himself being seen.

It was with almost a scream of joy and grief that he beheld in one of the occupants of that apartment his own, much-loved Maude.

She was sitting in a chair, gazing intently on some object which her young lover could not see from the position he occupied.

He pressed his hands upon his heart, which beat so violently that he feared almost its agonised throbs might be heard by other ears than his own.

And there was another figure in that apartment, standing close beside the chair in which sat the fair girl who was so idolized by her youthful lover.

The young man waited anxiously to hear some word or words spoken which would give him a clue to the mysterious proceedings of Maude.

"Behold!" said the male figure, who was standing close to Maude,—"Behold, maiden, your future destiny!"

The voice was that of a man still young, and the adventurous youth fancied in the tones of that voice, he recognised those which he had heard before, but at the time his whole soul was so taken up in the effort to catch Maude's reply, that he soon forgot the effect they had at first upon him.

At first Maude leant forward, clasping her hands in evident admiration and astonishment, while the eyes of the man by her side seemed bent upon her as though he would read her very soul.

" Well ?" he said at length, in a low whisper, " well, what think you, beautiful Maude, of the bright future which is there represented ?"

" Oh, it cannot be—it cannot be," sighed Maude, turning her beautiful eyes, and looking up into his face with such an expression of ingenuous simplicity, that her young lover could scarcely restrain himself from bursting into the room, and at once revealing his presence to her.

" No, no, not yet !" he murmured to himself, " not yet. I may be able to be of more service to her if I wait and hear more."

The man again spoke :—

" But I tell you, sweet one, that it is all true, or at least, it may be all true if you will but believe in the many protestations I have already made to you, that you are dearer to me than life itself."

Oh, how the young lover listened to hear what reply his Maude could make to such a profession.

" But I am kneeling at the altar, the bride of one far above me in worldly wealth. I see a coronet hovering over the head of the girl who is kneeling before the altar. It cannot be, I tell you it cannot be."

" And why not ?" asked the man, in still gentler accents than he had hitherto addressed to her.

" Because I know no such person as the one represented in that glass, and——"

" But if you did," interrupted her interlocutor.

" If I did—why then he would not love me."

No sooner had Maude uttered these words, then the man who was standing before her, raised his hand, and dashed from his head a wig, beneath which appeared fair hair.

He took, also, a beard from his chin, and now stood before her quite another being.

Maude almost uttered a cry, for in the man, who now fell on one knee before her, she recognised the living, breathing reflection in the mirror at which she had been gazing.

CHAPTER XXVIII.

FREDERICK, PRINCE OF WALES, MEETS WITH A SURPRISE. — THE MAGIC MIRROR. — THE UNEQUAL COMBAT.—THE UNEXPECTED FRIEND.— VICTORY.

SIMULTANEOUSLY almost with the action of the man who stood beside Maude, throwing off his wig, the young lover drew a small, bright sword from its scabbard, and rushed into the apartment.

" False friend !" he cried. " How dare you thus whisper words into those innocent ears, which from your lips become pollution. Frederick, Prince of Wales, I know and denounce you ! and with my own life will I protect that, which is far dearer to me than life, the innocence and purity of this young girl."

As the young man rushed into the apartment, Maude had risen, and when she heard her would-be lover denounced as the Prince Frederick, she uttered a shriek of dismay, and springing to her feet, she clasped both her hands round the arm of her youthful protector.

With one arm passed round the slender waist of Maude, the young man brandished his sword, and then his eyes fell upon the third occupant of that room, whom he could not see from his hiding-place outside the door.

" So," he said, turning to his Royal Highness, " it is thus that Kings and Princes amuse their leisure hours !"

Frederick, Prince of Wales, had been gradually recovering his composure, for he looked at the mere stripling before him, and felt quite certain of being master of the field.

" Beware, boy, how you address one so high above yourself in wealth, power, and station. Leave this place immediately, or we will find means of making you do so."

The young man turned to Maude and said, gently, " Will you trust yourself with me, dear one ?"

" Oh, yes—yes," said the young girl, " believe me, I was only weak and dazzled for a time by the bright prospects that bad man, whom you tell me is the Prince of Wales, held out to me."

" Yes, yes, I understand, but come quickly, the air in this place is polluted."

It was fortunate at this moment, that the young man happened to turn sharply round to take one look into the eyes of her he loved, for had he not done so, he must have fallen a victim to a deadly b low which had been aimed at him, by the pretended astrologer.

As it was, however, he had no difficulty in parrying it.

The Prince Frederick seemed to be waiting only for this signal, as it were, to begin hostilities; for clenching his teeth, he made a rush at the young man, which must have proved fatal had he not sprung aside.

Placing his back, then, against one of the walls of the apartment, and still keeping his left arm around the terrified young girl, he faced his enemies.

There was a look of high resolve and chivalrous courage on his commanding brow, which seemed at first to intimidate his two opponents ; but they soon rallied from the panic which had seized them, on perceiving that they had a skilful swordsman to deal with.

" Draw, villain, draw !" cried the pretended astrologer, at the same time throwing aside his flowing scarlet robe—" draw ! And know that few have left the field alive who have had me for an opponent !"

For one moment the young man seemed to be, so to speak, concentrating his whole strength into his right arm, and he spoke calmly to his two cowardly assailants.

He merely made a sign to Maude to retire towards the door, and then the conflict fairly begun ; but with all his courage and with all his consciousness that he was armed in a right cause, he could not but have some misgivings as to the result of the unequal strife.

While parrying a blow from the astrologer's sword, the Prince of Wales made a furious lunge at his sword-arm, and inflicted a serious wound.

" Ah," cried Frederick, Prince of Wales, " I had you there, fair sir ! Perhaps you are punished enough, and we will yet be lenient, and give you the option of ridding us of your unwelcome presence."

The blood was flowing copiously from the wound, and the young man began to feel sick at heart.

"Oh, Maude, Maude!" he cried, "must I indeed leave you to these unprincipled men?"

At these words, Maude rushed forward, and tied her handkerchief round the arm of her defender.

"Now," cried the young man, re-animated at this slight token of Maude's interest in his welfare—"now, have at you again, fiends that you are!"

As he spoke, he dashed the raven locks from before his eyes; but another lunge from the pretended astrologer compelled him to retreat again.

At this moment, there was a noise of hasty footsteps; and a young man, in a plain, but rich costume, stepped into the apartment.

"Hold!" he cried. "What means this unequal combat? Is it possible?"

As the young man who had just arrived on the scene of action uttered the last words, he lowered the point of his sword, and made a low inclination with his head.

The Prince Frederick stood aghast.

The new comer now addressed the seeming astrologer.

"Put up your sword, my lord, nor tarnish your ancient name by the recollection of engaging in such a conflict as this!"

Then turning to the young lover of Maude, he spoke in hurried accents, "Follow me; and let us hope that the transaction of this night will never be spoken of."

The young man mechanically sheathed his sword, and again drawing the arm of Maude beneath his own, he followed his new friend from the room.

They retraced the little passage, and passed thence out into the garden, where, having opened the gate which had been leapt by the young lover, they found they were free.

Maude's lover held out his hand.

"By what name may I remember him who this night has not only stood between me and death, but has also saved this innocent young girl from many a heart-pang."

The stranger spoke, and there was a soft melody, if we may so speak, in the tones of his voice, as he said, "My name is Sir Stafford Guy; and now, farewell! We may meet again under happier auspices."

As he spoke, he grasped the hand of the young man who that night had braved so many dangers for the sake of her he loved, and, bowing courteously to Maude, he disappeared from their view.

They were by this time at the water's edge, and there was the little wherry which had brought that brave young heart in search of her he held so dear.

Was it strange that now there were no eyes to note the love glances, no ears to listen to the words of love which were welling up from his heart to his lips, that the young man was silent?

And she—that young, fair girl—who had manifested so great an interest in the preservation of her protector, she, too, was unable to break the silence which fell upon each as the stranger left them.

He was the first to break the silence.

"Thank heaven!" he said, "you are safe!"

"Saved by you!"

"Oh, Maude, Maude! speak not to me thus or I shall forget that gratitude only has a place in your heart, and mistake it for something else."

"Mistake it for what?"

"Can you not guess?"

The maiden was silent; but had the obscurity been less, the young lover would have perceived a tell-tale blush upon that fair young face, which would have led him to hope that all his dreams of future happiness and bliss were fulfilled.

As it was, however, he could only hope that the maiden's silence was an earnest of some deeper feelings, and, for the time, he was resolved to be satisfied.

For his was a true and fond affection, and his noble heart would have spurned the idea of appealing to the gratitude of his fair companion and making her fancy that gratitude was love.

No, a thousand times no! He would not thus win his idol; he would not make her promise to return his deep affection while he had her, so to speak, at a disadvantage.

"Let us get into the boat," he said, gently drawing her arm within his own.

In another moment he had seized the oars, and was pulling with a will to the opposite bank.

When he had safely landed her, he again took her tiny hand in his, and it was a comfort to that brave heart to feel that that hand reposed in his so confidingly.

Silently they pursued their way towards the abode of Mr. Welling, the draper.

When about to enter with a latch-key, which her young lover was allowed, Maude placed her hand upon his arm, and said in a voice of deep emotion, "I know not how to thank you for what you have this night done."

"Speak not of it; but, oh! if I might claim the privilege of an interview to-morrow you would then make me your debtor."

Maude looked up into his face with an expression that could not be mistaken. It was full of deep gratitude.

Perhaps there might be something more in it, too; and without listening much to vanity, her youthful lover might have read it, "I would rather be thus protected by you than by any one I ever knew."

At length she said, "I will see you to-morrow."

"I will seek you, then, Maude—dear Maude! for I must speak to you on a subject which will create much emotion in your gentle heart."

Did Maude think, even for a moment, that he was too confident?

She did not; and if such an idea had presented itself for a moment, it would have vanished immediately, as he continued: "I know that I must greatly agitate and move you; for if my brightest and dearest hopes are true, that heart is too deep and too intense in all its feelings not to be agitated by the words you must hear, and the words you must speak. Maude, I want to tell you, not that I love you, for that you must have seen long ago."

"Oh, no, no!" she cried, looking up into his

face, upon which the bright moonbeams now shone, making it look almost unearthly in its beauty. "I might have fancied that you loved me, but I could not be sure of it."

Her lover smiled, and pressed her hand to his lips.

"Do not think me presumptuous," he said, "when I say that those words, and that look, have answered me, and made me supremely happy. But yet, tell me, dear one, tell me that those words, and that look are intended to make me as happy as I dream myself to be."

For a moment she made him no answer.

"Oh, speak!" he added.

"What can I say?" she murmured, in a low voice. "You who know the human heart so well, must have read mine too deeply, perhaps."

He gave up a few moments to expressions of thankfulness and joy, and then a deep shadow overspread his expressive countenance.

"Dear Maude," he said, "there is one question which I feel I must ask you!"

"What is it?"

"Did you ever fancy that you loved that man—I mean Frederick, Prince of Wales?"

"Oh, no, no—a thousand times no!" He has waylaid me often; and, like a foolish girl, at length I promised to go to Whitehall, and meet him there, for the purpose of looking into the future."

"Oh, how could you risk so much?"

"I was vain and thoughtless, and won over by his courtly address, and at last acceded to his wish."

"Alas! alas!"

"Why do you speak so? Surely I shall never now hear of him again?"

"I know not. I know not. Princes are powerful, my Maude, and I tremble lest you should be exposed to his vengeance now, while before, he only sought your ruin."

"Oh, how could he speak so fairly, and promise so much, when he is already married to another?"

The young lover was not anxious to enlighten her as to the proceedings of the profligate Prince, who, no doubt, had well laid his plans for the utter destruction of that fair young creature, but little more than a child in years.

The young man was lost in thought for a few moments, as he felt that his heart's idol would never be safe, until he could give her the sacred name of wife.

Then he felt that he could, and would bid defiance, not only to Frederick, Prince of Wales, but to all the world.

"You must go now, Maude, dearest Maude!" exclaimed the youthful lover; "and to-morrow, we will speak again of our love."

In another moment, Maude had gained her chamber, and locking her door, gave herself up to sweet and painful reflections.

There was joy in the knowledge that she loved, and was beloved.

There was grief, deep, poignant grief at the thought of what she might at that moment have been, but for the timely succour of her young lover.

CHAPTER XXIX.

MRS. HANMER IS ALARMED.—THE VISITOR WITHOUT A NAME.—A SURPRISE.—A VIOLENT INVALID. — REVELATIONS. — RECRIMINATIONS. — MISTAKEN CONCLUSIONS.

WE shift the scene to Mrs. Hanmer's house.

That lady is at home, but in anything but a pleasant frame of mind.

Affairs have not gone so easily, nor so prosperously as she imagined or wished, for all the circumstances attending the marriage of Catherine were of a most disastrous character.

With great difficulty she got rid of the dead Guardsman, who was found in her chamber; but scarcely was that one disagreeable cast off her shoulders, when another supervened.

A violent knocking at the outer door of her house about half-past two o'clock in the morning, on the same night the adventures of which we have recorded in connexion with Catherine Chudleigh, as we must still call her, aroused Mrs. Hanmer to a thousand fears.

It might be fire.

It might be thieves.

It might be that the officers of justice were upon her track, and intent upon a discovery of the more remote causes of the death of the Guardsman.

"House! house! Open! open! House here! House!"

"Gracious heaven!" cried Mrs. Hanmer, looking from an upper window, "who, and what is it?"

"Open! open!" shouted the voices again.

"A pretty thing," said a watchman, as he held up his lantern. "A pretty thing for the master of a house, when he comes home half drowned, should be kept waiting at his own door!"

Mrs. Hanmer was delighted at those words.

They seemed to her an assurance that some mistake had been made, and she was half inclined to forgive the disturbance in the felicitation of the moment.

"There is no master to this house!" she cried, "thank heaven! You have come to the wrong place. There is no master to this house, drowned or not drowned!"

"But he said this was the number. Open, open!"

There was a sedan chair, around which the watch were congregated.

A consultation seemed to take place with the occupant of the chair, and then the principal spokesman of the occasion held up his lantern again, and shouted aloud—

"The gentleman declines to give his name; but he says, if this is Mrs. Hanmer's house, it is all right!"

This communication again awakened the fears, along with a great deal of the curiosity, of Mrs. Hanmer.

The disturbance, likewise, had aroused several of the servants in the house, and by the time Mrs. Hanmer had huddled on some clothing, and descended to the hall, the outer door had been opened, and a pale, ghastly figure, was assisted across the threshold.

It only required a glance from Mrs. Hanmer to recognise her visitor.

It was no other than Captain Harvey himself, who, after receiving such assistance in the King's Warren as could be readily rendered to him, had, in reply to all inquiries as to who and what he was, declined all communication; but insisted upon having a chair, and being conveyed to the house of Mrs. Hanmer.

The fact that he was still under arrest by the order of Admiral Gascoigne made it a matter of necessity that he should conceal his identity as long as possible.

At his lodgings in Spring Gardens the fact of his still being in London would soon be known, and hence, he thought it a happy idea, to order that he should be carried to Mrs. Hanmer's, who had every possible motive to aid him, and nothing practically to fear from so doing.

But the sight of Captain Harvey, apparently at the point of death, was rather alarming.

She was about to utter an exclamation which would have contained his name.

But he had just strength enough to check her, and glancing at the watchmen and constables, he faltered out the words, "No name."

Mrs. Hanmer took the hint, and curiosity overcoming all other considerations, she dismissed the watchmen with a handsome gratuity, and received her visitor.

"Rest—rest!" said Harvey, faintly. "Some hot wine and rest!"

"But what is the meaning of all this, and what has happened?"

"To-morrow—to-morrow! Rest now—rest now!"

Mrs. Hanmer found she could get nothing from her drenched and pallid guest except those words repeated with more or less passion and violence as his strength ebbed and flowed.

And so Captain Harvey went to rest in Mrs. Hanmer's house, and slept the remainder of that night, and deep into the following day, in that very chamber from which Catherine Chudleigh had taken such headlong flight in order to avoid his hateful company.

The impression was fully upon the mind of Captain Harvey that his wife—if he might so call her—was no more.

The momentary recognition of her on the river, brief and flashing as it was, could not be a mistake.

If he, Harvey, had found the chill and current of the tide too strong for him, how was she likely to escape those influences with life?

It was afternoon, and the sun of that day was declining, when Harvey opened his eyes and gazed about him.

That room, how suggestive it was of the past!

The extinguished wax-lights upon the toilet-table.

The faded flowers in the vases.

All the little decorative odds and ends which had been crowded into that chamber in order to give it a festive and nuptial appearance.

What mockeries they all were now.

"Dead, dead!" he cried—"she is dead!"

Then all his wild passion for the beautiful girl rose up in his head with redoubled force.

It was but passion.

It would be a desecration of the more sacred name of love to apply it to the feelings of such a man as Captain Harvey.

He forgot all her wilfulness.

All her waywardness.

All her many mockeries, and the manner in which she had played with him until she had married him.

He only remembered how beautiful she was.

And what pains he had taken to make her his.

How he had fought for her—how he had bartered his honour as an officer and a gentleman for her, and the price, likewise, that he had paid to Mrs. Hanmer for her foul co-operation.

And all was lost now.

All had been gone through, endured, and suffered in vain.

He had sown trouble broad-cast, and still had much of it to reap.

And where was his reward?

Nowhere.

Nothing.

"Fool—idiot that I was!" he cried, as he dashed his head from side to side on the pillow. "Idiot, idiot! Thrice soddened fool, that I did not hold her with a clutch of iron when I had her! Oh, fool, fool! From the moment that she uttered the word, 'Yes,' in St. George's Chapel, I should have clung to her as though with hooks of steel, and never let her part from me! But now all is lost—lost!"

Again he dashed his head to and fro.

Then he uttered bitter imprecations.

Imprecations on himself—on Mrs. Hanmer—on the Princess of Wales—the Dukes of Hamilton and Kingston—on Admiral Gascoigne—and upon everybody at all connected with the history of the past two days.

"When you've done cursing and swearing," said a voice by his bedside, "perhaps you'll be kind enough to listen to me."

"Ah, Mrs. Hanmer!"

"Yes, in truth, Captain, I am Mrs. Hanmer, and a pretty return you make for all my kindness and consideration."

Captain Harvey uttered an exclamation of impatience.

"Mighty fine, indeed!" added Mrs. Hanmer. "Here am I the town's talk, and all through assisting you."

"Be quiet."

"I won't be quiet. A fine thing to tell me to be quiet when there's been murder done in my house—when my niece is, heaven only knows where—and when my nerves are so shaken, that I shall never get the better of it. Quiet, indeed! Captain Harvey, I am astonished at you!"

"When you've done chattering nonsense," said Harvey, "I will speak to you."

"Well, then, what is it?"

"Mrs. Hanmer, it is all over."

"What is all over? Where is Catherine? I suppose you've been hunting her from post to pillar, and know more about her than anybody else?"

"I do."

"Well, where is she?"

"Stiff, stark, soddened, and ghastly at the bottom of the Thames!"

Mrs. Hanmer uttered a shriek, and staggered back.

She had brought some chocolate for Captain Harvey, and placed it upon a chair by the bedside; but chocolate, chair, and Mrs. Hanmer reached the floor in one general crash.

"Drowned! drowned!" she cried, "drowned!"

"Yes, that's it—drowned!"

"But how? How?"

"I hardly know—don't ask me. It's more like a dream than a reality, but it is true, for all that: and she is drowned, and so there's an end of all. She will never be the Duke of Hamilton's —the Duke of Kingston will never carry out his idea of making her his, and she will never be mine, unless I plunge into the Thames after her, which I am half inclined to do, and so put an end to all my troubles at once."

Captain Harvey swung his head to and fro again, and gnashed his teeth.

"What shocking events!" moaned Mrs. Hanmer. "There is the death of poor Sergeant Holtham, too, whom you killed in this very room."

"That's of no consequence," said Captain Harvey. "The King's Mews is full of such fellows, but where shall we find another Catherine?"

"Alas! alas! what a mother I was to her!"

Harvey made a grimace.

"The poor dear thing," added Mrs. Hanmer. When we are left alone in the world, what a consolation it is to feel that we have done our duty to those who have gone before us."

"Mrs. Hanmer!"

"Well, Captain Harvey."

"I think the least that is said about that the better."

"As far as you are concerned, perhaps, you brute. I shall always lay the death of the dear child at your door; and without wishing you any harm, I hope you will never enjoy a moment's peace in this world, and will wallow in flames everlasting in the next."

It was evidently a piece of policy on the part of Mrs. Hanmer to quarrel with Captain Harvey.

"You may say what you like," replied the Captain, "but you sold her."

"Sold her! I sell the dear child?"

"You know you did, like any other piece of merchandise. I don't know that there is much morality in trade, but as you cannot deliver the goods, it is clear to me you ought not to have the money; therefore, Mrs. Hanmer, I call upon you to return the *post obit* which I gave you for her."

"Return it?"

"I said, 'Return it.'"

"Not while I'm a living woman. You ought to be hanged twice. I have no doubt now but that you've murdered the poor thing because you found that she had an unconquerable aversion to you. Now, indeed, I see you in your true colours, and the sooner you get out of this house the better."

"Infernal witch!" cried the Captain.

"Help! Murder! Watch! A constable!— a constable!"

"Hold your noise," said Harvey, "or it will be worse for you. I am a desperate man, and——"

He made a movement, as if to spring from the bed, but at that moment a tremendous appeal to the knocker of Mrs. Hanmer's house awed them both into silence.

A fashionable visitor was no such rare occurrence in that establishment as to make that loud knocking anything very peculiar.

But it so happened that both the parties who had been startled by it were in states of mind to be readily startled by anything bearing the semblance of alarm.

Mrs. Hanmer was in hourly and in momentary expectation of being called to account in some manner for the death of the guardsman.

Captain Harvey felt that all his professional prospects were at stake if it were found that he had broken through his arrest, and despite the strict orders of Admiral Gascoigne, remained in London.

But Mrs. Hanmer kept a hall-porter.

At that time no house could pretend to any degree of fashion without one.

The outer door was flung open, exhibiting a handsome carriage, with well-powdered footmen and coachman, and within which sat a lady attired in the most elaborate mid-day toilette.

The two footmen belonging to the carriage opened its door pompously.

The steps were let down with a rattle like a file of grenadiers handling their firelocks.

Then the footmen projected their arms.

The lady alighted from the carriage, making a slight use of those arms, as though they had been the balustrades of a staircase.

At this moment a mounted man rode up to the door of the carriage.

He reined in his horse, and slightly lifted the plumed hat from his brow.

He seemed almost like an apparition, for he wore a half-mask, which covered the upper portion of his face.

But something seemed to tell the Duchess who he was.

"Sir Stafford Guy!" she exclaimed.

"Even so," said the horseman, "and ever at the service of the Queen of Beauty."

Putting spurs, then, to his horse, he galloped from the spot, disappearing round the first corner that presented itself.

"It is my fate," said Catherine Chudleigh. "I feel that my destiny is henceforward mingled with that of the mysterious man who has already shown himself friendly towards me. But I will not forego my purpose of upbraiding my aunt Hanmer for her treachery."

The incident had not taken three moments in happening, and then she moved towards the threshold of her aunt's house.

"Lady Catherine Chudleigh!" shouted out one of the footmen.

The hall-porter was all amazement, for, in common with the other servants of Mrs. Hanmer's household, he was well aware of the marriage that had taken place between the fair Maid of Honour and Captain Harvey.

Mrs. Hanmer's own maid, too, uttered a shriek, for she had just descended the staircase after being an attentive listener upon her knees for the last ten minutes at the door of Captain Harvey's bed-chamber.

Occupying such a favourable position, with her ear flat against one of the panels, she had duly heard Captain Harvey's graphic description of how Catherine Chudleigh was lying dead at the bottom of the Thames.

CATHERINE FIGHTS A DUEL WITH HER HUSBAND.

To see her, then, alive, and getting out of a fashionable coach, was quite a shock.

No wonder that Mrs. Hanmer's own maid screamed.

All this tumult and all this vociferation could not but reach the chamber where the aunt and the detested husband were holding so unamiable a colloquy together.

They both heard the name of Chudleigh, but so prepossessed were they with the idea that Catherine was no more, that they never suspected the utterance of that name, or the consequence of her presence.

"More trouble! more trouble!" cried Mrs. Hanmer. "You will be found here, and I shall be accused of harbouring a felon."

"A felon!" shouted Harvey; "what do you mean by a felon, madam?"

"A pretty question, truly, when you've just

No. 10.—KATE CHUDLEIGH.

told me you have drowned the sweetest, dearest creature that ever lived, in the Thames!"

"I drown her!"

"Yes—who else? Was she likely to drown herself? Certainly not; all the men in the world would not have induced her to do so."

"Perhaps not," cried Captain Harvey, with bitterness; "but I am a desperate man, and let those who goad me to desperate actions take the consequences. I will not be taken."

He sprung violently from the bed, and sought for his sword.

"We shall have more murder," cried Mrs. Hanmer—"more murder, as I am a living woman. For heaven's sake, be still while I go down stairs and see what is the matter."

Mrs. Hanmer rushed from the room, and the first person she met at the head of the stairs was Catherine Chudleigh.

Then Mrs. Hanmer uttered a scream, and fell backward against the chamber door, slamming it shut with such violence, that Captain Harvey was nearly knocked down by his near proximity to it.

"So," said Catherine, "I have found you here!"

"Found me?"

"Yes; I was determined to visit every room in the house until I did so."

"Then you are not drowned?"

"Drowned! Certainly not! It is quite impossible I could come by any sort of death whatever, until I had had the opportunity of telling you to your face how false, wicked, and cruel I knew you to be. Wretch! robber! where are the Duke of Hamilton's letters that he sent to me once a week from Vienna."

"Letters?"

"Yes, letters."

"You don't mean letters?"

"I do, wretch! Did you not morning after morning taunt me until I was sick and dizzy, and could scarcely see out of my eyes, with his falsehood and fickleness, while all the time you had his letters, breathing nothing but unalterable affection, in your wretched Indian cabinet, beast, monster that you are!"

"Murder!"

"There ought to be, but, as it is, take that and that!"

Catherine flew at her aunt, and with one wrench, deprived her of her head-dress, bringing with it more than she expected, in the shape of a wig, the existence of which even she was ignorant of.

"Murder! murder! Help!"

"Yes, I will murder you, for you ought to be murdered; you have murdered me!—my peace! —my life! I did love Hamilton, and you knew it; and I love him better now than ever, that I have lost him! It was you who made me marry a wretch! a monster! a baboon!—whom I hate —hate—hate!"

Mrs. Hanmer was a woman of the world.

She could put up with a great deal.

Abuse.

Crimination and recrimination.

Perhaps a scratch.

But her wig!

That was the unpardonable offence!

"Captain Harvey!" she shrieked, in accents that rang through the house. "Captain Harvey, come, and look after your wife!"

"Harvey!" exclaimed Catherine.

A roar came from the chamber, as if it contained some wild animal imprisoned.

Harvey, in his eagerness to get out, had complicated the lock in some way, and impeded his own exit for the space of about a minute.

But Catherine heard the roar.

She had a musical ear.

She knew it in a moment.

Down the staircase like a streak of light.

Across the hall like an arrow shot from a bow, and into her carriage she flew, before either of the astonished footmen could strike an attitude.

"Home!"

Up went the steps.

"Home!" again shrieked Catherine Chudleigh.

Bang! went shut the door of the carriage, and off it went again to Mabledon House, as fast as its horses could drag it.

"He's alive! He's alive!" cried Catherine, as she clasped her hands over eyes, and sunk back upon the luxurious cushions of her carriage.

"She's alive! she's alive!" yelled Harvey, as he dashed his head through one of the panes of glass of the chamber window, and looked out into the street just as the carriage drove off.

CHAPTER XXX.

CATHERINE CHUDLEIGH AT HOME.—THE CAPRICIOUS BEAUTY.—A VISITOR ANNOUNCED.—THE YOUNG WIFE IS ANXIOUS FOR A DIVORCE.—THE BREAKFAST.

IT is the morning succeeding the day that Catherine Chudleigh had had so narrow an escape of being brought face to face with the man who was in deed and in truth her husband, that the spoiled and capricious beauty was reposing upon a couch in an elegant and luxurious boudoir of Mabledon House.

And surely it would have been difficult to find an object more in unison with all the elegance of that superb apartment than the lovely girl who there reclined.

Her arm supporting her head, which was thrown back, as the eyes were gazing upon the beautifully painted ceiling, as if in deep thought.

For Catherine Chudleigh did think sometimes.

And on this particular morning, as she remembered the preceding day, Catherine Chudleigh congratulated herself on the success which had attended what might be called her flight from her aunt's house, on hearing who was Mrs. Hanmer's guest.

"He is not dead, then!" she murmured to herself; "he is not dead!"

A slight noise made her turn her head in the direction of a door which led to her sleeping apartments, and Bella appeared.

At first the young girl did not address Catherine, but stood as if almost expecting her to give some orders which she wished carried out.

After a moment's pause, Catherine Chudleigh turned and uttered the single exclamation, "Well?"

In a moment Bella was by her side, and, kneeling down, pressed her hand to her lips.

Catherine Chudleigh—for such she still called herself—drew it away impatiently, as she said, "Pshaw! What now, Bella? You tire me with your maudlin sentimentality."

"Oh, how can I make you understand how much I love you?" sighed Bella.

"Now don't be stupid, Bella. I like you very well, because I think you wish me well."

"Think I wish you well! Oh, Catherine!"

"Well, well! because I know you wish to serve me——"

"With my life!"

"Don't interrupt me. But as I was going to say, I do not want such love and such devotion from a woman. I have determined upon waging war upon the hearts of men, who call themselves the lords of the creation, forsooth! Ha, ha! but

I will let them all feel that I hold their hearts—almost their lives—at my disposal !"

" Oh, Catherine, dear Catherine ! if you would but think and ——"

" Think !" interrupted the beauty. " Why what in the world is the girl talking about? Have I not been thinking for the last quarter of an hour, and does not even that effort make my brain grow dizzy, and bring lines into this fair brow, of which I have heard so much in praise ?"

" You are very, very beautiful, Catherine."

"Of course I am: I know that; and that is why you are so provoking, Bella. You will persist in telling me things that have been told me so often, and so much more to the purpose."

" But not with so much sincerity," timidly interposed Bella.

" What does that signify to me? But a truce to all this, Bella. What am I to do? That fiend, that wretch, that I was fool enough to marry, is not dead, after all ! What am I to do ?"

" But I think he loves you," suggested Bella.

" Think he loves me ! But what does that signify ? Have I not told you that I hate him, and that I love Hamilton ?"

" Alas ! it is too late now," said Bella.

" Bella, you are a fool. Why is it too late? Why should I, Catherine Chudleigh, consent to give up my name, my freedom, my beauty, to a man whom I detest, when I might have been happy with a man whom I loved ?"

" But it is too late now, dear Catherine, to think of this. You are married now to Captain Harvey."

Catherine Chudleigh sprang to her feet, and the look of fury that was upon her features made even Bella, who had had so many opportunities of witnessing ebullitions of temper, shrink back almost appalled.

" Is it from you, Bella, that I am to hear that I have made a sacrifice of myself in becoming the wife of a man whom I always despised ?"

" Then why did you marry him ?"

At this moment the door of the boudoir was thrown open, and a servant announced, " His Grace the Duke of Hamilton !"

" You may leave me," said Catherine, looking at Bella; " at present I have private business with his Grace."

With a sigh, Bella turned, and left the boudoir by the door at which she had entered.

The Duke of Hamilton sprung towards Catherine, as the door of the apartment was closed behind him, and pressing her hands to his lips, said, with much emotion, " Dear, dear Catherine, I was so anxious to see you, that I am sure you will pardon this intrusion at, I may say, an unusually early hour."

" Oh, don't mention it! I wanted to see you, to tell you that Captain Harvey is not drowned, as we both expected."

" Have you seen him, then ?" asked Hamilton.

" No, I have not had that pleasure. I called upon my Aunt Hanmer yesterday, and the first words almost that she addressed to me, made me aware of the pleasant little fact that Captain Harvey was her guest."

" And what did you do, Catherine ?"

" What did I do ? Why, what do you suppose? Do you think I flew into his arms, and asked him to forgive his runaway bride ? or, on the contrary, do you not suppose that I fled the house like one who was fleeing from a pestilence, lest I should see his odious face, or hear his hated voice ?"

" But you do not flee from me, my Catherine !" said the Duke of Hamilton, love lighting up every feature of his handsome face.

" Flee from you ?" repeated the spoiled beauty. " Why should I—you are not my husband."

" Oh, would that I were !" sighed the young nobleman, passionately.

" You would not love me then as you do now," said Catherine, softly.

" Oh, that I had the chance of proving how madly, how devotedly I love you !"

" Well, help me, then, to get a divorce from this monster I hate, and then I will be yours."

" But it is a work of time, Catherine ; and my heart aches, pines to call you mine."

" Well, call me yours, then," replied Catherine, pettishly.

The Duke of Hamilton drew her towards him.

" I have called you mine, Catherine, in still hours of the night, until this heart has ached ready to bursting; but then I was upheld with the thought that, when I returned to England, I should, indeed, be repaid for all my sorrows, when I clasped you to my heart, and called you my own—my beautiful—my wife !"

" Hush ! Do not speak of that ! When I remember what might have been, Hamilton, I feel as though even this frail arm could or should remove from my path every one who had had a hand in separating us ! Let us speak no more of the past, Hamilton, but tell me, have you breakfasted ?"

" No ; I thought you would not object to share that meal with me."

Catherine touched a little silver bell which was by her side, and the summons was immediately answered by a footman in livery.

" Bring coffee immediately !" was the order given by Catherine Chudleigh, as soon as the man made his appearance.

" Yes, my lady."

In a very few minutes a most *recherché dejeuner* was served to Catherine Chudleigh and her illustrious guest.

Little was said during the repast, which, certainly, from the frugal way in which the two partook of it, said but little for it.

Catherine Chudleigh was, in her own mind, wondering if Hamilton really loved her as much as he had said he did; and the Duke of Hamilton, as he gazed upon the beauty of his hostess, asked himself if it were not a stretch of morality to suffer one so young, and so enthusiastic, to pass her days virtually alone ?

He could not but confess to himself that Catherine was somewhat of a coquette; but then could he not read that he was the beloved in those sweet eyes, and hear it in the occasional tremulousness of her voice when she addressed him ?

" You take nothing !" said Catherine, perceiving, for the first time, his untasted breakfast.

" You mistake, dear Catherine !"

" How ? What do you mean ? I do not believe you have taken anything since we sat down to what I intended, at all events, to be an inviting repast."

"I have been feasting my eyes upon your transcendant loveliness, dear Catherine, and I care not for eating or drinking under such circumstances."

"Hamilton," said Catherine, with a look of ineffable affection, "I believe you do really love me!"

"Believe that I love you! Oh, Catherine!" cried the Duke of Hamilton, seizing her hand and pressing it to his lips,—"would that I could make you understand how inexpressibly dear you are to me!"

"And you to me!" was the low reply.

"Oh, speak not thus, dear—dear Catherine!" said the Duke of Hamilton, almost frantically. "In every look—in every tone, there is temptation—temptation to forget that the tie which binds you to one who cannot appreciate you is yet unbroken!"

"But what does that signify, seeing that we love each other so fondly?" sighed Catherine, as she drooped her head upon his shoulder.

The Duke of Hamilton was human—he was in love—madly in love, with the beautiful girl whom he had once hoped to call his own; but he had, at the same time, a chivalrous sense of honour.

With his constitutional strength of mind, and conformably with his acquired theories, the young nobleman determined to struggle against this strongest passion of his life.

It might have been seen by the paleness of his brow, and that nameless expression of sadness which betrays itself, in such natures as his, in the lines about the mouth.

Gently he unclasped the arms which Catherine had thrown around his neck, and holding her from him, said, tenderly, "I must save you, dear Catherine!"

"Yes!—oh, save me from him, Hamilton——"

"No, dear one!—I must save you from a greater enemy than even he of whom you speak —I mean I must save you from becoming the thing you would hate to be—I must save you from yourself, Catherine,—from——"

"No, no, Hamilton! Can you leave me—me who have loved you so well—so fondly? What can hinder us leaving this cold, noisy city, and seeking the shores of the sunny South, where we can wander hand in hand, and listen to nothing but the words of love which heart will whisper to heart? Tell me, my Hamilton?"

A groan burst from the labouring heart of Hamilton as Catherine uttered these words.

But he did not reply. His brain was in a whirl. He dared not listen to the suggestions of his heart at that moment.

"I see how it is," said Catherine, withdrawing herself from his arms where she had again nestled so fondly,—"I see how it is—the Duke of Hamilton rejects the heart of Catherine Chudleigh, whom he thought he loved."

"Oh, Catherine!" was all the Duke could say.

Catherine covered her face with her hands, and wept with a bitterness and anguish that was awful to hear and look upon.

Slowly the Duke rose, and took one of her hands in his. He pressed it to his lips—his manly heart was nearly broken.

Unbidden tears came to his eyes, and with one deep sob of anguish—a sob which smote upon Catherine's ears with more awful intensity than would the crack of doom—he tore himself from her and reached the door.

"No, not thus—not thus, Hamilton!" she cried. "That sigh would haunt me, and I should go mad! I—I dare not, Hamilton, part with you thus!"

He sprang towards her, and opened his arms.

"Catherine!" he said.

A radiant smile lit up his face as he spoke.

"Think over this interview, dearest and best, and tell me when we shall meet again?"

"Then we are going to part?" murmured the beautiful girl, again sinking into his arms.

"Yes, and let this very parting convince you of the intensity of my affection. Let us both reflect well upon the step we may take, and then——"

"Then we may be happy?"

"Then we may be happy!"

"Well, then, to-morrow night, you know, I have issued invitations for a masked ball, to inaugurate my taking possession of Mabledon House. Let us meet then, and, if you desire it, my heart may then be all your own, Hamilton— dear Hamilton!" she whispered.

"My heart's treasure!" was his reply, as he clasped her gentle form to his breast. "Mine— mine!"

"Yours only!" she gasped.

———

CHAPTER XXXI.

THE MASKED BALL AT MABLEDON HOUSE.—AN UNEXPECTED VISITOR.—CATHERINE CHUDLEIGH CANNOT FOREGO A FLIRTATION.—A SURPRISE. —THE CHALLENGE.

"CLEAR the way there! Get out, you ruffian! Constables!—constables! Clear off!—clear off! Thieves!—thieves! I've lost my watch! Move on!—move on! A link here, my boy! Help! Oh! I shall faint!"

Such may present a faint specimen of the cries, shouts, and general observations which took place at the door of Mabledon House on the evening of the masked ball given by the spoilt beauty of fashion, Catherine Chudleigh.

Thieves, constables, and demireps, and every variety of the idle and dissolute population of London, were mingled together in inexplicable confusion.

But we will leave the guests to assemble in the gay saloons as best they may, and take a look at the mistress—for such, indeed, she was—of that princely residence.

It is in the boudoir, which was elegantly draped with blue satin, and sparkling with mirrors, that we shall find Catherine Chudleigh, as she still called herself, giving, or rather suffering Bella to give, the last touches to her very becoming and *recherché* toilette.

"Here, Bella, quick—give me that bracelet! Ah, me!"

"Why do you sigh, Catherine?" asked Bella. "You, so beautiful, and so beloved!"

"That's just it, child—it is because so many

love me, that it is so difficult to make up one's mind which to listen to!"

Bella sighed.

"What's the matter now, child? There!—let me do it; you are stupid to-night, and can't even fasten on a bracelet."

As she spoke, Catherine raised a half-mask from the toilet-table, composed of white velvet, and fringed with gold, and placed it on the upper part of her face.

As she did so, a smile of gratified vanity sat upon her beautiful lips.

"Yes," she said, half aloud, "I am very beautiful, there is no doubt about it; and surely I shall be irresistible in this costume. Hamilton is all very well in his way; but the fact is, he is always preaching about——Ah! what is that?"

A slight tap came at the door of the boudoir, and then it opened, and a figure in a domino stood on the threshold.

"May I have the honour of escorting to the ball-room the most beautiful and fascinating of her sex?" said a voice.

Catherine, however, recognised in the tones of that voice one in whom she felt she must ever feel a deep and heartfelt interest.

"You here?" was all she could summon up resolution to say.

"Yes—I come to ask forgiveness."

"Forgiveness? Forgiveness of me?"

"Even so. You saved my life when nothing else could have stood between me and an ignominious death; but how did I repay the debt?"

"Think not of it—think not of it. It is passed away, and—and——"

Catherine paused.

"And you forgive me?" mournfully asked Captain Johnstone—for it was indeed he.

Again those tones seemed to thrill to the heart of the young girl, and she held out her hand to him, with a smile which he thought the most fascinating he had ever seen.

Captain Johnstone took it, and pressed it to his lips. He then added, quickly—

"Now let us go to the ball-room, for I fancy the music will not commence until the Queen of Beauty graces the ball with her presence."

Catherine's vanity was gratified, and she waved an adieu to Bella as she took the arm of her new friend, who now led her towards the ball-room.

"Will you tell me," she said, clinging confidingly to his arm—"will you tell me, now, what was the meaning of all I saw and heard at that strange house to which you took me?"

"It is better not—at least, at present. I had made up my mind that for one evening, at least, I would forget everything but the joy of basking in the beauty of those eyes."

Catherine shook her head coquettishly.

"It seems to me, Captain Johnstone—if that indeed be your name—that it is rather difficult to see whether I have eyes or not while I wear this mask."

"But having seen them once, they are ever present to my imagination."

By this time they had reached the ball-room, and Catherine Chudleigh looked anxiously round in hopes of seeing the Duke of Hamilton.

"Perhaps," she thought to herself, "this may turn out—this finding of Captain Johnstone, I mean—a lucky accident; it may induce him to

be somewhat less particular in regard to that divorce for which he was so anxious."

Just as the thought had passed through her mind, Catherine saw the individual who had occupied so prominent a place in her cogitations approaching the spot where she and the Captain stood.

Captain Johnstone was not slow to perceive that Catherine was interested in the approaching figure.

"Ah!" he said; "a favoured lover, perhaps?"

"That is as the case may be," replied Catherine, in an off-hand manner. "Surely you do not suppose that I am to be tied to your side the whole of the evening?"

"I submit; but may we meet again this evening?"

"I have no objection, provided you have as many pretty things to say to me as you have already said," laughingly replied Catherine, as she let go the arm of the Jacobite spy, and approached the Duke of Hamilton, with one of her most sunny smiles.

There was a haggard look upon the face of the young nobleman, as he stooped down, and imprinted a kiss upon her hand.

"Well, Hamilton! You look gloomy to-night; and I assure you I feel in the best spirits in the world."

"Alas! alas!"

"Good gracious! what on earth are you going on in that style for? What, in the name of all that is lugubrious, do you mean by shaking your head in that solemn way?"

"Catherine, dear Catherine, I love you!"

"Well, I thought that was all settled long ago. What is there in that interesting little fact to make you look so wretched?"

"Because we must part."

As he spoke, the young nobleman's voice faltered.

"Oh, very well! with all my heart! But I must say, after our conversation yesterday, I was unreasonable enough to expect a very different result to attend your reflections, as you call them. But I see how it is; you only fancied you loved me. Perhaps you have seen some one else since we parted, who has taken your heart by storm?"

"Speak not thus, Catherine, or you will break my heart. I love you with a deep and pure love; and to make you mine, would indeed be to make this world an earthly paradise."

"Indeed!"

"Do not speak so coldly, Catherine; I want to make you understand, dear girl, that you must first get a divorce from Captain Harvey, and then—oh! then with what joy and pride will I present you to the world as my bride—my stainless wife—my precious heart's treasure."

"A nice little arrangement, by all that is honourable!" shouted a voice close beside them.

With a cry of dismay, Catherine Chudleigh recognised Captain Harvey.

Hamilton stepped back a pace, and then he advanced, and laid his hand lightly upon the arm of Catherine.

"Remove your hand, sir, from off my wife—your touch is pollution! I claim her this night, and no one on earth shall rob me of the possession of the lady who——"

"Hates you!" exclaimed Catherine, almost

beside herself; and, by a dexterous movement, she had placed the Duke of Hamilton between her and her husband.

The two rivals both had their hands upon their sword-hilts.

"Not here—not here, Captain Harvey!" said Hamilton, with cool presence of mind. "It might not be convenient for Captain Harvey, who is under arrest, to be discovered brawling in a ball-room."

The whole had not taken more than five minutes, so that few, if any, of the guests were at all aware of what was going on among that little group of persons.

At length the Duke of Hamilton handed his card to Captain Harvey, saying, "There, sir, is my card, and I shall be most happy to meet you when and where you please, provided that the spot you choose be more fitting than the present scene for such a meeting as ours is likely to be."

Captain Harvey made a movement forward, as though he would then and there seize Catherine on the spot.

But Hamilton was too quick for him, for placing himself directly in the way, Captain Harvey made a false step and fell.

In an instant all was confusion, during which the Duke of Hamilton bore, rather than led, the almost fainting girl away from the scene, which might have had so direful a termination for her.

"Oh, Hamilton," she said, as soon as he had placed her on a couch in the boudoir, "Oh, Hamilton! why did you offer to fight that man?"

"Because, dear one, there was no other alternative in the first place, and in the next——"

The Duke of Hamilton paused, and a bright flush came over his face, for at the moment he had thought that if he should kill that man his way would be clear and straightforward; but the thought was banished as soon as it shaped itself into being, and he paused.

"And in the next place," said Catherine, looking up fondly into his face, "you thought that you might be the means of ridding me of his odious presence for ever. But now, Hamilton, I have a favour to ask of you."

"What is there in this world that I would not consent to if it took the form of a request from those dear lips?"

"To be sure, I know all that," said Catherine, with something of her old wilfulness returning. "I want you to send some one to this Captain Harvey, to appoint the meeting which is to take place."

"Are you so anxious then, Catherine, that this meeting should take place? Do you forget that I, perhaps, may fall?"

"Stuff!—don't talk nonsense, Hamilton, but go and do what I ask of you."

The Duke of Hamilton rose, and left the room.

In a short time he returned, and told Catherine that the preliminaries were all settled, and that the duel was to be on the following morning in St. James's Park.

"That's right," said Catherine, with a sigh of relief; "and now, Hamilton, let us sit here and enjoy ourselves while that tumultuous scene yonder is still at its height."

"Most willingly, my own love."

Upon a side-table was wine and fruit of every description, and hour after hour Catherine and Hamilton sat and gazed into each other's eyes, and thought not of the morrow.

That is to say—Hamilton thought not of the morrow.

Catherine, on the contrary, had made her arrangements, and at a moment when the Duke was not observing her, she dropped a few drops of a bright-looking liquid into a crystal goblet, and, holding it to him, after having filled it with wine, she said, with all the fascinating sweetness she could command, "Pledge me, Hamilton: 'To our new compact, and may nothing happen to mar its beauty, or dull the brightness of our love.'"

Hamilton eagerly seized the goblet and drained it to the dregs.

A well-pleased smile flitted for a moment across the beautiful features of the bewitching girl.

Ere long the Duke began to droop his head.

"I must shake off this feeling of drowsiness," he said, "or, I shall not be at my post to-morrow morning, and then, my Catherine——"

"On the contrary, my Hamilton, you must just compose yourself to sleep, and trust to me waking you in time for your duel."

"Can I trust to you?" asked Hamilton.

"Of course you can. Have I not a greater interest than even you can have in ridding myself of this man, who has become the bane of my existence."

"Then I will sleep," said Hamilton, as he let his head droop upon the end of the couch upon which he was reclining.

In less than two minutes he was in a profound repose.

"Now I must be up and doing," said Catherine to herself, as she gazed upon the sleeping form of him who really loved her well.

She stepped quietly across the apartment, and opened an inner door which led to an adjoining room.

Bella was there, waiting.

As Catherine entered she sprang towards her, and asked, anxiously, "Is all well, dear Catherine?"

"Yes, all is well so far, Bella; but I want you to assist me in disguising myself in one of those uniforms which, it seems, I ordered only just in time."

"Disguise yourself, Catherine! Oh, be careful!"

"Now, don't be a goose, Bella, or I will tell you nothing of my doings."

"No, dear Catherine, I won't be a goose. What are you going to do?"

"Going to do? Why, fight a duel, to be sure."

"You? You fight a duel?"

The consternation upon Bella's face was so ludicrous, that Catherine Chudleigh laughed outright, as she replied—

"Yes, Bella, I am going to fight my husband, and, if I can only succeed in running him through, the better."

CHAPTER XXXII.

THE DUEL IN ST. JAMES'S PARK.—THE TIMID ALLY.
—CATHERINE IS DISABLED.—AN UNEXPECTED
ARRIVAL ON THE FIELD OF ACTION.

THE sun rose brightly on the morning of that day, which was to witness so strange and unheard of an encounter.

A wife fighting a duel with her husband.

A husband seeking satisfaction of his rival—that rival being personated by his own wife.

Catherine Chudleigh dressed herself in the disguise of an officer of the King's Light Horse, but just as she was about to take leave of Bella, the thought occurred to her that she was not provided with a second.

"Will you go with me, Bella?" she asked, eagerly.

"Yes—yes, dear Catherine, to death itself."

As she spoke, Bella made a movement, in order to get her hat, which was thrown carelessly upon one of the chairs.

"How provoking you are, to be sure, Bella," said Catherine, impatiently, "do you suppose I want a puny girl with me. You must dress yourself in male attire, or you will be of no earthly use to me."

"Anything you like, Catherine, so that you will but believe how much I love you."

"Quick, then, show your love by your desire to assist me."

Bella disappeared, and returned in a few moments, tolerably well disguised, although she trembled violently.

"You will do," said Catherine, as she looked at her friend critically. "Now, let us be going, for I should not like to keep my husband, eugh! waiting."

Catherine and Bella met with no obstructions on their route to the Park, and it was some satisfaction to the former, to find that her antagonist had reached the rendezvous first.

As they approached the spot where stood Captain Harvey with a friend; these seemed to regard them with evident looks of suspicion.

Catherine Chudleigh, with a firm step, approached within a few paces of where Captain Harvey stood, and slightly bowing, said—

"I think I have the honor of addressing Captain Harvey?"

"That is my name, sir! And pray what may be your business."

"Merely to inform you that my friend, the Duke of Hamilton, is so indisposed, as to render it a matter of impossibility for him to keep his appointment with you this morning."

"Coward!"

"Hold, sir," said Catherine, sternly. "The Duke of Hamilton is no coward, and the thought of not having the opportunity of chastising you, as your deserve, renders him almost beside himself."

"Oh, indeed!"

"And, therefore," continued Catherine, without heeding the contemptuous interruption; "and, therefore, in order to ease his mind somewhat, I have undertaken to fight this duel for him."

"You?"

"Even I," said Catherine, drawing her slight figure up to its full height.

"Pshaw! I fight not with boys!"

"Have a care, Captain Harvey, or I shall begin to think that it is Captain Harvey who shrinks from this encounter."

"I shrink from it?"

"Yes; because it may not be convenient for Captain Harvey to risk being seen in St. James's Park, seeing that he is under arrest."

Captain Harvey turned pale.

"I will not fight with you!" he cried, again; "boy, go, I tell you!"

Whatever else Captain Harvey might have been going to say was put an abrupt stop to, for, at that moment, Catherine Chudleigh adroitly drew her glove from her hand, and threw it right in the face of her opponent.

"Fight now!" she cried; "or will you have it bruited abroad to the world that Captain Harvey is a coward!"

For a moment rage got the better of every other feeling in the breast of Captain Harvey.

"Come on, then!" he cried; "and your blood be upon your own head!"

As he spoke, he made a desperate lunge at Catherine's breast; but, by stepping a little on one side, she evaded it.

But that one thrust had been sufficient to show Catherine that, with all her skill—and that was by no means small—she was no match for her infuriated opponent.

This thought, perhaps, rendered both her eye and hand somewhat unsteady; and Captain Harvey, after two or three passes, made another thrust at her breast, and this time succeeded in wounding her.

Catherine turned sick and faint, and but for Bella would have fallen to the ground.

As she leant heavily upon the arm of Bella, the hat which she had worn fell to the ground, and, in an instant, her beautiful fair hair rolled in masses around her neck and shoulders.

The sight of those fair ringlets struck dismay into the heart of Captain Harvey, and springing forward, he cried, "Catherine! My wife!"

"Yes," gasped Catherine; "no doubt of that, villain! murderer, that you are! You have killed me—ha, ha! Yes—it—is—over!"

With these words she glided gently from Bella's supporting arms, and lay still and calm, as if in death.

"Oh, Catherine—Catherine!" he murmured. "I meant not to have killed you—I was deceived. Ah! who is this?"

A tall, dark man, dressed in black, approached.

"I am a surgeon," he said; "can I be of any service here?"

As he spoke, he stooped down beside Catherine Chudleigh, and felt her pulse, and then placed his hand upon her heart.

"It is too late for human skill to be of any avail. I should advise you, sir, to fly, and leave this lady with me. You can do no good by staying, but may get into trouble."

Captain Harvey, now that the first shock was over, began to think only of his own safety.

Apart from the duel, which had terminated, as he believed, so fatally, he knew that he would risk all his future prospects if he were discovered at large, after having been placed under arrest by Admiral Gascoigne; so, turning to his friend who had accompanied him, he said, "What say you, Lovatt—shall we go?"

"I should say, it is the only wise thing that is left us to do."

Captain Harvey, then taking the arm of his friend, after making an inclination with his head to the surgeon, who was busily employed in staunching the blood of his patient, left the spot.

He watched the two retreating figures, and then he said, softly, "Do you feel better now?"

"Yes—oh, yes! Who are you?" asked Catherine, faintly.

"Do you not know me?"

"Oh, heaven!"

"I have saved you: once you saved me!" was the low reply to Catherine's ejaculation.

"Where is he gone?"

"He will fly the country, and for a time, at least, you will be free from his persecution."

Catherine shuddered, and clung still closer to the arm of the pretended surgeon.

"But how came you here?" she asked, raising her eyes for the first time to his face.

"Because I knew I should be of service to you—therefore, I came!"

"Dear, dear friend!"

"Bless you for those words," replied Captain Johnstone, for it was none other. "Tell me where you wish to go."

"Home—home to Mabledon House," said Catherine.

Captain Johnstone raised her from her reclining posture, and carried, her as though she had been an infant, to a chariot that was in waiting at one of the gates of the park.

He placed her tenderly inside, and assisting Bella in, he stooped forward, and whispered in so low a tone that only Catherine could catch the words:

"Let us meet again!"

Catherine's only reply was a warm pressure of the hand that sought hers.

"To Mabledon House!" was the order she heard given to the coachman.

*　　*　　*　　*　　*

It is towards the evening of the day on which Catherine had fought with Captain Harvey, that she sat upon a low stool by the side of the couch upon which still lay the sleeping form of the Duke of Hamilton.

"He must wake soon!—he must wake soon!" she kept repeating to herself. "What will he say when he knows all?"

An uneasy movement from the Duke made her turn abruptly.

His eyes were open.

There was, however, a dreamy look about them which at first made Catherine feel uneasy.

She spoke gently and softly.

"Well, dearest, you have slept long. Have you dreamt of me?"

"Ah! are you there, sweet Catherine?" he said, as he shifted his position so as to catch a glimpse of her face.

"Yes, Hamilton," she replied, as she took his hand and pressed it to her lips.

His hand wandered over his clustering hair, and he gazed tenderly into her eyes as he said mournfully, "And I must leave you, dear one,

and perhaps for ever! You have been thinking so too, have you not? for you look pale and weary! How could I leave you to watch beside me, when it is I who ought rather to have saved you from anything and everything in the shape of care and anxiety!"

Catherine shook her head.

"I want you to forgive me, Hamilton!"

"Forgive you? What for?" he asked, rising to a sitting posture, and looking her full in the face. "Forgive you, dear one, looking so pale so unlike yourself? It will be easier to forgive you than to forgive myself, my precious one!"

As he spoke the Duke folded her in his arms, and kissed her brow, her eyes, her lips.

"You misunderstand me, Hamilton, I want you to forgive me for not letting you fight that man who calls himself my husband."

"But it is not too late surely for that!" said Hamilton, taking his watch hastily from his pocket.

"Half-past six! What does it mean, Catherine? Have you allowed me to oversleep myself?"

"Yes, Hamilton! But the duel has been fought without you!"

"Fought without me! What mean you, Catherine?"

"I kept the appointment!"

"You!"

"Even so! Nay, do not look so alarmed! He only tried to kill me—you see he did not succeed! I pretended to be dead lest he should carry the game too far!"

"But you are wounded, oh, Catherine!"

"Only a scratch here!"

As she spoke she opened her vest.

"It is nothing!" she said—"it will soon be well; and then, my Hamilton, we shall be very happy together!"

"But he—what has become of him?"

"Oh, I heard him advised to fly the country, —which he seemed not at all loath to do—so for some time, at all events, I shall not meet his detested face and form!"

"And who went with you, Catherine?"

"Bella!"

"Only Bella?"

"That is all!"

As she spoke Catherine felt a flush overspread her face, for at that moment the face and form of Captain Johnstone came before her mind's eye, and she felt how much she had owed to his opportune interference.

But Hamilton was too full of admiration—too full of affection at that moment for the beautiful but fickle girl, to heed the change in her countenance.

"But why did you risk so much danger, my Catherine?" continued the Duke, stroking fondly her beautiful hair.

"Because, Hamilton, I was in hopes I should be able to kill him, and I feared, also, that something might happen to you in an encounter with that man!"

"But, suppose, on the contrary, that you had fallen a victim, Catherine?"

Catherine Chudleigh looked thoughtful.

To tell the truth, the reflection that she might possibly have fallen by the hand of Harvey was not a pleasant one, for life to her now seemed to be

CATHERINE RESCUED FROM SHIPWRECK.

opening with so much beauty and brightness, that she could not bear to think of the annihilation of all her hopes of future conquest.

"Enough, Hamilton; let us talk of something more congenial to both our hearts. Shall I ring for coffee—say, Hamilton, for you are master here?"

"Say, rather, that I am your slave, bright being," replied the Duke, playfully; "and that henceforward I am here to do your bidding."

"Very well, then," returned the spoilt beauty, "that is all settled; so I will begin at once, by issuing my commands."

"So soon?"

"Certainly! I wish to make a cruise, and so I shall expect you to give orders for the fitting up of your yacht, and we will go together for a little sea breeze, for, in truth, the sight of that man has made me feel at least fifty years old."

No. 11.—KATE CHUDLEIGH.

"You do not look any older," said the Duke, gazing with admiration upon her beautiful countenance.

"Of course I should not expect you to tell me so if I did," she said, giving him a tap with her fan. "But now for coffee."

Catherine touched a small silver bell, which was by her side, and a footman in handsome livery made his appearance.

"Coffee!"

"Yes, my lady," was the reply.

In a few minutes an elegant equipage was brought in, and Catherine Chudleigh and the Duke of Hamilton partook of a slight repast.

"Then, to-morrow morning, dear one, I will go and give the necessary orders for our little cruise in the Channel."

"Do so—do so! for I am restless, and must be doing something, or it will be mischief."

"I hope you will never be weary of loving me, my Catherine."

"I don't know, I am sure. Heigho!"

"Come, come," said the Duke, kindly, "you seem low-spirited to-night! You must rest, and to-morrow all will be well."

Catherine was lost in thought.

"May I ask what you are thinking about?"

"No, of course you may not," said Catherine. "You might not be pleased if I were to tell you."

"Then I will not ask."

CHAPTER XXXIII.

THE CRUISE IN THE CHANNEL.—THE WRECK.—CATHERINE IS RESCUED FROM DEATH BY THE DUKE OF KINGSTON.—THE COTTAGE ON THE BEACH.—THE RETURN HOME.

SWIFTLY and silently Catherine Chudleigh and her favoured lover for the time being, the Duke of Hamilton, glided along in a beautiful yacht.

The sun shone, and as the water rippled the sunbeams danced and seemed to assume every fantastic shape.

Catherine for a time forgot all her causes for uneasiness.

For a time at least she was happy, and determined to enjoy the present let what clouds might hover in the future.

And the Duke of Hamilton, he, too, was for the time happy.

True, that at times he found himself looking sadly at the fair siren by his side, and then would come the question—

Did he really love, or was it but the mere fascination of her beauty that held his heart in thraldom?

Did she really love him? That was the question he would fain have had answered.

Both had been sitting, silently gazing upon the rippling waters and the bright sunshine, and both had seemed to be occupied with thoughts which had nothing whatever to do with the world around them.

Suddenly, they both started as though something palpable had come between them and the bright sky.

Catherine drew nearer to her lover, and he clasped her to his breast.

"A storm!" he gasped.

Catherine was silent.

The yacht had nearly reached the Isle of Wight when a sudden squall set in.

The howling of the wind at this moment—the ceaseless roar of the waves—the dashing of the high crested billows against the side of the yacht, and the cries of the mariners, made up a chorus of sounds that was perfectly bewildering.

A cry of dismay went forth from the floating vessel to Heaven; and at long intervals when there was a periodical lull of the wind, and when the fury of some huge wave had spent itself upon the labouring bark, the cry for aid was more awful than the raging of the storm.

The wind blows and howls over the devoted heads of all on board that trim yacht.

Sea and air seem confounded together, as the gale plows up the deep waves to the mirky sky.

There were cries, shrieks, tears, and prayers, and so with the living freight, the beautiful yacht speeds to its grave.

She strikes!

There is a harsh grating noise.

It is heard even above the roar of the wind, or the bewildering rush of the waters; the timbers break with a fearful crash; once more the waves and the wind force the vessel a-head; they have lifted her from the breakers, but they let her go again in wantoness, and she falls a total wreck.

"Forbear—forbear, my lord! No boat can live in such a sea. Forbear!"

"Seek not to stay me. I will go alone."

A tiny boat, which seemed too frail for such a sea, might have been seen, now rising, now falling, upon the waste of waters.

The single occupant of that boat was a man about thirty—handsome and well proportioned.

He seemed to be able to control the frail bark in which he had put to sea, and so, sometimes riding upon the top of huge waves, and then again being apparently buried fathoms deep in the dark waters, the fearless man made his way towards the doomed vessel.

For a time he was lost, and those who had tried to dissuade him from the perilous undertaking gave him up for lost.

But in a short time, far away in the distance, one of the men who had carried a telescope, said he could see a man in the distance battling with the waves.

It was the chivalrous man who had been addressed as my lord.

One arm encircled a something which, as he neared the shore, showed itself to be a female form.

With the other arm he swam well, and with practised skill he stemmed the retreating waves, keeping his head above their crests, and making for the shore at the only spot where the landing was at all practicable.

"Saved—saved, my Catherine!" he said, as his feet touched the sandy beach, and he found he had only to wade to the shore. "Saved, my Catherine!"

* * * * *

When Catherine returned to consciousness, she found herself in a small, but cleanly apartment, evidently belonging to the working classes, and beside her sat a matronly-looking woman, who seemed to have been constituted her nurse for the time being.

"Where am I? What has happened?" were the first exclamations of the young girl as she raised herself on her elbow and gazed about her.

The woman spoke in a low voice.

"Hush! Do not excite yourself, you are in good hands, and will soon be well again."

"But tell me," said Catherine, impatiently, "where I am, and who brought me here?"

"My name, lady, is Clark; my husband is a fisherman, and you were given into my charge by a gentleman, who, I think, had saved you from drowning."

"I remember now—yes. I thought it was all a dream; but, tell me, do you know the gentleman's name, my good woman?"

"No, lady. All I know is that some of the bystanders called him, my lord."

"I suppose, then, it was the Duke of Hamilton."

"I think not, madam, for I did hear say——"

Here the woman paused, as though she thought she was going to say too much.

"Well, what did you hear?" said Catherine, gazing at her full in the face. "You had much better tell me all you know. I can bear anything better than suspense."

"Well, then, miss, I did hear say that the Duke of Hamilton had gone down with the crew of the yacht."

"Good heavens!" said Catherine, starting from her recumbent posture. "Let me get up. I must get up and hear more of this!"

As she spoke, Catherine caught the hand of the half-terrified old woman, who vainly endeavoured to tranquilize her.

"Help me to dress, I say! Here are my clothes, I see. Help me, and I will ever bless you!"

"But are you able?" began the woman.

"I am quite well, I tell you. See here, how steady my hand is. There, that will do. Now my hat. There!"

"But where are you going, dear heart?"

At this moment there was a knock at the cottage door.

"That's the gentleman!" exclaimed the woman; "for he said he would come back again as soon as he had changed his wet clothes."

Catherine did not try to prevent her from hurrying from the little apartment, as she was not a little curious to see who her preserver could be.

A manly voice was heard inquiring for her, and then she heard the woman reply, "The lady seems quite herself now, sir, and was just going down to the beach, I fancy, to see if she could hear any tidings of those who were in the yacht with her."

"Ask her to see me, and I will give her all the information she can have on that subject," was the reply.

Catherine knew that voice, and her heart beat with a feeling of gratified vanity when she recognised in those manly tones those of the Duke of Kingston.

When the old woman had apprised her guest of the fact that the visitor wished to see her, Catherine slowly rose from the chair on which she had sunk on first hearing that voice, and entered the adjoining room where she was so anxiously expected.

The old woman seemed to be aware of the fact that her presence could be dispensed with, for she retreated to some of the back premises.

The Duke, as soon as he beheld Catherine, sprung forward, and sinking upon one knee pressed to his lips passionately the little hand he held in both of his.

Coquette though she was—vain though she was—Catherine could not repress a sigh, which seemed to come from the depths of her heart.

"Ah! why that sigh, dearest and best?" asked the Duke, love looking out of his eyes and speaking in every feature of his animated and expressive countenance, "are you not content that it was I who snatched you from the very jaws of death?"

Catherine could not reply; for at that moment, we must do her the justice to say, that her thoughts were with Hamilton, whom she had so lately seen full of health and life.

"Speak to me; tell me, at least, that you are glad to see me."

"I am glad to see you, and glad to have an opportunity of expressing some of the gratitude I feel——"

"Hush! Do not speak of gratitude. Love such as mine ought to receive something more than gratitude in return; but I see how it is, your love is another's!"

These words brought back Catherine to herself in a moment, and she began to feel that if Hamilton were really no more, it would not be wise to send the Duke of Kingston from her in anger.

He was wealthy, and what conquests and triumphs might not yet be hers?

Might she not yet aspire to a ducal coronet, and yet be the reigning belle of London?

Such people as Catherine Chudleigh seldom really love. They may fancy for a time that some one possesses their affection; but when that person is removed, either by death or any other circumstance, they find that they have yet a heart left for the next eligible offer which presents itself.

"Speak to me, Catherine, and tell me if I may hope one day to call you mine?"

"You forget, my lord," said Catherine, as the remembrance of the hated Harvey crossed her mind—"you forget, my lord, that I am the wife of Captain Harvey."

"But you do not love him?"

"Love him!—love him! Would that I could rid the world of him, I might then be happy!"

"But why not get a divorce? Surely, such a step could not be attended with many difficulties. No one could condemn you, so full of life, of love, of beauty, to drag on a dreary existence uncheered by the tones of affection, just because you happened in an unguarded moment to link your fate with such a man as Harvey."

"I know not—I know not," said Catherine.

"Will you depute me to make arrangements for such a step?"

"Indeed, I will," said Catherine, giving him her hand, and bending on him one of her most fascinating smiles.

"And then, what is to be my reward?"

"Whatever you may choose to ask," said Catherine, looking down and speaking in a low, tremulous voice.

The Duke of Kingston caught her to his heart, and as he pressed a passionate kiss upon her unresisting lips, he vowed then and there to make her his before many weeks had come and gone.

And was Catherine satisfied with this arrangement?

Yes, she was quite content to forget the past, in order thoroughly to enjoy the future, as she hoped and believed she should do as the bride of the Duke of Kingston.

For some time the lovers—for such, indeed, they now were—conversed with each other, almost forgetting, in the delight of interchanging vows of mutual fidelity, that time was waning, and that the shades of evening were gathering around them.

"You will allow me to accompany you back to Mabledon House, will you not, dear one?"

"Most assuredly I shall not think of going alone," was the reply.

"Then, while you make your preparations, I will give the necessary directions for our departure."

In half an hour's time, the Duke of Kingston and Catherine Chudleigh were pacing the deck of a Dutch galliot, which happened to be on its way to the coast of England, and, in less than an hour, the two passengers were seated in a private carriage belonging to the Duke, and were being whirled at a rapid pace towards Mabledon House.

Once there, Catherine felt a great relief, for the excitement and danger she had undergone during the last few hours had robbed her of all her joyousness, and made her but a dull companion for the fascinating and brilliantly talented man by her side.

At the door of the mansion, the Duke took his leave, being anxious not to appear too troublesome to one whom he could not but perceive was fickle and easily displeased.

"Adieu, Miss Chudleigh, we shall meet again!" he whispered; "and talk over our plans for the consummation of our mutual happiness."

"Adieu!"

Catherine hurried to her boudoir, where she was soon rejoined by her ever watchful and faithful friend, Bella.

"Oh, Catherine! I have been so unhappy about you—are you well?"

"Well? of course I am; what should make me otherwise?"

"I was afraid you had met Captain Harvey again, perhaps."

"Me meet Captain Harvey, child! what should make you think of such a thing?"

"He has been here," said Bella.

"Here!" exclaimed Catherine, starting to her feet; "what did he want here?"

"He said he wished to speak to you of something which he thought would give you pleasure."

"Something that would give me pleasure? Did he say what it was?"

"I could not exactly make out; but he said he was the Earl of Bristol, and——"

"Ah! then his father is dead!"

"Yes, that is it."

"And I am a Countess!"

At this moment the door was slightly opened, and the Earl of Bristol—or, as he is better known to the reader—Captain Harvey stood before the astonished eyes of his wife.

Catherine turned deadly pale, and would have left the room by the opposite door, but her limbs refused their office, and she sank upon a low ottoman.

"Leave us!" said Captain Harvey, in a tone of command, turning to Bella, who seemed uncertain whether to go or stay.

"Leave us, I say, again!" repeated the Earl. "I wish for a private interview with my wife."

At these words a groan burst from the lips of Catherine.

But yet, if the truth must be told, she was not so averse to that man now that she found that he had not only succeeded to the title of the Earl of Bristol, but, at the same time he had received an accession of fortune.

Catherine Chudleigh saw, that by assuming the title of Countess of Bristol, she would probably command increased respect, and would obtain greater power. Hence was it, that the interview which her husband claimed, was less repugnant to her feelings than any of their former ones had been.

As soon as they were alone, the Earl, as we must now call him, thus addressed her:

"Countess! I have come once more to claim you as my wife. Are you still disposed to carry on this unseemly warfare?"

Catherine expected to be addressed in a more conciliatory manner than these first words portended, and, instantly, all the fire of her impetuous disposition broke out, and she loaded him with invective which goaded him almost to madness.

There was a look of malignant triumph upon his countenance as he approached the door, and turned the key in the lock.

"Now," he added, as he put the key in his pocket; "we will understand each other, once for all, madam."

The instant Catherine saw that she was wholly in the power of the man who had made her his prisoner, so to speak, she began to see that she must change her tactics if she hoped to achieve anything for her future benefit; and little did he, Captain Harvey, or the Earl of Bristol, as he now was—little did he think that at that moment, the girl whom he had made his wife, and whom he really loved as much as such a man was capable of loving, was weighing in her mind the probable advantages which would be hers if she consented to be reconciled to this her lawful husband, or whether she should endeavour to persuade him to forego his claims in favour of the Duke of Kingston.

"Well, madam, I await your answer to my question. Do you consent to take your proper position and title of your own free will, or will you compel me to force you to be a Countess?"

CHAPTER XXXIV.

CATHERINE CHUDLEIGH HAS A SATISFACTORY INTERVIEW WITH THE EARL OF BRISTOL, HER HUSBAND. — THE DUKE OF KINGSTON PLEADS HIS CAUSE, AND IS ACCEPTED.

CATHERINE raised her head at these words, and spoke with some show of remorse.

"Alas! you could never receive me now as your wife, after what has passed!"

"Exactly; and now we have come to the real point. That is what I came here to say——"

Catherine looked up inquiringly.

"It is folly for you and me," continued the Earl, "to go on longer deceiving ourselves. The fact is, I did love you once but that love is now dead and cold!"

"Indeed!" scornfully returned Catherine, her colour rising.

"But nevertheless I am quite willing to prove the sincerity of my friendship by at once foregoing all claims to the hand of the flattered and caressed favourite of fashion, and allowing the fact of the stolen register to remain a secret between you and me!"

Catherine started and turned pale.

"Then you refuse to acknowledge me as the Countess of Bristol?" she almost screamed.

"Most assuredly I do, Miss Chudleigh—especially as I am myself on the eve of marriage with one whom I love devotedly."

Perhaps there is no woman who can bear to hear a man who has once professed to love her—even if she have no love for him—confess that he loves another; and Catherine was no exception to the rule.

A pang of jealousy—if such a feeling can exist where there is no love—shot through her heart, and she felt at that moment as though she would rather have heard that he loved her, rather even than the Duke of Kingston.

A well-gratified smile played about the lips of her husband, as he saw how he had succeeded in mortifying her self-love.

"Nay," he said, "you do not seem inclined to congratulate me on my approaching marriage. I should have thought that so old a friend as Miss Chudleigh would have been the first to rejoice in my happiness!"

"I do congratulate you with all my heart; but not more than I congratulate myself upon my emancipation from the hateful thraldom in which you held me!"

"Hush!—hush, Miss Chudleigh, not so fast, if you please! Such talk does not become the Countess of Bristol! If you vex me, remember I can easily prove the abstraction of the register, and you may yet be my Countess!"

Catherine bit her lips until the blood came, but she made no reply to this taunt.

"And now it only remains for me to take my leave, Miss Chudleigh, and to hope that some day I may have the pleasure of presenting to you my Countess, who is, I think, more beautiful than yourself!"

With this last arrow, which was winged at the overweening vanity of Catherine, the Earl of Bristol left the boudoir.

Catherine Chudleigh stood for some minutes immovably fixed where he had left her, and then a smile passed over her features as she drew herself up and glanced at herself in a mirror which was before her.

"Yes," she murmured, "this brow will well become a ducal coronet! I shall be a duchess, that is a higher rank than countess!"

She drew her chair towards the fireplace, for the day was chilly; and from the serene and contented expression she wore, a spectator would have guessed her reflections to have been all pleasing.

That night when the Duke of Kingston came to see if she had perfectly recovered from the fatigues and excitement of the preceding day, he was at once charmed and surprised at the unmistakable look of happiness which beamed from her eyes.

Deluded man! he thought that it was joy at seeing him!

Love at hearing him address her in words of fond affection.

He knew not that there was no heart beneath that fair exterior—but only admiration for his rank and wealth—by participation in which she hoped to figure in the world without apprehension or control.

"Tell me, dear one!" he said, as he fondly drew her towards him—" tell me, dear one, why you seem so happy to-night, and so like what I would ever see you?"

"I have seen——"

Catherine paused. She knew not what name to give the man who had once called her wife.

"Seen whom? I fancied that I was the cause of your happiness perhaps."

"And so you are!"

The Duke gave a cry of joy.

"Tell me, now, who your visitor has been."

"My husband—that was!"

The Duke started.

"Well, Catherine?"

"He wants to be married!"

"To be married!"

"Yes! And I have given my consent!"

Catherine put on an exceedingly comical expression as she said this, but one which had so much fascination in it likewise that the Duke pressed his lips to hers again and again.

"Then, dear one," he said, " you see there is no obstacle to my making you my wife—my Duchess!"

"Oh, yes, there is, though!" said Catherine, mischievously.

"And what is that?"

"My consent!"

"Of that I am sure! Tell me when I may have the happiness of calling you my own!"

"Well," said Catherine, putting on an air of deep thought, "suppose we say—well, Thursday —this is Thursday, and that will give me a week to make my preparations."

"So long do you require?"

"So long? Now if you say another word upon the subject, I will say next year. And remember, the wedding must be a public one!"

"Of course — of course!" replied the Duke. "I shall be only too happy to show the world the beauty of my bride. And do you love me, Catherine?"

"Of course, I do; but you must go now, for I have no end of things to see to."

"Adieu, then, fairest and dearest!"

"Farewell! There, go now! I declare I am almost tired of so much kissing!"

"Oh, Catherine!"

"Oh, Kingston!" was the reply of the wilful girl, as she darted into the adjoining room, in search of her friend Bella.

"Bella, Bella! Where are you?"

"Here, dear Catherine."

"I am going to be a duchess. Congratulate me! Why, what is the girl staring at? Can't you speak, Bella? I am not going to be a countess!"

"Alas, alas!"

"Now, really, if you are not the most provoking creature in the world, Bella!" cried Catherine, stamping her little foot impatiently. "Instead of being delighted, as I thought you would, here you are looking as woe-begone as if I had told you I had been measured for my coffin."

"I was thinking, dear Catherine, that your time will be so taken up, that you will never have any secret little chats with me, and no one loves you so well as I do."

"Oh, but they do, though; but I don't think I care so much for them as I do for you, if you would only be a little more lively, and help me to prepare for my grand wedding."

"Oh, thank you, dear Catherine, for saying you care so much for me! Now I will enter heart and soul into all your plans."

"That's right. Now call Perdita."

The waiting-woman soon made her appearance—in fact, so soon did she answer the summons, that if the two young girls had not been very much pre-occupied, the thought might have suggested itself to them that the abigail was not so far from the door of the apartment as might, under other circumstances, have been desirable.

"Now, Perdita," commenced her mistress, "you must see about getting me the necessary finery of my wedding; and remember that my wedding-dress must be as gorgeous and beautiful as that of royalty itself!"

"Never fear, my lady," replied the waiting-woman. "With this," she added, viewing a well-filled purse which Catherine had thrown upon the table, "I can promise your ladyship as magnificent an outfit as even she can desire."

"That will do, my good Perdita! Now, leave me."

The woman left the apartment, well pleased with the commission she had received from the careless girl, who she felt sure would never think of inquiring how the large sum contained in that well-filled purse had been spent, so long as she beheld a few articles of magnificence and beauty with which to adorn her exquisite form.

*   *   *   *   *   *

The wedding morning arose bright and unclouded.

All nature seemed gay and smiling upon the auspicious event that was at hand, and teeming with the incense of her silent congratulations; and nothing could rival the radiance that sat upon the brows of the bride and bridegroom.

As the bridal party entered the church—one of the most fashionable at that period—it was evident that nothing but the fact of the sacredness of the edifice restrained the cry of interest and admiration that hung upon the lips of the beholders; for fairer than the collective beauty of every flower which was wreathed in such gorgeous profusion around her, shone the beauty of Catherine Chudleigh, now for the second time about to take upon herself those vows which were to bind her for life to the manly and gallant nobleman who stood by her side.

The sacred rites were now proceeded with, and in less than half an hour Catherine Chudleigh had become the Duchess of Kingston.

The merry peals of bells greet the bridal party as it leaves the sacred edifice, and step into their well-appointed carriage which is to convey them to Kingston House, where breakfast, which awaited them, was served on a scale of princely magnificence.

And now Catherine Duchess of Kingston has been raised to the pinnacle of her fortune, and she enjoyed that which her later life had been directed to accomplish—the parade of title; but without the honour which integrity of character can alone secure.

Germany was the destination of the newly-married pair, and it was during the honeymoon that she visited the chief cities of its principalities.

Possessed, as her husband was, of introductions to the highest class, Catherine was gratified by obtaining the acquaintance of many crowned heads.

Frederick of Prussia conversed and corresponded with her.

In the Electress of Saxony she found a friend, whose affection for her continued to the latest period of her life.

On her return from the Continent, the Duchess of Kingston became the leader of fashion; she played her part well in every coterie, of which she was the leading star.

Now, the Duchess of Kingston was at this time the beauty of London.

Even the women confessed her pre-eminence.

Her wit was keen and court-like—lively, yet subdued; for her high breeding was very different from the lethargic and taciturn imperturbability of the English generally.

It was at a brilliant masked ball, given at Kingston House, where a crowd of loungers surrounded the chair upon which sat the beautiful Duchess, dressed in the character of Iphigenia.

She sat apart from the dancers, with the silent English dandy, Lord Baltimore, most exquisitely dressed, superbly tall, bolt upright behind her chair.

And a celebrated German Baron, covered with orders, whiskered and wigged to the last stage of perfection, sighing at her right hand.

And the French Minister, shrewd and eloquent, and gesticulating violently to his neighbour, occupied a position on the left hand of the belle of the evening.

The charming Duchess! she had attractions for them all: smiles for the silent—badinage for the gay—politics for the Frenchman—poetry for the German — the eloquence of loveliness for them all!

Catherine was looking her best: the slightest possible tinge of rouge gave a glow to her transparent complexion, and lighted up those sparkling eyes.

"Will you do me the honour of waltzing?" said the tall English lord.

"What Catherine might have replied was suddenly checked, for at that moment the Duke of Kingston, who had been in close conversation for some time with the Prime Minister, approached the spot, and, stooping down, whispered in the ear of the Duchess, "Come to the conservatory, Catherine: I have had a most important conversation with the Prime Minister."

The Duchess rose immediately.

"Not now—not now!" said the Duke. "In a short time hence. You will recognise this cloak, there is not another like it in the room."

"I will be there, never fear."

The Duke of Kingston turned, and left the spot, without perceiving that the whispered conversation which had been carried on between him and Duchess had another attentive listener.

CHAPTER XXXV.

AN UNLUCKY ENCOUNTER IN THE CONSERVATORY
OF KINGSTON HOUSE.—THE JACOBITE SPY IS
KILLED.—THE EARL OF BRISTOL A FUGITIVE
FROM ENGLAND.

"In the conservatory—in the conservatory!"

These were the words which one of the admirers around the chair of the Duchess kept muttering to himself, as he kept his eyes, from the moment the Duke had uttered them, fixed upon the Duchess.

It is not our intention to have any secrets from the reader of these pages, and so it will be quite in accordance with that determination if we state, at once, who the personage was who seemed to take such particular notice of the directions given by the Duke to his Duchess.

It was none other than Captain Johnstone, the Jacobite.

He whom, in the earlier pages of this history, Catherine had saved from certain capture, and probable death.

He who, likewise, had appeared at that opportune moment when Catherine, wounded by Harvey, felt that if she failed to play upon her husband's fears, feigning death, might terminate in his capturing her, and insisting on her going with him whithersover he might think fit to convey her.

There was also another person, then present, who marked, with jealous eyes, the admiration which the beautiful Duchess excited in all who beheld her.

That other was her former husband, Captain Harvey, now Earl of Bristol.

He had contrived to be present at the ball, in order that he might work upon her fears, and force her to use her influence in order to get him reinstated in his proper position; or, if she refused, to threaten her with exposure, by showing himself and her to the world as man and wife.

The Duchess continued to flirt and talk with her many admirers for some time longer, and then she rose.

Instantly there were at least twenty cavaliers who started forward to lead her whither she might wish to go.

But she declined their proffered assistance with, if we may be allowed to use the term, dignified condescension.

"I thank you, my lords and gentlemen all, but I do not feel in want of any assistance at this moment. Let me hope that I shall have the pleasure of finding you all here on my return."

A wish from her was looked upon as a command; and no one ventured to stir.

Catherine walked across the saloon, and opened a door which led into the conservatory—the place mentioned by the Duke as that where he wished to speak to her upon some diplomatic business on which his grace had set his heart.

At the farther end of the conservatory, half concealed by the large leaves of some magnificent palm trees, the Duchess at once perceived the purple cloak by which she was to recognise the Duke.

"Ah, you are earlier than I expected. Be quick, or we shall be interrupted. What have you to tell me?"

As she spoke, the Duchess leant her hand on the arm of the figure who wore the purple cloak, and looked inquiringly into the face; but only the mouth was visible, for the mysterious personage wore the half mask common upon such occasions.

As the Duchess spoke, the figure raised his hand, and removed the silk mask, and the Duchess recognised the features of Captain Johnstone.

"What means this masquerading?" she asked, almost gaspingly, for a strange fear crept over her, and she dreaded she knew not what.

"Is it so strange a thing to wear a domino and a mask at a masked ball?" he asked, in his gentlest tones.

Those tones now, even as they had done before, chilled through her, and she was silent.

Did she love this man?

Could Catherine, Duchess of Kingston, be said to love anybody? And yet, why did she tremble and turn pale, and clutch at some of the ornamental work of the conservatory to steady herself, as she stood gazing upon her strange visitor.

The Captain spoke again.

"Have you considered the subject of our former conversation? When I told you you might serve a higher cause, and be the magnet of attraction in a circle far superior to that in which you move at present?"

"Ah, I understand you. I gave you my answer then, as I repeat it now—never will I turn traitress, and become——"

"Hold! I thought—I hoped—that there was a warmer feeling at your heart, and that my love—my devotion, would repay you for any sacrifice you might fancy you would be called upon to make. Fly with me, most beautiful, and in another clime we will forget courts and palaces, and dream only of love!"

As he spoke, he drew her towards him; and for a moment Catherine gave herself up to the bliss of feeling that, for the first time in her life, perhaps, she really did love.

"Speak to me, dearest," whispered the Jacobite, "and tell me that you will consent to be mine!"

She knew not that the words of seeming affection which the Jacobite addressed to her were only prompted by the knowledge he had of her character, and that he believed it was by the means he was now using that he might be enabled to force her, even against her will, to join the cause he had so much at heart.

Whether or not he would have succeeded in gaining his point with the fickle Duchess, is uncertain; for, just at that moment, a third figure appeared in the conservatory.

The new comer was taller, and a much more powerful man than the Jacobite spy.

"So my Lord Kingston, I meet you at last," hissed the new comer, as he made a desperate lunge at the breast of the Jacobite.

"Help!—I am murdered!" was all that Catherine heard.

Indeed, so sudden had been the dastardly attack, that it seemed to her almost like a dream, and she stood gazing at the horrible spectacle as one in a dream.

"Now, madam!"

Catherine uttered a shriek.

She recognised in the tones of that voice none other than those of her hated and much dreaded foe, the Earl of Bristol, as he was now.

"Unhand me, monster!" she shrieked.

"Not so fast! Surely you ought to thank me for saving you from a tedious widowhood. If I have killed my Lord Kingston, you can yet, you see, be a Countess."

"What mean you? Oh, heaven! There is some dreadful mistake! Save me!"

As the Duchess spoke, she flew past Harvey, and threw herself into the arms of the Duke of Kingston, who, at that moment had entered the conservatory for the purpose of keeping his appointment with the Duchess.

"Ah!"

The Earl of Bristol saw the mistake he had made, and availing himself of the incoherence of the Duchess, who was endeavouring to make the Duke—her husband—understand that murder had been done, turned and fled.

"By Jove!" he said; "this is a pretty business! I must fly now with a vengeance, or all London will be on my track. Fool—idiot, that I was! I will fly—fly, and hope never more to look upon that fair, false one, who has brought nothing but disgrace and ruin to me ever since I have known her."

The Earl's horse was in waiting a few paces off.

His groom looked inquiringly into his face, but the Earl addressed not a word to him until they had galloped a considerable distance.

Then he turned and beckoned to the man.

"Go," he said, "and make preparations, for I leave England to-night; and, if you are so minded, you may accompany me."

"Yes, sir."

"What's in the wind now?" said the man to himself, as he turned his horse's head in the direction of town again. I've a great mind to go with him; who knows, it may be worth my while."

That night saw the Earl of Bristol on board a vessel bound for the Continent, a fugitive from his native land.

*   *   *   *   *

"He has killed him!—he has killed him!"

Those were the words which first met the ears of the Duke of Kingston, as he bent over the fainting form of his wife, whom he loved with a depth of affection which it was not in the nature of Catherine to understand or appreciate.

"Killed who? Speak, Catherine!"

"The man I loved!"

"Ah!"

If a cannon-ball had struck the Duke, he could not have staggered more than he did as he heard those words.

A pallor as of death overspread his features, and he was forced to hold by a chair to prevent himself from falling to the ground.

"Oh, Catherine! I think—you—have killed me! This is, indeed, a blow!"

"What more murder!" shrieked Catherine, not yet mistress of herself. "No, no, let me see!"

As she spoke she approached the dead body of the Jacobite spy.

"Alas! alas!" she said, speaking to herself, and unheeding the presence of the Duke. "So young, so gallant; and to fall by the hand of such a man as that! But, oh! I will have vengeance!"

As she spoke, the Duchess started to her feet, and, for the first time, apparently, was conscious of the presence of the Duke.

He looked at her mournfully, but tenderly.

The sight of him seemed to restore Catherine to a sense of her situation, for she forced herself to smile, as she said, "Truly, this has been a night of murder! Behold the handy work of him who once called himself my ——. No!" she added, checking herself, "I will not utter that word in reference to him; but come and look! Ah! why do you turn from me?"

"Catherine!"

"Well?"

"Did you love this man?"

"What, Harvey, or the Earl of Bristol, as he calls himself now?"

"No, not Harvey. I mean—I mean his victim."

"I love him? I know not who he is, even. What ever could have put such a thought into your head?"

"You said you did; but I hope you were not conscious of what you were speaking. Oh, Catherine, I think at that moment I should have blessed the hand that had sheathed a dagger in his heart."

"Oh, nonsense. You are more moved by this terrible transaction than I am; here, give me your arm, and let us leave this dreadful spot."

As she spoke, Catherine looked, shudderingly, towards the place where lay the cold, still form of the Jacobite.

The Duke looked fixedly at her.

"And you love me—and me only, Catherine?"

"Why, of course I do! Why do you ask me in that tone? You make me afraid to look at you, Kingston. You are so pale. Are you ill?"

"I feel sick at heart. I would that I were dead, Catherine!"

Catherine probably heard not these last words, for she was taking perhaps a farewell look at the Jacobite, who, for a time at least, had held captive her fickle heart.

Several of the guests now approached the conservatory, probably seeking her who was the attraction of the evening.

"Close the doors, Kingston—close the doors!" she whispered to the Duke, as she saw the guests approaching.

"Wherefore, Duchess?" he asked in a stern tone of authority. "Neither you nor I have anything to do with the actors in this scene. Then why should we strive to make a mystery of it."

"Then raising his voice," he said aloud:

"Come hither, gentlemen, and tell me if any of you recognise the gentleman who there lies a victim either to his own rashness or to the treachery of some foe, who has been pleased to make my house the scene of their brawls."

CATHERINE INTIMIDATES MR. JENKINS.

Several gentlemen now crowded into the conservatory; but no one was able to give a name to him who was lying still and stark before them.

"It is a bad business—a very bad business!" said a voice close to the Duchess. "Probably the gentleman came by his death by accident. Was it not so, Duchess?"

The Duchess turned sharply round to answer the speaker, but failed to detect who had uttered the words.

The Duke of Kingston, after giving some orders to the servants, who had been attracted to the spot, led the way from the conservatory, the Duchess still clinging to his arm.

"Let us leave these scenes for to-night, Catherine," said the Duke, in a weary kind of voice; "but I will not take you away; remain, if you will."

No. 12.—KATE CHUDLEIGH.

"No, Kingston, with you—ever with you!" softly whispered Catherine.

There was a well pleased smile upon the face of the Duke of Kingston, as he listened to these words, and, pressing her hand, he said, "Be ever thus, and I may perhaps forget those words which seemed to sear my brain as with a hot iron."

"Heed them not—heed them not! I knew not what I was saying. But come at once to the Green Drawing Room, for you look ill."

As she spoke, Catherine felt the arm of the Duke tremble within her own, and she had just time to conduct him to a couch, which was just within the room, when he fell back in a swoon.

Perhaps her heart smote her at that moment, when she saw the suffering her indiscreet words had caused the Duke.

She began to tremble for the consequences,

for should he die she saw in imagination all the wealth and influence which she now possessed departing from her to the next heir.

"He must make a will as soon as ever I can speak to him on the subject, or all that I have lived for—wealth, honour, title, everything will be swept away from me. Let me think—yes, let me think."

She sat down beside the senseless form of her husband, and sprinkling his face and hands with some perfumed water, which was in a crystal bottle by her side, she waited anxiously for his restoration.

At length he sighed.

That was a welcome sound to the ears of Catherine, for she knew then that he still lived.

And then she began to ask herself how she could introduce the subject of the will; but in this she was forestalled, for the Duke, after he had recovered, sat for some time in deep thought.

Catherine, at length, ventured to ask him if he felt better.

"No, Catherine," was his reply; "and lest I should get worse, I wish to read to you my last will."

"Oh, do not talk of wills now, dear Kingston," replied Catherine, with well-acted concern. "I do not wish to see it."

"But it is better that you should be cognizant of its contents. Take this key, dear Catherine, and you will find it in a small Indian cabinet in the library. Go and fetch it."

It is needless to say that Catherine was only too well pleased to think that she was now about to see that which would inform her of what her future prospects would be if anything happened to the Duke of Kingston.

CHAPTER XXXVI.

CATHERINE IS NOT QUITE SATISFIED WITH THE DUKE'S WILL. — THE INTERVIEW WITH MR. FIELD, OF THE TEMPLE.—THE FRUSTRATION OF THE DUCHESS'S SCHEMES.

CATHERINE, Duchess of Kingston, soon returned to the green drawing-room, where the Duke was anxiously expecting her.

"Ah! here you are, Catherine," he said, kindly. "Now, open the document, and read for yourself."

"But why read it now? You are so much better—you are looking yourself again."

"Read it, Catherine, and tell me if it is as you wish. I have tried to consider your happiness only in drawing up this will."

Thus pressed, Catherine took the will, and began perusing it.

The fortune which his Grace possessed was not entailed; and it was at his option, therefore, to bequeath it to the Duchess, or to the heirs of his family, as seemed best to his inclinations.

Now the Duke had bequeathed the income of his estates to the Duchess during her life, but under the express condition that she was not to marry again.

"Well, Catherine," asked the Duke, as soon as she had read the will, "does it please you?"

Now, the reader knows quite sufficient of our heroine to be able to imagine that the last clause was anything but agreeable to a woman of her disposition; but amongst her other qualifications she possessed also the ingenuity of effectually hiding from the observation of others what her real opinion upon any subject might be—that is to say, if she saw, or fancied she saw, any advantage in veiling her real sentiments.

In reply, therefore, to the Duke's question, she merely said, "I am perfectly satisfied, my dear Kingston, although I hope that will will never have to be carried out."

"Well, well, we shall see—we shall see," was the reply.

But now, as days and weeks passed, the Duchess could not hide from herself the fact that the Duke was very unlike himself; and at length he was seized with a paralytic affection, which ultimately caused his death.

Change of air and change of scene were recommended to the noble patient; and the Duchess spared neither time nor expense in hurrying about from place to place under the false idea of prolonging his life.

At length, when she felt convinced that nothing would save him, she remembered the will which, while it left her sole mistress of his vast wealth, yet at the same time shut the temple of Hymen against her.

She had recourse, then, to her solicitor, Mr. Field, of the Temple, to whom she despatched a messenger, urging him to come to Kingston House without delay.

Mr. Field obeyed the summons, and was shown into the library of the mansion.

He had scarcely entered the room before he was joined by the Duchess, looking almost as radiant and beautiful as ever.

"Your servant, your Grace," said the man of business, making an elaborate bow.

"Be seated, Mr. Field. I have business of the greatest importance to talk to you about."

There was a silence of some minutes, and then the Duchess spoke.

"The Duke of Kingston, Mr. Field, is, I fear, very, very ill; and it is necessary that his will should be revised."

"Hem! Yes, your Grace. Then my business is with his Grace?"

"Well, not exactly," replied Catherine, looking at the solicitor fixedly in the face. "The fact is, he has left the whole of the property to me during my lifetime, and——"

"A most proper arrangement," began Mr. Field.

But Catherine interrupted him.

"And so I was going to observe, Mr. Field, that I shall probably be one of the richest peeresses in England."

"Exactly so, your Grace, and one of the most beautiful——"

"Yes, yes, I know all that; but I have not yet told you what I require your services for."

"Anything that lies in my power——"

But Catherine held up her hand.

"Time is precious," she added. "What I wanted with you was, that you might induce the Duke to execute, and be yourself a subscribing witness, to a will made without his knowledge."

" Pardon me, madam," said Mr. Field, looking shocked.

" Oh, you need be under no apprehensions, Mr. Field. The will may be couched in precisely the same terms as the original one. The only difference I wish to suggest being so trifling that you need have no scruples about it."

" May I be allowed to ask your Grace, then, in what the alteration consists?" asked Mr. Field, looking somewhat puzzled.

" Why, you must know, Mr. Field, that it is anything but pleasant for a woman, still young, to be excluded from the privilege of giving her hand in marriage, if she be so inclined; and, therefore, it is the clause in which the Duke expresses his opinion on that subject which I want to have altered."

Mr. Field breathed more freely. It was not, then, an entire setting aside of the Duke's will that was required of him, but only an alteration of a single clause.

Catherine looked at him keenly, and then said, in a low tone, " Of course, Mr. Field, you would be amply rewarded for whatever trouble you might have in the transaction."

Mr. Field looked undecided; but rising from his seat abruptly, he said, " I will be guided by circumstances, your Grace; and if his Grace be in a condition to execute another will, more in accordance with your feelings than the original one, you may count on my good services. When may I be allowed to see his Grace?"

" Now, at once," said Catherine. " Follow me, and I will lead you to his chamber."

Mr. Field followed the Duchess up the second flight of stairs, and, opening a door to the right, he found himself introduced into the sleeping apartment of the Duke.

Surely, her evil fortune was in the ascendant, for the Duke's intellect seemed more clouded than usual; and when the Duchess approached the bed-side, he failed to recognise her.

Mr. Field was shocked in the extreme, and remonstrated with the Duchess against the impropriety of introducing a will for execution to a man in such a state.

" I cannot—I cannot, indeed, your Grace," he said, " lend myself to anything of the kind."

" What have you to fear, Mr. Field?" asked Catherine. " Have you forgotten that I am the possessor of vast wealth, and have I not already said enough to convince you that I can also be generous."

" I cannot do it," said the solicitor.

" Of what are you afraid?" almost shrieked Catherine. " You have no right to think at all about the matter; your province is but to obey the wishes of your employers."

" Not against the dictates of my conscience, Duchess; and some day you will perhaps be glad to think I have had the courage to withstand your brilliant offers. I beg to wish you good day!"

As he spoke, Mr. Field turned and left the room, and was soon making his way to his chambers in the Temple.

Catherine's ready wit, however, did not desert her at this juncture, and she resolved to use all the influence she possessed over the Duke, in order to induce him of his own accord to alter the will the better to suit her own tastes.

For this purpose she hastened to the sick chamber of her lord, and approaching the bedside, said, in her gentlest accents, " I trust you are none the worse for Mr. Field's visit?"

But there was no reply.

Catherine began to feel uneasy.

Was it possible that she was too late, and that she was to fail in this her last effort to procure an alteration in the will?

She hastily drew back the heavy drapery, but the face that met her gaze was rigid in death.

The Duke of Kingston had breathed his last while Catherine had been loading her solicitor with invective.

" Too late—too late!" sighed Catherine. " But I am still mistress of these princely estates, and for the rest, why——"

Even at that moment—while standing by the bedside of the man who had really and truly loved her, and whose kindly smile was quenched in death—even at that moment Catherine could not repress a smile of triumph and gratified vanity.

The young and beautiful Duchess gave orders for the funeral rites to be conducted with great pomp and state; and no sooner were these performed than Catherine laid her plans for the future.

About a week after the funeral, Bella Steinburg was summoned to her presence to hear what were the intentions of her ladyship.

" Bella," began Catherine, " I am going to travel."

" To leave England?"

" Yes, I am tired of London," replied this spoilt child of fortune, " and intend to visit Rome for a time. Will you go with me?"

" Oh, Catherine, if I might——"

" Might! Why, of course you may if you choose. What do you mean?"

" I was thinking that my duties as Maid of Honour——" began Bella.

" Leave that to me—leave that to me, child. I will settle all that with her Royal Highness."

" Do so—do so, dear Catherine, and I will devote my life to you," said the infatuated girl.

The Duchess looked at her friend in surprise.

She could not understand such devotion. She had never loved any one so well as to think for a moment of making any sacrifice for the sake of another, and she could not therefore understand the feeling which actuated Bella Steinburg.

In two days from that on which the above conversation took place between the two friends, Catherine, Duchess of Kingston, was on her way to Rome.

There her wealth, rank, and beauty procured her the *entrée* to the best society. She was even lodged in the palace of one of the Cardinals.

Even the Pope himself treated her with marked civility, and gave her many privileges.

Masquerades, balls, routs, all that could serve to gratify the vanity of such a woman, took place in honour of the beautiful Duchess.

And now nothing seemed to be wanting to make up the earthly bliss of the gay and fickle Duchess.

She was fêted and admired to her heart's content, and thought not of the future in the enjoyment of the present.

But other scenes were at this time enacting in

England, and little did the Duchess suspect that her present triumph would be of such short duration.

  * * * * *

It is about three o'clock—the sun is gleaming into the comfortable chambers of Mr. Field, and that gentleman is quietly reading the newspaper, after having had a rather busy morning, when a knock came at the outer door.

"Ah! another visitor."

Mr. Field spoke rather impatiently, for he had hoped that business was over for that day.

The summons for admission was answered by Mr. Field's clerk, who was busily writing at his desk in the outer office.

"Is Mr. Field disengaged?" asked a young woman—she was not a lady, but was evidently above the lower class of society.

"I will see," was the reply. "Take a chair. What name shall I say, if you please?"

"Mrs. Cradock."

The clerk disappeared into the inner room, and made known to Mr. Field the name of his visitor.

"Cradock? Cradock? I don't remember the name, Mr. Abbot. What is her business?"

"I don't know. Shall I ask her if she can leave a message for you?"

"Oh, no, never mind. Show her in."

In compliance with the orders of his employer Mr. Abbot returned to the outer office, where he found Mrs. Cradock seated in a chair, as though she had said to herself, "Here I will wait until I can make known my business to Mr. Field."

"Will you please to step this way, ma'am?"

Mrs. Cradock rose immediately, saying, as she did so, "Can I see Mr. Field?"

"Yes, ma'am, he is waiting to hear what your business may be. Follow me."

Mrs. Cradock soon found herself in the presence of Mr. Field.

As she entered, the solicitor looked inquiringly at her.

"Mrs. Cradock, I believe?" he began.

"That is my name, sir. You are the solicitor of the lady who calls herself the Duchess of Kingston, I believe?"

"I have the honour to be the legal adviser of the Duchess of Kingston."

"The Countess of Bristol you should rather say, sir," quietly remarked Mrs. Cradock.

"I have nothing to do with the lady you mention," returned Mr. Field; "but you spoke of the Duchess of Kingston. What have you to say with reference to that lady?"

"I have come to you, sir, for assistance. My circumstances are reduced. I am, in fact, in want, and, as the solicitor of the Duchess of Kingston, as you are pleased to call her, I thought you the proper person to apply to."

"But are you commissioned by her Grace to apply to me?"

"Oh, no—oh, dear, no; you can assist me without her being troubled. Besides, she is at Rome, and while my demand for assistance was on its road to her I might be reduced to the greatest poverty; so again I say, Mr. Field, I come to you as the proper person to assist me in behalf of the Duchess of Kingston."

"Pooh! pooh! This is gross imposition. Do you suppose that you, a stranger, without any means of showing me even that you know the lady, are to come here and force me against my sense and reason, to supply you with funds just because you say I am to do so? Nonsense! nonsense! young woman! Now leave me, I am busy."

As Mr. Field uttered the last words, he threw open the door which communicated with the outer office, and took up the newspaper again.

But Mrs. Cradock had taken too much pains to ensure this interview with the solicitor to be so summarily dismissed.

She merely rose quietly, and again closed the door.

Mr. Field looked up in surprise.

CHAPTER XXXVII.

THE TREACHERY OF THE CONFIDANTE. — THE LAWYER IS OUTWITTED.—DANGEROUS DISCLOSURES.—THE HUNT FOR THE MARRIAGE REGISTER.—PERSEVERANCE REWARDED.

"I HAVE not yet told you what I came to say—it would, therefore, be absurd to leave before I had been candid with you."

There was an air of quiet determination about this woman that at all events had the effect of securing for her a listener.

"Well, Mrs. Cradock—I think that is your name," said Mr. Field, leaning back in his chair, "I am quite prepared to listen to you, provided you will be as brief as possible."

"I have come to say, then, that it is in my power to strip the lady, whom you are pleased to call the Duchess of Kingston, not only of her wealth, but of her title."

Mr. Field smiled incredulously.

"Hear me out, Mr. Field, and judge for yourself," continued Mrs. Cradock. "I was present at the marriage of her Grace with the Earl of Bristol—then Captain Harvey, of the Royal Navy."

"Absurd!"

"Allow me sufficient to satisfy my few wants, and I care not whether the lady in question be called Duchess of Kingston—or, as she ought to be named, Countess of Bristol; but, on the contrary, if you refuse me——"

"Well," asked Mr. Field, looking up; "what then?"

"In that case, I give you fair warning, that I shall not fail to disclose all I know, and all I can prove, in the right quarter—namely, to the relations of the Duke of Kingston, who have been set aside by the late Duke, in order that she, who could not legally have been married to him, might enjoy the whole of his vast wealth. Do you understand me?"

"I hear what you say, Mrs. Cradock, but treat your information with contempt, and tell you to do your worst."

"I am answered: henceforward it shall be war, Mr. Field; and now, good day!"

As Mrs. Cradock uttered the last words, she sailed out of the room, and left the office.

"Upon my word," said Mr. Field, when he found himself alone,—"upon my word, she would not do badly for a tragedy queen! Surely there is no foundation in what she says! The marriage was publicly solemnised; and surely this Captain Harvey must have had some friends to inform him of what was going on, even if he was absent himself! Pooh! pooh! Idle threats, merely to extort money under false pretences!"

Mr. Field, having thus relieved his mind again resumed his newspaper.

He knew not that his client had, indeed, all to dread from the vindictiveness of this woman, who really had been a confidential servant in the household of Mrs. Hanmer, while her niece, Miss Chudleigh, was still free to bestow her hand upon whomsoever she would.

This woman had really been present at the marriage of her young lady with the Hon. Captain Harvey, of the royal navy, and had also been shown, by Catherine herself, the leaf of the book which had been taken from the register so expertly and so cleverly by the fickle bride of Captain Harvey.

It will at once be seen, then, how much Catherine had to fear from this woman's knowledge of her secrets.

Mrs. Cradock immediately set about her work of destruction.

Having been so much in the confidence of the Duchess, she was aware of the enmity which existed between the late Duke of Kingston and a nephew of his named Evelyn Meadows.

The Duke, even, went so far as to carry his feelings of dislike beyond the grave, and actually excluded this gentleman from the presumptive heirship to his property.

To him, therefore, Mrs. Cradock determined first to have recourse, reckoning upon Mr. Evelyn Meadows' co-operation in avenging his own wrongs, while, at the same time, she had every reason to believe that she would be well paid for the information she could give.

It was on the following day to that which had witnessed her ineffectual attempts to extort assistance from Mr. Field, that Mrs. Cradock made her way towards a house of some pretensions, situated in a tolerably fashionable part of London.

"Now, I wonder what sort of a reception I shall meet with here," she muttered to herself, as she rung the bell of the outer door.

It was soon answered by a respectable middle-aged woman.

"Is Mr. Meadows at home?" she inquired.

"Yes, ma'am," was the satisfactory answer to her question.

"Then, will you be kind enough to say that Mrs. Cradock wishes to see him upon business of the greatest importance."

"Certainly, ma'am. If you'll just step in here, I'll tell master that you want to see him."

"Thank you."

Mrs. Cradock waited, with some degree of curiosity and expectation expressed upon her features, for the return of her messenger.

She had not long to wait, for, in less than five minutes, the servant returned, saying, "Will you please to step in here, and master will be with you in a minute."

Mrs. Cradock rose from the chair upon which she had been seated in the hall, and followed her conductor to a kind of library on the ground floor.

No sooner was she within the room, than the door again opened, and admitted a tall, gentlemanly looking man, who appeared to be about forty years of age.

"I have not the pleasure of your acquaintance, I believe, madam, but did I understand that you wish to speak to me on business?"

"Most important business, sir," slowly replied Mrs. Cradock.

Mr. Meadows placed a chair for his strange visitor, and having seated himself at the table in a luxurious easy chair, he waited for Mrs. Cradock to begin the conversation.

There was a pause of a few moments, and then Mrs. Cradock broke it by saying, "Mr. Meadows, I will be candid with you, and then we shall get on much better. The information I bring you may be very advantageous to you."

"It may be so, madam," replied Mr. Meadows; "but after I have heard what you have to say, or to consult me about, I shall be the best judge of that."

"In the first place, may I ask you one question," said Mrs. Cradock, in the lowest of low tones.

"As many as you like, madam, provided you are not too long about it; for I have a pressing engagement in half an hour from this time."

As he spoke, Mr. Meadows gazed rather impatiently towards a little time-piece on the mantel-shelf.

"Tell me, then, sir, did it never occur to you that you might dispute the validity of the will of the late Duke of Kingston?"

"Bless my soul! No, certainly not. I have been injured—grossly set aside, madam, in that will—looked over entirely."

Mr. Meadows paused to take breath; and then Mrs. Cradock interrupted him by saying, "Do you know the contents of the late Duke's will, sir?"

"Know them, madam? Certainly I know them, madam. Did he not leave everything to his wife during her lifetime, and——"

"Stop—stop!"

"Well, madam?"

"Supposing he had no wife?"

"Why, then, in all probability, he would have made no will at all; and the estates would have descended in a regular line to his heirs-at-law."

"You think so?"

"Think so? I think it more than probable that the Duchess played her cards so well as to persuade him to make a will in her favour; and then he remembered how he had always hated me, and excluded me therefore from all participation in the vast properties which belong to the Kingston estates."

"I think so, too," quietly remarked Mrs. Cradock.

"But such being the case, Mrs. Cradock, I cannot see what can be your motives in seeking me, if they are merely to inform me of what I already know."

"Probably not. But now I will tell you that of which you do not seem to be aware—viz., that at the time Miss Chudleigh, as she called herself, was married to the Duke of Kingston, she was already the wife of another, and that other is still living."

"Ah, if you can prove the truth of what you

say, this shall not be the worst day's work you have done. How do you know she was married to another at the time she became the wife of the Duke, my uncle?"

"Because I happened to be present at the ceremony which made her the wife of the Hon. Captain Harvey, of the Royal Navy, now, by the death of his father, the Earl of Bristol."

Mr. Meadows drew a long breath.

"Are you—are you quite sure of what you say?"

"Quite."

"Then there is the register of the marriage to be obtained somewhere? Where was she married the first time?"

"In the Chapel Royal, at Whitehall."

"And to Captain Harvey?"

"To the Hon. Captain Harvey."

"And the register, then, can be easily examined?"

"No, that is destroyed."

"How destroyed?"

"By the bride herself, who, when it was too late, repented of her haste in marrying Captain Harvey."

"But are you sure of that fact?"

"Quite sure, for she showed me the original, which had been torn from the register kept in the church."

"But its destruction must be apparent to any one who will take the trouble to examine it."

"Perfectly so; for I have seen the register, and the missing leaf makes a decided gap in the entries."

"Mrs. Cradock, can you come with me to-morrow morning, and let me see for myself that the register has been torn, and then I will reward you for your trouble."

"I will accompany you, sir. My brother-in-law happens to be the sexton, and he can easily get admission to the registers."

"Good. And now, Mrs. Cradock, may I ask why you have sought me out to tell me all this?"

"Because I felt that you, like I, would have but one feeling in the transaction—viz., revenge."

"I have been badly treated, certainly; and truly I have no cause to love this haughty beauty, whom I never saw but once, and then it was to be almost insulted by her, I may say."

"And I, too, have been badly treated, sir; good services forgotten. But never mind, I will be with you by ten to-morrow morning."

Mrs. Cradock, as the reader may suppose, took her departure, well pleased with the success of her mission.

"Now," said Mr. Meadows, pacing up and down the library; "now, if all that this woman has told me turns out to be correct, I will at once prefer a bill of indictment against this Duchess of Kingston for bigamy, and have no doubt but I shall be amply revenged for the injury she has done me."

When Mr. Meadows returned to the drawing-room, where he had left his wife and daughter, he was met by a look of inquiry from each.

"Evelyn, you are troubled; what has passed since you left us?" said Mrs. Meadows.

Mr. Meadows threw himself into a chair.

"I have received information, Emma, which if —as I have no doubt I shall be able—I can verify to-morrow morning, may—indeed, will—place me on a very different footing. The will of my uncle—the late Duke of Kingston—was drawn up in favour of his wife."

"Yes, Evelyn—yes! but I thought you had no ideas of ever recovering your rights—for such, indeed, they were—for that will, while it made the Duchess sole possessor of all his property during her lifetime, dispossessed you entirely in favour of your brothers."

"I know all that; but the Duchess was not his lawful wife."

"Not his wife! what mean you, Evelyn! Why the marriage excited the wonder and admiration of the town."

"But she was married already to another, and therefore, she committed bigamy when she married the Duke."

Mrs. Meadows looked astonished.

"Is it possible?" was all she could say.

"It is not only possible, Emma, but too probable, with a woman so vain and fickle as the Duchess. But, to-morrow morning I am going to satisfy myself that the register of the marriage was removed from the book by Catherine Chudleigh herself; because, at the last moment, she fancied she would rather not feel that she was tied to Captain Harvey, whom she had pretended to love."

"How monstrous!"

"It is, indeed; and I feel that if I can be the means of exposing this woman to the world's scorn, she richly merits the disgrace that must be hers."

Ten o'clock the next morning, saw Mrs. Cradock true to her appointment, standing on the step of Mr. Meadows' house.

"Good morning, Mrs. Cradock!" was the greeting she received from Mr. Meadows, as he appeared in the hall, ready equipped for the little expedition to Whitehall.

"Good morning, sir! I am glad you are ready, as I have appointed to be at the chapel by half-past ten."

Together they proceeded to Whitehall, where they were met by the sexton, who had been previously named by Mrs. Cradock, to be at the appointed place at a quarter past ten.

They were not long in effecting an entrance to the little chapel, as the sexton was provided with the necessary keys.

The little chapel gained, the iron chest containing the registers of the births, marriages, and deaths were next produced.

The particular one was soon selected, and in an incredibly short time, Mr. Meadows had the satisfaction of seeing that he had not been deceived by Mrs. Cradock.

There were unmistakable signs of the missing register.

"It is enough—it is enough, Mrs. Cradock! I am satisfied; and for the present take this as an earnest of what may still be yours."

As he spoke Mr. Evelyn handed to Mrs. Cradock a well-filled purse.

At the door of the little chapel they separated.

In the course of a few days, Mr. Field, the solicitor of the Duchess of Kingston, received notice that an indictment against the Duchess, for bigamy, had been preferred, and had been duly returned a true bill.

The same notice urged upon him the necessity of immediately advising the Duchess to return to England, so that she might plead to the indictment, in order to prevent a judgment of outlawry.

On reading the notice, Mr. Field, it must be confessed, begun to feel that he had been rather premature in his self-gratulations in ridding himself of Mrs. Cradock's importunities, for he did not entertain a doubt but that she was at the bottom of the transaction.

He lost no time, therefore, in writing to the Duchess of Kingston, and enclosing her a copy of the notice which had been served upon him, and strongly urged her to neglect no time in hastening to England.

CHAPTER XXXVIII.

THE DUCHESS OF KINGSTON FINDS THAT THERE IS NOT UNMIXED HAPPINESS IN THIS WORLD. —THE UNWELCOME DOCUMENT. — THE VISIT TO THE BANKER.—THE PISTOL.—CONCORD.

CATHERINE was seated in her luxurious boudoir in the Palace, which had been her residence since she had been in Rome, listlessly turning over the leaves of a book of rare engravings which had been left for her inspection by one of her many admirers.

There was an air of calm repose upon her fair face, and any one to have gazed upon her youthful beauty would never have supposed that so many years of her life had been passed in wild excitement or disreputable intrigue.

To outward appearance, the Duchess of Kingston was still as beautiful and fascinating as had been the Catherine Chudleigh of other days; but the freshness, so to speak, of her better nature had departed, and had left her only the gay woman of the world and the heartless coquette.

She was roused from her contemplations, however, on the morning in question by an official looking packet being brought to her by one of the servants, who merely said, as he presented it to her on a silver salver, "This arrived this morning, your Grace; but I thought it would be quite time enough to trouble you with it at a later hour."

"Good Anthony, you are ever thoughtful," said the Duchess; and as she spoke she bestowed upon the man a smile, which, at all events, made him think her not only the most beautiful, but the most captivating woman he had ever seen.

As soon as Catherine found herself alone, she opened with some degree of curiosity the official-looking packet.

Scarcely, however, had she glanced at the first few lines, than the packet fell from her hand, and she sat as though she were paralysed.

Her lips moved, but no sounds came from them at first, and she pressed her hands upon her eyes as if to shut out from them the sight of the fatal document.

"Shall I never cease from being persecuted on account of that man?" at length burst from her lips.

"What can it mean? Who is busy with my name now? But I will read further."

She raised the document from the floor, and continued reading for some time; at length she said, "Cradock— Cradock? Ah, yes! I remember now. Louise was to be married to a man of that name, and she has betrayed me! Oh, fool, fool that I was to put any trust in her! But I must lose no time. I must return to England and see what is to be done. But I must see Jenkins first, I must have money—he must advance me a sum of money that will, at all events, suffice to place at my disposal the means of bribing this woman to withhold her dangerous testimony."

Mr. Jenkins had in reality large security in his hands for the advance of such sums of money as the Duchess might require. Catherine had had the forethought to do this as soon as she was settled in her new home.

She now rang for her maid, and, dressing herself with more than ordinary care, she proceeded at once to the house of the wealthy banker.

But Mr. Jenkins had also received notice of the proceedings which had been instituted against the Duchess; and, fearing that she would inevitably lose the vast fortune she had acquired, so to speak, under false pretences, he resolved not to see her if she called upon him, as he felt certain, indeed, she would not fail to do under the circumstances.

The consequence was that Catherine called upon the banker three several times, but each time was told he was from home, and was not expected to return for some days.

The Duchess then wrote, apprising Mr. Jenkins of her intended journey, and demanded a sum of money in order to enable her to return to England.

Still, however, he treated her letters with silence, and her applications to see him were as fruitless as had been her former visits.

There was a look of determination upon the beautiful features of the Duchess, which would in all probability have induced the banker to reflect twice before he trifled with her could he but have seen it.

It was on the occasion of the fourth denial, that Catherine turned from his door with the determined look we have mentioned.

When she entered her boudoir, she went immediately to a beautifully inlaid Indian cabinet, and took from thence an elegantly mounted pair of pistols.

"I think now," she murmured to herself, as she secreted the weapons—"I think now that I shall be able perhaps to convince this banker that I am not a person to be trifled with."

The Duchess then stepped into the carriage, which had been placed at her disposal, and ordered the coachman to drive again to the house of Mr. Jenkins.

Again she inquired if Mr. Jenkins had returned, and was at liberty to see her.

"He has not yet returned, your Grace," was the answer to the demand.

"Then, I will wait here until he does return," replied the Duchess, calmly, as she seated herself upon the doorsteps, which she kept open with the muzzle of one of her pistols.

Now, as it may be supposed, the banker was

not so far off as he wished the Duchess to suppose, and was by no means pleased with the appearance things were assuming.

"Confound the woman!" he muttered to himself. "It will never do to let her sit there. I shall be a byword to the whole city."

Catherine had not held this position for more than a quarter of an hour, when Mr. Jenkins himself appeared at the outer door.

"Really, Duchess," he began, in as plausible a voice as he could assume under the circumstances, "I was not aware——"

"Oh, never mind," said Catherine, replacing her pistol in a pocket of her dress which seemed to have been made for the purpose,—" never mind, Mr. Jenkins; no apologies. I want some money, that is all."

"Will you allow me to lead you to a more comfortable place for discussing your affairs than here on the doorsteps. Allow me, your Grace."

Mr. Jenkins gallantly offered his arm to the Duchess, and led her into the library.

As soon as the door was closed, Catherine made him acquainted at once with her position.

"And now for the money, Mr Jenkins. Give it me at once, for I have yet much to do."

"Really, my dear Duchess," began Mr. Jenkins.

"Now, no nonsense," replied Catherine. "Give it me at once."

"But, really, I have not so large a sum in the house at the present moment——"

"Nonsense! stuff! Give it me at once, or it will be the worse for you!"

As she spoke, Catherine drew out the pistol again, and presented it full in the face of the discomfited banker.

"Mercy! murder!"

"Will you give me the money I require, or must I fire?" asked the Duchess.

"For mercy's sake, take away that murderous-looking weapon, and you shall have whatever you require!"

"Here?—on the spot?"

"Here, on the spot."

Catherine slowly removed the pistol, and Mr. Jenkins hoped that he would be able to reach the door of the apartment, when he never doubted but that some assistance would arrive at this fearful juncture.

But Catherine was too wary.

"Have a care! If you value your life, Mr. Jenkins, you will not tempt me to pull this little trigger, which I certainly shall do, if you attempt to leave this room!"

"But you dare not murder me?"

"Dare not? Who dares to say 'dare not' to me, I should like to know?"

"But everybody would know that you had murdered me, and your own life would pay the forfeit."

Catherine laughed.

And there was a light-heartedness—a scornfulness in her laugh—which drove the banker almost to phrenzy.

"But would that knowledge—I mean, the knowledge that I had murdered you—bring you back to life, you stupid old man?"

A new light seemed to break in upon the bewildered brains of the old banker; and he returned to the chair he had quitted, and drawing from his pocket a small key, he opened one of the drawers in the table.

He took hastily from the drawer a roll of bank-notes, and, glancing at them, he handed them to the Duchess, saying, "Here, madam, is the sum you require: now go, and let me never see your face again."

"Not if I can help it," replied Catherine, saucily; "for you really do look shockingly old and ugly!"

With this, she bowed, and left the room, leaving the discomfited banker a prey to the most unenviable reflections.

Now that she had obtained all that she desired as regarded the means of proceeding to England, Catherine at once made preparations for her journey thither.

As she took leave of her friends and admirers at Rome, no one would have suspected, for one moment, that beneath that gay exterior the Duchess hid an aching heart.

She had not proceeded far on her journey, however, when she found it impossible longer to battle against a feeling of great weariness and distress; and just before reaching the Alps, orders were given to put up at the first place that looked at all likely to be suitable, for that the Duchess was seriously ill.

A small inn by the roadside was the only accommodation which offered.

The Duchess was carried from her carriage; a raging fever set in, and before night she was delirious.

Bella Steinburg watched beside her friend, but she might have been miles off for all the notice the Duchess took of her.

She raved incessantly of Harvey, the Duke of Hamilton, Captain Johnstone, the Jacobite spy, —all, in fact, who had played any active part in her chequered career.

The predominant feeling in her mind appeared to be that she was confined in some cell in Newgate.

"Take me out! take me out! Kingston— Hamilton! Help! help!"

It was in vain that Bella strove to soothe her troubled mind. She knew her not; but, on the contrary, seemed to fancy that she was the unhappy cause of all her misery.

"False, false! You have betrayed me! Go —go from my sight!"

These words almost broke the heart of the faithful Bella, who the more she strove to pacify, seemed only to add to her distress.

"You must leave her," kindly said the doctor, one evening when the paroxysm had been more violent than usual—" leave her to the care of the nurse, and in all probability to-morrow the fever will have abated.

Poor Bella supplicated with many tears to be allowed to watch beside her much-loved friend, promising however to keep out of her sight.

To this proposition the kind-hearted physician could make no objection.

About midnight Bella had the satisfaction of seeing the patient fall into a deep sleep—such a sleep as had not visited her eyelids since the commencement of the attack.

Hour succeeded hour, and day began to dawn, but still the Duchess slept the deep, calm sleep of exhaustion.

KATE DISGUISED AS A MIDSHIPMAN.

About ten o'clock the next morning Bella was rewarded by seeing Catherine's eyes fixed upon her with a look of recognition.

"Dear, dear Catherine, you are better?" asked the agitated girl.

"Yes, I think I am, Bella; but I am very weak. Have I been ill long?"

"Ten days."

"Ten days! Merciful providence, I must proceed this very day."

"Yes, yes, dear, you shall; but lie quietly until after the doctor has been to see you."

Bella feared that the natural impetuosity of the Duchess would get the better of her reason, and she knew not what to say to prevent any imprudent step on the part of her friend.

But she need have had no such fears, for the Duchess was by this time fully aware of the utter impossibility of her rising that day, at all events.

No. 13,—KATE CHUDLEIGH.

Towards the end of the third day, however, Bella was rejoiced to see her looking more like herself as she said, "Bella, if you will make all the necessary preparations, I think I shall be able to pursue this dreadful journey to-morrow."

"Yes, yes, dear; do not exert yourself, everything is prepared. I have had so much time on my hands, and was so afraid of you seeing me, dear, that I was forced to seek any employment to keep myself from contemplating you too much. Oh, Catherine, it was dreadful to hear you talk as though I, your own faithful Bella, had injured you."

And the affectionate, infatuated girl laid her head upon the Duchess's pillow, and wept bitterly.

"Hush, hush, Bella; do not think any more about it. I can sleep now, and to-morrow I will embark for Dover."

A refreshing sleep stole over the Duchess; and the morning, which was bright and spring-like, found her even stronger and in better spirits than could have been expected under the circumstances.

The journey was by no means so trying to the invalid as Bella expected it would be; and on her arrival at London Bridge the Duchess ordered a post-chaise, and drove at once to Kingston House.

"Welcome, welcome, Duchess!" were the first words which greeted her ear as she was led up the steps of the mansion by her faithful friend, Bella Steinburg.

"Ah, my Lord Mansfield!" exclaimed Catherine, some of her old coquetry returning. "Ah, this is indeed a pleasure! But what are they going to do with me? Shut me up in the cell of some horrid prison? Oh, I shall die! I can never endure it!"

As she spoke, the Duchess pressed her hands upon her eyes, and sobbed like a child and as if her heart would break.

"Hush, hush! There, lean upon me!" said the venerable Earl of Mansfield. "Why, what are you frightening yourself about in this fashion? Shut you up in a cell, most certainly not."

"You think they will not?" she asked, looking up into his face with all the simplicity of a child.

"Tut, tut! of course not! Yours is a bailable offence, and here are plenty of friends who are but too pleased to be of the slightest service to you."

At these words, Catherine again looked up, and beheld the Duke of Newcastle, Lord Mountstuart, Mr. Glover, and several other gentlemen of rank, assembled in one of the saloons of the mansion.

"Then I have no longer any fears, gentlemen," she said, gracefully. "I am now only anxious that my trial should take place as quickly as may be, in order that I may return to Rome, where I may have especial business to settle with his Highness the Pope."

But this was only seeming on the part of the fair Duchess.

She dreaded nothing so much as a public trial, for she could not but felt that, in the course of that trial, many revelations would inevitably take place which she was most desirous of keeping secret.

Her staunch friend, the Earl of Mansfield, strove all in his power to persuade her to accept a proposition which had been offered her, which was to give the sum of ten thousand pounds, in order to quash the prosecution, but Catherine, unfortunately for her, trusted too much to her own machinations for getting out of the scrape, and therefore refused the overtures which had been made to her.

"I shall be acquitted, I tell you, my lord; then why should I lavish money upon my implacable enemies, merely for the purpose of enriching them?"

In fact, she went so far as to petition for a speedy trial.

CHAPTER XXXIX.

THE DUCHESS CONTINUES TO CAPTIVATE ALL HEARTS.—THE CONFERENCE.—STRATAGEMS.—THE PLOTTER OUTWITTED. — THE SCHEME FRUSTRATED.—DISAPPOINTMENT.—THE LONELY APPOINTMENT.

BUT it would be impossible for a manœuvring disposition like that possessed by the heroine of this romance of real life, for her to desist long from some scheme or other, which would not only have an element of danger in it, but one also of romance.

There happened to be in the employment of the Duchess a boy of the age of sixteen, who was distantly related to her former servant, Mrs. Cradock.

This boy, like so many before him, conceived a violent passion for the beautiful Duchess, who was not slow to perceive the impression she had made upon the lad, and to use it for her own advantage.

Job Miller, therefore, was no less pleased than surprised one morning to hear that her Grace wished to speak to him in the library.

Growing red and white by turns, the youth reached the door of the library, and there paused, for he could not at that moment have turned the handle, even if he had been assured that, by doing so, he might have aspired to the hand of his beautiful and fascinating mistress.

"This won't do; I must go in, that's certain!" said the boy, giving his hair another touch, which he hoped would prove irresistible. "I will go in."

He turned the handle, and then his heart gave such a bound as almost to take away his breath.

"Come in, Job," said a sweet voice.

Job did go in, and felt as though he were standing in the presence of an angel.

If Job could but have reasoned more correctly, he would have told himself that he was, in reality, the superior of that heartless, beautiful woman, whose whole life had been a scene of intrigue and falsehood from beginning to end.

But Job did not reason correctly, and so he stood bewildered in the presence of his idol.

"Well, Job, I have sent for you, to ask you a few questions."

"Yes, ma'am—yes, my lady—I mean, your Grace."

Catherine appeared not to notice the confusion of the boy, but went on in her soft accents.

"Have you seen anything of your relative lately—Mrs. Cradock, I mean?"

"Yes, ma'am—I mean, yes, your Grace. I see her here sometimes."

"Here! How long ago is it since she was here, Job?"

It was surprising to see how calmly the Duchess put the question, when it lighted a volcano in her heart.

"One day last week, your Grace."

"And what did she come here for, Job?"

The boy turned very red, and hesitated.

"Never mind telling me if you had rather not, but I fancied you would be glad to be of service to me."

Deceitful Catherine! Full well she knew

that that boy would have given his heart's blood to be of service to me.

But her words had the effect she intended they should.

"Oh! don't think that I don't want to serve you—please don't," said the boy, almost beside himself with grief. "But I thought, perhaps, you would be angry."

"Angry, Job? Angry with you? Have I not told you that I sent for you because I knew you would serve me if you could; and you can serve me by telling me why Mrs. Cradock came here last week."

"To see Mr. Evelyn Meadows, your Grace."

"Indeed?"

Catherine forgot the part she had intended to play, and rose to her feet with flashing eyes; but happening to cast them upon the boy, his look of dismay recalled her to herself.

"To see Mr. Evelyn Meadows. Do you know what she came to say to Mr. Meadows?"

"No, your Grace."

"Well, now Job, I want to see Mrs. Cradock. Do you think you can manage to let her know that I wish to do so?"

"Oh yes, your Grace, quite easily."

"Stop!" said the Duchess, as if a sudden thought had struck her. "Tell Mrs. Cradock that I will meet her in one of the alcoves of Westminster Bridge, to-morrow night, at ten o'clock, disguised as a Midshipman of His Majesty's Navy."

"Oh! how beautiful you will look!" exclaimed the boy, with fervour, forgetful of all else but his admiration for the Duchess.

Catherine could not forbear a smile at the boy's looks, and tone, but she made no comment whatever with regard to his behaviour.

"And now, Job, you must remember my instructions. You must tell your relative that she will recognise me, by my using the word 'negociation.' Stay, I will write it on a piece of paper."

The Duchess approached the table, and taking up a scrap of paper, wrote upon it the word "negociation."

"There now, Job," she said, with a smile, "you will not forget the word, will you?"

"It isn't likely I shall ever forget anything you have ever been so good as to say to me," replied the boy, with natural courtesy.

When Job left the boudoir, he naturally directed his steps towards the servants' hall, where he found the domestics in a state of great excitement and curiosity, to know what the Duchess could want with him.

"Here he is!—here he is!" were the words that struck upon his ears, as he neared the hall.

Fain would he have escaped to the stables—to the cellars—anywhere, in fact. so long as he might escape the questions he felt sure would pour in upon him; but it was too late, he was seized by a footman, and dragged into the servants' hall.

"Now young'un, tell us all about it," cried his tormentors.

The boy fought vigorously for a few minutes, but he had sufficient wit to see that they were too many for him, and he accordingly began to cast about in his mind what he had better do under the circumstances.

"Speak!" again cried the man who still held him by the collar. "What have you been talking about to the Duchess?"

"I haven't been talking at all," said the boy, doggedly.

"Then what has she been talking about? Tell us directly, or we'll beat you black and blue."

"Well, then, if you must know, her Grace only wanted to speak to me about the grey pony."

"Oh! about the grey pony. Now tell us what followed."

"Nothing."

"Nothing? It's of no manner of use telling us such a tale as that; know we will, what passed between you, won't we Mrs. Upton?"

"Certainly! Mr. Rea," replied the housekeeper; "it is only proper that two individuals like ourselves, who are at the head of this establishment, should know exactly all that is taking place. So I should advise you to tell the truth at once, Job, or I shall find means to make you."

Job looked dubious.

He was turning over in his mind whether or not he should invent something to appease their curiosity, but then it occurred to him that if the Duchess had intended what she said to be kept a secret, she would have intimated as much, so he made up his mind then and there, to tell the whole truth.

Little did he suspect the effect the truth would have upon his hearers.

"Well, we are waiting. Tell us directly what else passed."

"Well, then, if you must know, the Duchess wishes to see my aunt, Mrs. Cradock."

The butler and the housekeeper exchanged glances, and the former said, "Oh, indeed! and when does she wish to see Mrs. Cradock, pray?"

"To-morrow night, at ten o'clock."

"Here? In this house?"

"No. In one of the alcoves of Westminster-bridge," replied the boy.

"Then her grace is going to meet her? Will she be alone?"

"Yes; and won't she look lovely, neither! She is going to dress herself up like a midshipman of his Majesty's navy."

Mrs. Upton held up her hands, and for a moment nothing but the whites of her eyes could be seen.

Mr. Rea burst out laughing.

"Well, this is a capital joke," he said. "I'll just witness this romantic interview."

"Well, now, Mr. Rea, perhaps you'll just let me go, for I've got to see Mrs. Cradock to-night."

"Oh, leave all that to me—I'll manage all that."

"But I must. The Duchess believes I am even now on my road to her house.

"But I expect you just to remain where you are. Upon second thoughts I will make sure of my prisoner. Go in there, young man, and when dinner is ready you shall not be forgotten; and, hark ye, my young friend, if I hear a sound I will come in and teach you how to hold your tongue."

"But will you go to Mrs. Cradock, Mr. Rea?"

"Of course—of course. Didn't I say I would manage all that part of the business for you?'

This assurance seemed to re-assure the boy, and he went quietly enough into the butler's pantry, and heard the key turned in the lock.

"Well, here's a pretty go," thought Job; "but it's better to keep in with Rea and Mother Upton; and after all, what does it matter as long as the Duchess sees Mrs. Cradock?"

As soon as Mr. Rae and the housekeeper found themselves alone, enjoying something warm in the shape of grog before retiring to rest for the night, the following conversation took place between them:—

"Well, Mrs. Upton, tell me," said the butler, "what you make of all this masquerading for the sake of meeting Anne Cradock, on Westminster-bridge."

"Think! Mr. Rea," replied the housekeeper; "why I think it is dreadful to talk about such things. The idea of a woman, and a duchess, too, dressing herself up to look like a man—I'm shocked!"

Mr. Rae did not seem to see that part of the transaction exactly in the same light; on the contrary, he was rather amused at the Duchess's eccentricity. However, he did not mention to his companion his difference of opinion, but only said, "I don't intend the Duchess to see Mrs. Cradock, that is why I have secured Job. It will be fine sport to see her Grace's disappointment when she waits in the alcove of the bridge, all for nothing."

"And serve her right, too," said the housekeeper, who never had forgiven Catherine for being so beautiful.

"But I think Mr. Evelyn Meadows ought to know of the little arrangement her Grace wished to make with her former servant."

"Of course he ought. Didn't he tell us to keep an eye upon the Duchess's movements when she returned, and that we should be well paid for our trouble?"

"He did—he did! And I intend to go this very day and inform him of this proposed meeting."

"Do so."

We will leave Mr. Rea to carry out his intentions with regard to informing Mr. Meadows of Catherine's intentions, and return to that lady, whom we shall introduce to our readers again about an hour before her departure from Kingston House, disguised as a midshipman.

Bella, as usual, had been assisting her in effecting the change of costume; and as she placed the cap upon the head of her beautiful friend, she could not restrain an exclamation of admiration as she gazed upon her.

"You will let me go with you, dear Catherine?" she said.

"What on earth for, Bella? Do you think then that I look so captivating that I shall have great difficulty in keeping the girls off?" laughed Catherine, in her old strain of coquettish vanity.

"No, no—that is, you do look fascinating, and captivating, and all that sort of thing—of course, you know you do; but suppose any one should recognise you?"

"Never fear, Bella; I don't believe you would know me in this jaunty little cap."

As she spoke, the Duchess settled the cap once more upon her head, and turned to leave the room, but stopping abruptly, she said in a low tone,—

"You go first, Bella, and see that the road is clear. I don't want to meet any of the servants in this costume. You know my reputation might suffer if they saw a handsome midshipman leaving my boudoir."

This was said with one of her arch smiles, which made Bella think her more beautiful than ever.

"All is quiet, said Bella," as she returned, after an absence of some three minutes. "Come, now, and I will open the door for you."

"But the hall-porter?" said Catherine.

"Is in the servants' hall, having his supper," replied Bella.

Catherine now sallied from her boudoir, and, with a light step, and still lighter heart, she made her way towards the front door of the mansion.

Bella had no difficulty in opening it, and, with a beating heart, she watched her as far as she could in the darkness, proceeding at a brisk pace in the direction of the bridge.

"Oh, I hope all will be well!" was her ejaculation, as she re-ascended the grand staircase.

The Duchess, in the meantime, continued her route towards the place she had herself appointed for the meeting to take place between her and Mrs. Cradock; and she was now resolved to offer even thousands of pounds to this woman, if she would not appear against her at her trial, after having refused her, not many weeks previously, a trifling remuneration to withhold her testimony.

"Yes," she said to herself, "I shall succeed now in foiling my enemies; and it is money, and money alone this woman wants, and I will—for I can well afford to be so—be munificent to her."

At length the alcove was reached.

There was no one there.

"I am a little too soon," said Catherine to herself. "I hope she will not keep me waiting here long."

In her impatience, the Duchess began to pace to and fro.

"Past ten o'clock, and a moonlight night!"

"Confound that fellow! Now, I suppose I shall be questioned as to my business here at this hour."

"Past ten o'clock, and a moonlight——Hilloa! who are you?"

The watchman raised his lantern to a level with his eyes, in order to get a better view of Catherine.

"Who are you, I say? Why don't you speak?"

"Go on, old fellow!" said the Duchess, speaking in as manly a voice as she could assume. "Go on, old fellow, and don't interfere with what doesn't concern——"

"But it do concern me; everything concerns me when I am acting in accordance with my duty; and, again I say, what are you doing here at such a late hour?"

"Why, you old spoony, you don't mean to say you fancy I am going to throw myself overboard, do you? What do you think I am doing? If I tell you will you keep the secret?"

The watchman had a slight suspicion floating in his mind that the young man was only making fun at him, so, putting on an authoritative tone, he said, "It will be the safest plan, I see, to convey you at once to the lock-up, so come along, and don't interrupt me in the discharge of my duty."

"Now, really, Mr.—what's your name—you are a most provoking fellow. Don't you see I am waiting here to say good-bye to my sweetheart before I go on another voyage? There, take that; and don't make a third party where two are only necessary."

"Humph!" was all the watchman said, as he pocketed the coin Catherine had had the wit to tender him.

The watchman soon remembered that he had not got to the end of his beat; so, in a much more courteous tone of voice than he had hitherto used, he said, "All right, sir! Tim M'Carthey knows when he's too many as well as any man breathing, so I wishes of your honour good luck and good night!"

The watchman continued his walk, and Catherine was again alone.

Another quarter of an hour elapsed.

"She will not come," she murmured to herself; "but I will wait yet another hour."

Catherine waited for an hour, and yet another hour, and then she felt that she was foiled.

"Let them do their worst," she said, as she shut her teeth firmly together. "I feel sure that I shall yet be acquitted. I will return home."

The Duchess left the alcove, and made her way as rapidly as she could, without attracting notice, to Kingston House, where the faithful Bella was on the watch for her.

"I am foiled—I am foiled, Bella; but I care not!" was all she said.

CHAPTER XL.

THE DUCHESS OF KINGSTON IS PUT UPON HER TRIAL.—THE SPECIOUS ADDRESS READ BY A BEAUTIFUL WOMAN.—THE EXAMINATION OF ANNE CRADOCK.

At length, the day arrived which was to witness the trial of the popular beauty, one who had played her part so successfully in every intrigue, and in every Court scandal.

The morning sun shone bright into the court, and thousands of spectators, some of the highest rank, crowded into Westminster Hall, not so much to hear the results of that remarkable trial, —but many went for that reason solely—but the greater number by far to look upon the Duchess, whom report said was looking more majestically lovely, if we may use the term, than she had ever done in her more youthful days.

Even royalty was present—consisting of the Queen, the Prince of Wales, and other members of the royal family.

No sooner had these high personages been conducted to their places by the Lord Chamberlain than the Duchess entered, accompanied by two or three ladies, her chaplain, her physician, and her apothecary.

As she came forward, a slight flush passed over her face, but she advanced firmly to the bar, and bent low before the royal family.

She then dropped upon her knees, and clasped her hands over her eyes.

All faces were turned towards her—so humble —so beautiful—so innocent even, did she appear in that touching attitude.

Then an official-looking personage rose, and, addressing Catherine, said, in kind tones, "Madam, you may rise."

The Duchess slowly availed herself of the permission; then, bowing once more to the royal personages present, she turned and bent gracefully to the official personage who had addressed her, and then to the members of the House of Peers—all of whom returned her salutation with great courtesy and gravity.

"Silence! silence!" was shouted by the ushers of the court.

Then the Lord High Steward rose, and addressed the Duchess.

"Madame," he said, "it is my painful duty to remind you of the fatal consequences which attend the grave crime of which you are accused —viz, bigamy. To think that one so young— so beautiful—and, from your social position, possessing so much influence—is at once overwhelming and melancholy in the extreme.

"If, however," he continued, "you have any means of proving that what your accusers bring against you is unfounded, then shall I, and all here present, including the august presence which has condescended to honour these proceedings with their countenance and support, be, indeed, rejoiced.

"If, on the contrary, however, what has been alleged is found to be true, then may you, madam, derive some consolation from the knowledge that you are about to be tried by the most liberal, the most candid, and the most august assembly in the universe."

Having delivered himself of this peroration, which really meant little or nothing, the Lord High Steward withdrew to a position a little behind the chair of the Queen.

Then Catherine rose, and, amid the profound silence, drew from the folds of her dress a paper, from which she read, in a clear, distinct voice, asseverations of her innocence of the crime of which she had been accused.

She wished, she said, to impress upon the minds of the august assembly that the agitation she manifested, was not that she felt the consciousness of guilt, but that she was overwhelmed with the painful circumstance of being called before so awful a tribunal to answer to a criminal accusation.

She begged, further, that if she had the misfortune to be deficient in the observance of any ceremonial points, her failure might not be understood as proceeding from any wilful disrespect, but should be attributed to the unfortunate peculiarity of her situation.

The paper further went on to state that she had travelled from Rome in a dangerous state of health, in order to undergo that trial—which she was perfectly sure would be in every way a fair trial—and on the result of which would depend her future honour and fortune.

Having expressed herself as being in every way content to abide by the decision of th august assembly who had met to sit in judgment upon her, the Duchess replaced the paper in the folds of her dress, and gazed around her with an air of such ingenuous candour, that if she had been an entire stranger to those present, they must then and there have acquitted her.

Again the Lord High Steward came forward, and having courteously requested the Duchess to be seated, he begged her to give her attention while she was arraigned on an indictment for bigamy.

He then told her that she must plead to the indictment—in consequence of which she was arraigned.

Then the clerk of the Crown rose, and asked, in a loud voice, "Madam, are you guilty of the felony with which you stand charged?"

Catherine, not in so loud a voice, but so as to be heard distinctly by every person in the court, replied, "Not guilty, my lords."

"How, then, does your Grace wish to be tried?" asked the clerk again.

"By God and my peers," was the brief but comprehensive reply.

"Then God send your ladyship a good deliverance," was the fervent ejaculation of the clerk, and the trial proceeded.

The first witness called was Anne Cradock.

The counsel for the prosecution rose to examine the witness.

"Your name is Anne Cradock?"

"Yes, sir."

"Where did you first see the Duchess?"

"At the house of Mr. Merrill, at Lainston, in Hampshire, during the Winchester races."

"Were you then living in Mr. Merrill's service?"

"No, sir, but in the service of Miss Chudleigh's aunt, Mrs. Hanmer, who was staying on a visit at Mr. Merrill's."

"Do you know whether Captain Harvey visited at Mr. Merrill's?"

"Yes, sir; it was at his house that he and Miss Chudleigh first met."

"Had you any reason for supposing that they were attached to each other?"

"Yes, sir; and Miss Chudleigh told me they were engaged to be married."

"Were you present at the marriage?"

"Yes, sir."

"At what time in the day did the marriage take place?"

"In the evening."

"Where were they married?"

"In the Chapel Royal of St. James's."

"And it was quite dark?"

"Yes, sir."

"Then there were really no means of seeing the features of the persons assembled in the church?"

"There were two wax candles burning on the communion-table, and the light they emitted was quite sufficient for every one to recognise his neighbour."

"Did anything extraordinary take place at the marriage?"

"Yes, sir; there was a great deal of confusion, and the Dukes of Hamilton and Kingston both claimed the lady for their bride."

"Were there any other claimants?"

"Yes, sir; some one fired a shot in at the window, but I do not know who it was."

"But you are quite sure Miss Chudleigh married Captain Harvey?"

"Yes, sir."

The Attorney-General sat down, and Anne Cradock was about to disappear, when the Duke of Grafton rose and detained her.

"I wish to put a question or two to you, Anne Cradock, before you leave. Have you not received a letter, offering you a sum of money if you appeared as a witness against the Duchess?"

After some hesitation, Mrs. Cradock admitted that such was the case.

"From whom have you received this letter?"

"I am not at liberty to say, sir."

"But we must know; so you had better state at once, without further trouble."

"It was from Mr. Fossard."

"And what else was in the letter besides the reward mentioned?"

"Mr. Fossard told me that I might show the letter to the Earl of Bristol, if I liked."

"Then you admit that it was for the sake of pecuniary assistance that you were induced to appear against the Duchess?"

"Yes, my lord."

"That will do."

Mrs. Sophia Pettiplace was the next witness called, but she said little. Indeed, what information she had to give mainly consisted in the fact that she lived with the Duchess at the time of the supposed marriage, but was not present at the ceremony. At last she admitted that she only believed the Duchess herself had told her of it.

Cæsar Hawkins, Esq., was the next witness who was called, and who deposed to the following facts.

The Attorney-General rose, and questioned him at some length.

"Your name, sir."

"Cæsar Hawkins."

"How long have you been acquainted with the Duchess of Kingston?"

"Many years."

"That is scarcely an answer. Can you remember how many?"

"I believe, about thirty."

"Did you ever hear of a marriage between the lady at the bar and Captain Harvey?"

"Yes."

"From whom?"

"Both from the Duchess and also from Captain Harvey."

"At the time of the marriage?"

"Almost immediately after."

"Did you ever have any private conversation with Captain Harvey with regard to his marriage?"

"Yes, once."

"Upon what occasion?"

"Captain Harvey sent for me, and asked me to see his wife, the lady now at the bar, in order that I might induce her to accede to the proposals he wished to make to her to consent to a divorce."

"Did you see the lady and propose the question to her?"

"I did."

"What was the result of your interview with the Duchess."

"She absolutely refused to listen to the proposals."

"Did you ever have any further conversation with the Duchess in regard to the

"Incidentally she informed me, that she was very unhappy, and that she wished that she had acceded to the proposals made to her by Captain Harvey."

"Is that all that ever passed between you and the lady on the subject?"

"On one occasion she told me that she had had an interview with Captain Harvey, and that she had consented to allow him to disavow her marriage with him."

"Is that all she said?"

"No; she said likewise that she had destroyed the proofs of the marriage, the consequences of which had caused her much uneasiness; but since Captain Harvey desired the divorce now quite as much as she did, she no longer dreaded the discovery being made."

"What discovery?"

"That she had removed the register from the book where a record of all marriages was kept."

The Reverend James Trebeck was next called.

The Attorney-General again rose.

"What is your name?"

"James Trebeck."

"What is your profession?"

"I am the Incumbent of St. Margaret's, Westminster."

"Can you tell me if you performed the marriage service for the Duke and Duchess of Kingston?"

"I did not."

"But have you any means of proving that that marriage really did take place?"

"I can; here is the register."

Mr. Trebeck handed the book to the Attorney-General, and the entry was duly read.

"Who performed the marriage ceremony?"

"The Reverend Samuel Harpur."

"Is he in Court?"

"He is, your lordship."

"I need not trouble you further, sir," said the Attorney-General; "let Mr. Harpur be called."

"Mr. Harpur — Mr. Harpur!" was shouted several times, and then a gentlemanly-looking man, in the dress of a clergyman, slowly made his way to the table where he was anxiously awaited.

The Attorney-General spoke.

"Will you kindly look at the lady at the bar, and tell me if you recognise in her the Duchess of Kingston?"

"Most undoubtedly, my lord."

"Why do you speak so positively?"

"Because I myself performed the ceremony which made her the wife of the late Duke of Kingston."

"I have nothing further to ask of you, Mr. Harpur," said the Attorney-General, slightly inclining his head.

Then there was a pause in the proceedings, during which the counsel whispered together, while the Duchess remained almost unmoved by all that had taken place.

To outward appearance, at least. In her innermost heart, however, she felt how mistaken she had been in daring so much for wealth, and power, and influence.

But perhaps it was too late, even if she had the wish to do so—to retrieve the past.

Again the trial was adjourned, for it was get-ting late, and again that remarkable woman left Westminster Hall with as firm a step and head erect, as though she had merely been a spectator of what had been passing within that Court.

Her carriage was in waiting, and she gave her orders to be driven home, in a clear, firm voice.

But as soon as the carriage was set in motion, the Duchess leant back on the luxurious cushions, and something very like a sob might have been heard.

But Catherine was alone, or, probably, she would never have so far forgotten herself as to give vent to the emotions which were contending in her breast.

"Will my enemies prevail?" she sighed, "or shall I yet triumph over them? Methinks all will yet be well, and I shall still be great."

She fell into a musing attitude.

"Yes, great!" she continued. "What else is worth living for, after all? My wilfulness has driven from me all the good. Even Mr. Pultney, who did really love me because he thought I was better than I appeared to be—even he withdraws his countenance, and has not called upon me once since my return to England."

Catherine clasped her hands over her eyes, and unmistakable tears—tears which really did her credit, for they were the offspring of a tardy repentance—trickled through her fingers.

— —

CHAPTER XLI.

THE PRONUNCIATION OF THE VERDICT. — ITS EFFECT UPON CATHERINE.—SHE IS COMPELLED TO SUBSIDE INTO A COUNTESS AT LAST. — AN UNEXPECTED FRIEND.

On the following Monday the court was again sitting, and the trial of the Duchess resumed.

As upon the former occasions, all the high and noble families in attendance upon royalty took their seats to hear the termination of this remarkable trial for bigamy.

The Attorney-General rose at the commencement of the proceedings, and informed the court that the evidence on behalf of the prosecution was at an end.

Then the Lord High Steward rose, amid a breathless silence—all eyes being turned upon the Duchess.

She, as had been the case during the whole of the proceedings, stood calm, cool, and collected.

"Madam," began the Lord High Steward, "you have heard what the witnesses for the prosecution have deposed to, and I would now urge you to plead your defence; and I trust that you will be able so to invalidate their evidence that you may be acquitted of the great crime wherewith you stand charged."

The Duchess gracefully inclined her head as the Lord High Steward uttered these words, and when he sat down Catherine rose.

She drew a paper from the bosom of her dress, and commenced reading it in a firm, clear voice, as follows:—

"My lord and gentlemen,—If I were not perfectly well assured of the justice and equity of those who are sitting in judgment upon my conduct I should tremble for the results of the accumulated evidence against me; as it is, however, I appeal to a higher tribunal—even to the searcher of all hearts, and declare that I never considered myself as lawfully married to Captain Harvey."

There was great sensation in court as the Duchess continued,

"Finding, on my return from the Chapel Royal, the gross deception which had been practised upon me by my aunt, and connived at by Captain Harvey, I made a vow that I would never act the part of a wife to that man—and I never did.

"On the very evening of my marriage with him I escaped from my aunt's house by the window, and ever considered myself as a single woman, and as such, received the addresses of the Duke of Kingston, to whom I gave my hand in marriage.

"I instituted a suit in the Ecclesiastical Court, when my marriage with Captain Harvey was declared null and void; but being anxious for every conscientious as well as legal sanction, I submitted an authentic statement of my case to the Archbishop of Canterbury.

"And what, my lords and gentlemen, was his decision?

"Nothing more nor less than his lordship's decisive and unreserved declaration that I was entitled to marry whom I would; and he even granted and delivered to Dr. Collier a special licence for my marriage with the late Duke of Kingston.

"On my marriage with his Grace, I had the happiness of experiencing every mark of esteem from their Majesties, and from my late royal mistress, the Princess Dowager of Wales, and was everywhere publicly acknowledged as the Duchess of Kingston.

"Under such respectable sanctions and virtuous motives for the conduct I pursued, if your lordships should deem me guilty on any rigid principle of law, I hope—nay, I feel sure, they will attribute my conduct as proceeding from a mistaken judgment and erroneous advice, and will not censure me for intentional guilt."

The Duchess paused, as if in hopes that some remark would fall from the lips of one or other of her judges.

But all was as silent as the grave.

With a little heightened colour Catherine continued,

"I beg, while I am thus permitted to plead my own cause, to be allowed to assure the honourable company here assembled, that I never in a single instance abused the influence I had over my late husband; and so far from endeavouring to engross all his possessions, it was I, on the contrary, who insisted that I was amply provided for, by that fortune, for life, which he, but for my opposition, would have settled upon me in perpetuity."

There was a murmur of approbation, mixed with applause, which was instantly quelled.

"With regard to Mr. Evelyn Meadows," continued Catherine, "I can only say that he has only himself to thank for being set aside in the will of his uncle, the late Duke. His behaviour to me, on two several occasions, was anything but that of a gentleman, or what I should have expected, considering the position I held as his uncle's wife; and I must say that I was pleased to see another nephew, although a younger one, substituted for Mr. Evelyn Meadows."

And now the Duchess paused, and refolded the paper from which she had been reading. After a few minutes' duration she again seated herself.

The Lord High Steward then rose, and requested Mr. Wallace, who acted in behalf of the Duchess, to proceed with the evidence he had to adduce.

Mr. Wallace then rose and said.

"My lords and gentlemen—I have great pleasure in stating, that the evidence I have to produce will prove that Anne Cradock has asserted at different times, and to different people, that she has no recollection whatever of the marriage between Captain Harvey and the lady at the bar, and that she was incited to appear against the Duchess in consequence of various promises which had been made her of sums of money."

Mr Wallace then called Mr. Berkley.

Mr. Berkley answered at once to his name.

"What is your name, sir," asked Mr. Wallace.

"Francis Berkley, sir."

"What are you by profession?"

"I am a solicitor."

"Do you act for the Earl of Bristol?"

"I do, sir."

"Did you ever have any conversation with the Earl of Bristol relative to his marriage with the lady at the bar?"

"I had."

"Tell us what passed."

"On one occasion the Earl informed me that he was very desirous of bringing about a divorce between himself and the present Duchess of Kingston."

"Did he state upon what grounds?"

"He said that she had never been as a wife to him, and that, moreover, he was desirous of entering the marriage state with a young lady whom he had recently met."

"Did he mention any person's name who knew of his marriage with Miss Chudleigh."

"Yes; he told me that Anne Cradock was the only person living who really could and would say that she was present at the ceremony, but that he hoped, for a consideration, she might be prevailed upon to find she had a short memory."

"Then you think that Captain Harvey was desirous of concealing his marriage with Miss Chudleigh?"

"That is my belief."

"Have you ever seen Anne Cradock before you saw her here?"

"Yes, in accordance with the Earl's wishes, I called upon her; and, in the course of conversation, Anne Cradock told me that she expected to be amply provided for after the trial, and, also, that she had influence enough in high quarters to be able to procure a situation in the Custom House for one of her relations."

"Have you any idea what induced her to make this statement to you?"

"None whatever; but I should say that she is just the sort of person to boast of her power and influence."

"Then, Mr. Berkley, I have nothing further to ask you."

Mr. Wallace sat down.

There was an uneasy movement in Court, as

KATE WITH DEBORAH BRAHAM.

though each person expected something extraordinary was about to take place.

The Lord High Steward then rose and addressed their lordships in a tone which indicated profound emotion.

"My lords," he said, "you have heard the evidence on both sides, it is now the duty of your lordships to proceed to the consideration of the case.

"The gravity and solemnity of the occasion," he added, "makes it advisable, as well as necessary, that you should each pronounce your opinions in the absence of of the prisoner at the bar. I shall, therefore, take upon myself to request the lady, who stands accused of this act of felony, to withdraw."

Catherine instantly rose, and was conducted, with some show of ceremony and respect, by the Usher of the Black Rod, to an apartment out of

No. 14.—KATE CHUDLEIGH.

hearing of what was taking place within the precincts of the Court.

There was now a scene of great excitement in Westminster Hall.

Every one seemed anxious to press forward, in order to catch, if only a few words of the conversation which was being carried on in low tones at the table, round which the Peers who had sat in judgment upon the Duchess were seated.

But all their efforts were vain, and after many ineffectual struggles to accomplish that which was impossible, the spectators were obliged to content themselves with waiting patiently for the return of the prisoner in order to come at their lordships' decision.

There was then a cry for silence, and the Usher of the Black Rod was desired to place the prisoner again at the bar.

Catherine re-appeared, and there was a look of anxiety, not unmixed with curiosity, upon her countenance, as she re-entered the Court.

Then the Lord High Steward rose, and, addressing himself to the Duchess, said : " Madam, it is my painful duty to inform you that their lordships have given their most mature and careful deliberation to the evidence which has been adduced against you, as well as the testimony of the various witnesses who have been called in your behalf ; and the result of their deliberation is that they pronounce you guilty of the felony of which you stand indicted at this bar."

Catherine started, and seemed about to speak, but the Lord High Steward, as though not noticing her intention, continued.

" It remains, therefore, for me only to ask, madam, if you have anything to say, or any reason to give, why judgement should not be pronounced against you ?"

The Lord High Steward paused, as though waiting for her to reply.

The Duchess, for a moment, seemed to gasp for breath ; then, making an effort, she controlled her emotions and quietly handed to him a paper.

He again handed it to the clerk, who was sitting at the table, who read aloud the following words :—

" I plead the privilege of the peerage."

A silence succeeded the reading of these words, which was broken by Lord Mansfield, who rose and whispered something across the table to his colleagues.

A consultation now appeared to be taking place amongst their lordships ; while Catherine stood, now pale and beautiful as a statue, her hands clasped, and her eyes fixed upon their faces, as though she would by that means read what was passing at that table.

But she heard not a word, and months seemed to her to be concentrated into the short space of time which intervened between her return to the bar and the announcement of their decision.

Then the Lord high Steward turned, and again addressed her.

" Madam," he said, " their lordships have considered your plea, and have agreed to allow it. As Countess of Bristol you will leave this Court, upon paying the usual fees."

At these words, Catherine turned of a deadly pallor.

She bit her lip until it bled.

She clutched nervously to the front of the bar, but all would not do.

Nature was fairly overcome, and she fell fainting into the arms of some of her ladies.

There was a murmur of pity as the mass of spectators witnessed the effect produced upon the Countess by the declaration of the judgment, and at that moment sympathy, however ill-placed, appeared to be the only feeling which reigned in every heart.

It was Bella Steinburg who was the first to rush forward and raise Catherine's head gently upon her arm.

" And this is what they have reduced her to !" she exclaimed, passionately. " It was jealousy—

nothing but jealousy, that made all the world her enemy—jealousy of her beauty—jealousy of her wealth ——"

A gentlemanly man here stepped forward, and placed his hand firmly but kindly upon the shoulder of the excited girl.

" Hush ! hush ! What you say is well meant, but your affection for the Countess of Bristol must not allow you to impugn either the justice or the judgment of those who have so patiently investigated this sad case. Stand aside, and allow me to convey the lady to a less conspicuous place."

Bella involuntarily drew back, and the stranger making nothing of Catherine's light weight, raised her in his arms, and bore her from Westmiester Hall.

In the ante-room, to which she had been conveyed, Catherine, after the application of such restoratives as were to be had on the spot, showed some signs of returning consciousness.

She opened her eyes languidly, and fixing them upon Bella, who was tenderly chafing her hands and temples, she said, faintly, " What has happened ? Am I to be shut up in some horrible prison house ?"

" No, no—a thousand times, no !" cried Bella ; " All is well, and, as soon as you have sufficiently recovered, your own carriage will convey you whithersoever you may please to direct."

" What—home to Kingston House ?"

Bella looked as though she knew not what to say, but the stranger who had carried the Countess into the ante-room, here came to her assistance.

" I should advise you, madam," he said, speaking in low tones, " to seek some other home under the present circumstances."

" Sir ?" said Catherine, in a haughty voice.

" Nay, believe me, I advise you for your good ; perhaps if I tell you that I am Sir Stafford Guy, you will believe that I am only actuated by the purest friendship."

" Sir Stafford Guy—Sir Stafford Guy," mused Catharine, as she gazed inquiringly into his face.

" Who had the happiness of once being of service to the most charming of her sex," replied Sir Stafford Guy, with a courtly bow.

" Of service to me ? Upon what occasion ?"

" When you were surrounded by a party of Mohawks, some few years back."

Then Catherine, or the Countess of Bristol, for by that title must she now be known only to the reader, remembered that memorable night, when she was returning to Mabledon House, accompanied by the brave and gallant Duke of Hamilton, how they had been assailed by a party of Mohawks, and, but for the timely aid of Sir Stafford Guy, she would inevitably have been subjected to insult, and in all probability much personal danger.

As memory brought to her mind the scenes of that night, a feeling of gratitude took possession of her, and she extended her hand to Sir Stafford Guy, saying, as she did so—

" I will trust you, and believe that you advise me for my good. I will go to Mabledon House ; there, at least, I know I shall not be intruding."

" Indeed—indeed, you will not ; and it is because I am the bearer of a message from Mr. Pultney, that you see me here."

"Ah! He then has not forsaken me."

"Far from that; he thinks that this is the time on the contrary, to prove his sincerity."

CHAPTER XLII.

CATHERINE IS AGAIN RE-ESTABLISHED IN MA-BLEDON HOUSE. — TRUE FRIENDSHIP. — THE MYSTERIOUS BILLET. — MUTUAL CONFIDENCE. — THE RESOLUTION CARRIED OUT.

A PANG of regret shot through the heart of the Countess, as she remembered how heartlessly she had trifled with the affection of that true and noble heart.

But she uttered not a word.

Bella bent over her affectionately, and as she did so, she whispered—

"Are you well enough to leave this place, it feels stifling to me?"

"Yes, Bella—I will go."

"Permit me," said Sir Stafford Guy, advancing, and offering his arm, respectfully.

Catherine did not decline the proffered assistance, and Sir Stafford led her gently towards the door.

There was still a number of persons lounging about the precincts of Westminster Hall, and Sir Stafford Guy looked annoyed.

"Wait here," he whispered. "If you will allow me, I think it will be advisable to dismiss your carriage, and mine will be at your service to convey you to Mabledon House, if that be your destination."

Catherine felt the delicacy and expediency of Sir Stafford Guy's advice, and bowed her head in token of assent; for her heart was too full to be able to utter her thanks.

Sir Stafford Guy having beckoned Bella to advance, and take his place by the side of the Countess, quickly disappeared amongst the crowd.

As the Countess and Bella were standing almost entirely concealed by a pillar, a man came forward hurriedly from the crowd, looking anxiously in every direction.

Both Bella and the Countess remarked the man, but neither of them gave utterance to the thoughts which his presence suggested.

At length he disappeared from their view.

Then Catherine spoke.

"Oh, Bella, he is gone. I feared he was looking for us."

"So did I. But why should he be looking for us? Did you recognise him?"

"Yes."

"Who was he?"

"I know him not by name, but I saw him once, at a house were terrible things were taking place."

Catherine shuddered, for she remembered the beautiful woman who had been executed in that strange house, the night she was carried from her aunt's house, by Captain Johnstone, in order to escape from the presence of the husband she learned too late to detest.

Just at this moment she was startled by feeling a hand laid upon her arm.

"Silence! Read! And attend to the advice of a friend."

As Catherine turned she beheld the same man she had before noticed.

He placed a small folded paper in her hand, saying in a low tone, so as to be heard only by her.

"A friend sends you this: follow the advice it gives, ere it be too late."

The Countess would have asked this mysterious messenger the name of her unknown adviser; but, before she could utter the words, the man had disappeared among the crowd.

Catherine looked irresolute, as she said to Bella, "What, do you think, is the meaning of all this? Shall I read this paper?"

"It can do no harm," replied Bella, "to read it; but as to following the advice contained in it is quite another thing."

Catherine was about to open the letter, when she beheld Sir Stafford Guy making his way towards her, through the crowd.

"Not now—not now," she whispered, to Bella. "When we are alone."

At this moment, Sir Stafford Guy stepped up to Catherine, and said, "Now, if you will allow me, I will conduct you to your carriage for the time being."

"My carriage for the time being? What mean you?" cried the Countess.

"Have you so soon forgotten, then," said Sir Stafford, "that I advised you to allow me to dismiss your carriage, while I placed at your disposal my own?"

"True—true—I had forgotten," said Catherine.

Sir Stafford now offered his arm, and in another moment she and Bella were being driven rapidly in the direction of Mabledon House.

There was a look of weariness and exhaustion upon the face of the Countess, which made her look, in Bella's eyes, perhaps more interesting than ever.

The beauty had become more classic—more refined, so to speak; and as she sat, slightly reclining against the luxurious cushions of the carriage, Bella could not but tell herself that she had never gazed upon so sweet a face.

Catherine was roused from her reverie by the carriage stopping suddenly, and looking from the window, she beheld Mabledon House, looking as though it were only yesterday that it owned her for its mistress.

Perhaps the sigh which escaped her was in memory of the chivalrous Duke of Hamilton, with whom she had spent so many happy days, in that very house.

Perhaps it was the remembrance of the disinterested friendship of Mr. Pultney, who, notwithstanding all her follies and all her weaknesses, still held out a hand to shield her from her enemies in this, her great need.

These thoughts, however, passed through her mind like lightning; and, as she slightly touched the footman's arm who assisted her to alight, no one would have detected, in the expression of her features, aught but serenity and triumph.

She went at once to the boudoir in which, in former days, she had delighted to collect around her all that could charm the senses and delight the eye.

As soon as she entered this charming apartment, Catherine threw herself on a divan, and unlike her usual self, began to think—to reflect.

An accidental noise at this moment caused the Countess to turn her head, and, looking up, she beheld Bella looking anxiously at her.

"Well, Bella, what now? Any more ill tidings?" asked Catherine.

"I was thinking, dear, that it would be as well, perhaps, to read that letter the man gave us as we were leaving Westminster Hall."

"I had forgotten it. Yes, I will read it, Bella——no, you read it for me. My eyes ache."

As she spoke, Catherine handed the billet to Bella, who, with a trembling hand, slowly opened it.

"Why, Bella, what makes your hand shake in that fashion, child? You don't suppose there is anything to fear from its perusal, do you?"

Catherine still called Bella "child." It was a term of endearment, so to speak.

"No, but——"

"But what? Would you rather not read it? If so, let me do so."

As she spoke, Catherine held out her hand; but Bella still retained the paper.

"No, Catherine; I was only fearful that it might contain something which would, perhaps, pain you; and oh, dear Catherine, I would rather a hundred times suffer myself, than be the indirect cause, even, of giving you pain!"

"Dear, kind Bella!" said Catherine, with more affection, perhaps, than she had ever expressed for the devoted creature who now knelt by her side; "dear, kind Bella, you will win me back to life again, if you treat me to so much flattery."

Poor Bella looked and felt intensely gratified at so marked a difference in the tone and words of the Countess.

She seated herself on a low ottoman by the side of Catherine, and at once commenced to read the mysterious billet, which read as follows:—

"Seek not to know the writer of these lines, but be persuaded that they come from one who has ever, and will ever wish you well."

"Come," said Catherine, with a look of her old playfulness, "that sounds well; and just fancy, Bella, the writer does not even wish to be known; but go on. Ah! what is the matter? you look pale; let me see."

"No, Catherine, let me read it."

Bella again read from the paper.

"Your enemies are now concocting a plan to confine your person to England, as also to deprive you of your personal property; in fact, I know the writ which is to carry out this project, is actually, while I write, in course of preparation.

"To be forewarned is to be forearmed; slight not the counsel of one who is, in deed and in truth,

"A FRIEND."

Catherine held out her hand for the paper, and seizing it, eagerly read it again.

Then starting to her feet, her eyes fiery with indignation, she gave vent to the passion which she could not control.

"Are they not satisfied yet? What more do they want? Mean, cowardly, dastardly wretches.

Not leave England. I say, I will quit this land, where I have never known aught but unhappiness and disappointment."

Bella, although she had for so many years been accustomed to these fearful outbursts of ungovernable rage, looked perfectly dismayed at the effects the little billet had produced.

She made a step forward, as though she would have clasped Catherine in her arms, but she shrunk back, for there was such an expression upon the features of the Countess at that moment, that she stood silent and irresolute.

"Bella, I will leave England; and this night——"

"Yes, dear. But——"

"But what? Do not seek to oppose me if you love me, for I am desperate."

Bella now ventured a little nearer, and throw her arm round the still slender waist of Catherine, she said, in soothing accents—

"Let us talk over this matter, dear Catherine, and see what is best to be done."

"What mean you by what is best to be done, child? Would you have me stay here because my enemies wish me to do so?"

"No, dear Catherine; but do you not think that if the information contained in this paper be correct—do you not think it would be advisable to frustrate their plans by others?"

"What mean you, Bella?"

"I mean, that if it be the intention of any of your enemies to oppose your leaving England, they will probably set a watch upon you every moment."

"True—true. I had not thought of that, Bella. Let me think—let me think."

The two friends sat long together on that evening, conversing upon the changes which had taken place during the last few years.

"Who would have thought—oh, who would have thought, Bella, that I, the spoilt child of fortune, so to speak—courted, and sought after by the highest in the land—who could have believed it possible that I should now be planning means for flying from my native land?"

As Catherine spoke, she rose and paced the room with hasty steps.

Suddenly she paused as she said—

"I have it. Yes, Bella, to-morrow I will drive through the streets, and appear unconscious of the machinations of these awful plotters; and while I am showing myself to the world as the triumphant Countess of Bristol, do you make our preparations for our departure, for you will accompany me, Bella, will you not?"

"To the world's end," replied Bella, pressing the Countess's hand to her lips.

"Then be it so. And Bella?"

"Yes, dear."

"Send out some invitations for as large a party to dine here as can be conveniently accommodated, next Wednesday."

"Yes, dear; but——"

"But what, Bella?"

"Should you not leave here before then?"

"Are you so simple, Bella, as not to have guessed that on Wednesday next I shall embark for the Continent?"

"But the guests?"

"What care I for the guests. These invitations, do you not understand, Bella, are merely for the purpose of blinding those who have it in their power to stay me. So long as they see me driving about in my carriage, and have an invitation to dine with me on a particular day, I can have nothing to fear."

"But does not the note seem to urge your instant departure?" asked Bella.

"Not at all. It says, on the contrary, that a writ is actually in the course of preparation. It cannot be fit for execution before I am really on my way to Rome."

"Then, I will set about my part at once, dear Catherine."

"Do so; and I will begin by taking my first drive, as soon as the horses can be put in the carriage."

Catherine's toilette on that morning was even, perhaps, more carefully attended to than usual; and certainly, no one, to have looked upon her face, and seen the smiles she bestowed upon several cavaliers, who approached to pay their respects to its beautiful occupant, would have guessed the world of anxiety that was pressing upon her heart at that moment.

The preparations for the journey were concluded by Bella in an incredibly short space of time; and Catherine, ever impetuous, was only too glad to accelerate her departure.

"My good Bella, you have, indeed, been expeditious. Nothing now remains but to convey secretly what little luggage we may have to some place where we may call for it on our route."

"I have thought of all that. But how are you going to travel?"

"Why, I will tell you. At the usual hour to-morrow, my carriage shall drive from the door. At first, no one will know but that I am inside it. Then, I intend to disguise myself in that sailor's suit of clothes, and travel in a post-chaise to Dover."

"The very thing! Oh, Catherine, you are so fertile in resources! I should never have thought of such a capital expedient."

"Of course you would not, Bella," laughingly replied Catherine; "but never mind. You are invaluable to me; for, at least, you are always willing to obey orders."

"And will no one else go with us, Catherine?"

"Not from the house, Bella: but I have apprized Mr. Hampton, who was the captain of the yacht I had built at Rome, of my intention of meeting him at Dover, where he is now staying on business of his own."

"I am glad to hear that you will not be quite alone, Catherine; that is a great relief."

"And why so, you silly Bella? Do you not think I can take care of myself yet?"

"Yes; but you are so beautiful——"

"But you forget that I am to be dressed as a sailor—in fact, I must be your sweetheart, you see—so that my beauty will attract only the admiring gaze of pretty girls who may chance to cross my path."

"I see," said Bella.

"Now go, for I have several things to arrange."

When Catherine was alone, she went to an inner room, where Bella had displayed to the best advantage the different costumes which she had ordered, when first she took possession of Mabledon House.

The smart appearance of the uniform of a captain of the Light Horse, almost determined Catherine to select that one in preference to that of the sailor boy.

"I will try on this one first, at all events," said Catherine to herself, as she took up the sailor boy's suit.

But she soon put it aside, as a sad expression passed over her countenance.

"No—no not this one—not this one. Poor Hamilton used to admire me so much in that costume! The remembrance of him would, I think, dissipate every joyous feeling; and I have yet much to live for. I am still wealthy: and certainly, many would still call me beautiful. This shall be the costume: this officer's dress of the Light Horse."

A tap came at the door of the apartment, and Bella entered.

CHAPTER XLIII.

CATHERINE DISGUISES HERSELF AS AN OFFICER OF THE KING'S LIGHT HORSE, AND MEETS WITH AN ADVENTURE.—THE BROKEN CARRIAGE.—THE RESCUE.—A STRANGE CONFESSION.—THE YOUNG JEWESS.

"WELL, Bella, shall you be as well satisfied with a military as with a naval lover?" asked Catherine, coming forward, dressed in the distinguished-looking uniform of an officer in the King's Light Horse.

"Oh, yes—yes!" cried Bella, with admiration. "You are more beautiful, I think, every day! That costume suits you admirably."

"Very well, then, Bella. We have only to wait patiently for four days to pass away, and then we will bid adieu to England for ever."

"Yes, for ever!" said Bella.

"What are we to do in the meantime?" asked Catherine, in her usual impatient way. "I can't sit with my hands before me, doing nothing, all that time."

"What can you do, Catherine?"

"I don't know, but I must find some kind of excitement, or I shall die of *ennui*. I shall take a stroll to-night in this costume, and then I will turn in the Opera House, and see what is doing there. It will be charming to see Dowagers and their daughters throwing admiring glances at me, which glances I shall, of course, return with interest."

"Be careful, dear Catherine," began Bella.

"Now, Bella, you are a very good sort of creature and all that, but you know nothing about my capital personation of any character which I take into my head; therefore, do not look so scared, but promise me you will wait patiently for my return, and not worry yourself about things that will never happen."

"I will, of course, do anything you tell me, Catherine, but as for not worrying——"

Catherine placed her hand playfully upon Bella's lips.

"Now really, Bella, you are a regular wet blanket, and I will only say this, that if you do worry and feel so as to make yourself look so unlike yourself as you have done lately, I can only say I shall look out for another sweetheart, for I must and will have a pretty girl."

As Catherine spoke she stroked the false moustache she had affixed to her upper lip, and acted the exquisite to such perfection, that even Bella, who was more than ordinarily doleful, could not refrain from laughing.

"Well, well, have your own way, dear," she said, "and I will be content, so long as you promise to love me a little."

It was nine o'clock when Catherine, fully equipped, stepped from her boudoir into the hall, where Bella was anxiously awaiting her.

"Quick, quick! all is quiet! The servants are enjoying themselves, and no one will see you leave the house. Good bye, dear Catherine, and take care that you do not run into mischief."

"Never fear, Bella. Good bye, and mind you are looking cheerful when I return."

As she spoke, Catherine turned from the door of Mabledon House, and was soon lost in the surrounding darkness.

She bent her steps at once towards the Haymarket, where a long line of carriages was waiting to set down their occupants at the Opera House.

The crowd was great, for on that night a new prima donna was to make her debut, and all the elite of London society were expected to be present.

Catherine stood by the door of a carriage, which had come to a standstill, and glancing in, she beheld a pair of admiring eyes fixed upon her face.

"Ah!" thought Catherine to herself, "here is a chance of a little sport. I will keep this carriage in view."

As she looked again, and glanced casually at the other occupants of the carriage, she recognised Mr. Evelyn Meadows.

"Oh," thought Catherine, "one of my foes, and the young girl is in all probability his daughter. I should like to know something more of her."

Scarcely had the thought passed through Catherine's mind, when a great jerk, given to the vehicle from the other side, caused her to step hastily aside.

But it was only for a moment that Catherine was inactive, for she perceived at once that a pole of another carriage had been projected into that in which were seated Mr. Evelyn Meadows and the two ladies whom she supposed to be his wife and daughter.

In an instant, Catherine had wrenched open the door of the vehicle, just in time to save the young girl from being seriously injured.

Instantly she seemed to cling to Catherine, who, even in that moment of terror and alarm, could not but feel amused at the deception she was imposing upon the owners of the injured carriage.

"Follow me! follow me!" she cried, taking the young girl from the carriage, and hurrying with her to the nearest shop, which presented itself.

The truth is, Catherine had no intention of being followed by the father and mother of her fair charge, as she hoped that she might perhaps,

by her instrumentality, be enabled to judge better of the real aspect of her affairs, which were indeed more serious than she chose to allow she believed them to be to Bella.

Mr. Evelyn and his wife were too much terrified at first, to be able to collect their thoughts sufficiently, in order to help either themselves or Blanche, who, as the reader is already aware, was not likely to give either of them any more trouble for the present.

As Catherine, in her military uniform, bore the young girl to the nearest shop, a crowd of persons was of course intent on following her—but the Countess had determined that such should not be the case, so bearing her burden right through the shop into a small apartment just beyond, she spoke in a tone of authority to the old man who was waiting behind the counter.

"Shut the door instantly, and do not let the rabble intrude."

"Yes, sir, if you please."

The little old man came out from his hiding-place, and partly by persuasion, and partly by threats, succeeded in clearing the shop.

"That will do. Now get me some water; this young lady is fainting."

"Yes, sir; yes, your highness."

It is evident that the old man was in doubt as to the rank and title of his visitor.

The glass of water was soon brought, and Catherine had the satisfaction of seeing her charge revive.

On first opening her eyes, the young girl looked round in a bewildered kind of manner, and then, for the first time, she encountered those of Catherine fixed upon her.

"Are you better?" she asked, assuming, as she could so well, the tones of a young man.

"Oh, yes! I am better."

Catherine made a sign to the old man to leave them alone; and when he had left the room, she stepped to the door and closed it.

As soon as she had done this, the young girl seemed at first seized with terror, and shrunk back as if to make her escape; but as she did so, she kept her eyes fixed upon Catherine, and the result of that earnest gaze seemed to be an entire alteration in her feelings and sentiments.

The look of surprise and alarm gave way to one of pleasure and confidence and; and well indeed, might these feelings be engendered by any one who was prepared to take a romantic view of the beautiful and the interesting; for, in addition to the handsome uniform in which the Countess was dressed, there was an exquisite beauty of expression, which no human eye could look upon with indifference.

Catherine was fair, and had a delicate complexion; while the young girl with her raven hair and dark flashing eyes, presented a true type of the daughters of the ancient people, whose claim to beauty is considerable still in those cases where regularity of features is to be met with.

It was evident to Catherine that her young and charming companion had led a secluded life of orientalism, and that none of the conventionalities of modern existence had any weight with her.

She spoke what she thought as freely as those thoughts came to her mind.

"Ah! I could not see you when you stood by the carriage before that dreadful accident; but now, even by this dim light, my eyes tell me you are beautiful. I thought I heard a sound of strife and cries for help; but I see you, and I am reassured and happy."

Catherine's first thoughts certainly were that there must be something the matter with the wits of this young creature, who addressed a perfect stranger in such extraordinary language.

"There was some confusion," said Catherine. "I think the pole of another carriage run into yours. I saw you were in danger, and I rescued you from it. May I know your name?"

"Deborah Braham," replied the girl.

"And who were the lady and gentleman who were in the carriage with you?"

"Only some friends of mine; a Mr. and Mrs. Meadows."

"Oh! And were you going to the opera?"

"Oh, dear, no! they were taking me home, after having spent a long day at their house."

"Well," said Catherine, "I happen to know your friends, then, well, by report. Doubtless, you have heard them speak while you have been staying with them, of the Duchess of Kingston?"

A flush came over the face of the young girl.

"Oh, yes, yes! Do you know the Duchess?"

"Well."

"Then are you——"

Deborah paused abruptly.

"Am I what?" said Catherine, seating herself by her side and taking her hand, which the young girl did not withdraw,—"am I what?"

"Are you, too, in love with her, like everybody else?"

"I thought I was."

"Thought you were?" repeated the young girl, snatching away her hand, impetuously.

"Yes," added Catherine; but I know now that I am not."

"What do you mean?"

"I mean that I am not in love with the beautiful Duchess of Kingston; because now I am looking at one much more lovely than she ever was."

There was a well-pleased look upon the face of the young girl as Catherine said these words.

"And now, Deborah—if you will allow me to call you by that name—will you do me a great favour?"

"Oh, what is it? How can I refuse you anything? I shall think of you by day, and dream of you by night; and if you will promise to let me see you again—I mean when I reach my home—I will do anything you ask."

"Then, Deborah," said Catherine, "if you really love me, you will try and remember all you have heard about the Duchess of Kingston."

"Oh, she is——But I forgot, you are a friend of hers?" said Deborah.

"I am; and therefore I am anxious that you, whom I have such a sincere regard for, should not think her worse than she really is."

"Oh, I have heard that she is vain, and a flirt and coquette, and that she is married to two husbands at once—in fact, everything that is bad."

"Then, Deborah, you must not think badly of her any longer. She was married to her first husband while she loved another, as you say you love me. She found out too late that her aunt and her first husband had been planning and scheming to bring about this marriage, while at the same time they were intercepting the letters she was expecting from the man she did really love."

"Oh, how wicked!" cried Deborah.

"And so you see, dear, this poor girl—for she was but a girl at that time—was more to be pitied than condemned; and do you not think you would have done the same thing if you found out after all that your first lover was faithful to you?"

"I am sure I should."

"Of course you would. And now tell me what else you have heard about her."

"Oh, so many things that I would rather not remember after what you have told me; but there is one thing I think you ought to know, if you are her friend."

"And what is that, dear Deborah?"

"I dare say I ought not to tell you; but I must. Mr. and Mrs. Meadows know some people who have received an invitation to a large dinner party at her house next Wednesday, and they hope by that day that some writ—I think they call it—will be able to be put into execution, so that she will never be able to leave England. I dare say I have not explained myself properly; but I dare say you will be able to understand what I mean."

"Yes, I think I understand. And now, Deborah, I want to say something else to you. Do you know it was very indiscreet of you to tell a stranger that you loved him."

"Oh, yes, it would be to any other stranger; but to you, whom I really love, it cannot be so."

These words were spoken with such an air of simplicity and candour that it was evident that the young girl thought them very conclusive in the way of argument, and Catherine felt that it was of no use contending about the matter.

"Then, now that I find you have quite recovered from your fright, I must bid you adieu," said Catherine; for in truth she wished to see the end of the adventure.

"I see your friend's servants are making their way towards this house; so, as my services will be no longer required, I will now bid you farewell, dear Deborah, in hopes of seeing you again some day."

Deborah looked from the window into the street.

"Are you going to walk in the streets?"

"Yes."

"How strange and delightful it must be to walk in the streets!" sighed Deborah.

"Can it be possible," cried Catherine, "that you have never done so?"

"Never. One of my uncles brought me two years ago from Cairo, and I have never been out except in a coach."

A glance from the window warned Catherine that if she would avoid encountering Mr. Meadows she must leave the shop without delay. Therefore, turning and pressing a kiss upon the jewelled fingers of her strange companion, she turned and left the house just as Mr. Meadows entered it.

The Countess's object now was to avoid being questioned; and she therefore made her way as quickly as she could towards Mabledon House.

"I have had enough for one night; but it has been a most fortunate circumstance that threw me in the way of that young creature. I know now where to look for danger. We shall yet see who is the cleverest—myself or my enemies."

When Catherine reached Mabledon House she was met by Bella, who darted from the portico, and seizing her eagerly by the arm, she said, "Oh, I am so glad to see you safe once more within the walls of Mabledon House. I have been so anxious about you."

As she spoke, Bella opened the hall door with a small latch-key with which she was provided, and she and Catherine went at once to one of the drawing-rooms of the mansion.

CHAPTER XLIV.

CATHERINE BIDS ADIEU TO ENGLAND.—THE DISAPPOINTED GUESTS.—THE ARRIVAL AT DOVER.—THE TRIP TO CALAIS.—CATHERINE REVISITS ROME.—BAD NEWS.

"QUICK, quick, Bella! My desk at once. I must write a letter to Captain Hampton, in order to apprize him of the alteration in my plans, for I must leave England by the early dawn, or it may be too late."

Bella looked bewildered, but, as was her custom, she obeyed with alacrity the orders given her by Catherine.

The writing materials were soon placed at her disposal, and a letter was soon despatched to Captain Hampton, appointing him to meet her at Dover the next day instead of on the following Wednesday, as had been at first agreed on.

This done, Catherine looked and felt less anxious; in fact, there was so much novelty in the excitement which she proposed to herself in frustrating the schemes of her enemies, that she began to regain all her usual spirits, much to the intense gratification of Bella.

After the two friends had been busily engaged in talking over the arrangements for the following day for some little time, Catherine proposed that they should both retire to rest for some little time, in order the better to meet the fatigues of the morrow.

Perdita alone knew of her mistress's intention of leaving England, and a well-filled purse, together with a promise of future favours, were amply sufficient to bind the waiting-woman to her interests for life.

It was agreed before retiring to rest that Perdita should have everything in readiness by an early hour the next morning, and that she was to contrive that at the usual hour the carriage belonging to the Countess of Bristol should be driven from the door into the park.

Their was a smile of satisfaction upon the face of Perdita as she left her mistress.

"I shall be a lady to-morrow, at all events," she said to herself, "for I see no good in the carriage being empty. I shall therefore take a drive myself."

The remainder of that evening was spent by Perdita in packing and arranging for her mistress's departure.

At an early hour the next morning Perdita was standing beside her mistress's bed with a cup of hot coffee on a silver salver.

"Ah, Perdita, is that you?" said Catherine, rousing herself. "I am glad to be awakened, for my dreams were none of the pleasantest. But where is Miss Steinburg?"

"She has been up some hours, my lady," replied the Abigail, "and is now busy with the luggage."

"Is everything ready?"

"Everything, my lady."

"Then assist me to dress, and be sure you remember the instructions I gave you last night."

"Never fear, my lady, you will always find me faithful."

Perdita was a clever waiting-maid, and in an incredibly short time Catherine was equipped for her journey.

When the final touches had been given, Catherine descended to the drawing-room, there expecting to find Bella.

She turned impatiently to Perdita.

"Where is the luggage, and where is Bella? There is no time to lose."

"I thought, my lady," began Perdita, "to have found Miss Steinburg here; but I remember now I heard her say something about going on first with the luggage."

"Ah, to be sure, to be sure; that is a wise precaution. I know where I shall find her. Good bye, Perdita; don't forget to have the carriage ordered at the usual hour."

"No fear of that, my lady. But you are not going out alone, and on foot?"

"Yes, Perdita. I shall meet Miss Steinburg at the corner of St. James's Street, where she will be waiting for me in a post-chaise."

Catherine almost ran down the steps of Mabledon House, for the deserted state of the streets filled her with hope and spirits.

"I would give something," she said to herself, as she tripped gaily along, "to see the blank expressions on the faces of one or two of the old epicures I have invited for Wednesday. Oh, it will be a glorious joke to have them all assembling, and fancying they are going to have a feast, and then to be told by Perdita that her mistress went away two or three days ago, and has not since been heard of."

True to her promise, Bella had made all the necessary arrangements with the post-master, and was impatiently awaiting Catherine, whom, when she did observe emerging from a street opposite, almost cried out for joy.

"Oh, Catherine, I am so glad you have come," she whispered, as she assisted her into the chaise. "It has seemed so long to wait, and I began to get quite frightened."

"Frightened, Bella? What at? In case the post-boy should begin to make love to you?"

"Oh, no, no; not that. You are so full of mischief and fine ideas; but I was beginning to be afraid that some one would pass who knew me, and might inquire what I was doing here all alone."

"Well, could you not say you were waiting for a gentleman?"

CAPTAIN HAMPTON LEARNS KATE'S FICKLENESS.

"Catherine, Catherine, you are so indiscreet! Do not talk so loud, or the man will hear us."

After some further parley, Catherine at last settled herself in the chaise, and the postillion received orders to drive as fast as possible on the road to Dover.

The journey was performed, certainly not so rapidly as journeys are in these days of railroads, but quickly enough even to give satisfaction to the impatient Catherine, who had gradually recovered all her old girlish spirits by the time they reached Dover, where they were met by Captain Hampton, a handsome, gentlemanly-looking man about thirty years of age.

"Ah, you are true to your appointment," cried Catherine, as he gallantly offered his arm for her to alight from the vehicle.

"Nothing but death itself," was the reply,
No. 15.—KATE CHUDLEIGH.

"ought to prevent any one from keeping an appointment with which you honour them."

Catherine's eyes sparkled with gratified vanity; then, pausing abruptly in the middle of a coquettish speech, she said:

"But what has happened? You look as though you had some evil tidings to communicate. What have you to tell me?"

"Then you still have the power to read what is passing in the thoughts, Duchess?" gaily replied Captain Hampton. "I must be careful, or you may sometimes think me presumptuous."

"Nonsense! Don't talk nonsense; and don't call me Duchess. I am only a Countess."

"But still the most beautiful of women," replied Captain Hampton, in a low voice.

"A truce to compliments," impatiently said Catherine. "Tell me what is the matter—what you have heard, for I know you have unpleasant news to communicate by your looks, your manner. Speak! Do not be afraid; I am used to ill fortune, Captain Hampton."

"Then if I must speak——" began Captain Hampton, with some hesitation.

"Was there ever such a provoking creature?" exclaimed Catherine, stamping her foot. "Speak! Of course you are to speak, and not keep me here any longer in suspense."

"Well, then, I have heard from Rome."

"Oh, is that all? I suppose the Pope is in despair at my long absence?"

"Worse than that."

"Worse than that? Then some man who fancied he was in love with me, or I with him, has gone and committed suicide, perhaps! Well, these things cannot be helped, you see, Captain," added Catherine, shrugging her shoulders.

"Probably all that may have taken place," quietly replied Captain Hampton; "but I refer to the much more serious fact that the friar, Father Ambrose, whom you left in charge of your palace and furniture at Rome, has found the means to convert all the property you left in his hands into money, and has absconded."

"Father Ambrose!"

"Even so."

Catherine seemed, for the space of a few minutes, to be transfixed to the spot where she stood, so utterly unexpected were these tidings.

Then she turned suddenly towards the Captain, and laying her hand gently upon his arm, and looking up into his face, almost as ingenuously as a child might have done, she said, "You do not mean this? You are only telling me this just to try me."

"Is it possible that you can think me so cruel as to play you such a sorry joke? It is but too true; and had I not received your note, appointing to be here to-day, I should by this time have been on my way to England to apprise you of the fact, and to ask you what you would have me do."

Catherine no longer doubted of the truth of the sad news that had been imparted to her; but, ever energetic, she did not now allow her presence of mind to desert her.

"Let us go immediately, and see what can yet be done. I have yet some property left in Rome, for I was fortunate enough to deposit the whole of my plate in the public bank, so all is not lost."

"Brave woman!" exclaimed Captain Hampton, in a tone of admiration.

"Why, what would you have? It is of no use sitting down and repining over that which is irretrievable. Let me make the most of what still remains. When can we begin our journey to Rome?"

"This very night, if you please."

"That is right. Thanks. Now, remember, I must have no more gloomy looks about me, for that bores me to death."

"I will be careful not to offend," was the reply of Captain Hampton, as he left Catherine, in order to expedite their arrangements.

But Captain Hampton was doomed to meet with a surprise which he least expected.

When he parted from Catherine, a man, enveloped in a long cloak, emerged from beneath a doorway, and, turning round, followed Captain Hampton rapidly.

At the corner of the first street, he quickened his steps, and then, when he was sufficiently near, he laid his hand firmly, but not roughly, upon his arm.

Captain Hampton drew himself up; but at that moment the gleam from a lamp fell upon the face of the stranger.

"Hargrave! You here?"

"Yes, here and anywhere that I am likely to come upon the track of the heartless seducer of my sister!"

Captain Hampton removed his hand from the hilt of his sword, with which it had been toying for the last few minutes, and his head sunk upon his breast.

"Where is Annie?" at length he asked.

The man in the cloak raised his hand, and pointed to a house not far distant, saying, as he did so, "Beneath that roof lies a dying girl, almost a child still in years."

"And does she curse the author of her misery?"

"Would that I could say yes; but, on the contrary, her wish to see you—her belief that you will arrive, even at the eleventh hour, seems to inspire her with new life and energy."

"Oh, let me go at once, Hargrave!"

"For what purpose? To tell her that you have just left the society of a woman whom it is a disgrace to mention in the hearing of one so innocent as my sister—to tell her that you have deserted her for one who has numbered so many lovers already, and who still hopes to see as many more sighing at her feet? Me take you to Annie? Never!"

"I entreat you——"

"Hold, sir! I came not here to sue to you, to come and blast again the life of one so dear to me, that I would fain have lain down my life for her! I came here, sir, to avenge her wrongs! Draw, sir, here, at once, unless the cowardly heart that can win the affections of a young girl only to trifle away an idle hour, shrinks from the chastisement his crime—for such it is—deserves!"

As Hargrave commenced speaking, Captain Hampton laid his hand again upon the hilt of his sword, and, with flashing eyes, he took his station at a proper distance.

For a moment, the two men regarded each other in silence.

"Draw!" shouted Hargrave, as his sword-blade gleamed brightly in the afternoon's sun.

Captain Hampton mechanically followed his example, and their sword-blades dashed together in deadly combat.

"Forbear! For my sake, forbear, Frederick! Henry!"

With a shriek of despair, a white figure rushed across the road; and had it not been for Captain Hampton's sustaining arm, Annie—for it was, indeed, that unhappy girl—would have fallen to the ground.

"You here, Annie!" exclaimed her brother; "it will be the death of you!"

"I care not, so that I have saved his life! Dear Frederick, how my eyes have longed to look upon your face!"

As she spoke, she clung frantically to his bosom.

Captain Hampton wound his arms about her, and sped over the small space she had traversed with as much ease as though he carried a baby.

Her brother made no opposition now, for his sister's critical situation absorbed every other consideration.

As he laid his light burden upon a couch, and sat down beside her, Hampton saw but too plainly that her hours were numbered.

"Oh, tell me you forgive me, Annie! I deserve it not; but for mercy's sake, leave me not doubly bereaved!"

"Doubly bereaved, Frederick?"

"Yes, bereaved of your love and your forgiveness!"

"Both are yours, dearest! Forget the past, and be happy!"

"Happy? Me be happy with this load upon my conscience?"

As he spoke, the strong man bowed his head upon his clasped hands, and wept tears such as men seldom weep.

"Do not, if you love me. Rejoice rather that I am very happy, now that I have looked once more into your dear face and heard once more the tones of your loved voice!"

He bent over her, and kissed her.

Hargrave stood by; there was a look of despair upon his handsome countenance, which was painful to behold; but he did not try to prevent this last interview, which seemed to bring such comfort to Annie.

They had sat thus for about the space of half an hour, for they thought she slept.

Suddenly she raised her head, which had been pillowed upon Hargrave's arm, and with a gasping voice she spoke.

"Henry—Frederick—promise me that your quarrel shall end here!"

"Hush—hush!" groaned the wretched brother.

"Promise me, you will neither engage again in mortal fight! Oh, let me think of you both as forgiving and forgiven! Speak! Answer me, for my moments are numbered!"

Simultaneously the hands of those two men—who but a short time before had each determined to slay the other—met and were clasped in friendship.

"That is well! Now I die happy! Air, brother—air!"

Henry flew to the window, which he flung open.

"Farewell, Henry—kind, dear, faithful brother of my childhood! Frederick, dearest—best beloved—we shall meet again where there is no parting, no sorrow, no fading away!"

Her eyes closed, and the spirit took its departure from the mortal tenement.

"It is over! and I am, indeed, alone!"

These were the words that fell from the lips of Captain Hampton, as he threw himself into a post-chaise.

"I cannot go to Rome now. Another will soon supply my place in the affections of the fickle woman, for whom I have sacrificed an angel!"

A few lines to account for his absence were despatched to Catherine, which only caused her to shrug her shoulders and say, "Let him please himself, he is no loss to any one!"

And while Catherine is gliding over the blue waters to her home in the sunny South, the guests whom she had invited to dine at Mabledon House were *en route* for their destination.

Lord and Lady Mansfield were the first to arrive; and on the footman communicating the fact that his lady had left Mabledon House two days previously without leaving word either where she was going, or when she might be expected to return, the kind-hearted old peer was not only greatly astonished, but mortified; for it was a known fact that the Duchess of Kingston gave the most *recherché* dinners of all the aristocracy; and his lordship was always well pleased to receive an invitation to one of her dinner parties.

At first, he was about to re-enter his carriage, but, upon second thoughts, he determined to stay a short time; hoping even against hope, that Catherine, remembering the dinner party, would surely yet return in time.

Having returned, then, to the carriage from which Lady Mansfield had not yet alighted, after a few minutes of whispered conversation, the lady got out, and both she and Lord Mansfield were shown into the green drawing-room, there to wait with as much patience as might be for the expected dinner to come off.

Lady Harrington was the next to arrive, and the same footman who had admitted Lord and Lady Mansfield, opened the door, and at once ushered her ladyship into the drawing-room.

There was a strange look of solitude pervading the apartment, which seemed to strike her ladyship at the first glance.

Advancing, however, straight towards Lord and Lady Mansfield, Lady Harrington, after the first salutations had been gone through, ventured to inquire if the Countess of Bristol were well.

"That is more than we can inform your ladyship," replied Lord Mansfield; "for I have been informed that the mistress of this house left it some two or three days ago, and has not since been heard of."

"Merciful providence!" exclaimed Lady Harrington; "something has happened to her."

The peer looked puzzled; but the remark that was on his lips was put a stop to by one of those thundering rat-tat-tats in which footmen are so apt to indulge, when they happen to find a knocker that yields easily to their touch.

"Another arrival," said Lady Mansfield.

"Yes," replied her husband. "At all events we have the satisfaction of not being singular in this very absurd farce."

"It is abominable!" exclaimed Lady Harrington, as she glanced at her very becoming dress in a mirror on the opposite wall.

The new arrival was no less a personage than Lord Chesterfield, who had come as much for a game at whist with the fascinating Duchess as for the good dinner he made sure he was about to partake of.

As his lordship entered the drawing-room, his quick eye soon detected the absence of its mistress.

His look of inquiry was answered by Lord Mansfield detailing to him as much as he himself knew of the extraordinary disappearance of the Duchess.

"Well, I do not see the use of remaining here to be the laughing-stock of all the servants in the house," said Lady Harrington; "so, with your permission, I shall get into my carriage and return home."

"The wisest thing that has been said yet," returned Lord Chesterfield. "What could have induced her to play us this trick?"

From the good humour which beamed upon every feature of his handsome countenance, it was quite evident that had Catherine appeared at that moment, nothing was farther from his thoughts than finding fault with the beautiful woman who had captivated his fancy years before.

And so, one by one, the guests departed to talk over, and wonder at, the strange caprice which had led to so much disappointment.

Amongst those who were the most disappointed, probably, was Mr. Evelyn Meadows, who had pictured to himself the dismay of Catherine when one of the guests who was in his interests, should bring forward the writ which would have had the effect of making the Countess a prisoner, although at large, but still a prisoner in England.

He had not dreamt of being so forestalled, and his rage was proportionably great.

In the meantime Catherine had reached Rome.

She had had an interview with her admirer, the Pope, and received from him the most flattering attentions both in public and in private.

But still she was anxious and uneasy.

She was fully aware that her enemies were still endeavouring to compass her destruction in so far as her prospects in life were concerned; for they seemed determined to leave no means unturned in endeavouring to set aside the will of her late husband, the Duke of Kingston, and, thereby depriving her of the vast wealth she inherited from him.

In order, therefore, to frustrate these projects of her enemies, Catherine resolved once more to leave Rome, and repair to Calais, and there take up her residence.

Her reason for selecting Calais as her place of abode, was on account of the expeditious modes of communicating with her friends in England, who failed not to keep her fully advised of all that was taking place for or against her in London.

—

CHAPTER XLV.

CATHERINE ARRIVES AT CALAIS AND TAKES POSSESSION OF HER NEW HOME.—SHE IMPROVES HER ACQUAINTANCE WITH CAPTAIN HAMPTON.—ANOTHER CHANGE.

CAPTAIN HAMPTON had been previously dispatched by Catherine to Calais, to select a residence for the fickle but enterprising woman whom no reverse seemed to affect beyond the passing moment—for, as she stepped on to the pier at Calais, Captain Hampton thought he had never seen her looking more lovely than she did at that moment.

And he did not lose the opportunity of telling her so; and, by the pleased smile which played about Catherine's lips, it might have been supposed that his whispered words of admiration were far from being unwelcome to her.

The fact is, Catherine had always bartered everything for admiration.

She was a coquette in the real acceptation of the word; for, while she strove to bring all hearts to her feet, and was not slow to perceive her advantage when she had succeeded in so doing, her own was untouched, and she could smile calmly at the misery she beheld in her mistaken worshippers.

She had lived for conquest all her life.

She had attained the summit of her wishes, for she had but to will to subjugate the heart of her intended victim, and the wished-for result was sure to happen.

So it was that she smiled upon Captain Hampton, who, albeit that he knew of her former conquests, yet, with his man's vanity, he hoped, and believed that she did really love him, and in that belief he was willing to live and die.

"Well, and have you succeeded in finding me a house to live in, Captain Hampton?" asked Catherine, as she walked the length of the pier.

"I have taken a house—the only one to be had—but I have my misgivings as to whether you will think it good enough. However, I thought it advisable to secure it, as you stated so distinctly that Calais was your destination."

"I dare say I shall like it, and if not, it will then be time enough to look out for something better; so let us hasten."

There was a carriage in waiting to convey Catherine to her new home.

Captain Hampton was about to take leave of her for a time as soon as he had handed her and Bella into the carriage, but Catherine, with one of her most fascinating smiles, requested him not to leave her to seek her new abode alone, but to take a seat, which she indicated, by her side.

Nothing loth, the gallant Captain sprung into the vehicle, and having given directions to the coachman to drive to the Rue de Vauban, they were soon *en route*.

In a very short time the carriage reached the Rue de Vauban, No. 7.

The house was of white stone, and in a small court before it were two small beds full of beautiful flowers.

The carriage, as it drove up to the door, was compelled to turn in order to avoid a fountain that played in a basin of rockwork in which sported a quantity of gold and silver fishes.

The house, raised above the kitchen and cellars, had besides the ground floor, two stories and attics.

The breakfast-room was of oak, the saloon of mahogany and blue velvet, the bedroom was decorated with green damask; there was also a library and a music-room.

"Charming! charming!" cried Catherine, as she flew about the house from room to room, as delighted with everything she saw as though she had been a child; "you have more than pleased me, Captain Hampton, you have charmed me!"

Captain Hampton looked scarcely less delighted than the speaker—but from a very different cause.

While she was looking at, and admiring the

many beautiful things he had there collected together to give her a pleasing surprise, he, on the contrary, was regarding her with an odd mixture of pleasure and pain upon his handsome features.

Did he begin to feel already that new places and fresh faces were sure to make a good impression upon that fickle heart, and that the time would come when he too would be left to curse his evil fortune for ever bringing him into contact with that charming and fascinating coquette?

The remainder of the day was passed by Bella and a French waiting-maid, in arranging the various articles of furniture more in accordance with the tastes of the mistress of the house; and by Catherine and Captain Hampton in improving their acquaintance—the former bringing all the artillery of her charms to bear upon his sensitive heart—and the latter in drinking in fresh draughts of love for the beautiful being, who that night promised to love him, and him only.

Some weeks passed by, and then Catherine began to feel a desire to remove to gayer scenes than those in which she mixed at the quiet little town of Calais.

"Ah! I could pass the remainder of my days here in peace if blessed with your society only," was the remonstrance of Captain Hampton one day when Catherine was complaining more than usual of weariness.

The fact is, she had begun to tire of the man who never opposed her most extravagant wishes or commands. There was not excitement enough for Catherine in the love which yielded everything to her. Hers was a disposition which required a little opposition in order to make her present vain and useless life at all tolerable.

Having no other aim in life but conquest, as soon as that was attained, all energy ceased, and she was unhappy.

"I tell you this house is not large enough, nor grand enough!" she exclaimed, one day, to Captain Hampton, "to please me. I must be nearer to Paris—dear Paris, and then I shall know what it is to enjoy life."

"And do you not enjoy life now?" asked her lover, in a tone of sadness.

"Enjoy life in this prison-like house?" asked Catherine, in a provoking tone; "most certainly not. I must attend balls, assemblies, concerts—in fact, I shall not be happy until I can again feel that I am the reigning *belle* of the season, for my glass tells me that I may yet aspire to that honour."

The Captain sighed.

"And so the sooner you can find me a house that you think will suit me the better; and, remember, I shall always be glad to see Captain Hampton, provided I am not better engaged."

"Oh, Catherine!"

"Oh, Frederick! Why what on earth are you looking so sombre about? Any one would think, to look at you, that I had given you the right to approve or disapprove of my actions."

"I thought I had."

"You?"

"Yes, the right of love."

Catherine burst into an immoderate fit of laughter.

"Well, of all the dear, eccentric, stupid, love-sick creatures I ever met with, you beat them all."

The Captain regarded her with a sorrowful expression.

"Did you suppose," she continued. "Did you suppose, for one instant, when I allowed you to love me——"

Here she burst out laughing again.

"Did you suppose, I say, for one instant, when I allowed you to love me, that no one else was to be admitted to that honour at my age. The idea is absurd—ridiculous!"

The Captain's eyes flashed fire.

"There, now you are angry, and really look almost handsome with that hawk-like glance. But I am not afraid of you."

"Catherine, you have nothing to fear from me," gently replied Captain Hampton; "but the day will come when you will yourself be shocked at your own heartlessness and cruelty."

"Me heartless? Me cruel? Why have you not told me a hundred times that my heart was——"

"I knew it not so well as I do now," interrupted Hampton.

"And since when have you been so fortunate as to read that intricate thing — viz., a lady's heart?"

"Within the last quarter of an hour."

"Indeed!"

Catherine saw that she had gone a little too far, for it was not her intention to drive from her a heart that really and truly loved her, until some new face had replaced it; so she spoke more gently as she said, "Indeed! and must I cease to give way to the natural mirth which has ever characterized me, or feel that you no longer love me?"

Captain Hampton was by her side in an instant.

"Love you! I not love you? Oh, Catherine, you know not, you can never know, how inexpressibly dear you are to me!"

"Well, don't hold me so tight, then, or you will have the satisfaction of knowing that I am, indeed, only mortal; for another such grip, and I should probably lie senseless at your feet."

"Pardon me—pardon me, angel—my life, my love, I knew not what I did! I not love you?"

The Captain pressed his hands to his throbbing temples, and Catherine gently twined her arms about his neck, and whispered into his ear words of affection, which he had often listened to before from her lips, and he was happy—oh, how happy, no one knew but Catherine!"

"And now," she whispered, still nestling close to him,—"now you will find me a house nearer to Paris, will you not, Frederick?"

"Anything—anything you wish, dear one! Only command me, but love me, too, and I am your slave for life."

A well-pleased smile flitted over the face of the Duchess, as she listened to this speech. Hampton saw it not, or his dreams of bliss would no doubt have been less bright.

The next day, Captain Hampton commenced his search after a house near Paris for his heart's idol.

* * * * *

About the centre of the Faubourg St. Honore, and at the back of one of the most distinguished-looking mansions extended a large garden, whose widely-spreading chesnut trees raised their heads

above the walls, high and majestic as those of a
rampart, scattering each spring a shower of
rich and delicate pink-and-white blossoms into
the large stone vases placed at equal distances
upon the two square pilasters supporting an iron
plate, curiously wrought after the style and manner of Louis the Fourteenth.

The house, or rather mansion, which stood in
the centre of a kind of park, could only occasionally be caught sight of in summer through
the branches of the trees.

Such was the house which Catherine deputed
Captain Hampton to purchase for her.

She was charmed with her new home, and
loaded her admirer with benefits and smiles to
his heart's content.

But Catherine was not likely to settle down
even in this pleasant spot, and lead the life of a
recluse. She had no difficulty in making acquaintances, although some of her friends, so
called by courtesy, were not always of the most
reputable class, still they answered her purpose,
for her saloons were filled with guests.

And she was again the centre of attraction.

Catherine's sense of enjoyment, however, in
this earthly paradise was soon brought to an end,
for it was soon found that the house had been
only superficially beautified, while in reality
it was in so ruinous a condition as to be in momentary danger of falling.

By the advice of some of her friends, Catherine instituted a law-suit against the owner of
the estate.

It was after a lengthened interview with a
lawyer respecting this, that Captain Hampton
called one day, anything but pleased to find that
Catherine had such important business to transact
with any one for the space of three hours, during
which he had not ceased to pace to and fro the
dining-room like some infuriated caged animal.

At length Catherine appeared, and made no
secret of the fact that she considered him wanting even in common sense, to have taken for her
a house that threatened every moment to fall
about her ears.

The Captain was astounded at what he heard;
it had never entered into his head to give more
than a cursory glance at the mansion, seeing it
was in every respect a desirable residence, as far
as appearances went. He at first imagined that it
was only made a pretext for quarrelling with
him.

"Then, what are you going to do, Catherine?
Am I to look out for another residence for you?
Only tell me how I can serve you, and you know
how gladly I will do so."

"No; I shall travel again," was the petulent
reply.

"And whither would you—to Italy?"

"Italy! No. At least, I possess one friend
who will never look coldly on me."

There was an anxious look upon the countenance of the Captain, as though he expected
to hear the name of some detested rival.

Catherine was not slow to perceive the effect
her words had produced, and resolved to torment
him for awhile, as a punishment for his want of
care in purchasing a house which she found to
be untenable.

"Well," she resumed, "I suppose you have
no objection, Captain Hampton—you surely do

not wish me to remain here, to be buried in the
ruins of this house. I am not yet tired of life."

"But you seem tired of me, Madam," was the
reply.

"Well, now, really I had not put it in that
light to myself; but, now you come to mention
it, I think I do feel a little weary of your eternal
love speeches."

The Captain turned away to hide the emotion
her words produced.

"They are all very well, you know, in their
way; but one gets tired of hearing the same
things from the same lips. There's nothing
like variety, and, therefore, it is my intention to
pay a visit to Saxony."

"To Saxony?"

"I think I speak plainly. Yes—Saxony, and
I shall be very happy to see you on my return,
which will not be, by-the-bye, until this law-suit
is concluded."

"And you are going alone?"

"As far as you are concerned—yes."

"Oh, Catherine! Catherine! do not play with
a heart that really loves you! Why this acting?"

"Acting? I beg to state that I never was
more in earnest in my life."

"But tell me—who is my rival?"

"The Electress of Saxony!" said Catherine,
laughing heartily. "Oh, you men!—you are so
vain that you think a woman cannot possess a
friend unless it be one of the opposite sex!"

"Pardon me—dearest—most charming of
women! If I could but feel that you would
think of me when far away——"

"Oh, I can promise to think of you fast enough,
whenever I remember all the expense and trouble
your stupidity is likely to put me to. Oh, I
promise to think of you."

"But not in that way!" urged Hampton.

"In any way you please, then, so that you do
not have anything more to do with taking houses
for me."

The Captain looked somewhat crestfallen, but
he was nevertheless compelled to appear satisfied
with the terms of the agreement, and he and
Catherine parted the best of friends.

CHAPTER XLVI.

CATHERINE PAYS A VISIT TO HER FRIEND THE
ELECTRESS OF SAXONY.— HER RETURN TO PARIS.
—THE NEW HOME.—PASSION AND ITS CONSE-
QUENCE.—DEATH OF CATHERINE.

TRUE to her word, Catherine left the dilapidated
house in the Rue de Vauban the very next day,
and proceeded to Saxony, where she was received
by her friend, the Electress, with every mark of
distinction and affection.

Strange it is, but it sometimes happens in life,
that not only the very opposite dispositions seem
to amalgamate and form the strongest friendships,
but those often the most opposed in religion and
morals also conceive an affection for each other
which is perfectly incomprehensible to the looker-
on.

But so it is.

The Electress of Saxony had ever regarded
Catherine with all the tenderness and affection
of a mother, while Catherine, it must be confessed,

certainly felt for her more love than she ever conceived for any one else, and a desire to deserve her good opinion was strong within her, so long as she was under her immediate influence.

But the honour, virtue, and religion of this kind friend soon became rather irksome to the vain woman, who seemed to live but for the sake of receiving the adulation of her admirers, and hence it was that at the end of a fortnight Catherine announced to her friend that she intended to return to Paris as soon as she could make her arrangements for the journey.

"Oh, stay with me," said the old lady, kindly, clasping both Catherine's hands in her own; "you have long experienced my love. My protection—my fortune—everything I possess, you may command!"

Catherine was visibly affected.

"Come and live with me," continued the Electress; "leave a country where you have experienced so much coldness and unkindness—forget the world in which you have hitherto mixed, and be the child of my old age."

There is no telling what effect these words of the Electress might have had on Catherine, but just at that moment she happened to glance up, and caught the sight of her own graceful figure and beautiful face in a mirror.

"I may yet be the belle of any assembly I choose," was the thought that flashed across her mind, and then she almost smiled to think how weak she had been to be influenced so much by that kind voice.

"Well, Catherine," asked the Electress, "will you come and be my child—the child of my affections?"

To any one with less tact than our heroine possessed, the difficulty of refusing so kind an offer would have been great; but Catherine's presence of mind seldom or never deserted her.

"Thanks, dearest friend!" she replied, in her softest accents. "I may some day only too gladly accept your offered kindness; but urgent business obliges me to leave you for a short time; but when that is concluded——"

"You will return to me?"

"I will return to you."

The simple-minded and affectionate friend was satisfied, and Catherine congratulated herself upon her singular skill in extricating herself from any dilemma in which she had the misfortune to be placed.

Catherine was now only too anxious to expedite her return to the French capital, where she had already despatched a letter to her still devoted admirer, Captain Hampton, to be in readiness to receive her.

The leave-taking between her and the Electress was most touching and affectionate.

Again and again the aged gentlewoman pressed Catherine to her heart, and entreated her to make her absence as short as possible.

Such scenes, however, were little in accordance with Catherine's feelings, and she, therefore, hastened to bring the adieu to a termination as quickly as possible consistent with her ideas of courtesy.

At length Catherine was free.

Free to pursue her journey whither she would; and in an incredibly short space of time she was again treading the soil of France.

Her first intention was to visit her former house in the Rue de Vauban, at Calais, with a view of again taking possession of it; but whether it was on account of the comfortable quarters she had lately been occupying at Dresden, or whether it was merely her own fickleness of disposition, which was always looking out not only for new faces but new places, we will not take upon ourselves to say; but certain it was that the house in the Rue de Vauban now appeared to the spoilt beauty as something far too small and insignificant for her ever to take a fancy to it again.

"I shall look out for myself this time," she said, laughingly, to Captain Hampton one day; "and you shall see what my ideas of a house are."

The fact is Catherine had employed agents up and down to keep her advised of any which were to be sold or let that came up to her ideas of splendour and magnificence; and having ample means at her command, she soon found herself inundated with letters setting forth the beauties of at least twenty or thirty mansions or hotels which might be at her disposal whenever she chose.

The one, however, which pleased her most belonged to the brother of the reigning French monarch, fitted up on a most costly scale, and to which were attached ornamental pleasure grounds, besides excellent shooting.

This was, perhaps, the place of all others best suited to Catherine's tastes.

The mansion itself was large enough to be fit for the residence of a king. It contained no less than forty bed-rooms, to say nothing of music-rooms, billiard-rooms, ball-rooms, and reception-rooms innumerable.

Of course the sum of money needed to purchase such an estate was something almost fabulous; but, never deterred by trifles, Catherine agreed to pay the sum of fifty-five thousand pounds by instalments.

The necessary arrangements were entered into, and Catherine was duly installed as mistress of one of the most princely abodes in the kingdom.

And now she resolved, it seemed, to make up for lost time, for no sooner was she well established in her new abode than she issued invitations right and left to a grand evening party and ball, with which she intended to inaugurate her taking possession of her new home.

It was at this first ball—at which she wished to appear with as much *éclat* as had marked her entrance into the courtly circles of England years before—that she was fated to receive tidings which every one supposed really caused her death.

She had just been handed to her seat after having executed a most beautiful piece upon the harp to the delight of every one present at that gay assemblage, when Bella Steinburgh was noticed to approach her, and whisper something in a low tone.

Catherine gave a half shriek, and covered her face with her handkerchief.

In an instant twenty—nay, three times that number of arms were at her disposal.

"The countess is ill! Air! air! Bring some water! Make way there! Carry her to the conservatory!"

Amidst this babel of sounds Catherine, faint and unconscious, was carried to the conservatory and there laid upon a couch.

Upon removing her hands it was found that her handkerchief was saturated with blood!

Bella, bewildered—almost beside herself, stood by her side, looking as though she had been the unhappy cause of all.

"Oh, Catherine! Catherine! look up—look up! and tell me you forgive me!" cried the almost frantic girl.

"Hush! hush!" said Catherine, faintly; "no more of this. I am well now. Lead me to my chamber."

The guests fell back in order to allow Bella to take the place by her side which Catherine indicated.

No one attempted to follow them, and one by one the guests departed, wondering within their own minds what could have caused so sudden a change in the beautiful Countess, who that night had certainly gained sufficient admirers to satisfy even herself.

When the two friends were once alone together, Catherine seized Bella by the arm, and said,—

"Tell me again, Bella—is it true that the law-suit is decided against me?"

"Alas! yes."

"Then I shall never be able to meet the expenses. But let us not talk any more about it to-night; I would rest; and to-morrow I will think what is to be done."

But Catherine did think that night, and the consequence was the next morning she was too ill to rise, at least so Bella thought, as she endeavoured to persuade her to lie still.

"But I must and will get up! I am not well, I confess; but I am well enough to get up, I tell you."

"Nay, rest awhile, dear Catherine," urged Bella.

"I will get up, and at once," was the impatient reply. "If you do not assist me to dress, I will do so by myself."

Bella was too wise longer to oppose the wish, imprudent though it was, and she assisted her to dress.

"That will do; now let me walk about the room. Bella, your arm!"

Bella was by her side in an instant.

"I am parched with thirst, Bella; give me drink."

Bella, from a side table, brought a cool beverage, of which Catherine was particularly fond.

But she put it aside with her hand.

"No, no—not that. I must have wine—nothing but wine, I tell you. Make haste, Bella. Madeira, I say!"

"But, dear Catherine, you are so feverish! Wait until to-morrow."

"I will not wait!" she cried, stamping her foot impatiently. "Bring me Madeira at once, I say!"

Bella reluctantly brought her the wine, saying, as she gave it to her,—

"It will be the death of you, Catherine! For my sake, if not for your own, forbear!"

Without making any reply, Catherine seized the glass and drained it.

"I am better already!" she said, with a strange laugh.

Bella shuddered.

"Another glass! Another glass, Bella!" cried Catherine, "and I shall be quite well!"

After drinking the contents of the second glass, she walked about the room for a few minutes unassisted, and then throwing herself on a couch she expressed a wish to sleep.

Bella knelt by the couch, holding one of her hands in hers, and in a few minutes Catherine had fallen into a deep sleep.

From that sleep Catherine never awoke in this world.

When Bella moved her hand to adjust the pillows, she was startled to find that the beautiful face was rigid, and the throbbing bosom cold and still.

Catherine, Duchess of Kingston, was dead!

THE END